Her Lips

Clove Finch

Contents

1. No man's an island...but this woman is

A aaand 3 ... 2 ... 1 ... Happy New Year to me! Ugh, not much to celebrate, is there? I swapped channels while I could still hear the fireworks outside, but on TV, other than the fireworks themselves, there were only couples kissing and people hugging. Cue the eye roll.

I changed to some crappy movie to use as background sound. I was ready for my yearly ritual: slumped on the couch, dressed in red flannel pajamas, empty pizza cartons on my coffee table, along with Coca-Cola. Starting from this year, there were also Reese and Shaw keeping me company; well, more like friendly wrestling with each other. However, the most important feature was ... the book in my hands.

That's my ritual. I like to enter the new year by starting a new book. Lame for most people, simply perfect for me.

Oh, the name's Joanna, Joanna Brooks, but most people call me Jo. Reese and Shaw are my kittens, one black and the other white.

I'm 28 years old and I work as a waitress at the diner a few blocks from here, while for the rest of the time ... nothing, I just go in search of a job that suits my degree. Needless to say I haven't had any luck so far.

I should be an editor. Emphasis on the should. Considering that I've been rejected by ... I don't know, 30 magazines since I started my hunt? Although I could do more than the editor. I mean, with my degrees, I could do different things, but for each and every single one of them they want experience, so ... here I am.

I live in New York City, of course. The city where dreams come true. Mmh, weird, I've been living here for about 2 years already and no opportunity has fallen from the sky for me yet. Not one.

What else, let's see ... normally at this point there's a physical description. I'm 5'8", which is a bliss, considering it doesn't quite allow me to expand endlessly, but I still weigh way more than I should, with a body shape that's halfway between apple and hourglass, so yeah, I'm on the chubby side and, actually, expanding. I've been putting on weight lately. Thank my ever so high self-esteem and Joe's pizza just downstairs, always too inviting to refuse. Besides, I'm too lazy to cook and I am not a great chef either.

You'll say, size doesn't matter, Jo, what matters is the beauty inside. And you're right. But, you know, there aren't really many men willing to pick this side of the fence when they can have the other one. Although, I'll admit that it's my fault, too. I mean, it's not like I really take care of myself.

Last time my face saw makeup was ... I don't know, 15 years ago maybe? And only because my crush was to come to my birthday, so my friends convinced me to dress up for him. I did get a kiss on the cheek from him, so I guess it was worth it.

I'm the lonely type. The one that prefers to stay at home on a Friday, other than go partying, the one that, few real friends are better than hundreds of shallow ones. That's why my circle is really, really restricted, namely two girls I met when I moved to New York. The others are acquaintances, which means that, likes on Facebook maybe, greet on the street, nah. I like to think of myself as a lone wolf, but I've often been reminded that wolves are pack animals, and the lone one is the one that's gone crazy, that's why he remains alone. Well, fine with me. I don't like being ordinary. I like uniqueness.

I'm not exactly the perfect prototype of beauty. I mean, girls like Faith and Hope (yes, yes, I know, quite a sense of humor their parents had), they're gorgeous, but me ... please. I am nonexistent to the male population. Although, my friends often remind me that it's also because I always look so grim that guys think I'm always mad. I never smile much, never talk much, I'm always lost in my lala land, most certainly daydreaming. I like to think I'm made to be alone, but I like hanging out with the girls. Well, when they don't try to drag me to some silly party: in that case it's a huge no.

Now, back to New Year's Eve. Faith and Hope normally go to Aspen with their posh friends, and even though they always invite me, I always say no. I'm just ... uncomfortable around people I don't know. Besides, I know what kind of parties they attend and ... thanks, but no, thanks. I think I'm gonna die alone on this couch, with Reese and Shaw waiting for the rigor mortis to start nipping on my flesh.

I've always wanted to travel, but never had the money. The most I've seen is ... well, New York. I love this city, really, it's the perfect combination that allows you to see everything without going anywhere ... yeah, I know, I take that too literally, as the twins say. I mean, if they suggest we go see a movie or a play, yeah, gladly, but pubs, bars and whatnot? Nah. Not even in a million years.

Honestly, I barely have the courage to show my face to the world outside sometimes, how could I enjoy a wild party? I don't easily relate with the male universe either. It's even worse when they're handsome. Ah, handsome faces make me very, very nervous.

Don't get me wrong, I believe in myself; better said, I believe in myself that much enough to be sure I am good at something, which is what I took as major in college, and there was a time when I was good at sports too, before the couch decided to declare his undying love for me and keep me chained to him for life. But as for the rest ... well, no. I lack social skills, I'm one inch away from being socially awkward for real. That's because, as a child, I was shy – and I mean super-shy, almost pathologically shy –, then less and less, till shyness just turned into introversion, a type of introversion that makes every single social gathering not just hideous, but also source of anxiety at times. So yeah, if I had to describe myself, I'd say introvert and asocial. Completely and utterly locked up in my own world. Openly despising the word love but then longing for that fool who'll look at me like I look at pizza.

Ah, yes, this is me, the epitome of awkward, your favorite type of cliché. I'm that one girl that flees when a cute boy deigns to talk to her. Well, those rare times that that happens. Well, ok, that happened with my crush in college. Oh, that was a huge and utter mess. I mean, I couldn't have fucked it up worse even if I tried, I swear.

But ... let's get back to New Year's Eve. The movie I picked absentmindedly was some western with Clint Eastwood, just not to hear anything sappy or cheesy, not wanting to depress myself even more. I don't even like western, but Reese and Shaw seemed to enjoy it.

After a couple of hours spent reading, entirely ignorant to the world outside, I yawned, followed by my kitties, so I stood up, and dragged myself to bed, Reese and Shaw on tow; that usually means that tomorrow morning

I'll find them both cuddled up on my pillow, above my head. As lame as that sounds, it feels like being cuddled for once.

Ah, the perks of being single and lonely. It's awesome yet awful sometimes. Not everyone's made to be lonely. No man is an island. Well, this woman is. Kind of.

2. Hello, Mr. Sexy

Lucky thing my boss decided to be kind and close the diner from 31st to 2nd January, so I could relax a little. This morning Faith and Hope called me from Aspen, asking if I wanted to join them, I was still in time, they said. I'm supposed to go back to work tomorrow, I argued, so they asked if I could plead with my boss to have a few days of vacation. I snorted. Just that.

Scott would laugh in my face if I asked even half an hour off, imagine a few days. He's closing the diner these days only because his mom forced him to, he's visiting her in Alabama.

I spent the first day of New Year just being lazy. My perfect kind of day is very simple: just me, food, books and movies/TV shows, plus now Reese and Shaw keeping me company. Although, yesterday I had a Person of Interest marathon, so my cats are learning about their homonymous.

Weirdly enough, this morning I woke up in a good mood. Well, aimlessly scanning through job offers wasn't exactly joyful, but 2 days away from Scott always do wonders. The only glitch in this perfect day were the noises I heard all morning in the hall. Not sure what was it, neither did I care to inquire, but they were too loud for my tastes.

Taking advantage of today being Tuesday, therefore normally no one's laundry day, I decided I'd do mine. I figured I'd do my business without anybody around ... I was wrong.

The moment I set foot in there, I spotted a guy fumbling with one of the washing machines, seemingly trying to understand how it works. I could only see his back, so all I could tell was that he was .

Being the socially awkward klutz I am, I felt the strong urge to turn on my heels and come back later, but that would have been really childish, right? So I settled for heading to the machine that was farthest from him, highly hoping he'd be too focused on figuring out its functioning to notice me.

As silently as I could, I placed the basket with my things on the ground and opened the washing machine. I learnt to be silent long ago, enough to be invisible, so it was easy to pass by unnoticed.

However, I forgot one detail ... washing machines aren't amidst the most silent creations of the human mind. I was ready to grab my basket, and leave, but the damn thing gave me away.

"Hey, there. Don't flee. Please. Care to give me a hand here? I'm kinda hopeless." The guy said while I already had a foot outside the room.

Part of me wanted to smile at his cuteness, the other ... the other was pointing out that he sounded handsome. I mean, his voice was kinda sexy, and it's never a great idea to have anything to do with men like those. Then again, he just needed help with a damn washing machine, he'll forget me as soon as I'm out of this place and ... well, indulging in eye candy sometimes doesn't hurt, does it?

So I turned around slowly, and tried to do my best to smile, poorly succeeding ... opposite to Mr. Stranger, who exposed for me his pearly white teeth, my ovaries already screaming in delight. His light brown hair I'd noticed earlier was a perfect frame to an amazing pair of light brown eyes. He was handsome, yet commonly handsome. Not the, is he even real type, but definitely not the kind I see regularly in my life.

I realized I looked like a twig, with my slightly open mouth, kind of drooling over him already, when he grinned but kindly avoided to point out my pathetic stunt. He grazed the back of his neck, messing his already tousled hair, and asked me to give him a hand to make the washing machine work.

Gulping down my shyness, I walked up to him and, having given him a half, well, more like a quarter smile, I started fumbling with the machine. I thought I'd quickly just start it for him, then I'd be free, but no ... the guy came closer, making me more nervous ... have I mentioned that handsome faces make me very, very nervous? Well, they do. Really.

"Hey, wait, could you ... explain what you do? Please? I know I'll sound like a dummy but really I can't wrap my head around it."

I didn't even have the courage to let him hear my voice. Better said, words were stuck in my throat and I couldn't make myself talk. Yet I had to, be it only to explain to him how the washing machine works. Normally I don't talk much, but I can manage to say a few words, yet now ...

After having inhaled deeply, I hope silently enough not to let him notice, I started talking lowly. Maybe too lowly, because he came closer, claiming he couldn't hear me, given the noise the other machines were making.

My heart started racing, and I probably started sweating and blushing, especially when he came so close that I could feel his hot breath against my neck as he was watching me fumble with the machine while explaining what I did. I just hope my voice didn't quiver.

I'd talked so fast that I was done in a minute, but it felt like eternity, because his hot breath against my neck had me close to hyperventilating. Once I was done, I moved abruptly ... bad idea. Like a perfect klutz, I ended up bumping into him, who grabbed my hips to keep me in place, smiling gently as he asked if I was ok.

Nervously, I nodded and slipped away from his grip, my heart already doing somersaults. As red as a tomato and stumbling a little, I dashed out of the room, not even saying goodbye, my heart racing faster than a Ferrari while I sprinted to the elevator, but I'd obviously forgotten it was broken, so I had to resort to climbing the stairs. I felt like a murderer fleeing the crime scene.

Once I'd reached the second row of stairs, I paused, taking a deep breath, and slowed down, chastising myself for being so silly. It's not like he was running after me with a chainsaw.

Jeez, girl, hold your horses. The guy's probably just there laughing at you, maybe already texted his friends to tell them about this weird chick he just met.

I took a deep breath, and restarted walking, this time calmly, climbing the stairs till I reached the fourth floor, more than a bit wheezing, seeing as I'm not exactly in a great shape and not used to exercising, but I made it.

Behind my door I could already hear Reese and Shaw scratching, as they always do when they hear I'm about to enter, almost as a manner of greeting.

Putting the key into its hole, I heaved a big sigh, discomforted at the thought of the very poor impression I just made, highly hoping not to see the guy again.

"Hey, uh ... you forgot your basket in the laundry." The same voice as earlier mentioned just as I thought I was lucky. Karma, huh? When I turned around, I saw my blue laundry basket in his hands. Nervously, I waited until he was close, and I thanked him, omitting to inform him I'd left it there purposely, so that if someone else arrives before me when the machine is done, they'll put my clothes in the basket and won't dirty them by leaning them on the washing machine or worse, on the ground.

Pretty Face decided to make my coronaries explode, though, because I'd only cracked open my door that he leaned against the doorframe, giving me a sexy smile as he grabbed my arm to stop me: "Hey, wait, I didn't say thank you for helping me." I remained staring at his hand on my arm for a bit, and he noticed that, but didn't pull back, actually, he took one step closer. "I'm Ben."

He stretched his hand for me to shake it, so I nervously did, praying to whatever God for it not to be sweaty, and nervously muttered: "Joanna."

He gave me a wide smile as he squeezed my hand in his, making my heart race only faster. "Nice to meet you, JoJo. Unfortunately for you you're gonna see me often. I'm your new neighbor."

So much for being an island. Now I've got Mr. Sexy living right next door. Yay.

3. I hear you singing, you know

I hate this place. I hate this place. I hate this place. I kept chanting in my head as I cleaned up the umpteenth table, which was left purposely dirtier by some snob skinny girls that kept snickering all the time, glancing at me. Ugh. I so hate this place. It's not that it's bad per se, actually, it looks like a nice place, but it's frequented mostly by high school girls that believe they own the world, middle-aged perverts that ogle those girls, then very, very old people. Then add that my employer is a huge asshole with capital A, and you'll understand why do I hate this place so much.

Besides, I'm not supposed to serve tables. I'm supposed to be behind a desk writing articles about thrilling events happened in this or that far country or about whatever floats my boat. But no, I'm stuck here serving haughty toothpicks that think they're better than me only because they can eat like pigs without putting on one single pound. Well, I'm unfair. They don't eat like pigs. They don't eat at all. Those girls come here at least thrice a week and all they ever order is a very light salad they share, plus water. Wow. So riveting. No wonder they look like they've just popped out of a mode magazine. Me, I think I'd be good for the Michelin commercial, I even have the same flab.

Once I'd cleaned up the table, I went back to the counter, having heard the bell that informed me another order was ready. Of course, my co-worker was there polishing her nails, as usual, because, hey, don't you dare ask Your Highness to raise one single finger, she's so delicate! Aaaand ... she kinda fucks the boss so she's paid to do nothing while I do both my and her part. Yay. Technically, Scott would be married. But you can't really expect such a stallion as Scott to keep it in his pants, can you?

Poor Edith, she's such a nice woman, I wonder how the hell did she end up with an ass like Scott. I guess she was blinded by his good looks. I mean, now he looks like pretty much an incident between a snake and a goat, but she swears he was really handsome when he was younger. More than good looking, I think he's good with flirting, that's why his lame pickup lines always work with clients. Mandy here, my co-worker, she's been his lover for four months at least. But, she's also in bed with our cook. It doesn't concern me anyway. I just live my Hell 12 hours a day then I go back home and wash away the stench of failure, trying to convince myself I won't die in this horrible place ... I hope.

Ignoring Greg, the cook, flirting with Mandy, my ever so professional co-worker, I grabbed the order, and scuttled to serve the waiting clients, who didn't even bother to say a very simple thank you, as usual. Then again, when were New Yorkers ever kind? And who's that freak that ever thanks the waitress just because she's brought you your food still warm without even spitting in it?

Glancing around, I saw nobody needed anything and all tables were clean, so I took a moment to rest, but of course, I'd barely leaned against the other side of the counter, opposite to Mr. and Mrs. Let's Have Sex Wherever At Least Thrice Per Shift Every Day, that I already heard that booming voice: "Joanna! I don't pay you to sleep! Move that fat ass of yours!"

Please, Lord, take him. Please. Before I murder him among sauces. Or at least give me patience, because if you give me strength, I'm gonna kick that ass so much he's gonna end up on Mars. Rolling my eyes, I stood straight and turned to the sauces, pretending to be reordering them, trying to tune out Scott going to flirt with his bimbo.

Having finished with the sauces, I sighed, careful to look still active, although Scott was gone. I had only one moment of peace, because then I heard the door opening, a new client entering, so I turned around, ready to take care of yet another impolite jackass – you'd think it comes with the diner client job, being a rude jackass. However, at the sight of the newcomer, my throat dried as much as Mandy's eyes bulged out. I think I've never seen her adjust her merchandise so eagerly and sprint so fast towards a client. "Hello, there!" She greeted the guy perkily, a huge smile on her face, the kind I've only seen the rare times someone actually decent comes to eat in here.

On the other side there was a pretty tall guy with broad shoulders and tousled light brown hair that barely reached the back of his neck. Does that sound familiar?

"Hello." Ben greeted Mandy politely. Politely. Men don't greet Mandy with the kind of smile they use for a cute child or an elderly. Men drool first, then stutter their way to a hi when they have Mandy in front of them. Especially when, clearly, she has her eyes on them.

She didn't seem to detect that tone, she just smirked, and went to set onto his table, making sure to show off as much of her legs as possible. "What can I get you?" She asked, leaning in enough for him to get a pretty clear idea of what's her bra size.

"Uh ..." Ben's eyes moved to the menu on the table, much to my surprise. Since when the crappy food in this diner is more interesting than Mandy pretty much throwing herself at you, averagely handsome but charming guy? He seemed halfway between flustered and uninterested.

"JOANNA!!!" Scott thundered from his office before I could hear Ben's full response. With a sigh, I dutifully dropped the cloth in my hand and went to my boss, before he could start insulting me loud enough for the whole diner to hear. Not that it would be anything new, regular customers are used to it, but I'd rather my brand-new neighbor with whom I haven't even really spoken yet didn't witness one of my daily humiliations.

As I dragged my feet to the back of the diner, I could faintly hear Mandy turning every dish on the menu into something R-rated, as if she were some brothel hostess presenting all the things her girls were available for. Don't get me wrong, I'm not slut-shaming her. Mandy isn't a slut for wanting to sleep with whatever hot guy she can get her hands on, no. If anything, she's a whore for shamelessly sleeping with married or at any rate committed men without a care for the families she destroys. However, most of my concerns were going in one direction: what if she actually starts dating my neighbor and I have to endure this bitch for the remaining 12 hours of my day where she can't make my life more miserable than it already is?

--

With a heavy sigh, I shouldered my bag once I'd changed into my plain clothes – which, even as unfashionable as they may be, still are better than the crappy excuse for a uniform Scott forces us to wear, and I headed for the back exit. It's technically not very safe, but the diner gets crowded on Friday nights due to the Karaoke on the opposite side of the road, and I didn't want to make my way through the horde of 20-something college students, so happy and full of dreams, while I smelled like French fries and overcooked fish.

I had dreams. A long time ago. I don't know what crushed them. Maybe my own self-deprecating and self-loathing behavior that led me to not trying enough; maybe the "crisis" that affected the publishing world so heavily that even an internship seems like asking for the moon. Or maybe I just missed my proverbial train because I was too busy being afraid of the world outside my room. Yeah, I know, I'm "only" 28, there's time. But 28 is that age when you're still young yet not enough to keep dreaming without ever setting your feet on the ground. Especially not when you can barely make ends meet.

Clutching my bag, having plugged my earphones in, I headed to the bus stop near the diner. The only reason I got the job is that when I applied for it, Edith was in, her husband was in Alabama to visit his mother. I didn't realize why was Edith so quick with formalities such as contract and whatnot until her husband plainly told me I had a job only because his wife took pity on me. Right then and there I swallowed it, thinking it would be just a temporary thing not to starve, but ... 3 years have passed. 3 years, can you believe it? 3 entire years of putting up with Scott's crap. Mandy only arrived a few months ago, and I gotta say, Scott's mood has improved ever since he started sleeping with her, but I'm still devil incarnate for him. Mainly because he cannot fire me, even though he'd love to. His wife added a clause in the contract, according to which only she can send me away. The diner is technically hers, or rather it was her father's, but when she married that caveman, she became a housewife and he took over.

When I got to the bus stop, I found only a couple of teenagers busy making out. I did my best to keep my eyes elsewhere. I've never had that. High school romance. I was invisible at best as a teen, and not much has changed. Hope and Faith say it's because I do nothing to take care of myself, which may be true, but I don't see why should I make my life uncomfortable just to accommodate someone else. It's not like I'm much interested in a social life anyway. Like I said, I'm an island.

One bus came and the teen couple left, so I remained alone. It was only when I turned around to check the arrival times that I saw Ben lazily leaning against the wall, listening to his own music. I kind of wanted to say hi, be it only to apologize for having been rude the past few days – I avoided him as much as I could –, but I didn't know how. I chose to sit on the bench and stare at my phone, to pretend I didn't see him. Unfortunately for me, the bus I usually take home is always late, and this time was no exception. As much as I tried to focus on the music in my ears, it was still awkward.

I wonder what he must have thought. He moved in about a week ago and his only neighbor still hasn't said a word to him other than a shy hi when we meet in the hallway. Every time he smiles cheerfully, as if he's even glad to see me, and I clearly see he wants to start up a conversation, but I just always run off. Most words I've ever spoke to him were: I'm 28, I'm a waitress. He's a photographer from Nebraska and he's my age. I often hear him talk on the phone – walls are really thin –, so he probably has a girlfriend. Maybe that's why he didn't respond to Mandy's attempts today. Could he be one of the last gentlemen standing?

When the bus finally arrived, I felt relieved yet at the same time disappointed. I should have said something. We stepped inside from different doors, and I was careful to sit as far as possible from him, but I could see him clearly. He seemed preoccupied. Mindlessly staring outside the window while listening to music. That's something I normally do, ending up plotting ways to murder Scott and get away with it.

Deciding it wasn't polite nor sane to keep staring at my neighbor from afar, I went back to my daydream, but right before I got to the killing part, my playlist shifted to my ringtone, signaling and incoming call. I didn't even need to look. Only my parents call me and always exactly when I get off work.

We don't say much to each other, there isn't great communication in my family, it's all about how are you, did you finish work, are you alone, have you eaten ... the questions a mother asks. It's not that we don't care, it's just that we're not one of those openly affectionate families, which I appreciate.

By the time the bus arrived near my building, the call was over; however, before I could restart with my music, I felt someone tap me on the shoulder, so I turned around. "Hey, neighbor." Ben greeted me sweetly, to which I barely cracked a smile.

"Hi." Well, that's a start, I guess.

"How are you?"

"I'm ok. You?" The driest conversation ever, but at least I managed not to stutter.

Ben shrugged. "A bit tired. Between relocating and work, plus classes, I haven't had much time to breathe lately."

"Classes?" Way to go, Joanna, way to go. One word at a time can help sustain a whole conversation without you turning into the reddest tomato ever seen.

"Yeah, I'm a Photography & Imaging major at NYU."

"Oh." That wasn't exactly a word, but close, right?

Ben cracked a small smile and ruffled his hair a bit. "I started late, I know. I do photography for weddings, bar mitzvahs and other ceremonies right now, but that's just one of those jobs you do not to starve. What I really want, is to be a National Geographic photographer. Or it was that as a kid." He pursed his lips, as if thinking of something.

"Not anymore?" Oh, wow, two words together. Progress, Jo, big progress. We still were standing just outside our building, by the way, and for some reason I didn't want to go inside.

"I mean ... if National Geographic called, I'd be ecstatic, but realistically ... it's not gonna happen. I'll settle for anything that'll allow me to take interesting photos."

"Nice."

"What about you?" Ben asked, starting to walk towards the condo and I instinctively followed. "I can't believe working in a diner is your biggest ambition."

I remained quiet. No, it isn't. But as I said, my dreams are gone. Yes, I do look for a new job every day, but realistically I have as many chances of making it that Ben has of somehow catching the eye of someone that works for National Geographic.

"I'm sorry, I didn't mean to offend you ..." Ben mended quickly, looking at me worried. "What I meant is, it's a diner and ... ugh, no. I mean, a girl like you ..." He stopped walking and rambling, and ran a hand over his face, sighing. Then he turned to me, and my heart skipped a beat, because he looked straight into my eyes. "The thing about photography, is that it teaches you to really look at people, learn about them without talking, capturing their most hidden sides without them realizing it or even wanting you to."

I blinked my eyes, confused. He wasn't gonna say he secretly took some pictures of me, right? Just now that I was starting to consider him just a cute, innocuous, nice guy.

"I can see that you're unhappy at the diner."

You don't say? Who in their right mind would be happy working 12 hours a day every day in that dumpster?

Ben cracked a small smile, restarting to walk, to which I followed. "I hear you singing, you know." He mentioned, and my cheeks reddened. I sing when I take a shower, sometimes when I cook – the rare times I don't order takeaway. "Someone that sings like you, I can't believe your greatest ambition is to serve mediocre food to rude people every single day for the rest of your life."

I remained silent, unable to answer. How could he read me so well just by listening to me singing?

4. What would I know about dates?

S undays are mildly tolerable at the diner. There's less people to serve, because it's Sunday and they all prefer to go eat somewhere less depressing and dirty; Scott is in a good mood because he has his boys night on Saturdays, meaning poker and strippers; and, the weekend cook is at least nice – then again, it doesn't take much to be nicer than Greg. All that together makes Sundays at work good enough for my mood to be lifted the slightest. Not enough to be happy, but enough not to want to smash my head against the glass door of the diner every time I get to work.

As I neared Ben's door, I heard his voice. He was on the phone again. I wonder how come he moved here without his girlfriend, because, clearly, he can't stay more than a few hours without hearing from her.

I haven't talked to him since that night when he pretty much profiled me at the bus stop. It's rare that someone notices me enough to see behind the curtain. As a matter of fact, I don't think anyone ever has. You know that feeling you get when you reappear on the radar of humanity after having gone AWOL for years – that's what I felt when Ben mentioned my singing. I only sing when I'm sure no one can hear me, and since there are only two apartments on my floor, it's really easy. I just never considered someone could be listening and even make something of it.

"You have a really nice voice, by the way," Ben told me that night, while we walked home, "and you sing with such a passion that it's almost heart-breaking, given the songs' themes." Most of them are sad or at any rate talk about broken dreams and difficult lives. "It's not about the voice, it's about the story behind it. Like I said, photography teaches you to read people, and what I read when I look at you, or rather, listen to you sing, is broken dreams that you think are gone, but they're not. Someone like you, JoJo, is worth much more than a filthy diner."

It's not the first time I hear I have potential, my teachers and all told me the same, but coming from a complete stranger that has nothing to gain from it neither is compelled to give me pep talks (teachers are, due to professional bias, pretty much forced to), it sounds completely different. It's not some old lady that's known me my whole life, it's some random guy with whom I've barely spoken.

Beware, I'm not saying there is some sort of weird connection between us just because he appreciates my singing. I'm not about to go off on how he must be my soul mate and how am I gonna die if I don't end up spending the rest of my life with him. I'm just saying that, I don't get that often. Someone actually seeing me behind all the layers. If he understood so much just by listening to me sing, I wonder what would happen if we grew close. Not that I want or need to, just ... wondering, that's all.

Yawning, I unlocked the door, already hearing my kittens scratch it, eager to get dinner. Poor babies, I leave them alone most of the day. "Yes, yes, I know, you're hungry ..." I grumbled as I made my way to the kitchen, Reese and Shaw on tow, "you should feel lucky you have a home, so many strays starving and you complain about the quality of your tuna." I scoffed, reaching for the cabinet where I keep their food. Only 2 things I spend a lot on: my books, and the kitten's food. Cats are haughty, they want what they want, so it's either that very specific brand and that specific type of food, or hunger strike. Obviously, no faucet water, needs to be the cool store-bought one that's in the fridge.

Reese and Shaw barely gave me time to put food and water in their bowls that they jumped to it. I fell back against the wall with a heavy sigh, to check my phone. Predictably, there was a missed call from my mom, who, after all this time, still doesn't remember my work hours hence calls me when I can't answer. There were a couple of pics from Faith and Hope as well, just the twins enjoying themselves in Aspen. The last one was peculiar. It wasn't just the two blondies, there was a third one. Faith and Hope were hugging a guy that looked just a bit older than them. I didn't even need to read the text: blonde, early 30s, pretty hot, eyes as blue as theirs ... Nathan Hill, Faith and Hope's older brother.

Nathan – Natey, as his sisters call him, much to his dismay –, is the exact type of guy that would intimidate me. I never met him, but his looks say it all: successful, self-confident, handsome ... the exact opposite of me, my worst nightmare when I was in school. That's why I don't understand why his sisters are so adamant on setting us up.

The text Faith sent me with the photo read: Natey is so excited to meet you! I sighed, inevitably, already prefiguring the awkwardness of a meeting none of us really wants. I'm sure "Natey" has better things to do than waste his time like this. But, it's hard to say no to Faith. She's the dominant one of the twins, always finds a way to get what she wants, but I'm way more stubborn than she can handle ... so when she fails, she sends Hope to guilt trip me.

Having left Reese and Shaw to eat alone, I opened the fridge, hoping it would be less empty than yesterday, but, surprise surprise, it wasn't. Working at the diner doesn't leave me much time to go grocery shopping, mostly because I always end up doing overtime on my 12-hour shift; plus, I don't really cook, so ... takeaway it is. Luckily there's a great pizzeria nearby. Needless to say, I ordered pizza. Actually, didn't even need to say much, I just sent a text: the usual. They already know full well what I order. Predictably, the reply came right away: 20 mins tops, Joy. The thing about having a name so prone to nicknames, is that everyone changes it to how they want. Joe calls me Joy to mark a difference between my name and his, he said, and, because I don't smile much, so I'm such a "joy". I always get that. You don't smile, you don't talk, why are you so quiet, are you ok? Just because I'm not hyper and happy all the time, doesn't mean there's something wrong with me, you know.

I mean, sure, my life sucks, but I'm not always miserable. Quoting Jane Eyre, I'm not unhappy. I'm happier on my own, that's for sure. People are complex and complicated and so much hard work. Even only the twins tire me out. Then again, Faith and Hope Hill would tire out anyone. I always wonder how are we even friends, and I'm sure everyone else does when they see us together.

I went to take a quick shower, aware that the only thing I can be certain of in my life, is that Joe is never late. And in fact, the minute I stepped out of the shower, I heard someone knocking on my door. "I'm coming!" I shouted, trying to get dressed at the speed of light, which, let me tell you, is not a piece of cake when you're largely overweight as I am. But I managed.

When I opened the door, however, I remained petrified. There was pizza, alright, but it wasn't Joe. "Pizza is always the answer, huh? I can't disagree." Ben commented with a light chuckle, reading the writing on my t-shirt. I blushed, obviously. "I heard you were home, thought we could split this giant pizza," he said, pointing at the box in his right hand, while the other held two cans of beer. How to tell the him that, one, I already ordered my dinner and I never ever share my food, two ... I don't drink, at all. Or at

least not with people around me. Can't risk losing control and making a
fool of myself.

Ben stepped inside without me saying a word, a warm smile etched on his
lips. "I take that as a yes." He said, placing pizza and beer onto my coffee
table, and sitting on my couch. I was at a loss for words. Even more when
Reese and Shaw curiously went to him, sniffed him a little bit, then started
purring around his legs, especially Shaw. My cats are asocial like me, since
when do they show such affection towards anyone that isn't me? A stranger
even? "So? Aren't you hungry?" Ben asked me, patting the seat beside him.

"I ..." I murmured, blinking my eyes repeatedly. Am I dreaming? Did he
come to the wrong apartment? We've barely spoken a few words since he
got here, now he suddenly feels free to invade my home like this. Not even
my only 2 friends dare.

"I swear, there's no pineapple." Ben chuckled, opening the pizza box. "I
know some people like it, but," he grimaced, "I hate it. Don't tell me you-"

"No." I blurted out, feeling my cheeks redden more.

"Great." He took a slice, then put it back, grimacing a little. He looked
around, and once he'd eyed the paper towel roll on the kitchen counter, he
stood, and went to grab it. I followed him with my eyes all the time, utterly
baffled. "Come here, JoJo, I don't bite." Oh, so he didn't come to the wrong
place. I didn't move, though. Ben turned to me, and cracked a small smile.
He stood up, and walked to me, stopping a few inches away.

I took in his features. He looked a bit disheveled, hair ruffled, light stubble
– the kind you leave on a day like Sunday, when you don't go to work –,
kind of nerdy glasses on his nose. Oh, wait. Glasses? I mean, I'm used to
people wearing glasses out of trend, but his looked as real as mine. He was
unkempt, the kind of look you have when you've been home all day and

don't care about appearance. But he was still cute. The glasses especially made him cuter.

"Joanna?" Ben called me back to Earth. He was perusing me, yet not amused by my inability to speak a word. He seemed a bit concerned. "I shouldn't have barged in like this, I know," he admitted, curling his lips, "I just thought ... it's been a week and you're my only neighbor, it's about time we get to know each other." I blinked my eyes again, my lips parting to speak, but I didn't know what to say. Luckily, a knock on the door behind me saved me.

"Hey, Joy!" Joe greeted cheerfully, coming in. "Sorry, I'm a bit late, some idiot made me fall and the pizza was ruined, and I didn't want to-oh ..." he stopped the moment he saw Ben, I bet thinking the same as anyone would: a man? In Joanna Brooks' apartment? Is the world coming to an end?

"Hello," Ben greeted with a cheerful smile, extending his hand to shake Joe's, "I'm Ben, JoJo's new neighbor."

Joe blinked his eyes. Joe is a 17-year-old boy that's really just as nerdy and awkward as me, which is the whole reason why we get along well, despite the age difference. He's pretty much the brother I never had, which is why sometimes he even comes over for dinner and we watch a movie together. He knows the kind of life I lead and he doesn't judge me for it, because it's the exact same as his. "I'm ... Joe." He said, still dumbfounded. It was probably a miracle that he didn't drop my order.

"Nice to meet you, Joe." Ben claimed gleefully, grabbing said order – embarrassingly big for 1 single person, by the way –, and placed it next to his on the coffee table. "Thank you," he took out his wallet, "how much is it?"

"Uh ... no, Joy already ... I mean, Joanna doesn't pay."

I bit my lips, embarrassed. He meant I don't pay on Sundays. His uncle, the pizzeria's owner, said I'm such a great client that I can have anything I want for free once a week. It pretty much implies that I eat pizza all the time, which is kind of a subtitle for 'oh that's why she's so fat'. Heard that one before, yes. When, like me, you're not graced with a nice frame, anything you eat is watched carefully, or at least I always felt like everyone watched me eat and judged me for my eating habits. I know my cousins and aunts did.

Ben, however, was surprised but still, not amused. "Oh, ok," was all he said, then put back his wallet. "Well, time for dinner." He smiled. "Joe, would you like to stay?"

"I would, but ..." the 17-year-old glanced at me, suspicious and mildly amused as, slowly, an impish grin made its way to his lips, "I've got other deliveries to make." No, he didn't. He just thought oh, she finally found a man, can't spoil this miracle of the century. To no use were my pleading looks, Joe winked at me, then left, closing the door behind him.

"Well?" Ben invited. "I can't eat all this by myself."

How do I politely ask him to leave? I don't know him and I hate having people over when I'm eating – again, big girl eating, it's easy to feel like a pig when someone's watching –, plus I came from a tiring week and this was the only day when I actually got off early.

"So, what do you want to watch?" Ben asked me, turning the TV on. Shaw went to seat on the couch's arm beside him. I guess if even my cat likes him ... I could try.

Slowly, I marched to the couch, sat down, and grabbed the remote from his hands – careful not to brush his skin, obviously –, so that I could go to my selection. "I ... I was going to rewatch Infinity War."

"Great! I love Marvel!"

I couldn't help but smile the slightest. I guess at least we have something in common. I exhaled lowly, nodding, and started the movie, praying I could go on a couple of hours without embarrassing myself and at the same time trying not to think that this looked so much like a date. Then again, what would I know about dates?

5. That sounded like a threat

Awkward. Awkward. Awkward. The first part of this weird dinner with my neighbor was somewhat easy: I just needed to be chewing most of the time. Not that Ben didn't try to chat, but with food in my mouth, I had an excuse to just nod or shake my head all the time. However, once the food was over, how could I still keep on being quiet? Especially since he didn't seem to have any intentions of leaving. I shouldn't have agreed to watch such a long movie.

"So, are you an only child?" Ben asked, seemingly absentminded. I blinked my eyes, mildly confused. So far, since I wasn't talking, he'd done a monologue. We really hardly watched the movie, actually. He talked about every single thing he could think of: from the whole Avengers saga to Marvel vs DC, and then cartoons and Netflix, and how he likes New York and his new job ... seriously, anything.

"Yes." I mumbled, trying to focus enough on the movie not to blush.

"I have two younger brothers. Both in high school." Ben said. I could feel his eyes on me; it was uncomfortable because I hate when people watch me, but it didn't feel creepy.

I knew I had to say something, but I couldn't make myself. So I just nodded. He'll probably think I have some sort of speech impairment.

Luckily, I was saved by the bell. Literally. Or almost. Because before Ben could say anything – like, do you have some mental issues I should know about? Can you talk? Do you understand my language? – someone knocked on the door. Part of me hoped it would be Joe coming back to save me from this awkward night, but deep down I knew it was something that would throw me deeper into the abyss of embarrassment. And I was right.

Because when I, somewhat relieved but also anxious, went to open the door, on the other side I found a double pearly white grin to greet me. Of course, Faith and Hope normally crash on my couch when they go clubbing, so I'm used to them coming over late at night. "Surprise!!!" The twins yelled in unison – it's creepy, by the way, twins talking in unison. They didn't even wait for my answer, just pushed past me, Faith half yelling she needed a shower. I don't know how she totally missed the guy sitting on my couch, petting one of my kittens, but she did. Hope didn't, though.

"Hello." She greeted politely and gently, going over to him.

"Hello." Ben replied with the same kindness. "I'm Ben, Joanna's new neighbor." He introduced himself, extending a hand to shake hers, which she welcomed with a small smile.

"Hope. And the rude hurricane that just passed you is my sister, Faith."

He smiled. She smiled. I felt uncomfortable. It's as if I was a third wheel, witnessing something I wasn't supposed to. Or rather, the beginning of something special. Usually in movies this is the moment when the two feel some sort of electric shock as their hands touch, and they stare into each other's eyes for a long time, seeing the future: white dress, black tuxedo, a nice and quaint church, a house in the suburbs, at least 3 kids and a dog.

They didn't. But only because Faith called for her sister, needing her to unzip her dress. Oh, right. I forgot the details. I should have described their perfect dresses worn on perfect frames and perfected by a perfect makeup on their perfect skins, right?

Faith and Hope are good friends. But they're also the kind of girls with looks that make those like me feel less than mud under their stilettos.

Much to my surprise, when I tore my gaze away from Hope, who'd just disappeared behind the corner, I realized Ben wasn't as much busy staring at her. Instead he was looking at me, his head tilted. He was probably wondering how could I be friends with such beautiful girls. He opened his mouth to say something, but before he could, there was a light knock on the door, which I'd left ajar. Turning around, I saw him entering. Nathan Hill in all his splendor. Man, the Hills must be pretty high up in God's list of favorite people, otherwise I can't explain how can they all be so breathtaking.

"Hello." Nathan greeted. "You must be Joanna, the girls have told me a lot about you." He grinned, extending his hand for me to shake it once he'd gotten closer. What is wrong with these people? Shaking hands is so overrated, do you really need to touch someone to introduce yourself to them? Don't they know hands are the main source for germs?

I must have looked at his hand a bit too long, because Nathan retrieved it with that leer on his face, the one I've seen many times directed at me in my life. The one that pretty much reads: she's a weirdo. It doesn't hurt, it's just embarrassing, because the underling feeling people ooze when they do that, is pity, and I hate it.

"I'm Ben." I heard my neighbor close, so close to me that I almost jumped out of my skin when I realized he was standing right next to me.

"Nathan. Faith and Hope's older brother."

The guys nodded and started conversing with each other. I'm used to it, people having their own conversations while I'm there sitting or standing still. Sometimes I do it purposely, in order not to attract attention on me, but more often than not it's just how it goes. Happens when you're invisible. When you're like me, you get used to it: sometimes you're concealed by the noise of more relevant happenings, others you're so big you feel like a dinosaur loose in San Diego – impossible not to notice. It's a blessing and a curse.

--

Two hours later, I felt exhausted. I didn't participate much in any of the conversations happening in my living room, yet I felt like I'd just given a day-long seminar to hundreds of people.

Obviously, the twins asked me all sorts of questions before leaving, wanting to know everything about Ben, but I dodged them all. Not like I could answer, really. All I know is that we're neighbors and he's keen on us being friends for some reason. If I was paranoid I'd think he's an agent come to keep an eye on me because I accidentally saw something I shouldn't have. Then again, how could I have seen something I shouldn't have, if I never even go out? My life is all a street from home to the diner, from the diner to my home; once or twice a week I extend that road to include the grocery store.

"Nice friends."

This time, I did jump out of my skin, my heart beating fast. Why does he always need to sneak up on me like that?

"Sorry," Ben chuckled, lifting his hands in surrender, "force of habit ... in my line of work you come home at the weirdest hours, you get used to being as quiet as a burglar." I guess that's why I never know whether he's home or not unless he's talking on the phone.

"It's ok." I mumbled, keeping the door open in hopes that he would catch the hint and leave. The cats were sleeping already, and I needed to start getting ready for bed. The twins forget not all of us can afford to stay up until late hours, some of us need to get up at 6 to get ready for their personal Hell.

"Well, I gotta admit, JoJo," Ben said, not moving an inch, but persistently staring at me like some maniac that doesn't know we live in an alienating society where you're not supposed to give someone your full attention when you're talking to them, "I'm surprised."

My right eyebrow arched the slightest. "About?"

He walked up to me, definitely breaching my personal space, which is something I most definitely hate, but at least he smells nice. "Your friends." Oh, here we go. How can someone like you be friends with beautiful girls like Faith and Hope? I hear that so much, I swear. "I thought you hung out with ..."

"People like me?" Fat, sad, awkward crazy cat moms?

Ben cracked a small smile. "Yeah." Ugh, not you too, Ben, not you too.

"I understand."

"No, you don't." He chuckled, stepping into my comfort zone, which made me back up against the door, so he leaned back as well. "You're think-ing the exact opposite of what I mean." Huh? "Don't get me wrong, Faith and Hope are nice, their brother is an interesting guy, but ... I wouldn't think they're your crowd."

"Why not?" Don't mind me, I was tired as hell, which makes me less aware of how much I talk and what I say.

"You're a dreamer, JoJo. A complex type, delicate yet full of rough angles, while the girls ... they are what you see," having noticed my half offended look – they are my friends after all –, he raised his hands again, "which is not a bad thing, of course. Just ..." he sighed, "I guess what I'm trying to say is, they are what you expect, while you, you are way more than what the eyes meet. Does that make sense?"

No. Not at all. I don't have a clue what are you talking about. You sound crazy, and I don't like having crazy, possibly dangerous neighbors that show up in my apartment, pretty much spending most of their time profiling me.

"Well," Ben clapped his hands once, finally stepping out of the door, "time to sleep. I'll see you tomorrow." Somehow that sounded like a threat.

6. Teen boys are dumb

"Sooooo ..." Joe leaned in, yet pulled back at the same time, pretty much invading my personal space yet keeping the pizza from me. Yes, yes, I am eating pizza for dinner two nights in a row, don't judge me. I gave Joe a dirty look, because you don't dare keep food from a starving woman, but he only chuckled, letting himself in. Again, the only guy ever allowed into my safe haven. He's pretty much the baby brother I never had. Sometimes I think I would have been less awkward, had I had a sibling to practice sociality with.

"Joe ..." I warned, not in the mood, when he plopped onto my couch, leaving the pizza onto my coffee table.

"Yes, Joy ...?" He grinned sheepishly, you know, that teenage grin boy scouts have, halfway between annoying know-it-all and impish little monster that torments you. I like how he feels comfortable with me, to be honest.

I sighed, walking up to the love of my life – pizza, obviously, duh –, "I warn you," I said, grabbing a slice, and taking a bite, "Scott was a bigger asshole than usual today, so I'm not in the mood."

In response, Joe scoffed, grabbing a slice of pizza for himself, and leaning back. "Is Scott ever not an asshole?"

I shrugged, sitting beside him, leaving a seat in between. Joe is probably the one person in my life that understands the importance of personal space. He's the same, doesn't like people getting too close. "I guess those 3 minutes after his quickie with Mandy. So, what do you wanna watch?" I asked. He doesn't work on Mondays, but he does pick up dinner for us and we watch movies together. Told you, he's my brother from another mother, and one of the very, very few people I am comfortable around. Actually, he's probably the only one I am really close to, even more than Hope and Faith. To think I've always hated teenagers, even when I was one.

"Hmmm ... Transformers?" Joe gave me a pleading look.

I rolled my eyes. "You only like that because of Megan Fox."

"Well, duh!" He laughed.

"What happened to 'I don't like skinny'?"

"I never said that, did I?" He munched on another slice of pizza.

I sighed, taking a bite for myself. "I liked you better when you were an awkward kid only interested in his videogames." I teased.

"I still am." He plopped his head back against the couch, suddenly in a mood. Ahhh, to be a teenager prey of raging hormones that change your mood quicker than you can say your name.

"Chloe still not giving you the time of day, huh?"

Joe sighed, staring at the ceiling. Judging by his antics, sometimes, you'd think he's 20 years older than he actually he is. "She's a 10, I'm a 2 at best ... what can I expect?"

I rolled my eyes, taking another slice of pizza. "You're a nice guy."

"Which means I don't get the girl."

"That's not true."

"Don't girls like bad boys?"

I chuckled a bit. "Say, have you been on your sister's Wattpad again?"

"Maybe."

"Joe ..."

"Well, I'm 17 already and I've never had a girlfriend. That makes me a pariah, doesn't it."

"Using the word pariah at 17 years old makes you a pariah, Joe." I teased.

He rolled his eyes, but secretly chuckled. "Where's Ben, by the way?"

I gulped, my hand stopping mid-air as it was bringing another slice of pizza to my mouth. "How would I know?"

"Well ... he seemed pretty taken the other day ..."

"He's just lonely," I took a bite, "says he doesn't have much time to make friends, with work and everything."

"And you believe that?" Joe laughed loudly.

"Why wouldn't I?"

"Aren't you the one always telling me how guys always lie?"

I frowned. What reason would Ben have to lie?

As if he'd read my mind, Joe continued: "Clearly he's after something."

"Like what?"

He rolled his eyes, this time. "Uh ... I don't know, you, maybe?"

I scoffed. "As if."

"Why not?"

Oh, I love you, Joe, but let's not go there. "It's more likely that he's a spy working for the CIA."

Joe scoffed one more time, lying down on the couch to prepare for the movie. "You're really blind, sometimes, Joy."

"Says the guy aiming for the cheerleader when his best friend pines for him."

Joe furrowed his brow, which made him look like a cute puppy. Seriously, I often forget he's pretty much a baby. "What the hell are you talking about, woman?"

I rolled my eyes. Cleverer than most boys his age, but still clueless when it comes to the other gender. "Nothing." I stood up to go get glasses for the both of us. I may not understand a single thing about love and relationship, but it didn't take me much to see that cute little Phoebe, Joe's Chemistry partner, is head over heels for him. And I saw her like, once: she was at the pizzeria when I went to get my dinner on my way home. "So, Transformers?" I decided to change subject when I saw his quizzical look.

Joe remained like that for a few seconds, seemingly doing some mental relationship Math, then his features softened, clear sign he'd given up, and, having plopped back against the couch, he grinned, nodding. I threw the remote at him. "I still think Ben wants to be Mr. Joanna Brooks, though." The little rascal teased as I walked to the sink.

"And you say that based on your vast knowledge and experience in the field?" I teased, to which he threw me a pillow that hit my back, and we both laughed.

Ben into me. As if. The guy just needs friends and I'm his only option since he lacks time to go out and whatnot. Wanna bet the moment he starts making actual friends he'll forget his neighbor?

--

I rolled my eyes for the umpteenth time as I heard Joe snore. He decided to crash on my couch last night, I guess deciding we're at a point in our weird friendship that it was time for me to discover the worst things about him.

Number one: he talks in his dreams, which are mostly all about Chloe Jensen, the superhot cheerleader every boy at his school wants, finally giving him the time of day. Teenage boys are unequivocally dumb, and I hoped Joe would be smarter, but you know, hormones. I don't know Chloe, but if she's as smart as the stereotype, then I'm sorely disappointed in my teeny friend.

Number two: Joe snores. He's not loud ... he's Jurassic Park T-Rex preparing to attack kind of loud. First time I heard it I thought a Mr. Hammond had actually brought dinosaurs back to life. It's true that my apartment is the size of a shoebox, but this kid has some serious problems.

Sighing for the billionth time, I blindly grabbed the phone, to check the time. Four am. The only times I woke up at this hour are when Scott is extra-assholey and claims I can only do inventory before we open, not during, not after. I must have slept 3-4 hours. Deciding it would be useless to try again, I got up. Even my cats were still asleep.

I tiptoed my way around the house, executing my usual routine: prepare food for the cats, shower, get dressed. I even prepared breakfast for Joe, even though I never eat it. All this, and I was out by 5 am.

Since it was way too early for everything, and I had no intention of prolonging my stay in that wretched place that pays my bills, I decided I'd get on with other stuff I'm normally too tired or too lazy to do, like laundry.

Last time I did it, I met my sexy neighbor with whom I haven't spoken since the night he spent amiably in my apartment chatting with my friends and their brother.

Lupus in fabula, Romans would say, meaning, speak of the devil ... the moment I stepped out of my apartment to go do laundry, Ben was about to enter his. He looked disheveled and exhausted – clearly, he'd spent the night out. Is he cheating on his girlfriend?

"Hey, neighbor!" He greeted me, too cheerful and lively for 5 am, even for him.

"Hi." I murmured, holding my laundry basket tight against my hip while simultaneously trying not to blush because I was wearing my uniform – I'm allowed to wear leggings underneath, but skirts, every kind of skirt always makes me nervous, they mercilessly expose my chunky legs.

"How come you're up so early?" Ben asked, unfortunately walking up to me. "Or you didn't sleep at all?" He tilted his head to the side, fainting a malicious smirk. "I heard you had a guest last night." My eyes widened. How would he ... "These walls are really thin," he chuckled, only to then wince a bit, "actually ..." he grazed the back of his neck, wearing an apologetic look on his face, "I should apologize ... you probably hear me on the phone a lot."

I wanted to say no, I don't, I'm not an eavesdropper, but it would be a lie. Sure, I can't really hear what he's saying, but I definitely hear his voice a lot. "It's ok." I mumbled, staring at my feet.

Ben raked a hand over his face, clearly sleepy. "I had a wedding yesterday. Italians. It went on until 4 am. Actually, I think they're still there, but the groom had mercy of me and sent me home."

Why did it sound like he was trying to justify to me? Because of that, I felt the need to justify as well. "My friend crashed on my couch, but he snores, so ..."

Ben chuckled again. Nice sound. "That must have been torture," he continued laughing, "my ex was like that, it was definitely a deal-breaker, hope it isn't for you, too."

My eyes widened for the second time and I blushed. "It's not like that!"

"Why not?"

Because he's underage and I'd go to jail? Or because the idea of me and Joe together makes me puke? Or just both? "We're friends."

"The same kind of friends I've been trying to be with you?"

I blinked my eyes, perplexed. What did that even mean?

Ben covered his mouth with a hand, "time to go to bed, clearly I'm not in control of what I say anymore." He backed away. "See you tonight, JoJo!" And then he vanished. Well, that was hella weird.

7. Ben The Serial Killer

You know, if I was Hindu, I would be happy to live the shitty life I'm living, because it would mean my next one would be splendid. Unfortunately, I'm Christian. Or not. I haven't really thought about it. The point is, every day of sufferance in that diner, every day I come home without having knocked Scott over his head and sold his organs to the black market should be a day I get back in the next life, otherwise it's not fair, is it? Why endure all this if there's no reward? The measly wage he gives me doesn't cover a quarter of the insults I gotta swallow every day.

Today was family day, even. This new ludicrous event my employer came up with offers free meals to mothers with children under 3 years old. Do you have any idea what does that mean? You guessed it: a diner packed with bellowing toddlers and uncaring mothers that gave up on any sort of civil education for their offspring.

Obviously, we're not talking about rich moms with nannies following them, we're talking about neighborhood youngish moms that would have locked up their mothers-in-law in a retirement home, hadn't they realized those old women are quite handy when it comes to babysitting: don't need to pay them, they work around the clock. I pity the poor ladies, to be honest. Their sons must have been deaf and completely idiotic to choose such life companions. Then again, it's usually ex cheerleaders that married straight out of high school, so you can guess what's their best quality. And yes, that is why Scott decided to do this event. He saw a group of these mothers at the mall nearby one day, and decided he needed to see more of them.

Don't get me wrong, I have nothing against (ex) cheerleaders nor girls that choose to be mothers instead of career women. It's their choice. But also neglecting their children and subsequently making of them future serial killers is a choice, a choice these women seem to have fiercely embraced.

Naturally, Mandy is always conveniently sick every family day, and Scott is too stupid, or rather, too distracted by breastfeeding mothers to notice. I don't think I've ever taken one single day off since I started this job. It's a good thing I never get sick.

I was more than exhausted, I was worn out, completely drained of my every energy, and when that happens, absurdly, I lose control. That's why, when I saw Ben standing against my door, I growled loudly, not in the slightest mood to deal with his chatty self tonight.

"Well, hello, there," he greeted cheerfully, "I ordered Japanese, it'll be here in a few minutes. Hope you like sushi."

This is the problem introverts always have to deal with: extroverts just don't know the meaning of boundaries. They don't think about how would someone react, if something makes the other person uncomfortable, they just go ahead and do whatever pops up in their gleeful minds. "I need to sleep." I murmured as I walked to my door, not minding my gruff tone.

"Bad day?"

"Worse than awful."

"Sorry to hear." Ben sounded truthfully sorry and I regretted being rude. He was just trying to be kind.

Sighing, I put my key into the lock. "Can we reschedule? I really badly need to be alone tonight."

"Why?" Ben perused me.

"What do you mean, why? I just-" I stopped when I realized he was smiling. Why was he smiling? Is he some kind of sadist that enjoys people's misfortunes?

"I'm sorry, but," he chuckled, "this is the first time you actually speak to me! I'm amazed and freaked out and happy at the same time."

"What?"

"JoJo ... I've lived here for about a month now, and this is the first time we actually have a conversation."

Oh. Right. I obviously blushed, which didn't help my predicament, but I was way too tired to really mind. "I'm sorry." It was the only thing I could think of.

"No need to be." Much to my surprise, my neighbor opened my door for me and, having grabbed my hand, he pulled me inside. I was even too tired to feel the tingles on my skin at his touch, but they were there. "Mmh ... bathroom?"

Blinking my eyes, I answered without thinking: "In the bedroom."

In other circumstances, I probably would have screamed or at least planted my feet on the ground not to move, but with barely 3-4 hours of sleep and coming from a 12 hour shift during which I hadn't been able to sit for one single minute, I barely realized Ben – this weird guy I met in the laundry

room about a month ago and that has been obsessively lurking around me
– was taking me into my bedroom.

He made me sit on the bed, then headed for the bathroom. "I was sure you
had a bathtub!" He screamed, excited. Normally, I would see a murdered
using the bathtub to store the blood he will drink once he's finished slicing
me up to throw me into the river, but his voice was too genuinely naïve to
think bad. Even in my tiredness, I doubt he realized what he said sounded
ambiguous.

I heard him fumbling in the bathroom, but my eyes were kind of closing
and I unconsciously lay down on the bed. Five minutes, just five minutes
to rest my eyes.

--

When I reopened my eyes, the sun was filtering through my curtains. I
jumped. Late for work? Last time I was late, like, 3 minutes late, Scott
made me clean the old bathrooms. The ones that hadn't been cleaned
since Clinton was president. Panicking, I scrambled to get out of bed, and
started searching for my uniform. Where the hell did I put it?

"You're wearing it." Ben's voice filled my ears, and I screeched. Literally screeched, which obviously made him chuckle. "Sorry, I should have
knocked."

Eyes wide, I stared at him, freaked out. Where did he come from? What
happened last night? Why was he in my bedroom? Unconsciously, I backed
against the wall, creeped out. Was I right? Is he a murderer?

"I already fed the kittens, so you don't need to worry about that. And I
called the diner and told them you're sick."

Is this how I am going to die? Trapped in my bedroom, no one knowing
where I am? The only thing I could hope for was that Scott would be

furious enough to show up here and yell at me. At least I could feed him to Ben The Serial Killer.

"I have to go to work, but I can make you breakfast first." My neighbor slash assassin went on. "You should rest."

"What ..." I mumbled, my heart beating fast.

Ben took a few calm steps, and came to stand right in front of me, close enough for me to smell him, but not enough for me to have to look up to see his face. "You pretty much passed out last night." He said. "I thought I'd prepare you a bubble bath to soothe your nerves and relax you, but when I came back into the room you were sound asleep," he chuckled, "I just took fed the kittens then took them to my apartment for the night. I brought them back just half an hour ago, to feed them. Then I thought I'd look in to see if you were okay but saw you panicking while looking for your uniform. It was a funny sight, I'll admit."

"What ..." I repeated, "why ... I ... who ..."

"Call it neighborly kindness." Ben shrugged, digging his hands into his jeans pockets, as if to assure me he meant no harm. "Or ... friendship, if you like."

I blinked my eyes so many times, I probably looked like I was having a stroke. Was this him trying to prove we can actually be friends?

"I'll leave you to it now," Ben said, finally walking away, "I can be back for lunch, I think. I'll bring some takeaway ... not Japanese though, sushi last night was awful. Is there a decent restaurant around here?"

"I ... I don't understand ..." I stuttered, disbelieving. Was this a dream? Or a nightmare?

Ben smiled the slightest. "It's simple, JoJo. I finally realized you don't hate me, you're just shy. And I can work with shy."

"But ..."

"If it helps, I'm gay," he shrugged, "so you have nothing to fear."

8. Just keep swimming

"So ... tell me about yourself."

Ugh, not that line. What am I supposed to say about myself? That I'm 28 and never had a boyfriend? That my crippling social anxiety mixed with nonexistent self-esteem keeps me not just from enjoying life but also from progressing in any way? Let's be honest, if I was any more sociable, I might have at least gotten a reply from the magazines, publishers, newspapers and everything whose jobs ads I answered to. Well, that or I'm really mediocre, which is also possible. Which also means I am going to die a virgin in Scott's diner, between mustard-stained walls, indecent bathrooms and rude customers.

I nearly jumped when I felt Ben patting on my arm, like a kid wanting you to buy him something. "Sorry, I forgot, no touching," he raised his hands in mock surrender.

I wanna say I wasn't shocked by his revelation, but I was. I mean, it's more likely than him having a thing for me, as Joe thought, absolutely, but if anything I thought he was already taken; then again maybe he is, all those times on the phone he talks to a boyfriend, not girlfriend.

I owe him, though. When Scott called to make sure I was really sick, Ben pulled a concerned doctor act that's worthy of an Oscar. He even kind of terrorized Scott when he implied that I was sick because he was overworking me (which is true, after all). Of course, my employer still demands that I go back to work tomorrow and he won't pay for this day I skipped, but it's still something. I slept all morning, then Ben came back in time for lunch, bringing takeaway, and now there we were, in my kitchen, intent on eating.

"Do you have siblings?" He asked, restarting to eat his lunch.

I shook my head in response, keeping my eyes on the plate. "Do you?"

"Yeah, two younger brothers." He reached for his phone while still chewing, and scrolled a bit. "Here." He handed me the phone.

The picture on the screen was clearly a family photo, I mean the professional ones, which makes sense, Ben being a photographer. It was a really nice family. One of the brothers looked to be 16, while the other looked 14; they looked a lot like the man standing next to their mother, but the woman didn't resemble any of them. She reminded me a lot of Ben, though: hair color, eyes, even the nose.

As if he'd read my mind, Ben pointed out: "They're my half-brothers, technically."

"Oh."

"I never knew my dad. My mother says he died in a war, but she never said which one, so as I grew older I realized she was just lying to protect me."

Oh dear ... too much too soon. Not that I don't want to know more about him, I do, but this is a lot, and we've barely started talking and I don't know how to deal with sad stories ...

"It's not that bad," Ben laughed, probably able to read my thoughts on my face, "my mom married Austin when I was 9, he's a nice guy."

I looked at the picture again. It was clear that the woman had Ben that she was really young. She was probably fresh out of high school or barely 16. "What about the child?"

Ben widened his eyes for a quick second. "The child?"

"Yeah, it's barely visible but there's a child in the corner." The picture had been taken in their backyard, I think, or in a playground, because I saw some sort of playfield in the background; and it's in that playfield that I saw the child. There was a young woman – probably early twenties – watching him, but he'd sneaked out and you could see him hiding behind a tree, watching the family take a photo. Maybe it was some random curious kid, but he was smiling at the camera.

"Oh, uh ..." Ben seemed taken off guard; maybe it was really just a random kid that'd photobombed their family moment and he'd never noticed.

"Do you know him?" I asked, eyes back on the picture. I couldn't see much of the child, but it was an interesting sight. Dark hair, lively and kind eyes.

"Uh ... that's ..." Ben grabbed the phone from my hands, not even looking at the picture, and put it back into his pocket, "my cousin."

His cousin? I guess that would explain why the child was photobombing but he wasn't in the picture officially: he knew them but it was something amongst core family, no cousins or uncles and stuff.

Ben seemed very nervous, though. In fact he immediately stood, leaving lunch. "I should get back to work, it's late." Having said that, he rushed out, barely saying bye.

Something definitely spooked him, but I don't understand what could have. He's always so calm and peaceful.

--

"Well, well, Her Majesty finally deigns us of their presence!" Scott barked the moment I stepped foot into the diner. I had to do all I could not to roll my eyes in front of him. "Did you rest? Poor baby is overworked." He mimicked a child whining.

I ignored him completely, and headed straight to the first table I could see, to clean it. I didn't think he would be glad to see me, but I gotta admit, I thought his reaction in seeing me back to work would be way worse. In other circumstances, Scott would have listed all the possible insults he could come up with, in order of hurt, starting from the least offensive to the worst offense possible, which, I guess in his mind, was supposed to make me snap and turn in my notice. I would have, long time ago ... if only I had somewhere else to go.

Obviously, Mandy was late. She has her mani-pedi on Wednesdays, and the off to the hairstylist to revamp that pale red she still claims to be her original color. The good thing is that she's normally in a better mood on Wednesdays, so she's nicer to Scott, and in turn he's nicer to me. If cutting in half the number of daily insults is what you'd call being nicer.

I went on with my morning, even though Scott now and then came shouting and yelling. I didn't really hear him, I was thinking about Ben. No, not in that way. I was just confused by what happened yesterday at my place. Why react so weird at the mention of his baby cousin?

"Helloooo! Earth to Fatass!!!" Scott bellowed so loudly that a) I could hear it echoing in my head; b) a couple of clients winced. Not that they'd give two shits about an employer belittling his employee, it's just that he was too loud for their delicate ears. "What the fuck is wrong with you, today!!"

He went on. "Are you deaf now??!" Nothing new here. What was new was that I felt his hand on my arm, and too late I realized he'd pushed me, so I lost my balance, and wound up crashing against a set of tables, which in turn broke – either due to my weight of because they were too old. I landed on my butt, and my back hit one of the tables, which hurt way more than if I'd hit a stone wall. That table hadn't been cleaned yet, which I guess is what Scott had been yelling about, so the remnants of what the clients had eaten crashed onto me entirely. None of the clients turned to look at what happened or see if I was ok. None.

I could see the cook laughing as he watched me, same as Scott, who was smirking in triumph, probably thinking this would be the proverbial straw that broke the camel's back to make me quit. And it probably would have been, had I, again, had somewhere else to go.

Insults have always been a daily routine in this diner, but Scott, as much of an asshole as he is, had never once come this far. Sure, he'd pushed me at times, but no like this. I should have been livid, furious. But I wasn't. I remained calm as I removed the chewed food from my hair and my uniform, some even got into my bra, but I couldn't remove it right there. All the while, Scott kept ranting about how I should have cleaned that table, this wouldn't have happened, how I was such a lazy ass, he didn't know why did he still keep me on.

I was in a whole different dimension. When you've worked for such a bastard as long as I have, you learn the long-lost art of self-control very fast, which comes in handy when such things happen. I could probably become a Tibetan monk thanks to Scott.

"What's going on here?" A stern voice asked from the door, just as I was struggling to get back up.

Scott's grin faded as he anxiously replied: "Nothing, just a clumsy waitress."

This clumsy waitress could feel her bones aching as she stood up. I realized why did Scott start acting all nice and serious, when I noticed the person that had just entered wore a police uniform.

She was somewhat short, or at any rate shorter than me, her hands were at her hips, her stance was combative, as if she were ready to arrest someone. The look on her face said she didn't buy a single word of what Scott said. Hence, she turned to me. "You okay, honey?"

I nodded without replying, and Scott filled in for me: "It's alright, ma'am, Joanna falls all the time, breaking things," like the plates that by miracle hadn't cut me, "I only keep her on because I don't want her to go back to her old habits," to which he mimicked a "glub, glub" that was meant to mean I was an ex alcoholic.

The officer didn't seem convinced, but because there was some chatter on the radio, she focused on that, during which time Scott saw to send me meaningful looks: play along. Play along, or you're fired. Play along, or this doesn't end here. I wasn't scared for my life, but I was for my livelihood, so I nodded.

I know, I know, it's not a very feminist approach, nor self-respecting, really. But you're barely above water as I am, you swallow all the dirt and the hurt, and keep going. Just keep swimming, Dory would say, no? Just keep swimming.

9. The very heart of everlasting clichés

"**W**hat's that?"

I jumped out of my skin when I heard Ben's voice. "You need to stop doing that." I muttered, my heart still beating fast.

"Talk to you, you mean?" He teased, to which I rolled my eyes.

"Sneak up on me." I don't know why I'm so tense lately. Oh, wait, I do know. Remember that cop that came in after Scott pushed me? She came back, asking all sorts of questions, and as a result, Scott has been a breathing on my neck, wanting to make sure I give her the right story: that I'm clumsy, that he only hired me as an act of charity, some pastor of some church convinced him to because I was in the AA and needed a second chance to rebuild my life. I don't know why he didn't just say I accidentally fell, instead of making up a whole good Samaritan tale, but that's what it is and I gotta stick to it if I want to keep my job. Which I don't want to, but I must.

I know my parents would do somersaults to support me financially, but they can't afford it and I don't want to bother them. Besides, I know that even only trying to ask for help would raise the major argument they have been hassling me with: why don't you just come back home? Find a job here? Clearly the big city isn't your place. I love my parents, but they're very pragmatic, and after 28 years, it's still difficult for them to accept that they birthed an idealist for a daughter.

Well, truth is, the idealist has left her place to the pragmatist that can barely make ends meet, but it's still better than going back home, riding that glorious horse named Failure.

"Is everything alright?" Ben asked, staring straight into my eyes, which is so, so uncomfortable, I swear, I don't know why people still keep it up.

"Yes." I shouldered my bag, and went on walking towards our building. For some reason, Ben has started waiting for me at the bus stop near our condo. The first time we accidentally took the same bus, it was because he'd been running some errands, but then it happened again and again for various reasons, so in the end he realized that our schedules aren't that divergent, so he could make an effort and escort me home like a true gentleman. His words, not mine.

It's been two weeks since that time I "accidentally fell" at work, my back is fine, but you know, someone has realized that literally mistreating me – as opposed to verbally – not only is more efficient, but it also makes his day better. So yeah, I had a few bruises here and there. Not that Scott truly beats me or hits me, no, just ... pushing a little harder than normal, or accidentally making me trip; you know, the whole school bully portfolio.

I'll admit it's becoming increasingly difficult to hide the bruises. One, because they're multiplying; two, because he's becoming careless about where do these bruises appear; three, because Officer Ford has decided something's weird in that diner, so she's become a loyal customer; and finally four ... because I have a nosy neighbor that insists on knowing every detail of my day and my life and when I'm exhausted – which I am every day more because mobbing involves wearing out the employee you want to fire but can't – I don't really control what I say. In short, January wasn't my month, and February didn't start too excellently either. I'm gonna go out on a limp here and say March isn't gonna be a happy hour.

"Are you sure?" Ben asked as he caught up with me.

"Yes."

"We're not back to monosyllables, are we?" He wondered, pouty.

"No." I opened the building's door, and headed to the elevator.

"You sure?"

"Yes." When I replied that, Ben chuckled, and I could barely hide a faint smile, too. "I'm sorry, I'm just tired."

"You're always tired, maybe you need a vacation."

I let out a loud wry laugh. A vacation. Scott would skin me alive if I even dared mention the word. "I need a new life." I murmured, without thinking.

"That too."

I turned to Ben, embarrassed – my face turned red already, that goes without saying – but also surprised. Do you know that feeling when someone actually pays attention to you? Like, actually listens to what you're saying? Because I don't. Or, I didn't ... until Ben.

"I mean what I said," he went on as we stepped onto the elevator, "I don't think your highest ambition is to slave away in a diner."

Of course not, but beggars can't be choosers and dreamers can't afford reality. "It's what keeps me above water." I muttered, not much keen on discussing my private business with him. It's true that we talk more, but not enough for me to just spit out everything.

"But that's the thing," Ben went on, turning to me, "it doesn't have to be like that."

Said every rich kid ever. I mentally rolled my eyes. How easy do people make it sound. Find a job, find a boyfriend, get settled, have kids, have a life. Easier said than done. When you're like me, you don't have many choices, so you take whatever you can get. When you're mediocre, at best, you can't exactly aspire to grandeur. The biggest lie I've ever been told was: you can do anything. No, you can't. You can do anything if you have money to invest or beauty or charm to use as weapon, not if you're poor, ugly and lame as hell.

You think I haven't been to interviews? I have. But let's be honest here, this isn't The Devil Wears Prada or Ugly Betty, you don't get hired as a test of some sort then turn into the most perfect employee ever and they realized you're just too essential to let you go and they offer you your dream life on a silver plate.

In real life – my life – it usually goes like this:

1. I apply for a job concerning my area of expertise

2. Option A: I get denied because I'm not qualified enough

3. Option B: I get selected for an interview based on my academic path

4. Option A: I go to the interview and stun them with my absolute lack of charm and ability to speak fluently in my own language – result, application denied

5. Option B: I go to the interview, force myself to be normal – result, application denied on grounds of lack of above-mentioned charm (read beauty)

6. Option C: demoralized by the enormous string of failures, I don't even go to the interview

I guess I lied when I said I don't have choices. I do. It's just a mix of terribly choices born out of the terrible one: deciding to do things on my own instead of remain in my hometown, marry the first guy my ever so intriguing aunt introduces me to, have a thousand kids, be happy slaving away in the kitchen. In the end, is it even that different? I'm still slaving away in a kitchen, pushed around by a sad little man whose apical expectations on life have been nipped in the bud by and overlord mother that asphyxiated him by deciding every single detail of his life. Is that so different from life as a housewife?

Don't get me wrong, max respect for housewives. I'm talking about life as a housewife of a husband that has been chosen for me, and, believe me, my aunt's taste in men has only 2 colors: handsome and rich for her daughters; sad, lonely but averagely wealthy for me. Of course, she couldn't introduce and ugly duckling to a swan, could she? It's merely pragmatic.

"I mean it, JoJo." Ben said, his expression serious. "Don't you think you owe it to yourself? To be the best version you can possibly be?"

I sighed. Where have I heard that one before. "This is the best version of myself."

"Bullshit. This is nowhere near your max potential and you know it. You're just too lazy to do something about it."

"Lazy?" I scoffed, outraged, "lazy? I'm lazy?!" I nearly yelled as I got out of the elevator, sick and tired of his new age mantras about infinite possibilities. News flash, honey, this world only rewards the bold and beautiful, it doesn't give a rat's ass about the fat, sad and lonely. And you know what, it's even fair. Survival of the fittest and all that. I just accepted that I'm part of the latter category and there's nothing I can do about it. Might as well make this ride the least painful possible by enjoying the little things in my life, like my cats, my books and my food.

"Yes, lazy." Ben insisted, pissing me off. "You decided life is an unchanging, immobile monster you can't fathom to face, let alone defeat. Like a princess locked in a castle protected by a ferocious dragon, you're there waiting for the valorous champion to show up and save you."

"Now, wait a minute ..."

"Life doesn't give, JoJo." He stated solemnly. "It's up to you to take. Quoting my favorite author: Life is a storm, my young friend. You will bask in the sunlight one moment, be shattered on the rocks the next. What makes you a man is what you do when that storm comes. You must look into that storm and shout as you did in Rome. Do your worst, for I will do mine! Then the fates will know you as we know you."

I rolled my eyes, this time literally. "Dumas? Really? Aren't you being a little bit overdramatic?"

Ben laughed. "First of all, note to self: it takes books, to really make you speak. Secondly, kudos for knowing Dumas," in saying that, he tipped his imaginary hat, "and thirdly ... it's the truth, JoJo. You remember when Montecristo was trapped in that prison for life? Forgotten by all, including his fiancée? Did he give up?"

"That's different ..."

"How is it different?" He asked rhetorically. "How is it any different, when you're just as trapped in your own prison? Your mental prison." He flicked my head, which annoyed me immensely. "I'll repeat myself, JoJo: life doesn't give. Forget that nonsense about lemons and lemonades. Life doesn't give you shit, it's up to you, whether you want to just lie down and crawl your way to the end, or stand up proudly and be able to shout "I did it my way", as you so like to sing when you think no one can hear you."

Inspiring words, really. But nothing I've never heard before in movies and whatnot. "That's all very well, but how am I supposed to work on my future when I don't even have time to live my present?" I don't know why I said it out loud, and I know that my cheeks were as red as tomatoes, but the cat was out of the bag now.

"Simple," Ben shrugged, "you start by letting go of the past. Present and future will thank you for it."

"The past?"

He fainted a smile. "Let me guess: working class family, not able to afford much but not destitute either; shy and introvert child that finds comfort in her books decides that the world outside isn't worthy of her attention, but at the same time, her inner world is too little to be confined within, so she needs her own space – and that's where New York comes in. The city of possibilities. But no possibilities ever come your way, and if they do, they swerve and head to the opposite direction out of the blue."

Frighteningly accurate. Like I said, it's different when someone actually listens and pays attention to you, even when you don't notice.

"It's time to archive the past rejections and start working for future success-es, JoJo. It'll sound cliché, but the only way to thrive, is to think positive."

He could be one of those overly paid life coaches, I swear. "And where should I start, oh Wise One?" I asked sardonically, gaining more confidence by the minute, if only just with this one weirdly sympathetic, kind, altru-istic guy.

He grinned, I would have said mischievously. "From the very heart of everlasting clichés: a makeover.

Oh, no. Oh, no, no, no, no, no.

"Tomorrow we'll go shopping."

10. Ben The Magnanimous

"**Y**ou realize I don't have money for this, right?" I grumbled when we got to the mall. Last time I went to a place like this, I was 13 and I needed a bra. After that, thank heavens, e-commerce became a thing.

"Makeover doesn't need to be expensive." Ben argued.

"No? It literally involves buying things, which entails spending money I don't have." I scoffed, to which he turned to me, half smiling. "What?"

"Nothing. I just like that you're finally coming around."

"Coming around?"

"Talking."

"Oh." I blushed a little. "Well, I'm not a Tibetan monk, I'm just ..."

"Selective."

I cracked a small smile. He totally nailed it. "Yeah."

"Well," he brought a hand to his heart, "I'm flattered to be included in your tiny circle," he tipped off his imaginary hat, but because he was walking backwards, he almost tripped into the dustbin behind him. I tried not to laugh, but a small chuckle came out.

"So where do we start?" Or rather, what should I prepare to first?

"The clothes, of course."

"Ben ..." I grumbled as he marched straight towards one of those shops that 9 times out of 10 don't sell plus size clothing.

"Yes, we're on a budget, I know ... don't worry."

No ... they're not gonna have anything that fits me and I don't wanna make a fool of myself. Why do you think I always buy online? You can pick anything without having to worry about scornful or worse, pitiful looks from clerks or other clients. When you're a certain size, you just learn to live based on a different standard. Your clothes will cost way more, they'll be less easy to find and less pretty; 99% of the clerks in female clothing shops are thin and skinny, and 99% of them is a haughty little witch that thinks your weight is your own fault and you're disgusting, which, I mean, in a way, is true.

I wish I could say my weight is to blame on genetics or metabolism and whatever, but the truth is, I've just never done anything about it. Of course, genetics does play a role – being born from two chubby people, it's hard to come out incline to thinness –, but it's also true that the years I should have spent shaping my pubescent self into becoming at least skinnier, were instead wasted declaring my undying love for the couch and hiding from, well, pretty much everyone.

Case in point, the moment we entered the shop, I noticed the above-mentioned haughty clerks. More specifically, I caught their bewildered look on their faces when they realize this humpback whale that just entered their domain wasn't alone, but was accompanied by a pretty handsome guy. I don't even think Ben is out of the ordinary in the scale of male beauty, but anyone would look 10 times better when next to me.

"Hello," a blonde super skinny clerk approached us as soon as we stepped into the dresses area, a big fake grin splattered on her white porcelain teeth.

"Oh, hello!" Ben greeted in his usual perky manner, clearly missing the x-ray she did to his body. I guess not being interested in women, he doesn't even notice when they check him out.

"What can I do you for?"

Weird inversion.

"Well, we're looking for a dress for my lovely friend here," Ben pointed at me, which gained me yet another perplexed look from a woman in the same shop, "do you think you can help?"

"Absolutely!" The blondie grinned like a Cheshire cat, and for some reason in my head resonated an 'off with her head!!!' meant to warn me I was going in the wrong direction.

Still, I followed Blondie – I'm not kidding, the name on her tag actually read Blondie – deep into the rabbit's hole called back of the store, where, I'm guessing, they keep the super large clothes no one ever asks for in here – because, let's be honest, no sane woman of my size would dare step foot into the untethered from reality, ethereal realm of the skinny. The last plus size girl that entered this place was probably catapulted out or swallowed by a black hole so that she wouldn't ruin the pureness of the store.

I did notice that the other clerks were looking at me, even more so when, having realized I was moving at a snail pace, Ben – my lovely but oh, so oblivious Ben – placed a hand on the small of my back and started gently pushing me towards the direction Blondie had taken. Yes, obviously I was terrified at the thought that he would feel how sweaty my back actually was, despite the multiple layers of Winter clothes, but it was still a nice feeling, I'll have to admit.

We stopped when we finally reached our destination, which felt like a hundred miles away from the front of the store, might I add. "Wait here," Blondie said, then disappeared behind a sliding door.

"Don't be nervous." Ben said, finally removing his hand from my back, "it's just a shop, like any other."

Except every other shop isn't purposely made to make you feel worthless, meaningless and a billion times more of a loser than you already feel. I could swing it at a shoe shop, you know. Sure, I've got big feet, but it's not so bad. But clothes? Dresses even! "I don't like dresses." I mumbled.

"Have you ever tried one?"

"Yes."

"One not made for a child and worn at a religious ceremony?"

Ugh. Damn you, Ben, why do you have to read me so well? "No ..."

"Case in point." He grinned, shrugging, then dipped his hands into his pockets. "This is part of the makeover, JoJo."

"You said clothes, not dresses." I pointed out, mildly bitter, as I stared at the sliding door Blondie had disappeared from, expecting her to come back with a squad of beauty experts ready to torture me like in Miss Congeniality.

"Dresses are clothes."

"Not in my book."

Ben chuckled. "The point is to open you up to possibilities, JoJo, prove you that the world outside isn't that evil."

Then we've come to the worst place possible. These shops are incarnated evil for those like me.

Finally, after what felt like forever, Blondie came out, with another girl on tow. This one looked ... normal. She was curvy, yet so beautiful. Is that even possible? That's an oxymoron, no?

"This is Valerie." Blondie introduced, pointing at the curvy goddess I could not believe existed. "She will help you."

Valerie offered us a gentle smile, then nodded at Blondie, who left, the noise of her heels clicking away rumbling in my head.

"Hey! You came!" Valerie took me off guard when she jumped into Ben's arms, squeezing him in the kind of tight hug you'd expect from a long lost friend.

"I told you I would drop by." He laughed, kissing her cheek and reciprocating the hug, which left me more befuddled than the clerks we saw at the entrance. Especially because their hug was quite long.

Finally, when they parted, Valerie turned to me, a big smile on her face. "And you brought a friend!"

"This is JoJo-I mean ... Joanna." Ben corrected when he remember I only accept his nickname when we're alone.

"Hi, Joanna, I'm Valerie!" The curvy goddess extended her hand for me to shake it, which I did, without thinking.

"Valerie and I went to school together." Ben explained, seeing me baffled.

"Oh." That explains it.

"More than that." Valerie grinned, rolling her eyes at him. "But this one ..." she flicked his head, "went AWOL after graduation."

Ben chuckled nervously, scratching the back of his head. "It happens, high school uh friends get lost."

"Uh huh. More like you just forgot about me." She pouted.

In all that, I remained speechless, staring at the both of them. It's weird, I'd almost gotten used to being Ben's only friend in New York, and it was nice, we started spending a lot of time together. I guess now it's over.

"So, Joanna," Valerie turned to me, "you and I ... are going to have some fun!" she entwined my arm with hers, and stuck out her tongue to Ben, "you go do some boy stuff, I'll send her back in a couple of hours."

Oh, no, no. Don't leave me with a stranger. Please, please, no.

"I'll stay." Ben sent me a sneaky glance, which was meant to say, much to my relief, that he knew I would be way too uncomfortable if left alone.

Valerie looked in between us, somewhat thoughtful. She probably thought it was kind of him to be so nice to such a lost cause. Ben The Magnanimous, helping disastrous girls find themselves.

"That'll spoil the surprise effect, but if you insist ..." Valerie murmured, leaving my arm to start walking the same path we'd just come from, "follow me, please." We did. It took a little bit, but when we finally reached our destination – the opposite side of the shop, again, because these damn places are larger than my whole neighborhood back home –, I was surprised to find way more normal women than I'd ever expected.

With normal I mean normal size. As in, overweight or even straight plus size: the kind of women you wouldn't expect to see around here. They were roaming that side of the store eagerly and anxiously, as if worried their preferred items might go out of stock.

"Valerie is a stylist," Ben explained as we followed her towards the dresses, "her clothes are in this store only for now, but will go nationwide soon enough, I'm sure."

"You're too nice!" Valerie yelled from behind the stack of dresses she'd just taken out of the racks.

Ben laughed, which made his presence known to the other women in that side of the store. It wasn't surprising to see how their eyes widened when they saw him. I dare say a couple even ran away.

Valerie grabbed my hand, and dragged me into one of the changing stalls. "Try these on!" She ordered, handing me the dresses, which felt like a thousand, but it was only something less than ten. "Meanwhile I'll look for other clothing items and everything else."

"But ..." I wanted to argue that she shouldn't go through such troubles, because I can't afford this stuff. It probably costs more than my rent.

"Don't worry, honey, you're on a friends discount." She grinned, to which I frowned.

"I ..." I blushed, so I lowered my gaze, "Ben ..."

"We go way back, sweetheart. As a favor to him, anything you buy to him is 50% off." I still can't afford it. "Officially ..." Valerie winked at me, "unofficially ... all free."

"What ..."

"My clothes, my prices," she shrugged, which didn't make any sense, considering she's selling this stuff to shops. But I didn't have time to argue, she disappeared behind the curtain, leaving me alone with the stack of dresses I didn't know what to do with.

"JoJo?" Ben called from the outside, making my heart thump, as if he could see me naked, even though I was still fully clothed."

"Y-Yes ...?"

"Try them on."

"But ..."

"Try them on. Trust me. If you start thinking I'm actually doing this to help, not to set you up for a prank or whatever else, it'll be a lot easier and the day will go a lot smoother."

11. If you sleep with a pig, you get what comes with it

Why. Why, why, why does it have to be dresses? Why can't it be just new jeans and shirts? What's this dictatorship where a woman isn't a woman unless she's exposing her skin? Why does it have to be dresses? I thought we'd reached enough equality for me not be forced into a dress. There's pantsuits, you know, and a woman can look good even wearing just large clothes that hide pretty much everything. But dresses! Dresses hide nothing! Especially not those that Valerie seemed keen on torturing me with.

"You ready, Joanna?" She yelled from outside the dressing booth.

Of course I wasn't not ready. How could I be ready. The dresses she gave me were for totally different people. This isn't me, not in the slightest, tiniest, flimsiest bit.

"JoJo, come on, let's see." Ben called.

I sighed, trying to make myself as small as possible. My face was as red as a tomato. It's a miracle that I shave regularly due to my work uniform, even though I always wear either leggings or thick stockings with it. But a dress!

A dress without stockings, revealing my ultra-imperfect pale skin! That's just not going to happen, no, no.

"JoJo?" Ben called again, this time a bit closer, "are you dressed?"

"Not yet."

"You sure?"

What do you mean, am I sure? How can someone not be sure whether she's dressed or not?

"Joanna, either you come out, or I come in. You pick." Ben claimed, probably stern for the very first time, which did surprise me, but it also scared the hell out of me; because by now I know him enough to be 100% he would keep his word and come into the booth. I couldn't allow that.

Heaving a deep sigh, and trying to pull in as much of my chubbiness as possible, I grabbed the curtain, and opened it. I felt like I was boiling, so my face was surely inventing new shades of red, and my armpits were beginning to cry profusely. Long, agonizing, moments of silence followe d.Then, Ben cleared his throat and scratched the back of his neck, looking perplexed. Valerie's eyes were on him, seeking approval. "That's-uh ..." he blinked his eyes, "that's ... that's a lot of pink, Val ..."

"Yes!" She screamed excited, finally turning to look at me. "Do you love it or do you adore it?!"

I loathe it? Hate it? Abhor it? I think this dressed should be prosecuted for crimes against humanity?

Ben bit his lips, eyes still well focused on me, but I could see clearly that he was trying to repress a chuckle. I guess I looked that bad that he was dying to just laugh of me.

"So?!" Valerie asked, impatient.

He grimaced as he turned to her. "Val ..." he bit his bottom lip again, "Joanna hates pink."

I do? I mean, yes, I do. But how does he know that? Well, he did ask me once what was my favorite color and I said I don't really care for colors, it's everyone except pink and purple, and I love black and white. But ... I didn't think he would remember. Who actually remembers what people tell them? Answers to those silly routine questions like what's your favorite color even!

"Oh." Valerie's excited smile faded away, only to be replaced by a disappointed frown. It looked as if Ben had just offended her in the worst possible way.

"I mean ... don't get me wrong, it's a nice dress," he mended, I guess seeing as much as I that her heart had been broken in a thousand pieces, "it's just not ... her. I mean ... JoJo wouldn't wear something like that, and the whole point of this is to make her comfortable in her own skin." He gave her a sweet smile. "You do remember how this process goes, don't you?" They exchanged meaningful looks. Clearly, I missed some secret reminiscence.

After a few seconds during which Valerie's smile went from uncertain to sweet, to finally grateful and proud, she nodded. "You're right, I'm sorry." Does this mean I can avoid dresses? She took a few steps, and entered the dressing booth behind me. She then reemerged with all the dresses she'd told me to try on and I hadn't. "Take that off, I need to rethink this entirely."

I obeyed without a word, glad I could finally get rid of that absurd dress and that none of them had even looked at my ugly chubby thighs and crooked legs, not to mention my giant flat feet. As I undressed, I could hear them talking lowly.

"You should have been a stylist." This was Valerie. "Or a personal shopper. You've always had incredible eye for these things."

Ben laughed. "You know it's not my thing."

"But you're so good at it!"

"Not really. It's just ..."

"What?" She inquired, and I instinctively leaned closer to the curtain, in order to better hear what he was about to say; that, unfortunately, almost made me fall, but I kept myself miraculously, yet not without thumping against the wall behind me.

"Everything alright in there?" Ben asked, his tone latched with concern.

"Yes!" I nearly screamed, afraid he'd enter. I was halfway through taking off the dress, that's why my balance had been unsteady. After a moment of silence, they restarted talking, and I heaved a sigh of relief. I wanted to hear their conversation if it resumed on the same note as before, but I needed to focus on a) taking off that blinding trap Valerie called a beautiful dress; b) avoid making a fool of myself again. However, one thing was certain, I this insane attempt at a "makeover" will not end well for me.

--

"Starting with dresses was a mistake." Valerie claimed as she handed me a pile of clothes whose colors were various nuances of black and white but also a couple of navy blue and bordeaux (the only two colors outside the rainbow that I actually can recognize, despite what they say about women and their ability with colors). "We need to work our way up, step by step. Hell, this might actually be a job that requires multiple sessions!"

She was even too excited for my liking, but I would have done anything to get things moving and go home as fast as possible, at this point. Hence, I tried on the various outfits she'd handed me: all jeans with different kinds of shirts and tops. Ben and Valerie approved of half, which were placed onto the small couch where Ben sat, waiting for me to parade before him every time.

When Valerie disappeared again, this time to take care of a couple of customers that needed her, I stepped out of the booth, to take a deep breath.

"Tired?" Ben asked, smiling faintly, to which I nodded. He glanced at this watch, "no wonder, we've been here 3 hours already."

"Three hours!" I exclaimed without being able to restrain myself, "no wonder I'm starving."

Ben chuckled. "You wanna go grab something to eat?"

"But ..." I nodded towards Valerie, who was all smiles and giggles with the customers she was helping.

"Oh, she'll be away for a while, might as well take a break. It's a long process, remember?"

"How ... long, exactly?"

He stood up, and after having typed something on his phone – a text to Valerie, I assume, since she received one immediately after –, he pocketed it, and walked up to me. "As long as it takes."

"But why ..."

He started walking towards the exit of the shop and gestured for me to follow him. "Because you need it," Ben claimed.

"I'm fine."

"Are you, though?"

I decided not to answer. An awkward silent walk to the food joint was easier to handle than a full-on discussion on why am I like this and how can I change. I've been there. You think I don't know my parents would prefer it if I was different? It would be a lot easier to have a daughter they don't have to explain. Or one they understand. Yes, I know they love me. But love doesn't always come with appreciation and understanding, a parent can love you without really knowing or understanding who you are.

--

"Oatmeal?" Ben eyed me carefully as we headed to the first table available while waiting for our orders to be ready.

"Yes." I tried to answer firmly, but I know my voice wavered.

"You said you were starving."

"It's ... breakfast."

"Not yours."

"Well, I can't order milk and cereals at a McDonald's, can I?" I tried hard not to blush, obviously failing.

"But you don't like oatmeal." Ben arched an eyebrow.

"How do you know what I like and what I don't like?" I asked, curious. He talks as if he's known me all my life.

He smiled faintly. "I'm a good judge of character."

"Well, I like fruit. I just don't eat it as much as-" I cut myself off when I noticed the guys behind Ben were snickering while staring at me. Ashamed, I lowered my gaze, and nodded. "I like oatmeal." I murmured, wanting to end the discussion. Clearly, those guys were laughing at my eating habits. A humpback whale doesn't eat fruit, otherwise she wouldn't be a humpback whale, would she?

"JoJo ..."

"Can you please not ..." I sighed, eyes fixated on the table. I felt like hiding under the floor. This is why I don't go out unless I absolutely have to. People judge. Every single time. Those people, those kind of guys, they see someone like me at a McDonald's, they immediately start laughing, expecting to see a pig in her natural habitat. I hate eating in front of people. I ordered the healthiest and lightest choice possible on purpose.

"Not what?"

"Nothing." I murmured, then heard Ben sigh.

"I guess this is going to be way more uphill than I thought. But I don't mind." He murmured, probably to himself. Then, he gently touched my foot with his so that I would look up, which I did, unconsciously, and Ben smiled at me. "Do you trust me?" My eyes widened in surprise. That's a big question, coming from a guy I barely known and that's literally trying to make me as uncomfortable as I can bear. "Let me rephrase that ..." he chuckled, "do you believe I'm not setting you up for a prank?"

"Y-Yes ..."

"So you do think that I am here to really help you?"

"I guess ..." I averted my gaze from his, feeling ashamed. He doesn't deserve my attitude.

"Joanna." Ben called, serious, and I looked back up, because he only calls me by my full name when it's a big talk. "Can you believe Valerie was just like you in high school?"

"What ..."

"Shy, no confidence whatsoever."

"Oh. You ..." That's what they were talking about earlier while I was changing. Ben helped Valerie the same way he was trying with me. Does he have a thing for makeovers or something?

"We helped each other." He smiled, and I frowned. "Do you honestly believe I was always like this?"

I didn't dare ask what "like this" meant. Hot? Cute? Handsome? What I did notice was that the guys behind him stopped laughing and started eating, but one of them still looked at me, making a weird face. When a pig noise escaped his mouth, I realized what he was doing. Making fun of me. Our orders had just arrived, and the waiter had mistakenly given me Ben's order – 2 sausage burritos, hash browns, and a coffee.

My neighbor didn't notice anything, he just swapped our orders. "Are you sure you don't want to try one?" He hinted at a burrito while he took a large bite of the other.

I shook my head, having lost all appetite. I still forced myself to eat a spoonful or two of my oatmeal, just so he wouldn't get suspicious. Ben went on talking in between bites, but I couldn't hear a single word. You know what they say where I come from? You can wrap it up nicely and call it chocolate, but it's still shit. You can try to dress me up and all, but there's no mistake, I am what I am, and there's no changing it.

And it comes with hurtful jokes like those faces and sounds that kid was making, or with seemingly innocuous lines like "why don't you try to go on a diet?" or "you look fatter, have you put on weight?", or "are you a boy or a girl?" and "if you fall, is there going to be a crack on the floor?" It's just the way it is. And there's no handsome neighbor or curvy goddess that can change that. I learned to live with it, push through and live as comfortably as possible.

I'm 28 and I've never had a relationship. I put everything into my studies, convinced it would give me the career I dreamed of, but it didn't, and now I'm stuck with nothing on both sides, and it's too late.

As lost as I was in my self-shaming mantras, I barely noticed that Ben had stood up and was now not very amiably conversing with the guys that had been sitting behind him. Wait, what?

"Come on, man, it was just a joke." The kid that had been making those pig faces and noises defended. "I mean, if you into the shit, props to you, great guts, my man."

Ben's jaw clenched. "Apologize." He hissed.

The guy and his friends laughed. "Truth hurts," the kid claimed, shrugging.

"Ben ..." I called lowly, hoping he wouldn't do something stupid.

"Apologize." He insisted, pointing at me.

"What's going on here?" A manager butted in, coming to stand in between Ben and the teenagers.

Ben snapped to him. "You probably allow your customers to be shamed and belittled. I don't sit by and watch my friends be hurt."

"What ..."

"Bro, you sleep with a pig, you get what comes with it." The main teenager laughed obnoxiously, and his friends followed.

Before Ben could take another step closer, evidently wanting to hit the guy, the manager went to stand in front of him, but facing the teenagers. "We do not condone such behaviors here," he claimed, "kindly leave the premises."

Everyone in there was staring at the scene. I wanted to make myself as little as possible. The kids protested a bit, but when they saw mall security approaching, the scuttled away. I faintly heard the manager apologizing to Ben, I was too busy trying to hide my face. However, when I heard other people murmuring, I couldn't resist any longer: I stood up in a hurry, and slipped away.

Ben called me loudly and repeatedly, but I didn't listen. I headed out of the building as fast as I could without running – no need to give people more reasons to laugh of me by having all my flab jump up and down –, and once I was outside, I stopped, and caught my breaths.

I don't think I've ever been as embarrassed. Believe it or not, I wasn't bullied in school. Sure, the odd looks and jokes here and there, hurtful words and innuendos, but nothing like this. Never. That's what happens when I let some random cute guy talk me into leaving my comfort zone.

When I heard Ben calling me again, I restarted walking fast, heading to the nearest bus station. I caught a bus just in time, before he could reach me. Obviously, my phone started ringing – Ben calling. I rejected. Feeling lost and hoping to God and all saints above that the other passengers on the bus hadn't noticed the horrible state I was in - sweaty, face red, teary eyes -, I started typing a message just to get it out of my system, but I wouldn't send it.

I'm not Valerie. I know you want to help, but you're making everything worse. Please, stop. I'm sorry I wasted your time, enjoy NYC.

The bus came to an abrupt stop because of a cyclist, and my phone almost slipped out of my hands. I saved it just in time. However, my heart jumped to my throat when I noticed the two icons that told me the message had been delivered. I frantically tried to delete, which I did. But not before those icons turned blue. Ben read the message.

12. Let me tell you a story

W hen I heard a knock on my door for the eleventh time, I hid deeper under the covers. Of course, he read the message and he immediately followed me home. If he wasn't such a nice guy, I'd seriously believe he's a stalker and a serial killer, because who in their sane mind would put this much effort into bonding with someone like me?

It must have been a couple of months since he arrived, and at this point he must have made some friends. There's Valerie even. So why keep this up? Why insist so much on me? I don't understand it. Not even Faith and Hope pay this close attention to me, and we've been friends since college.

That's the kind of friends I like, you know. Those that check in now and then but mostly stay away. Ben, however ... Ben seems to be one of those friends that need to obsessively hear from you every day and be absolutely sure you're okay. Nothing wrong with that, but for someone like me, it gets suffocating. Don't get me wrong, in a way, deep down, I appreciate it. In other ways ... it's too much.

We barely know each other, yet he barges in claiming I need a makeover and that he's determined to drag me out of my shell. What's so wrong with a safety shell? All the animals with shells die if they are left without it. It's a safety net.

Finally, Ben stopped knocking on the door. Reese and Shaw, who had been there meowing at him - I'm not sure whether they'd been wishing he could just teleport in or just go away -, came running and jumped into bed. I turned off my phone right after that message, but the chances someone other than Ben himself had tried to contact me were pretty slim. I would have to get up soon anyway: Scott changed my shifts for the month, because of that "sick day" Ben extorted out of him, so now I have to work the night shift. It's not as much of a punishment as he thinks, to be honest: the diner is mostly empty at night, people go eat in fancier places, so I can even relax and maybe read a bit. The only problem will be going out with bumping into Ben and his persistence.

--

Phew. I made it. Seems Ben gave up, finally. I won't deny I half regret it, but I can't handle this, it's just too stressful.

The diner was wonderfully quiet. The second shift is usually like that: it starts super busy, even more than in the morning, but then by 8-9 pm, it dies down, and the only clients are 20-something people on their way to some party. The most beautiful thing about the night shift, however, is that Scott goes home halfway through it. Well, he doesn't exactly go home, but he leaves, and that's enough for me. Everything is better when Scott isn't there, I think even the diner looks somewhat more decent when it's over isn't around.

Aside from the 20-something people I mentioned above, most of the night shift customers are law enforcement: either cops patrolling or coming to get something to eat before their shift begins, sometimes firefighters, since there's a station nearby. And no, none of the firefighters that come in here are anywhere near hot, in case you're wondering.

If this was a chick flick, I would be the lucky lonely girl that gets swept off her feet by a handsome and heart of gold firefighter, but this is the Joanna Brooks Show, where most of the luck was used up to get the final candy bar from a vending machine about 15 years ago.

"Well, hello, there!" Officer Ford greeted as she came in, taking me off guard while I was reading – like I said, no Scott, barely any client, a lot of time to myself, which I always use to read.

"Hi." I greeted, uncertainly looking up from my book. Scott hasn't 'accidentally' hit me in a week or two, but it's probably due to this woman putting the proverbial fear of God in him. She comes here regularly now, and sends him those stern looks that are meant to say 'I don't like you, I'll be happy to take you down'.

As she made her way up to the counter, I stood straight, and closed my book, albeit regretfully. I forced to smile a bit, not because I don't like her, but because I'm just not the smiley, chatty type, you'll have learned that by now. Not even Ben could succeed.

"I didn't expect to find you here!" Officer Ford exclaimed, surprised yet seemingly glad, as she came to sit at the counter. "Since when you work the night shift?" She asked, placing her cap onto the seat next to her, as if saving it for someone else.

"This is the first night." I replied, trying not to look to unhappy. Officer Ford is a kind woman, if she seems me even the slightest bit downcast, she'll immediately think it's Scott's fault and start tearing him down. Not that I'd mind seeing that asshole thrown off his self-made pedestal, but you know, if the diner closes, I lose a job, and I've always been a fan of not starving.

"For how long?" She tilted her head to the side, halfway between doubtful and observing.

"Just this month."

She pursed her lips for a long, long moment, then finally she erupted in a huge grin. "Great! I'm on night shift, too, this month. At least it means I meet a friendly face before starting my patrol through this dumpster."

I smiled faintly. "Nice."

"So, how are you?"

"I'm ok."

"You sure?" Read: do I have to come back in the morning and shoot your employer? She's a peculiar lady and an even more peculiar cop, I'll say that. But she's nice, and it's not very often that people are nice to me.

"Yeah."

"Then what's that frown, girl?" She furrowed her brows.

I chuckled a bit. "I'm ok, thanks, Officer Fo-"

"Ah ah! What did I say?"

"Michelle."

"Better." She grinned, then glanced at the menu. "So, what are you gonna give to a starving woman?"

I thought about it for a little bit, then finally nodded, and headed over to place the order for her. She likes my tastes, she says, so she always lets me order for her.

"Can you make that two?" Michelle asked the cook, to which he nodded. When I turned to her, a little bit confused, she shrugged, explaining: "I've got my rookie with me tonight." That explains why she kept the seat next to her occupied.

I felt my phone vibrate in my pocket for the umpteenth time since I started my shift. Nope, Ben didn't give up. He sent me so many messages while my phone was off, and even more after I turned it back on while heading to work. Anyone would be happy he's so persistent, I know. But I'm not just anyone, am I?

While I was busy deleting my notifications, I heard the front door bell ring, and Michelle exclaim: "Finally! What took you so long!"

"I'm sorry, ma'am, I ..." A young guy in his late twenties cleared his throat nervously, "I couldn't find anywhere to park, ma'am ..."

"You're a cop, you park wherever you damn well please, honey." Michelle rolled her eyes as she turned back to me. "Can you believe this guy?" She scoffed, while at the same time removing her cap from the seat next to her, so that he could reach her.

I remained dumbfounded, though. Not at her manners, no. But at the realization that hit me the moment the guy sat down beside Michelle. Me being so blind, it was difficult to make out his features from afar, but now ...

"Joanna?" He called.

"Hey, Jeremy ..." For the billionth time today, my face went crimson red and my heart started doing somersaults. This time, however, it was for a different reason than humiliation. You'd think New York is big enough for people to never meet, yet lately it's so damn small. Who is Jeremy, you'll ask? Well, let me tell you a story.

13. The way you make me feel

A FEW YEARS AGO

When I saw them, my heart immediately went ablaze, and in one of my most expected fight or flight responses, I hid behind the wall. When Faith told me a new friend of hers would join us for lunch, I expected it to be someone from the public relations department, since that's what she's majoring in and never ceases to talk about the wonders of it. I never thought it would be the one person I desired to see the most yet at the same time always ran away from.

I should have kept my mouth shut. It's typical of Faith to jump the gun like that. She caught me off guard that one time I was staring at him from afar, so I blurted out everything. Yes, I have a crush; no, I barely know him, we're just in the same criminology class together; yes, we've spoken but we're not friends. Jeremy Fahey. Bane of my existence yet the only ray of sunshine in this bleak universe called college life.

I've never been great at making friends, that's a given. And my fight or flight response is heavily unbalanced towards flight. So, when cute and nice Jeremy started talking to me in class, I went from zero to awkward real fast. No wonder he hasn't spoken to me since. That's why more than a crush, this is just the ludicrous product of a creative mind that's been overworking. That or, delayed adolescent idiocy. Maybe both, who knows. The fact remains, Jeremy is my kryptonite, and my alleged best friend was just about to ambush me with it.

I shouldn't have been much surprised, though. Ever since I told her about him, Faith has been dead set on pushing me into talking to him, claiming I ought to at least try. But why?

You never know, if you never try, she says. I don't need to try, because I already know, I say. It's not rocket science anyway. If he wanted to talk to me, he would have, instead he just glances at me now and then, probably wondering whether I'm just awkward or crazy-awkward. Then again, he wouldn't be that wrong in deeming me crazy, because it wasn't so hard to memorize his schedule.

Don't get me wrong, it wasn't just so I could hide behind a wall and stare at him with hearty eyes, no. It was more self-preservation: one of the basic rules of war according to Sun Tzu is, know your enemy. Some random cute guy that melts your insides at every smile and makes you feel like the world might actually be a better place only because he's in it, is indeed your enemy.

I have plans and ambitions, and I will realize them. Love life isn't contemplated in these projects, at least not until my career situation is stable. Not to mention the fact that Jeremy is way too cute for me. Just look at him, friendly and nice to talk to, while I'm a walking disaster that can barely utter a few words altogether unless it's for an exam. That's actually the funny part: in exams, be it written or oral, I shine, but in casual conversations? I don't even know where to start.

However, I'll admit that seeing Jeremy talk so amiably with Faith did make me a little bit ... jealous. No, it's not sane to be jealous when the person isn't even your friend, let alone boyfriend, yet I did feel that awful pang to my heart. Faith is a knockout, no doubt about that, any guy would be lucky to be with her.

Sighing, I dropped back against the wall, hidden from their sight. Not all of us can afford to be romantic, Charlotte Lucas came to my mind. Well, her movie version, to which the quote belongs.

But I've always been Charlotte Lucas. I love Pride and Prejudice to bits, but I was never Lizzie. I was always halfway between her sister Mary (who many often forget) and her best friend Charlotte. You know, those wall-flowers that are well aware nothing too exciting is going to come her way, romantically speaking, so they just set their eyes on a reachable horizon. Well, I wouldn't marry Mr. Collins, not even I am that desperate, but you get the point.

The dangers of being a reader involve this, too, you know. Setting your expectations too high, which inevitably results in scorching disappointments. So why set myself up for failure by looking for a Mr. Darcy, when I know full well my choice is between Mr. Collins and the celibate that presumably ended up being Mary Bennet's life?

My phone vibrated in my pocket, so I immediately grabbed it, even though I knew full well who it was.

Faith: where are you?? I'm starving!

I sighed once again. There's no chance I'm joining this awkward lunch, especially because I am 100% sure that Faith will have to suddenly leave with who knows what excuse. I don't get why she's so determined to get me a boyfriend. According to her, I need to be non-virgin before the end of this year, otherwise it'll mean I'll have wasted the best years of my life.

College is a time for explorations, she says, it doesn't matter if it's male or female, I need to get a move, she claims. As if it were of vital importance, which it isn't. Career first.

Me to Faith: I'm sorry, I ran into a problem. I'll see you after class.

I could distinctly hear her huff: "Ugh, this girl ..."

"What is it?" Jeremy asked, seemingly confused.

"It's that-"

Right then and there a group of loud freshmen passed by, laughing and chatting, so I couldn't hear what Faith said. As I watched them walk away, heading to the cafeteria, I sighed heavily. Maybe one day I'll get over myself, but not today.

--

TODAY

Taking a deep breath, I dared look up to meet that chestnut brown tousled hair, those vivid green eyes I used to dream of so often, that handsome face that used to make me as nervous as ever ... all I could utter was: "How ... are you?"

"I'm great!" He smiled up to his eyes, as if he was as happy as he'd never been before. "What a funny old world! I had no idea you were still here!" Was he actually excited to see me? Nah, that can't be.

I forced my lips to curve into a tiny, polite albeit ashamed smile. "Yeah, I ..." would rather be destitute in New York than go insane back home?

"You guys know each other?" Luckily Michelle butted in, saving me from embarrassment. My heart was pounding.

"Yeah, NYU." Jeremy answered. "We went to the same Criminology class."

Michelle tilted her head in surprise, looking at me. "Criminology? I thought you were a journalist."

"Not exactly, but ..." How to tell cops that you have a creepily dark interest in serial killers and everything that has to do with heinous crimes?

"Miss?"

Oh, thank God. Some clients have a perfect timing. "Excuse me." I murmured, then went to take care of the customer that had called me. He just needed a refill of his coffee, but I managed to take as much time as I possibly could. Once done, I thought I could sneak away into the kitchen, but Michelle called me back.

"You could have been a cop!" She exclaimed when I reached them.

"Well ..."

"Fahey says you were top of the class!" She continued, excited, as if thinking I missed out on a huge chance.

I never wanted to be a cop, or law enforcement in general. I just followed that Criminology class because I needed an elective and I'm a fan of the thriller genre. It was interesting and it led me to writing some short stories that are still tucked away in some directory in my laptop. For a while I actually fancied being a thriller author, but it faded away pretty quick, as my passions usually do.

"No, not really ..." I murmured in response, pretending the counter needed a thorough cleaning so that I didn't have to look up while speaking. "Jeremy was."

He chuckled. "You always got better grades, though."

"Only in written exams." I smiled to myself, remembering the old days. Criminology was one of my favorite classes, that's true. Sure, at first I got distracted staring at Jeremy from afar, kind of daydreaming, but when I realized it was gonna be a problem for my grades, I started sitting in the front row. It didn't help entirely, because Jeremy did the same, sitting just a few seats away from me, but that way it was also easier to keep focus.

"She kept me on my toes." Jeremy laughed, serving himself and Michelle the coffee I'd left on the counter while I was pretending to count the sugar bags. "I've always been competitive in school, and finding someone that passed me, it was a challenge."

I couldn't help but smile, remembering how Jeremy sometimes joked with me, pretending to steal my notes so that he could beat me at least once. I was never outspoken in class, I've always been the quiet one that gets things done without ever asking for help.

"I shouldn't be surprised anyway," Jeremy went on, for some reason beaming, "she graduated among the first of our year."

"Oh, a proper Rory Gilmore, I see." Michelle grinned.

I was dreading the question that followed. It usually happens when my academic successes are exposed, people stop and ask: then what happened? Meaning, how could you fall so low as to end up working at a filthy diner?

"So, what have you been up to?" There you go. Different form, same dilemma. How did someone that graduated top 5 in her class at NYU, end up scrubbing toilets? Where did all those dreams of either writing for a big paper like The New York Times, or editing manuscripts for Harper & Row just like Skeeter Pheelan? In the trash. That's the correct answer. In the trash.

"Joanna?" Jeremy called, clear sign I'd started spacing out, losing myself in my self-pity and self-hatred.

I will admit that my heart skipped a beat when he said my name. It's been a few years, but Jeremy was, without a doubt, the biggest crush I've ever had. "Uh ... not much, really." I murmured, without looking at him. By now that same spot on the counter was more than clean, it was becoming translucent. I cleared my throat, awkwardly asking: "I ... didn't know you wanted to be a cop?"

"He doesn't." Michelle butted in, making him laugh.

"I failed the firefighter exam, so ..."

"New York's Bravest didn't want him, so he joined New York's Finest. Better choice, if you ask me, but His Highness here doesn't like it." Michelle scoffed, pretending to be mad.

Jeremy smiled, a little embarrassed. "Well, I do like it, but ... it's a demanding job."

"And firefighter isn't?!" Michelle's voice was a little high-pitched.

Jeremy rolled his eyes, as if they'd had that same discussion many times already, then he turned back to me. "Honestly, Joanna?" He shrugged, and his candor took me off guard, "I come from a pretty long list of failures, so when a friend told me NYPD was hiring, I thought why not. I only have that criminology course, to make a career in the police force you need better than that, but I guess for now ..."

"As if." Michelle scoffed. "Once NYPD, always NYPD." She claimed proudly.

They went on bantering like old friends. It was a sweet scene, there seemed to be some sort of master/student relationship between them, or even mother/son, given the difference in age, but it looked comfortable, which I wouldn't have expected it, as annoyed as Michelle sounded when she said her rookie was with her.

--

At 2 am, the last customer left, and I finally headed to the door, to lock it and start cleaning up. It was a surprisingly easy shift. Michelle and Jeremy didn't stay long, they had to get on with their own shift, but the little they remained, it was pleasant, albeit awkward and embarrassing for me. It's sheer luck that Michelle was there as buffer between me and Jeremy, otherwise I'm not sure I'd have been able to really talk to him.

We were never friends. Sure, Faith tried many, many times to ambush me into a lunch or a dinner or a party just so I could remain alone with him, but I never budged, and finally when she started dating regularly, she forgot about my love life to focus on her. Funny enough, she almost got married with that guy, but it didn't work out in the end.

The most Jeremy and I exchanged were a few words here and there during the only class we had together. That's why I'm amazed he even remembered me. Of course, I remembered him all too clearly. How could I not? He was my torment and delight for a couple of years. Yeah, my crush lasted that long. Probably even more than a couple of years, but I didn't see him again after we graduated. I never had the courage to accept his friend request on Facebook. I never thought I'd meet him again, but despite the awkwardness and the fact that my heart was still in a state halfway between ecstatic and dismayed, I was happy to see him.

Jeremy is one of biggest regrets, I don't deny that either. If only I'd been any braver, I'd have at least cultivated a friendship with him, but ... it went how it went, nothing to be done now.

Once I'd locked the front door, I started cleaning up the tables that had been occupied until now. If every night shift is like this, I should pretend with Scott that I'm more unhappy than usual, that way he might remain convinced it's a punishment. Sure, Brooklyn is a little scary this late at night, but I'd rather get shot in a dark alley Mr. and Mrs. Wayne style than put up with Scott's bullshit and abuse during the day.

The cook went home an hour ago, so I was completely, totally alone. Of course, Scott made sure to call me by midnight to tell me I ought to give the kitchen and the bathrooms a thorough cleanse after closing, which meant I would remain until dawn at least, but again, I didn't mind. I turned the TV on, to have some company, but as much as I enjoy a good true crime show, maybe watching it while I was all alone in a diner in the middle of the night, wasn't a good idea. So, I switched to radio, keeping the volume low on the classics channel. Michael Jackson's voice started immediately filling the silence. I'm not much into pop, but he's one of my favorite singers, so it was difficult not to start dancing like I do at home, but I did start humming to The way you make me feel while moving my hips a little bit.

I was so into it that I literally jumped, scared, when the song ended and I heard someone clapping outside. The shutter was only halfway down, damnit. My heart thumping as fast as if I'd run a marathon across the entire city of New York, my faced as red as the juiciest tomato, I remained there frozen, staring at a grinning Jeremy, who was giving me thumbs up. I couldn't pretend I didn't see him, could I? But talking to him now, after this ...

I swallowed my saliva when he gestured for me to open for a minute. It's almost as if after all the times I ran away from him years ago, he finally learned the trick: trap her, don't give her any chance nor route to escape. Flushed and flustered, I went to the door, and opened the shutter first, then unlocked the door itself.

"I didn't know you could sing!" He exclaimed, excited, as he took a couple of steps into the diner.

"I don't." I let out inadvertently.

"Are you kidding? You were awesome."

"Y-You heard me?" Shit.

"Yeah. I mean, it's a glass door, after all, and the shutter was only halfway down." He chuckled.

Great. So much time spent evading him not to make a fool of myself, and here I was, seven years later, making that same mistake I worked so hard against. "Oh." Was all I could say.

"You have a nice voice, I never knew."

"Thanks ..."

There was some noise on his police scanner, to which he listened closely; after having concluded that the call wasn't for him, he turned back to me, apologizing. "So, Joanna, uh ..." he seemed flustered, "I'm glad we met again," he smiled, although a little embarrassed.

"Me too." I let slip. Clearly the fumes of the products I was using to clean up this dumpster did something to me, I wasn't thinking straight. The only thing that kept resonating in my head was the shame I felt for having been seen dancing and singing like that, by a guy I hadn't seen in years and that time ago I would have even said was my one and only. Idiotic, I know.

However, my simple answer seemed to encourage Jeremy, because his smile became wider, and his voice became more steady. "So, uh ... well, I forgot earlier, but I thought ... maybe we shouldn't let another 7 years pass?" I gulped inaudibly, my heart skipping a few beats. What was he aiming for? "I thought I'd befriend you on Facebook or follow you on Instagram, but I don't use any of those anymore."

"Me neither."

He nodded. "Yeah, so ... old fashioned phone number?" He let out an awkward laugh as he scratched the back of his hair. "I mean uh ... your?" Seeing me befuddled, Jeremy let out a heavy sigh. "Sorry. I swear, I've done this before."

"Done ... what?" I asked, uncertain.

"Ask a girl out." Another nervous laugh. "I ... I have, I swear I have." He rolled his eyes to himself. "Nice one, Jeremy, you sound desperate."

I had no idea what was going on, it felt like an extra-body experience. For a moment, I actually thought I was dreaming; or that that wasn't the real Jeremy, just some lookalike.

He took a deep breath, a hand over his heart, the same way I used to when I needed to calm it down after having come face to face with him years ago. "I'm just saying ..." the scanner interrupted him again, and this time it was indeed for him: Michelle telling him to get back to work. "Ugh, shit." He ruffled his hair, disgruntled. "Uh ... when do you go home?"

I blinked my eyes, surprised, and he slapped a hand over his face, cursing himself again. "Jesus, Jeremy." Then back to me: "I meant, when do you get off work?"

"I'm ... when I'm finished cleaning."

"Will that be ..." he took a look at his watch, "anywhere near 7 am?"

"Uh ..." I glanced at the watch hanging on the wall on the left – it was already 4 am, what the hell! – "yeah, probably ..." I wasted too much time dancing and singing, still had kitchen and bathrooms to clean."

"Great!" When he noticed my puzzled and mildly scared look, he let out a nervous laugh, once again tormenting his tousled hair. "Can we ... have breakfast together?" I think my heart nearly jumped out of my throat. "It's not a date!" He hastily pointed out. "Just uh ... to catch up?" He laughed nervously again, "talk some criminology like the old days?"

No. No, no, no, no, no ... us alone, talking, not a good idea, terrible, awful, absurd idea. No, no, no ... "yes." Ugh.

"Great! I'll drop by around that time then." And like that, he left. Jeremy went back to his patrol, leaving me with my heart ablaze, my insides churning, and such an emotional, psychological and physical tiredness that I slid to the floor, unable to believe what I just did. Am I insane? It's going to be a disaster, I know it.

14. Take a deep breath

- -

I should have known it was going to happen. Why did I even hope it wouldn't, when it was the only obvious and natural outcome? Nope, Jeremy didn't show up. As I knew he wouldn't. At first I was a little disappointed, but in the end I made peace with it. It's not like I could expect him to actually stay true to his word. He probably changed his mind halfway through his shift, realize what an absurdity it would have been, to get stuck at breakfast with me.

I did wait. I was sleepy as hell, and the last thing I wanted was to be there when Scott arrived to open the diner, but I resisted through it, thinking it would be worth it just to talk to Jeremy a bit. But he didn't come. Oh, well.

After a night spent working, I pretty much crawled home. My sight was so blurry that I barely saw the silhouette crouched beside my door. At first I thought it was a package, so I tried to remember whether I'd ordered something that big on Amazon.

"Good morning."

Right. I should have expected this. When will people learn the meaning of boundaries? "Morning." Ben stood up with a sigh, and stretched, to which I frowned. "You didn't ..."

"I did."

"Ben ..."

"Since you weren't answering my phone calls, I decided I'd wait out here," he hinted at the pizza box next to him, "then I guess I fell asleep."

I rolled my eyes, bypassing the pizza box to open my door. "You shouldn't have."

"Where have you been?"

Ben, I like you, but you're not my husband nor my father, and I'm way past the age where I need to ask for permission to anyone. It's what I wanted to say, as snappy as I felt, since he clearly disregarded my request. "Work."

He checked his watch. "It's 9 am."

"Yes."

"You need to report your employer, it's illegal to make you work like-"

"Ben." I interrupted him, exasperated. "Please. I'm worn out, I worked all night, can we please not do this right now? Please? And you need to stop sneaking up on me when I'm most vulnerable, it's unfair."

"It's the only times I manage to actually get through your thick armor." He grumbled.

Because he came to stand between me and the door, being quite unfair and rude, not to mention mildly creepy, I sighed, sliding against the floor to sit down. Most of the night shift might have been chill, but cleaning up the whole diner wore me out. Those restrooms, I swear, I clean them every day yet every day they get worse. "I'm going to speak now." I said, tired of all this drama that suddenly entered my life.

Between him and his obsession with dragging me out of my comfort zone, Faith sponsoring her brother in every single message, for who knows what reason, my parents hassling me about going back home if I can't make it in New York, and now even Jeremy coming back into my life for a split second, only to disappear just as quickly, yet in time to remind me of the dreamy little thing I was and how she died horribly, lost between one toilet scrub and the other ... I was finally about to blow up.

"Finally."

I sent Ben a dirty look, but he was unfazed. "I'm going to speak now," I repeated, "please, don't interrupt me. I am exhausted, physically, mentally and emotionally, so please, just let me say this, then we can call it a day once and for all." I paused, waiting for his reply.

Ben sat down beside me, yet far enough not to be able to touch me, crouching his legs. I hadn't asked him to, but I guess he prefigured it, because before nodding, he closed his eyes, leaning back against the door. He knew I would feel more at ease if I didn't have to look at him while speaking, and he was right.

I took a deep breath, and began: "I didn't mean to send that message, but I meant what I said in it. I appreciate all your efforts in helping me be more confident, but there is no need. You're not the first person to tell me I need to change, I already know that. But has it ever occurred to you that, maybe, just ... maybe, I'm fine like this? That I like spending my free time at home reading or watching Netflix? Has it ever occurred to you that I might prefer the company of my cats to actual people not because I'm desperate and lonely, but because I just like cats better than people?

Yes, I have a lot of issues. I do, I know I do. And I should probably work on them, but a makeover won't do anything about it. It just won't. This is not a movie, where the ugly nerd just removes the glasses, puts on some makeup, loses the ponytail, and suddenly becomes the beauty of the ball.

Maybe some people just are what they are, unpleasant. I made my peace with it a long time ago, and being dragged to the worst place possible for an introvert, only to be shamed and ridiculed, it wasn't the right approach.

I'm sorry I ghosted you, it was rude of me, but truth be told, I only partly did that. I left my phone untouched since I came back from the mall. I needed silence. Because that's also me, you know? Sometimes I need utter silence. Sometimes I need a break from everything and everyone. Yes, I was kind of mad at you. But then I reminded myself that you just wanted to help. It's not your fault, really, you don't know me that well, you thought the generic approach would work on me as it probably has on Valerie." I paused, my heart thumping in my chest.

I wasn't improvising, that's why I could put all those words together. During the breaks at the diner, I wrote a "letter" on my phone, and that's what I was reading to him. Before Ben could speak, I went on: "You were kind enough to try and help a desperate cause like I am, but the very definition of desperate is, in fact, impossible to change. So why waste your time? Just because we're neighbors, doesn't mean we must be friends. There's no rule for that. That's why I meant it when I said enjoy New York. For a guy like you, it'll be fun." Done. So I locked my phone, and stood up, wanting to leave before my self-preservation instincts kicked in. "Now I need to sleep."

Ben reopened his eyes, and looked at me. "You wrote it down?"

"Yeah."

"I guessed so." He stood. "Joanna ..." he dusted off his pants, "I'm sorry if I embarrassed you, I should have seen you were out of your depths. But I do believe you need to live a little. It doesn't have to be in loud places and surrounded by people, it can be Internet, you know. You can get out of your comfort zone even with people online. That's how it works nowadays. But whatever the means you prefer, you should do it."

"I ..."

He held up his finger to silence me, and came a little closer. Taken off guard, I backed up against the wall. He was so close that I could smell his usual perfume mixed with a little natural scent – he did spend the night outside my door, after all. "Whatever you may think," Ben stated, "if I talk to you, if I spend time with you, it's because I want to." He chuckled, "I'm way past the age of forced playdates, JoJo. If I want to be your friend, it's not because you're a forced choice, it's because I think you're funny – note that I said funny, not amusing, because if I laugh, I laugh with you, not at you."

This was a time for confessions, I see. 7 am, most people wake up, Ben and Joanna have the talks they never thought they'd have. Or at least I thought it. Somehow, he always catches me when I'm not thinking straight. Or maybe I don't think straight because I feel free around him. Some people are like that, naturally able to make you at ease.

I yelped when Ben fixed his light brown eyes on mine and left his hands at my sides, leaning in, until his forehead grazed mine. At this point I could really feel his hot breath against my mouth, as cliché as that may sound. If I was anyone else, I might have even thought he was about to kiss me. But ... he would never. First because I'm me, second because, well, he's gay.

"We good now?" Ben spoke softly, as if he weren't just casually causing my heart to nearly explode. At this rate, I'm gonna need a pacemaker soon.

I tried to nod, but it would have meant really touching his forehead with mine, so I just stuttered a flustered: "Y-yes ..."

Why was he so close, though? No touching, no touching, friends don't get this close, Ben, where did you learn this. Maybe it's normal for extroverts, but introverts abhor this sort of invasion of personal space. My legs were beginning to shake, both because of the embarrassment, and because I was so exhausted I could fall asleep just like that. "I ... I need sleep ..." I murmured, my throat dry.

Ben nodded against my forehead, yet his hands made me recoil when they actually touched my hips. "Yeah, you should go ..." he whispered, yet unmoving.

"Ben ..." he was acting weird, was he sick? He'd never breached my personal space like that, getting so close as to touch me, even.

Much to my surprise, Ben closed his eyes, his grip on my hips getting stronger. "Take a deep breath." He said, not sure if to me or to himself.

"I ..." I wasn't sure what I was going to say, but I didn't have time to say it. Yeah, you guessed it. Ben kissed me.

15. Joanna loves Harry Potter

I froze. Of all the possible things I could have done, I did the worst. I froze. I mean, what are you supposed to do anyway? When your allegedly gay neighbor comes up and kisses you?

At first it was just a peck on the lips, but as his grip on my hips tightened the slightest, I started feeling he was pushing for more. And when those very same hands moved to cup my neck as Ben deepened the kiss, I realized. This was no mistake, no random moment. He wanted it.

It was painfully slow, but in the end I unfroze, bit by bit, and started following his movements. I had no idea what I was doing, this was the first time ever, but even though I've never been impulsive, something told me I had to follow my instincts just this once. I had to.

I realized I'd been gripping his shirt only when, much to my own surprise, I pulled him closer. Ben was glad. He smiled against my lips, which he traced with his tongue, until he finally went in. So this is what a real kiss looks like? The feverish search for each other, the frenetic beats of the heart, the dizziness that blurries your sight, even though your eyes are closed, so you're not seeing anything at all. Is this what it feels like to be kissed?

I was tired, sleepy, worn out in every possible way; my uniform was sticking to me and I'm pretty sure I smelled of fried chicken mixed with bleach; I was probably sweating too, not to mention my breath was way less than ideal. And yet ... Ben was unmoving.

He finally moved only when I half choked on saliva – whether it was his or mine, I don't even want to know –, so he realized he'd kept me from breathing for too long. Now I know the true meaning of breathtaking.

Ben left his forehead against mine, and I didn't have the courage to open my eyes again, but I did hear him let out a tiny chuckle against my lips. He seemed just as out of breath and mentally, physically, emotionally exhausted. It was as if that single kiss had been enough to leave everlasting scars on the both of us. I know I felt scorched, and not just because it wasy my first real kiss, or because it came from the most unexpected person, but because I felt something deep within me. A fire I'd only known years ago, back to when I was passionate about my dreams and working towards that goal was the limitless fuel that kept me on, pushing me further and further.

"So ..." Ben finally spoke, his voice hoarsely low, then let out a small nervous laugh as his thumb traced my lips, "I ... someone's looking for you."

I blinked my eyes open, confused. Did I dream of it? "What?"

Ben pulled back the slightest, hinting at my pocket. "Your phone."

"Oh." I don't need to answer, do I? "Uh ..."

"Go on." Ben pulled back with a small smile, yet remaining just a few inches away from me.

Albeit confused as to why would he think that a call - probably my parents - would be so important as to break that fairy tale moment, I fished my phone in my pockets, and I did what I normally never would, in my right mind: I answered the call without checking the ID first. Now, if you're an introvert, you know that we need some preparation before human interaction, calls included, and in the state I was in - flustered, cheeks flushed, my heart racing - I was in the worst possible predicament to have a conversation with anyone else that wasn't Ben. But maybe he wanted to use that interruption as an excuse to get out of an otherwise awkward moment arisen from an impetuous act he most definitely regretted already.

"Hello?" I couldn't tear my eyes off Ben – and I hate eye contact, mind you –, but neither could he. His juicy lips were curved in a sweet smile as stared at me the same way I'd stare at a smoking hot pepperoni pizza that just came out of the oven.

"Joanna?" A male voice called from the phone.

"Yes?"

"Oh finally the right number! You have no idea how many Joanna Brooks live in New York City."

I frowned, befuddled. Do I have a stalker now? Because a sexy allegedly gay neighbor that just kissed the hell out of me wasn't enough, right? "Who ..."

"I'm sorry, it's Jeremy."

"Jeremy?" I did notice how Ben's smile faltered the moment I called that name.

"I probably shouldn't have, but I had to make it right before you came to the wrong conclusion ..." Jeremy explained, "I'm sorry for this morning, I got stuck at work."

"Oh."

"I didn't have your number, so when I was finally free I had to resort to uh ... police methods." He let out a nervous laugh. "I swear I'm not stalking you." That's not what it sounds like, Jeremy. "I just wanted to make sure you didn't think I stood you up ..."

So that's why he didn't show up for breakfast? There was no need for this call, I would have been fine knowing he just changed his mind. Ben was staring at me intently, as if trying to guess who was on the phone just from my expressions. But he could never guess right.

"So?"

"Huh?"

Jeremy chuckled. "I was saying ... can we try again? Maybe dinner this time?"

"Dinner?"

Ben's eyes widened in surprise at that word. He may not know who it was, but certainly he was beginning to guess what it was about. Picture this: Joanna Brooks, at the utmost epitome of her worst, standing outside her door, trapped against it by a guy that until yesterday was supposed to be gay yet had just finished kissing the hell out of her; and on the other side of the phone, her long lost crush, the one guy that had come as close as ever possible to owning her heart – actually, he probably had. Trapped between an allegedly gay neighbor that just gave her her first kiss in one of the cheesiest, most cliché yet most romantic ways possible, and an old crush, the guy of her dreams, finally asking her out – after years spent believing he was barely an acquaintance, imagine a possible love interest.

Not very believable, is it? If I didn't know any better, I'd have thought I was actually dreaming. I don't know why would I have dreams about Ben kissing me, but a dream sounded more believable than the truth.

"Joanna?" Jeremy called, probably thinking I'd hung up, instead of having been sent to a whole different dimension made of guys that actually see me.

Seeing me at a loss for words, or maybe impatient to get on with what we were doing, or just both, Ben decided it was cool to grab the phone from my hands, and put it on speaker. When Jeremy called my name again, Ben clenched his jaw the slightest, but nodded for me to answer.

"Yeah, I ..." I swallowed hard, not knowing what to say.

"So dinner?" Jeremy went on.

"Uh ... I ... I work at night." My voice was quivering, both because of this unexpected turn of events – my old crush asking me out, ladies and gents! – and because Ben didn't seem happy about it, not one bit. But wasn't he the one that'd been saying I ought to get out and live more?

"Oh, right. Night shift." Jeremy laughed. "Then coffee? Or we could grab a bite before we both start our shifts tonight?"

What do I say now? Yes? No? Maybe? You have the worst timing ever and you literally just interrupted the most exciting moment of my entire life, as sad as that may sound? I can't go out with you because my allegedly gay neighbor just kissed the hell out of me and I need to first of all deal with that before venturing out with anybody else?

"I understand if you don't want to ..." Jeremy commented, discouraged.

"No!" I blurted out. "I mean, yes! I mean ..." Oh, for God's sakes.

"Yes." Nope, that wasn't me. That was Ben answering for me.

"Who ..." Jeremy was baffled when he heard a male voice, of course.

"Yes, Joanna will meet you before work." Ben went on, his voice resolute. "3 pm, Leaky Cauldron."

"Leaky ...?"

"Leaky Cauldron." Ben repeated. "It's a Harry Potter themed bookstore café." He looked at me. "Joanna loves Harry Potter."

Well, I do, and Leaky Cauldron is one of my favorite places in Brooklyn, but I didn't think he was listening when I told him. It was just a place in the list I made for him when he asked me about stuff to see in the neighborhood.

"Okay." Jeremy agreed, somewhat uncertain. "3 pm, Leaky Cauldron. I'll be there." Then he hung up, without as much of a goodbye.

Ben slid my phone in one of my uniform's pockets, and cracked a small smile. "Shock therapy, I guess." He said. "I'll call Valerie to help you with the outfit."

"But ..."

"You can change into your uniform when you get to work, no?"

"Yes, but ..."

"Great." He clapped his hands, somewhat excited. "Now go to sleep, you need to rest before the big date." Ben claimed, turning me around so that I could unlock and open my door.

"Ben ..." I called as he headed to his own apartment.

He smiled – a weird smile, not one of his signature ones where his eyes smile, too, brightening up everything and everyone around him –, "believe me, it's for the best."

16. I'm onto you

- -

"Where's Ben?" I asked once Valerie was done dolling me up. I did tell her I would go to work right after, and a filthy diner is the last place ever to be dressed nice and wear full makeup, but she said I ought to look great for my first date. No, it didn't matter either that I told her it wasn't a date. Jeremy did specify it the first time, when he asked to grab breakfast together, didn't he? He said it wouldn't be a date. So it's only presumable that this one wouldn't be either. Makes sense, no?

Valerie, head tilted to the side as she stared at me, left finger on her lips, clear sign she was left in thought, answered absentmindedly: "Work."

I frowned. "I thought he was off on weekends."

She laughed. "Darling, he's never off."

"But ..." I pressed my lips when she looked at me weird. He told me we could spend the weekend on this ... new path I'm supposed to get onto because he's off, now it turns out he went to work on a Sunday?

"Do you have a purse?" Valerie asked.

"Uh ... yeah ..." I pointed at the wardrobe.

She headed there, and fumbled a bit. Needless to mention, my room was a mess of clothes and beauty products, all stuff Valerie had brought. "Just this one?" She held up the black messenger bag I used in college.

"No, there's a smaller one."

"You mean the worn-out brown shoulder bag you always use?"

I nodded, halfway between embarrassed and annoyed. I don't care about bag or shoes or clothes, I thought that was clear by now.

Valerie sighed, throwing the messenger bag back into the wardrobe. "Good thing I brought those, too." She claimed, then went over to the last paper back she hadn't opened yet. Case in point, there were a few bags of different types.

"How did you manage to take all this stuff here?" I couldn't help asking.

She chuckled. "Honey, I never lift a finger." When she saw me frown, she rolled her eyes, and pointed at her body with her bejeweled hands. "Womanhood 101, Joanna. Men are happy to play knight in shining armor if they believe they have a chance at a reward later on, if you get what I mean." She winked.

"Uh ..."

"Tell me, do you carry your own suitcase when you travel?"

"Well, I don't travel much." Or at all. Most I've been to was to and from New York and my hometown.

"What about when you arrived to New York? Or during college?"

I thought for a moment. "When I got to the dorms I usually found some-one that would help me with the suitcase if they saw me struggling, yeah."

Valerie grinned. "Boys?"

"Uh ... yeah."

"Then you see what I mean, don't you?"

Not really. "They were just being nice."

"They were trying to get to know you, honey."

Oh, come on. Do I really have to believe that guys don't do anything just for the sake of being nice or polite? Should I believe Ben has ulterior motives, too? He's been even too helpful. I mean, he did kiss me, but that doesn't mean anything, he regretted it immediately.

"Now ..." Valerie inhaled deeply as if tired yet proud of her work, "let's check you out." She dragged me to the bathroom, where there was the only big enough mirror in my apartment.

I gulped when I looked at my reflection. That was me? Joanna Brooks? The same Joanna Brooks I see in that same mirror every day? Nah, that's not possible. Valerie had me wear a red jersey dress that reached below my knees, with something she called body chain – which I heard for the first time existed – as accessory; black boots. All in all it was an easy attire, yet it was a mix of casual and elegant. I could have just as easily worn it in the morning or at night, I think.

She'd left my hair cascading over my shoulders in small ringlets; the body chain she said also worked as necklace. Valerie had spent at least half an hour, if not more, doing my makeup, so I thought it would be something heavy that made me look like a clown, instead ... it was simple. Almost natural. Sure, it hid my skin flaws perfectly, from my blackheads to the heavy bags under my eyes, but it looked as if that was my skin, without any product on it, except for a bit of eyeliner, eye shadow and mascara, not to mention the strawberry red lipstick. The last one was probably the only racy element in all that outfit.

"Do you like it?"

"I ..."

"I wasn't talking to you." Valerie laughed.

When I turned around, I noticed Ben was standing there, mouth agape. When did he arrived? He looked sweaty, as if he'd just come from a run. Well, duh. He wore black soccer shorts over workout tights, and a grey hoodie, his earphones still hanging from it. "I thought you were working." I wondered out loud, unable to keep myself.

Ben didn't reply, he was too busy staring at me, his eyes wide in amazement. Only when Valerie pinched his arm, he finally woke from his reverie. "Uh ... no, I mean ... I ... I have a uh wedding in a couple of hours. I thought I'd ... work out a little bit first."

"Won't you be running around anyway during the wedding?" Valerie teased, reading my mind, to which he sent her a dirty look. "Right." She pressed her lips to hide an impish grin. "So, what do you think?"

"Yeah." Was all Ben replied.

"Yeah what? Good, bad? Could be better? Could be worse?" Valerie insisted.

"Good."

"Come on, Benny!" She laughed, giving him a loud pat on the back. "You're so good with words!" Cue the second dirty look he sent her.

Ben sighed, averting his gaze from me to wrap up his earphones, and pocket them properly. "I see curves, I guess it's a good start."

Valerie laughed. "I know right?!" She turned to me, beaming. "My God, Joanna! You might be my best work so far!"

"What?"

"The makeover." Ben explained, rolling his eyes. He was clearly in a bad mood, which I didn't understand. He was the one that accepted this ... date/catching-up on my behalf.

"Oh."

"Valerie has launched a makeover program for ..." he hinted at me, "uh ..."

"Fat girls?" I blurted out, tired of his half stuttered words.

"Curvy." He corrected. "I was gonna say ... curvy girls."

"Tomato, tomahto." I shrugged.

Valerie looked in between us, curious. She was probably wondering why did Ben look annoyed at me, and why was I so mad at him. How couldn't I be? First he kisses me, then he ships me off to a date with a guy he doesn't even know. Talk about mixed signals.

Not to mention his being gay. I may not be a woman of the world, as my mom would say, but even I know the basic difference between gay and not gay. One likes men, the other likes women. Am I such a tomboy that for a moment he forgot I was a girl? Or was it just a joke? Or maybe a way for him to make sure he is indeed gay; like, let's see, I'm not quite sure whether I like women or men, let me kiss my ugly neighbor, see if she arouses me or not. Bad idea, Ben. If you wanna be sure you're gay, you should try kissing a woman like Valerie. That'll really put your hormones to the test.

"Well then. He's here." Valerie announced, so that I finally broke the stare contest with Ben – a pissed one, at that –, to turn to her.

"What?"

"Nah, he's not." She laughed. "But you should get going, or you'll be late."

I nodded. Valerie handed me a small purse, to which I frowned, but she explained it was necessary for the outfit. "Where do I keep my stuff?" I asked, skeptical. "And I need my uniform for work."

"Valerie will take you to Leaky Cauldron, you can put a bag with your uniform and everything you need for later in her car." Ben butted in, already walking out of my room. "Presumably ... he'll take you to the diner afterwards. But if he doesn't ... call Valerie."

"Not you?" Shit. I thought out loud.

I could see Ben's back tensing up, but he didn't reply, Valerie did for him. "Uh ... he's got that wedding, remember? I'm free today." Right. Somehow even dumbass old me could see through the bullshit this time.

--

VALERIE

"Uh ... Ben, can I use your bathroom?" I asked after Joanna had locked her apartment. He looked at me funny, I guess seeing through my old trick. I gave Joanna the keys to my car. "I'll join you in a couple of minutes." Reluctantly, she walked down the corridor. Ben opened his door, and gestured for me to go in, annoyed. I entered, but only spoke when I was sure Joanna had taken the elevator. "So?"

"What?"

I rolled my eyes. "Since when you're 'gay'?" I air-quoted the last word. I couldn't believe my ears when Joanna told me what he'd said to her.

He shrugged, walking into his kitchen to grab a bottle of water. "One can find out at any age, you know."

I scoffed, following him. "Bitch, please. I know you, Benjamin Harris. If you're gay, I'm a nun."

He fainted a smirk. "Now, that would be a miracle."

I hit his arm, and he laughed, I guess forgetting his horrible mood for a second. "So why did you lie to her?"

"Who says I did?"

"Ben ..." I rolled my eyes.

"Hey, you know things change." He drank some of his water. "I found this guy after you left, you know. I guess it was epiphany."

And there I went, scoffing once again. I stole the bottle of water from his hands, so that I could stare him dead in the eye. "This isn't you, Ben."

"And who is me?"

"Come on!" It's true that we haven't seen each other in a long time, but we've been good friends. Hell, more than good friends, if you know what I mean. "Honeybooboo, I know you. Biblically." I eyed his second half, to which he rolled his eyes. "That ain't gay material, babe."

"There's plenty of gay men that have been with women before realizing their true nature. Or I could be bisexual, you know?"

"Yeah, why not pansexual?" I scoffed.

"Yeah, that, too. You should open your mind, Val."

"Benjamin, don't make me spank you like I used to."

"Maybe you should have guessed since then ..." he joked, clearly trying to throw me off the scent. Too bad it doesn't work with me.

"Ok, so what's his name?" I leaned in, the island between us.

"Huh?"

"This ... amazing guy that made you realize you're part of Freddie Mercury's crew. What's his name?"

"Uh ..." There you go. He's a good liar, but not good enough to fool me.

"You can't think of a name, can you?"

He looked around, from his phone to his watch. "Cas ... Cassidy."

"Or Casio." I laughed, knowing that was the brand of the watch he was wearing.

"Shouldn't you go downstairs? You'll be late."

"For the date you forced the girl you like into?"

"I didn't force anyone." He rolled his eyes.

"She said she wasn't sure she wanted to go, but you agreed on her behalf."

"Only because she needed a push."

I sighed. "Alright. I'm giving up for now only because I can't let Joanna be late." I walked back towards the door. "But I'm onto you, Benjamin." I did the 'I'm watching you' gesture with my fingers. "I'm onto you."

"Bye, Felicia."

Here's Joanna's outfit, if you were curious:

That's very McGonagall

JOANNA

Biting on my lip, I stared at my phone. I didn't want to think about what was going to happen, because it would make me ultra-nervous, so I thought I'd text Ben, to see if he was okay. He was weird earlier. We haven't known each other long, but I am pretty sure he would have done anything to be the one driving me to this date/non-date. It was his idea after all.

Instead, he dismissed me with a generic excuse. It's true that being a photographer means having to up and leave at the weirdest times, but ever since that kiss, he's been acting strange. Even I can see it. I mean, if I, obliviousness personified, can see there's something fishy about his attitude, you realize how clear it is.

"You ok?" Valerie asked, taking me off guard.

I turned to look at her for a moment. "Yeah."

"Nervous?" She inquired, taking her eyes off the road to look at me.

I nodded. How couldn't I be. Sighing, I locked my phone, and pocketed it. Why did I agree to all this. It's not going to end well. Jeremy probably remembers the wrong person, someone more interesting he would have wanted to keep in touch with, another Joanna, who knows. People tend to romanticize memories, make them better than they actually are, maybe this is the case.

"It's gonna be ok."

No offense, Valerie, but that doesn't help me. I just nodded, though. She only wanted to be nice. This would be my first date. Technically I did go on a date a few years ago, with a guy I met online, but it didn't go further than that. If one counts dating apps, technically I have "dated", even if not in the proper sense. Back to when I used those apps, I usually would get messages from different guys, then focus on one for a couple of weeks, until it died down. Probably my fault. I mean, a guy only can wait so much before meeting, if you stubbornly refuse, of course they'll move on to the next one.

"We're here."

My eyes bulged out. "Already?" I blurted out, my heart picking up a faster pace.

"Yeah." She chuckled, then turned to me. I hadn't even noticed she'd parked already. "Look, Joanna, we don't really know each other yet, but, I think I know you, I was you. I was just as shy." Here we go again. Is it a thing where Ben and Valerie come from? Like, a town tradition, breaking boundaries and reading people. "It'll sound cliché, but believe me, it will be okay. Whether it works out or not, it's still experience."

I nodded, not knowing what else to say, other than: "Thank you." I gripped the handle, trying to convince my heart to be still. "The dress, uh ..."

"Oh, it's yours!" Valerie exclaimed with a big grin.

"No, I meant ..." I blushed therefore lowered my gaze to my lap, "do you think it's ... maybe it's too much? It's early afternoon, and we're going to a bookstore ..."

"It's perfect, believe me. And you look beautiful! Ben thought the same."

I looked up, surprised. "He did?"

Her grin widened. "He didn't know what to say, you saw him."

He looked pretty cold to me, as if he didn't even want to look at me. And I couldn't blame him, after that kiss, I would feel awkward, too – I did feel awkward. If there's one thing I've never learned how to do, that's read people. Of course, being taciturn means you observe a lot, but I don't understand my fellow humans, not in the slightest, so I will never, for the life of me, figure out why what happened between me and Ben, happened.

"Good luck." Valerie said, gesturing for me to get off the car. I nodded, and opened the door, but before I could step out, she stopped me: "Oh! Wait!" She scribbled something on the back of a half torn receipt from a bakery, then handed it over to me. "In case you need to be rescued." She winked.

When I looked at the receipt I saw her phone number written in a neat and cute handwriting. What do you know, maybe I've finally made another friend. At least this one understands the pains of not being a size 2. Don't get me wrong, Faith and Hope are awesome, but ... way above the average girl. It's difficult not to feel inadequate next to them. Valerie is a curvy goddess, yet being around her is easy, she's always so happy and her positivity can be contagious. Or it would be, if I wasn't such a Miss Grumpy Pants.

When I got off the car, she winked and smiled, thumbs up, then left, after having pointed at the tall guy standing outside the café just a few steps ahead of me. Well, then, here goes nothing.

When I saw Jeremy, I felt a bit overdressed. Valerie dolled me up in this fancy dress, but Jeremy was more in tune with the place: simple jeans, sneakers, a white shirt under a pullover sweater that looked a lot like the one worn by Hogwarts students, in fact it sported black and yellow lines near the bottom – Hufflepuff colors. I guess I missed a chance to wear my Ravenclaw sweater.

"Hey!" Jeremy greeted me with a smile. He took a step closer, as if uncertain whether he should make physical contact or not, but in the end he opted for a no.

"Hi."

"How ... how are you?"

"I'm okay. You?" Wow, this date began in the lamest possible way.

"All good." He turned to the café, which seemed half full. "Have you ever been here?"

"No, but I did hear about it."

Jeremy nodded again. Hands stuffed in his pockets, he seemed even more nervous than I was. But why? "So ... shall we?"

Having nodded as well, I followed him into the café. I felt my heart skip a few beats when he accidentally brushed my hand as we entered, but it definitely did do somersaults when he placed a hand over the small of my back to lead me to a table. A table that, later I realized, was reserved for us, as a small note specified. In an attempt at actually being present to the situation, I commented: "I didn't know you could book café tables."

"Me neither," Jeremy chuckled, "but it was nice of you."

"Me?" The note did read Brooks. But I didn't do anything ...

Jeremy gentlemanly helped me sit, then he took his spot in front of me. We both took a chance to look around. At the entrance there was an an ancient-looking counter, behind it, 3 large bookshelves that took up half the wall; by the window there was a spiral staircase that led to the actual bookstore ... an entire corridor of books. I was in awe. But if that weren't enough, the ground floor was also surrounded by bookshelves, with a few tables scattered around; there was also another room behind us, with more tables, but the one we were in was breathtaking. I've always loved the ancient look, as in old furniture, but the combo ancient look + Harry Potter vibe was just ... Stendhal Syndrome worthy. The walls were full of those classic Hogwarts portraits – Dumbledore included, yes.

"This is awesome!" Jeremy breathed out, just as in awe as I was.

"I didn't know you were a fan." I murmured, trying to actually make up a conversation.

He grinned like a child on Christmas morning. "You kidding? I grew up with this! I always wanted to go to Wizarding World, but never got the chance. I did visit Hogwarts in England, though."

"You mean Alnwick Castle?" I asked, amazed. That one's been on my big list of places to visit since forever.

"Yeah!" Jeremy said, excited. "I went to England after graduation, and," his cheeks flushed the slightest, "yeah, I saw King's Cross, Hogwarts-I mean ... Alnwick Castle, and some others." He scratched the back of his head, ruffling his hair, as usual, but this time embarrassed, then admitted: "As nerdy as it sounds, the places I saw in England were all uh ... kind of ... book related. Like, you know ... Baker Street, The Sherlock Holmes Museum, the British Library, and of course ..." he laughed nervously, "Stratford-upon-Avon, because-"

"That's where Shakespeare supposedly was born." I filled in for him without thinking.

Jeremy looked at me with a beaming smile as he finally quit tormenting his
hair. "Yeah."

I mirrored his smile, even though mine was less bright. "It's funny ... those
exact places are on my list as well."

"Really?"

"Yeah." I sat a bit more comfortably, while a waitress made her way to our
table. "I mean, the museums as well, even though I don't know much about
visual arts, but ... yeah."

"I'm guessing you'd like to see Highclere Castle, too." Jeremy mentioned.
"Or Chatsworth."

I gulped the slightest. "Well, yes, Chatsworth is pretty much Pemberley,
from-"

"Pride and Prejudice." He nodded. "Would you find it weird if I said I read
all Jane Austen novels?"

"I thought guys normally don't like her."

"Well, yeah I was a bit skeptical at first, but ..." he stopped, and probably
for the first time, he allowed himself to take a long, lingering look at
me, from tip to toe. Well, he couldn't see my toes, but you get what I'm
saying. Jeremy gulped visibly, and nodded to himself, "you read in class,
remember?"

I blinked my eyes, surprised he remembered. I always brought a book with
me at every lecture, I would read during breaks or whenever I had some
time. College doesn't leave you much free time, so I carved it out as much

as I could, and, as far as I can remember, so did Jeremy sometimes. "Yeah …"

He nodded. "I noticed your choice often landed on Jane Austen."

"She's … one of my favorite authors, yeah."

"Yeah, so …" he cleared his throat, suddenly uneasy on his chair, "I-uh … read her novels, thinking it would be, you know, something we could talk about …"

"Oh."

"It's creepy, I know …" he sighed, relieved when the waitress finally got to us after having been distracted halfway.

"No, it's …"

"What can I get for you, guys?" The girl – probably just a bit younger than us – cut me off, tablet in her hands, ready to write down our orders.

"Uh … we haven't had a chance to look at the menu yet," Jeremy told her, "is there anything you'd suggest we try?"

She nodded, then scrolled through her tablet a bit, until she seemingly found the right. "Want me to surprise you?" She looked in between us.

"Sure." Jeremy answered, and I nodded in agreement.

When she left, he turned back to me, a sweet smile covering his lips. "Do you think that was a good idea?" He asked, completely ignoring his confession from earlier. "Hopefully she doesn't bring back some weird English dish." He laughed a bit more than the joke required, probably to cover up the embarrassment.

"So, uh …" I started, only to be soon cut off by another waiter coming our way.

"House?" He asked, ready to take notes.

"Hufflepuff." Jeremy answered proudly.

"Ravenclaw." I murmured when the guy turned to me. He nodded, then left, to which I frowned. "What do you think that was for?"

Jeremy shrugged. "Maybe some survey." He chuckled. "Normal people would have asked what did he mean ... we knew immediately."

I chuckled, too. "Well, I mean ... Harry Potter, he says house ... so you're a Hufflepuff?"

He nodded, pulling back against his chair. "I wouldn't say I'm a Cedric, though. I'm more of a Newt."

"You mean weird and eccentric but loyal and kind?"

Jeremy grinned, nodding once again. " You're a Hermione," he claimed, "but also kind of a McGonagall."

"You mean old inside?"

He laughed. Wow, I actually made someone laugh, and not at me. "I mean, back in the day, you were always so calm, that's very McGonagall."

I nodded in agreement. The waiter from before came back, and placed two drinks in front of us. Both tea. "We have special blends of tea for the four houses." He explained. " Chinese black tea, ginger, calendula petals, dandelion leaf, citrus granules, raspberry leaves, raspberry essence, apricot pieces, apricot essence – for Hufflepuff. Chinese black tea, lemongrass, blue cornflower, ginkgo, lavender, blackcurrant essence – for Ravenclaw." He claimed proudly. "Your orders will be here soon, the teas are on the house." Then he scuttled away.

My eyes were still on the disappearing waiter, so when Jeremy spoke, I thought I'd heard wrong: "I should have told you before," he said, "but ... you look beautiful today." Inevitably, I blushed. I didn't know whether to pretend I didn't hear or just answer, so I remained quiet, which made him think he was supposed to explain or worse, justify: "I mean ... you're always ..." he cleared his throat, "damn, one attempt at being smooth, and it failed." I could barely retain a chuckle, my lips curved the slightest. "It's ok, you can laugh." Jeremy said. "I'm a weirdo."

"I wasn't laughing." I turned to him, so that I caught him staring at me, much to my surprise – I thought it was safe to turn around because he would be staring at his lap, embarrassed.

"Ok, how about this one ... you make the nerdy look sexy." He winked, feigning a bad boy attitude he definitely wasn't credible enough for. This time I definitely laughed – both because he was funny and because this sort of smooth/sexy talk always makes me laugh.

I remember those times, those very few words we exchanged, he often made me laugh. I guess lost in the whole, suppressing my crush drama, I forgot Jeremy was never really this impossible to get girl magnet. He was a cute nerd with a passion for ancient history and books. A lot more alike to me than I ever really considered. Maybe this is gonna go way better than I could have ever expected.

18. All it takes is you

<hr>

"So ..." Jeremy sighed, stopping the car in front of the diner.

"So ..." I repeated, suddenly embarrassed. We spent a great afternoon together, I never thought it could happen. I was convinced I would be awkward and quiet and he'd get bored and give up, instead ... we talked, like we used to back in the day, or even more. We found out we have a lot in common, we're more alike than I ever imagined.

"I had fun." He said with a small smile.

"Me too." I admitted. I glanced at my watch. "I ... need to go or I'll be late."

"Yeah, but ..." he cleared his throat, "breakfast when we both get off work in the morning?"

I remained shocked. He wanted to see me again? It's true that it was a nice afternoon, but I didn't think he'd want to repeat it, so soon even.

"It's okay if you don't ..."

"I do." I blurted out, my voice weak. "I ..." Come on, Jo, say it. "Yes, I ... yes to breakfast together." Damnit, that sounded like an indecent proposal, didn't it? I grimaced to myself for sounding so stupid.

"Great." Jeremy grinned. "I'll … I can pick you up at the diner, or … we meet at the café down the road?"

I nodded, not answering, but hoping he understodd what I meant. I'll wait a bit outside the diner when I finish work, just in case he comes pick me up, if not, I'll go to the café he said. I can't believe this is really happening, and it probably won't last, but I guess I should at least try to enjoy it for now.

News travels fast. It took one picture, just one single picture that Jeremy recklessly posted on his Instagram, one picture that didn't even include us, just books we bought at Leaky Cauldron … and everyone came to know we went out on a date. And by everyone, I mean everyone.

You know how social media are, people you knew in school follow you even though you haven't seen them nor talked to them in over 10 years. So from his school friends, it arrived to our college mates, including, yes, Faith and Hope. I know, I know, they're my closest friends, I should have told them first. But I guess we've never really had that relationship where we tell each other everything.

Obviously, they texted me, and I explained it was nothing to really worry about. It was barely a date, imagine if it's worth making a fuss out of it, but they didn't believe me, so they've been stressing me out to know the details. Luckily, I could use the work excuse to avoid answering messages. Valerie too asked how it go and wanted to know everything, not to mention Joe who also saw the picture on Instagram. Even my parents called, because my cousins saw that damn picture, so everyone wanted to know – you realize how impossible it might have semeed to them, given the fuss –, only one person never spoke a single word about it all. Yeah, Ben.

I haven't heard a single word from Ben since before the date, while nor-mally he would randomly text me just to keep me company – according to him, I may be forced to work in this shithole for the money, but doesn't mean I have to be alone in it; so when I'm at work he usually texts me, saying irrelevant shit just to hear from me. But this time ... nothing. It's been nothing since that stupid kiss, actually. It's as if the moment he kissed me, he totally switched sides, being a totally different person with me.

That's why, much against my very own nature, during a peaceful moment at the diner, I was once again staring at Ben's contact, trying to find the courage to text him. What am I even supposed to tell him? In the end it was just half a day without talking to each other, I go on way longer than that not talking to the twins or even my parents. I guess I just got used to hearing from him and seeing him often.

Maybe I'm just paranoid. The night shift just messed up our routine, he probably sleeps at this hour, and why wouldn't he ... yeah, stupid me, of course it's just that.

"Hey, girl!!!"

I unconsciously smiled when I heard that crazy cheerful voice. Looking up, I saw her: "Hey, Michelle." As she came in, I half checked behind her, wonderind if her partner would be with her, but she seemed to be alone.

"Romeo is in the car."

I blushed at her words. Damnit, she caught me. "No, I ..."

"Yeah, yeah ..." she grinned, sitting at the counter, "you know, I should be mad at you."

"Why?" I blinked my eyes, marveled and mildly worried.

"Because ever since you two met, he's gone on and on about you! And tonight? Ugh, tonight!"

"Oh." Jeremy talks about me. That can't be right. My heart immediately started thumping in my chest. It's true that he immediately asked to get breakfast together in the morning, but ... I kinda thought he was just being nice.

"Yeah, yeah ... listen, I don't have much time, can you get us our usual for the night?"

"Sure." I started preparing their coffees to go and burgers.

"He wanted to come, you know." Michelle mentioned while I started the coffee machine.

"Mmh?" I asked absentmindedly. Scott and his weird choices. The diner needs to remain open until 2 am, but the cook can go home at midnight. Pretty sure this is just a new idea he had to make sure my night shift is just as bad as my day shift. He can't be here to bug me, so he's getting creative, I guess. Too bad for him, every shift without him around is still better, no matter what.

"Fahey, I mean." Michelle went on, munching on a cupcake that had been there all day. When I turned around I tried to warn her about it, but she dismissed it. "He wanted to come see you," she went on, "but then thought against it."

"Oh?"

"Well, he changed his mind a few times, going back and forth. I almost slapped some sense into him." She laughed. "But in the end he opted for a no."

"Why?" Did he change his mind? Maybe breakfast isn't happening any-more?

Michelle shrugged, then licke her fingers that were covered in cupcake icing. "I guess he didn't want to seem too eager."

"Eager?" I asked.

She laughed, as if I'd missed some big important revelation she'd just made. "Oh, honey, how little you know men!" That's true, but what does that have to do with anything? "He doesn't want to be clingy. You had a date today, you have one in the morning ... two plus two equals four, you can get there, honey."

"He ... clingy would look desperate?"

"Bingo!" She grinned, then frowned. "Um ... you're burning the coffee."

"What?"

She hinted behind me. "The coffee."

"Oh shit!" The machine was hissing like crazy, as if it wanted to burst right in the spot. "Shit!" My hand got scalded when I removed the mugs too fast and got ultra-hot coffee on it. "Shit! Shit! Shit!" I blew on the back of my hand, trying to ease the pain.

"You ok?"

"Yeah, I just ... fuck!"

"Water, honey, water." Michelle chuckled, coming behind the counter.

"You can't do that, I ..."

"I'm a cop, baby." That's her standard response to everything, but it made me chuckle. She guided me into the kitchen, and helped me put my hand under the water after having opened the faucet. "Looks pretty bad."

"I'm fine."

"You're not." She frowned. "Now I feel bad for laughing."

I smiled. "Don't. It was kind of funny."

She rolled her eyes, though smiling. "Well, you may need to see a medic."

"It's not that bad." It did hurt a whole hell of a lot, though.

"Honey, it's gonna get blistered."

My eyes widened. "What?"

"I mean, it's probably just second-degree, but if you don't treat it, it's gonna get blistered and it might leave a scar."

"Oh, no."

"It's fine." Michelle pulled back a bit. "Keep it under the water. Don't move." She grabbed her radio, and spoke into it. "Yes, this is Officer Ford, can I get a medic on Flatbush? Mary Lou's Diner."

"It's not that bad," I murmured, but she shushed me with her finger, to which I sighed. It did hurt like hell, though. And there it goes, breakfast with Jeremy skipped again.

Trying to fetch my keys with one hand was proving to be a long, long quest. Michelle's friend, the medic, said it's only a second-degree burn so I shouldn't get any scars, but I should rest the hand at least for a day or two, and he bandaged it, of course. He also gave me painkillers, so I felt a little bit weird, but nothing too bad.

As soon as Michelle told him, Jeremy came, and he took me home after the medic had decided I couldn't go on working. Needless to say that Scott was pissed when he was called in the middle of the night to be told his worst nightmare had to close the diner early and take a few days off. Long story short, I got fired. Well, technically I fired myself.

"What happened to you?" I jumped at his voice, and dropped my bag. He sounded worried, but also mad. "I'm sorry, I didn't mean to scare you." Ben sighed, walking up to me.

I nodded, to assure him I was fine, even though I felt a little bit dizzy. Probably the painkillers. When I bent down to get the bag off the floor, my head started mildly spinning, and I almost lost my balance but I didn't fall. When I felt Ben's strong arms around me, I blushed, my heart starting to race as it does a lot lately. Between Ben and Jeremy, my heart's been doing overtime so much that if it doesn't stop I might just start having problems with arrythmia.

"You ok?" Ben asked, worried, his hot breath against my neck, his hard chest against my back.

"Yeah."

"What happened?"

"You should be sleeping." I drawled out, leaning on him because I felt my legs weak, either because of the dizziness or because being in Ben's arms made me weak to my knees.

Damnit, Joanna, what are you even thinking. He's gay. Or bi but not interested. Whichever it is, it's not the right road.

"I heard you arrive." Ben murmured, moving us enough for him to grab my bag from the floor. "So what happened?"

"Work accident."

Ben sent me a side look. "Scott?"

I smiled at his worried tone. "No ... just clumsy me." He didn't even smile, weird. Actually, he looked pretty distressed, heavy bags under his eyes. "Are you ok?"

He left me against the wall. "Can you stand still without falling?"

"Yeah, I'm fine."

"That's one word for it." Ben rolled his eyes.

"You ignored my question."

"I'm trying to get you home." He claimed, searching my bag, probably looking for my keys.

"That doesn't answer my question either." I laughed to myself.

"Say, how many painkillers did they give you?"

"Um ..." I held up my hand to show him. "Two."

"That's a four."

"Maybe I don't know how to count." I laughed a bit hysterically.

Ben sighed, not at all amused. When he got tired of looking for the keys, he groaned. "Alright, come with me."

"Where?"

"To my place, where else."

"I've never been."

"There's a first time for everything. Come on."

I tilted my head to the side, unsure. "My mom wouldn't approve."

Oh, finally, he chuckled a bit, although he tried to hide it. "I'll sleep on the couch, don't worry." He claimed, throwing my bag over his shoulders. I felt even more dizzy when Ben circled my hips, leaning me onto him. Together we walked to his door, and once we got there, he opened it with a small kick, since it was only ajar.

"I can walk." I murmured.

"I know."

"But you're still holding me."

Ben smiled faintly as he pulled me closer into him. "Maybe I like holding you."

Wait, what? That can't be it. It's the painkillers, I imagined it. We headed to his bedroom, which made my heart race faster than a Formula 1 car. When we got there, Ben sat me on the bed, then kneeled before me, hands on my thighs.

"You sure you're ok?" He asked, his penetrating gaze boldly and arrogantly pushing through my defenses.

"Yeah."

"What happened?"

"I told you, I was clumsy." Normally I would have stuttered my way through this conversation, instead, be it the painkillers, be it the pain itself that made me freer, be it ... well, Ben, I felt like I could say just about anything. Ben wouldn't judge me. He never does. No matter how weird or awkward I am, he doesn't judge me.

Ben leaned a bit closer, and once again caused my heart to go into override as he cupped my cheeks. "You need to take better care of yourself."

I smiled a bit. "I don't." Bold as ever, even though my heart was racing, I looked into his eyes. "I've got you for that."

He smiled for a moment, then went serious. "Not Jeremy?"

"It's different."

"Different how?"

I shrugged. "Just different."

"Right." He pulled back enough to not to touch me anymore, then stood up. "You can sleep here tonight. Tomorrow we'll see what to do."

"I can go home." I looked up. "It's not like you really want me here."

"If I didn't want you here, I wouldn't have brought you."

"But you've been so cold with me."

He rolled his eyes, yet his lips curled up in a tiny smile. "When I'm nice, I'm too nice, when I give you space, I'm too cold ... typical girl, huh?"

This time I rolled my eyes. "Just say you're sick of me."

Ben frowned. "What makes you think that?"

"Well," I shrugged, "first you kiss the hell out of me, then you just throw me into someone else's arms and disappear ... you didn't even text."

"You always say I shouldn't text you while you're at work."

"I say a lot of things, I don't mean them all, Ben. I'm a girl!"

He laughed, kneeling before me again. "It really takes mind-numbing drugs to get you out of your shell, huh?"

"No."

"No?"

"All it takes is you."

Ben blinked his eyes, marveled. And I bet he was just as shocked as I was when I moved. I felt like I was watching myself from a third person point of view while in slow motion I leaned in, ever so spontaneously and lightly, and went in for it. Yeah, I did it. I kissed Ben.

19. Friends in need

It felt like eternity, but it only lasted a few seconds. Me not having the slightest idea how to kiss, it was obvious that it would fail miserably ... which it did. Ben didn't respond to the kiss, either shocked or disgusted, so I pulled back, feeling ashamed as my heart thumped and my head ached.

I kissed Ben. What the hell was I thinking! I kissed Ben even though I already knew too well he's not interested. Jesus, Joanna, why can't you ever do one thing right!

Letting out a shaky breath, I looked for a way out, but he was still kneeled before me, so I couldn't exactly run away from the embarrassment. I opted for just looking away, turning my head to the window on my right, hoping I could just be an ostrich and hide my head beneath the sand. I felt even dizzier than before, and kind of nauseous, not sure if because of the whole awkwardness of the situation or because I only ate a candy bar when I took the medicines – or just both.

Finally, Ben reacted. He heaved a deep sigh, hands at my sides without touching me. "Joanna ..."

There you go, my full name, bad sign. "I'm sorry." I blurted out, my face as red as a tomato. I felt myself hyperventilating, but not entirely because of the mortification. "I ... I shouldn't have. I'm sorry." I tried to take deep breaths, but my head was spinning faster now, and I really felt like I couldn't hold it in any longer – I was gonna throw up. I brought a hand to my mouth, "I need to ..." I pretty much toppled Ben as fast as I jumped up to run to the bathroom.

"Joanna!"

I faintly heard Ben call. I barely had time to kneel by the toilet that I hurled into it. It felt like I vomited everything I ever ate in my entire life. Much to my disgust, my hair was caught in it; I would have moved it away but it was already soaked in vomit, so no point. I felt my stomach tighten as nothing seemed willing to remain in it.

I heard a loud curse in the air, and when I felt my hair being pulled back, I noticed Ben was crouched beside me, an arm around me while his other hand kept my hair out of the way.

"Ben, no ..." I drawled out, not wanting him to touch that disgusting hair, as soaked as it was in whatever I just hurled into the toilet. But even speaking was enough to trigger another jet, so I lowered my head as much as possible to avoid getting any of that revolting liquid on Ben. Only after two or three more fits, did I finally feel like I'd entirely emptied my stomach. My breaths were hitched, I was sweaty and exhausted, not to mention reeking of that insufferable smell. And in all this, Ben was there to witness it. Ugh. As if it wasn't bad enough. "Ben ..."

"Take a deep breath." He said, rubbing my back.

I shook my head. "Go home."

"I'm not going anywhere. Now, can you stand?"

I nodded in response, but he didn't let me go. Instead, he helped me up, always holding me against him. Ben guided me to the sink, and after having grabbed a hairband from the mirror cabinet, he tied my dirty hair. I grimaced when I saw my reflection in the mirror. I looked hideous, with my face all puffy and red and sweaty, my eyes were also kind of red; and in all that, Ben still looked flawless. I looked away, ashamed, and freed myself from his grip. "Go away. Please."

Instead, he opened the faucet. "Don't be silly." He splashed some cool water on my face with one hand while the other rubbed tiny circles over my back.

"Ben ..." I sighed, exasperated.

"Shhh ... you just need some rest. But first, let's get you cleaned up."

"No." I said firmly, moving away from him. I was flushed and flustered, mortified and ashamed, but I had to do this. It's like I'm some charity case he's obsessed with. "You need to leave. Now." I tried to be as steady as possible, but I felt weak to my bones so even my voice was quivery.

"JoJo ..."

"Please, just go." Damnit, even the tears now. There's just no end to this humiliation. My hair was soaked in my own vomit, my face was red and puffy, my eyes were hurting because I hadn't been wearing glasses for a long time now, since I'd probably left them at the diner after the whole steamy coffee incident, and because of the tears that now fell unabashedly, not at all wary of Ben's humiliating presence. He took a step closer to me, but I backed up, holding my hands up in order to get some space between us. My injured hand still hurt a whole hell of a lot, despite the painkillers. "Please." My voice broke as tears took over. "I ... I need to be alone."

"No." He took another step towards me, one after the other as I kept backing up, until I hit the wall and had nowhere to run, so he could easily cage me against the cold tiles.

"Ben ..." my bottom lip quivered as I tried hard to hold back my tears. Stupid makeup didn't do anything but add to my discomfort, I should have taken it off when I went to work.

Ben caressed my cheek, shaking his head in disagreement. "I'm not going anywhere."

"But why ..." I drawled out. "Look at me! I'm a mess! It's disgusting!" I cried out. "Why would you want to witness all this! Do you just enjoy seeing me humiliated? Is that why you stuck around? You found a laughing stock that can provide you all the fun you need, is that it?" I realized I was yelling only when my own high-pitched voice hurt my ears, but I was far gone now, too much over the limit to stop. "I don't get it, Ben!" I pushed him off me, although he barely moved an inch or two. "I don't get why you stay no matter what! What, you have a bet going on? Let's find the most embarrassing girl possible, see how far can she humiliate herself!"

"JoJo ..."

"NO! Don't JoJo me!" I slid away from him, feeling my knees weak yet again. If I didn't hold it together, I would crawl to the floor once more. "What do you want from me?! You just come here, out of nowhere, and start being all nice and chatty, but why! Why would anyone in their right mind decide to stick to me! I mean I get it, first days in New York, you didn't know anyone, but now you do! I'm sure you've made friends, how couldn't you! And there's Valerie! You've got a job, and friends, a family that loves you, a ... I don't know what, girlfriend, boyfriend, what! That calls you every day and night! You've got people in your life! People that are way more worth it than I am so why waste time with me! Unless it's all a joke! I mean, what else could it be! A joke, a bet, something! I don't see another reason!"

When I stopped, I was wheezing, my heart racing like a fool, my head thumping as if it'd been knocked with a hammer, even my bones ached.

It's always like that. The rare times I blow up, it affects me physically, so much so that I can barely breathe. Feeling lightheaded, I brought a hand to my chest, falling against the wall.

"Joanna!" Ben shouted, but I held my hand up.

"Leave."

"You know, I-"

I shook my head. "Just go."

"No."

"What do you mean no! I asked you to leave!"

"You don't know what you're asking." He stated solemnly, once again breaching my personal space.

"Ben ..."

He shook his head. "You need a shower, and some rest."

"What I need, is for you to understand the meaning of boundaries every once in a while." I wheezed, trying to calm down. Fun fact, if I blew up more often, maybe it wouldn't be this bad. Another fun fact, anxiety attacks are a thing, and I have it. This wasn't even a bad one, believe me, just a mild episode.

"Oh, I know the meaning of boundaries." Ben scoffed, taking off some of the vomit from my hair. "I just don't give a shit about them."

"Proper stalker talk." I scoffed back, looking away from him.

"If caring enough about you not to leave when you clearly need me the most is stalking, then I guess I'm a stalker." He claimed, deadly serious.

I turned to him, amazed. "You ..."

"Jesus, JoJo, why do you think I've been around? All those stupid reasons you gave, all bullshit. The only reason why I'm around you, is that you're my friend and I care about you. Simple as that." He went on removing the sticky grimy glop from my hair."

"But ..." The kiss. What about that kiss?

Ben ignored my objections, he just reached for the shower, opened the door, and then the faucet, letting water run for a bit until it became hot enough to be comfortably steamy, then he closed the faucet. "Can you manage?" He hinted at the shower.

I blushed. "Yes."

He feigned a little impish grin, and I would have sworn that when his eyes raked over my frame, there was something in them, but I'm not quite sure what. "Then I'll wait outside."

When he left, I closed the door behind him, and finally let myself restart breathing. What the hell just happened? Unable to retain myself, I went to stand in front of the mirror. My hair was up in a messy bun, makeup was all smudged, due to tears and water; I felt sticky, the dress was glued to my frame, and not in a flattering way – it just exposed my every unappealing curve.

Ben saw this entire mess ... I doubt he can really see me any worse than this. But the weird part is, he would stay regardless. I guess that's what friendship is. Oddly enough, the word friendship had a sour taste this time.

After having taken a deep breath, I opened the faucet to wash the makeup off my face, but then I remembered that the doctor said I shouldn't let the bandage get wet unless it sticks to the wound – in that case I should use cool water to unstick it. I looked around, trying to find something I could cover the bandage with, but I couldn't find anything. Sighing, I opened the door with my good hand, only to then yelp when I found Ben lying in my bed, cozily reading a book. "What ..."

"Well, that was a lightning speed shower. Wow." He commented sarcastically as he looked up from the book.

"I ... didn't ... you shouldn't be in here."

"I said I would wait outside the bathroom, didn't I?"

I rolled my eyes. "Yes, but not ... here." Unless you wanna see me naked, you freak, I almost said.

Ben sat up, placing the book on the bed – I'll admit the gentleness with which he did that, surprised me –, "you can't manage on your own, can you?"

"I just need something for the ..." I unconsciously showed the bandage. A bit embarrassed – which was still nothing compared to everything that happened just a while ago –, I reached for my bag, knowing there would be a plastic bag in there. Yeah, I always have a bag of chips in my bag, for when I get snacky. I guess I just proved him there's indeed a reason why I'm so fat.

Ben watched me fumble with the bag of chips as I tried to open it with my teeth, and only when he got tired of yet another one of my humiliating stunts, he stood up, and came over to me. He took the bag of chips from me, and threw it onto the bed, then much to my surprise, he took out an empty plastic bag from his back pocket.

I furrowed my eyebrows as I watched him wrapped that bag around my bandage. "You enjoy this too much."

He chuckled. "Guilty as charged." He looked me up and down for a moment, then reached for the hem of my dress, and lifted it.

"What ..."

"Lift your arms."

I obeyed without thinking, which left me clad in my underwear, my entire imperfections exposed. Instinctively, I tried to cover myself, but Ben rolled his eyes, pushing me into the bathroom. Standing behind me, he unclasped my bra, making me let out a small screech. "Ben ..."

"Arms stretched out in front of you." He ordered.

"This is not ..." He stretched my arms for me, which caused him to get closer, enough for his hard chest to graze against my back. "This is so humiliating."

"You need a shower and you can't do it on your own. I'd say this is the only possible solution." He explained. "If you'd rather I called Valerie, I can do that, but she's working."

"No ..."

"Then let's just get on with it, okay? I'm not even looking; my eyes are closed." Indeed, they were – I noticed when I turned to look at him –, but what difference does it make? It was still embarrassing as hell. Gay or not gay – which is still unclear to me, given the whole kissing business –, it was still a guy seeing me completely naked, my fat rolls and stretch marks exposed. Oh, sure, his eyes were closed, but were they entire time?

"We'll never say a word about this, okay?" I murmured, ashamed.

Ben chuckled. "Alright." His chest pushed against my back when he patted me down, trying to blindly find his way to my underwear.

"Ben?" I called when I felt something odd against the small of my back.

"It's my phone." He explained quickly, sounding a little embarrassed. He made sure not to brush any particular area he shouldn't have, so it took way longer than necessary, but after that phone incident, he also made sure not to get too close to me physically.

I always thought this kind of episodes wasn't believable in real life, but I guess I was wrong. Then again, I am not much believable as a human being, so I suppose it figures. It still remains that never, even in my wildest dreams, would have I imagined that one day I would be standing in my bathroom, with a bandaged hand, while my gay (or not so gay?) friend undresses me and helps me hop into the shower. It's more believable that Sheldon would suddenly kiss Penny when he helped her do the exact same thing Ben was helping me with – except she had a strained shoulder, not a scalded hand.

Like in a trash comedy movie, once he was done undressing me, I had to guide Ben to the shower door, since he still had his eyes closed. He cleared his throat. "Uh ... you can take it from here. I'll wait outside." And without letting me reply, he made his blind way out of the bathroom. Well, if this doesn't make us friends for life, I don't know what will.

20. Living in a lie

B^{EN}

I closed the door behind me, but only once I'd heard the shower running I opened my eyes, and let out a heavy sigh. That must have been one of the hardest and most awkward things I've ever done in my entire life – and believe me, I've had plenty of embarrassing and surreal moments.

I don't know how long I can go on with this. She's not stupid, she'll figure it out eventually; it's already odd that she hasn't questioned me despite that kiss.

Looking down at my pants, I groaned. Sweet, naïve Joanna even believed me when I said it was the phone. What damn phone? Mine was blatantly sitting on her bed, always blowing up with texts and missed calls. Valerie's been giving me a hard time about this, I try to take her off my trail, but we've known each other all too well for her to just believe I suddenly had some sort of homosexual epiphany in my mid-20s.

Yeah, I'm not gay. Duh. The revelation of the year, isn't it? Anyone less naïve than my sweet JoJo could have told you that much. Seriously, not even that kiss woke her up. Just how deeply lost in her self-loathing denial is she?

I mean, set aside the fact that if your friend is gay, he would never even accidentally kiss you, but a guy that loves his friendzone wouldn't kiss you like that, believe me. I almost felt free, I could finally say the truth, but then I chickened out.

I loved that kiss, though. I don't know what's going on with me, why did I just lie to her like that, why do I keep on lying even though I am perfectly aware that once she finds out, she will cast me out and never forgive me. And how could she?

She's slowly starting to trust me, open up to me, if now I come up with such a revelation, she'll not only hate me forever, but she will never ever trust a human being again, and I can't let that happen. She's spent the past 28 years surviving in her cozy bubble, far from the madding crowd, if now I prove her she was right to stay away from people, she'll never emerge from under her safety blanket again.

Raking a hand over my face, I tried to take my thoughts off Joanna for a moment, in order to fix the problem where the sun doesn't shine. But considering she was just one door away taking a shower, it wasn't easy not to let my dirty mind wander.

My eyes were closed the entire time, out of respect for her, but I did see. I saw with my hands, as they traced her voluptuous body ... and my God, was it mind-blowing. Those maddening curves, I could lose myself just tracing their lines, up and down, along that rollercoaster I wouldn't mind trying even just once.

Ugh. Damnit, these thoughts don't help. I opted for going out onto her balcony, to get some fresh air, hoping that would do the magic. There's nothing more off-putting than a lousy view on a filthy Brooklyn restaurant. The awful smells penetrated my nostrils, which was enough to distract me, thank God.

But this mess, this isn't going away. You can't lie to someone like her and still think she won't drop you. Sighing, I leaned over the balustrade, but even in the noise of the city, I could hear my phone buzzing from Joanna's bed.

Coming to New York was a big sacrifice, but I did it for the right reasons, and I know she'll thank me for it soon enough, but right now it's hard to convince her. The only compromise I could find was that we'd text all day and that I'd be her good morning and her goodnight every time. I still miss her, though, so much.

"Ben?" I heard Joanna call from the inside. I didn't have time to answer, when she didn't see me, she just went ahead and took off her bathrobe, remaining completely naked, no undergarments either. I covered my mouth before I could groan out loud, but not wanting to be a pervert, I turned around immediately, facing the alley below.

God, this is going to kill me. Good thing I'll go home this weekend, at least I can try and get my head straight. Getting time off work wasn't exactly easy, but I had to, Elle wouldn't forgive me if I missed her birthday.

How did I get myself into this mess, I have no idea. Between Elle and Joanna, my family, my job, university, I feel like I'm going insane. And the worst part is, I've been telling so many lies to so many people that I'm not even sure anymore which is which. I dread the day I'll slip up and lose everything all at once.

When I heard Joanna curse, I unconsciously smiled. All of this might be ultra-complicated, but I guess it is kind of worth it if I get to spend some time with such a lovely girl. I am 100% sure she wouldn't have eased up with me so soon, hadn't I lied about being gay. Not because she feared I might hit on her and become a creepy neighbor that stalked her, but because she's uneasy with men, so I thought that seeing me as pretty much a woman would help. I'd have told her I'm a drag queen, if that would have helped. Anything just to break through that hard shell of hers.

Believe it or not, at first my intentions were utterly pure. How couldn't they be? I've got Elle at home in Nebraska, I would have never dared. In the beginning, all I wanted was to help this shy girl find herself, the same as I did for Valerie, and the same as I was helped in my teen years. But then, I don't know ... it's as if she sucked me into her crazy awkward, nerdy world, and I found myself being a happy captive. Now I don't know how to get out of it alive.

I'll admit Jeremy was pure luck. He arrived at the right time, otherwise I would have had to explain that kiss. But she got so caught up in her date that she forgot about it, thankfully. Hadn't it been for those painkillers making her dizzy, she wouldn't have kissed me either.

I'm just gonna have to rely on her shyness this time, and hope she tucks this entire episode tonight far, far away in some uncharted corner of her mind. That way I can still live this lie a little more. One day I'll tell her everything, I promise, just not yet.

☆☆☆☆☆

"He can't just fire you." I furrowed my eyebrows when she told me her stupid employer sacked her. I've got half a mind of going over to the diner to teach Scott some manners. You think I didn't notice the bruises? Dipshit is lucky I didn't want to get her in trouble, otherwise he'd already be in a hospital crying for mommy. But unfortunately I am well acquainted with the pains of having to swallow the crap every day just to make ends meet.

"He didn't fire me," Joanna explained as she took a spoonful of her white rice – much against her will, I convinced her it was better to eat something simple after having thrown up like that. "I quit."

I blinked my eyes, surprised yet also proud of her. "You really did?"

"Yeah. I mean, I was probably too confused by the pain together with the meds and the fact that Jeremy was coming to pick me up, but ... I did it."

Ugh. Jeremy again. He called her earlier, wanting to make sure she was okay, he said; he'll come over when he finishes work, he said. I know, I threw her into his arms ... doesn't mean I have to enjoy it. He seems nice and all, but you know, we are still rivals, how am I supposed to like him?

Then again, technically we're not rivals. I can't do anything about this, there's Elle. I have to think about Elle. She was already mad that I missed her calls tonight because I was busy either taking care of Joanna or trying to push away all those thoughts about her. I haven't even told her about my neighbor, she'd get crazy jealous and would most likely come to New York.

"So what now?" I asked just in time, before Joanna realized I was spacing out.

She shrugged. "I don't know."

"Are you ok with ..."

"Don't even think about it." She sent me a dirty look, to which I chuckled.

"What? I said nothing."

She pointed her spoon at me, like a weapon. "Rent."

"What about it?" I played innocent.

She glared, unknowingly looking cuter. "I can make it while I find another job."

"For how long?" I inquired, only now realizing that if she can't afford to stay, she'll have to go back to her hometown.

"A month or two. It should be enough."

"You seem pretty positive, I'm impressed."

She grinned, glancing at her phone. "I'm just in a good mood." Ugh. Right. Fucking Jeremy again. "You know, Jeremy said his captain is looking for an assistant."

"What captain?"

"Oh, right, I didn't tell you." She laughed, giddy. "Jeremy is a cop." Great. Hard to beat a uniform. Ugh. What am I even saying? I'm not supposed to do anything. Elle, think about Elle.

"Nice." I commented dryly.

"Yeah. Well, we wouldn't work on the same floor, of course," she blushed therefore lowered her gaze, "but of course ... we'd see each other more often." Fantastic. "I know it's silly, but ... I wouldn't really mind seeing him more of him." Great. Stab me while you're at it.

Lucky, or unlucky, for me, my phone buzzed. This time I couldn't ignore it. "Sorry," I said as I stood from the kitchen table where we'd been eating dinner, "I have to take this." I went out the door before she could reply. After having taken a deep breath, I answered the phone. "Hey, sweetie?"

"Where have you been?" She cut straight to the chase, clearly mad.

"Just busy, honey. How are you?"

"Busy how?"

"Well, you know, work and university, the usual thing."

"I don't believe you."

I sighed. "Why would I lie to you?"

"I don't know, but you never have time anymore ..."

"Well, don't worry, I'll have all the time in the world for you this weekend, okay? I'll be all yours."

"So you're really coming?" I smiled when I heard the excitement in her voice.

"Of course I'm coming. In the 10 years we've been together, have I ever missed your birthday? Why would I start now? I miss you more than you could possibly imagine, honey, I can't wait to see you."

"Me too. Can I come to New York with you, though?" Elle asked, hopeful.

I sighed, raking a hand over my face. "Not yet. Remember I said I'd try to settle first, then I'd come back for you."

"Yeah, but ..."

"Just give me a few more months, okay? I love you so much, I'm doing this for us, to give us a better future. Staying away from you is pure agony, but it's a small sacrifice if compared to the happiness that awaits us." She wasn't convinced at all, but finally she agreed, then we hung up. I felt guilty for lying, but I can't let her come here yet. Things aren't going as well as I thought they would, and with Joanna ... I really don't know how could I explain it to Joanna.

21. Onceover plus smile equals flirting

JOANNA

"Have you heard from Ben?" I wondered, unable to retain myself, as I played with the ice cream. Somehow, Valerie convinced me to have a girl day that was supposed to be all about pampering ourselves, but it ended up being an interrogation on Jeremy. She wanted to know every single detail about that first date and everything that followed, which wasn't much, but according to her it was a big deal.

Jeremy and I really just have been texting, and he calls me when he's on the way to or from work. He hasn't come see me, but mostly only because I try to avoid it, it would be way too awkward to have him in my apartment while I'm nursing this silly wound.

"No, why?" Valerie sent me a side glance as she played with her own ice cream. The fact that I picked a cookie dough ice cream sundae, while she chose a whipped coffee one says a lot about how different we are, I think: I'm still a little girl deep down, she's a classy woman.

I shrugged. "Just asking." He said he'd be gone just for a weekend, but it's been a couple of weeks now.

"He hasn't texted?" Valerie inquired.

"He texts seldomly, just hi, how are you." I pouted, taking another spoonful of my ice cream. Two weeks ago, Ben said he would go back home for the weekend, because it was his mom's birthday; he said he'd be back on Monday, but there's been already two Mondays since then, and no trace of him. Oh, sure, he texts, once every 2-3 days, asking how am I, but for the most part he's been quiet. It's true that I've been more taken by this whole ... Jeremy thing, but doesn't mean I didn't notice that Ben detached abruptly.

"He's fine, probably got caught up in family life, you know how it is." Valerie dismissed it, only to then moan at the ice cream, "oh, Jo, you should try this, it's so good!"

I nodded distractedly, thinking about Ben. I'm just worried about him, is that bad? Between trying to understand why Jeremy even still talks to me, and looking for a new job plus reassessing my finances to make sure I don't end up starving too soon, I've been quite busy, but still not enough to notice the void caused by his absence.

It's odd, you know. It's odd how you can go on a whole life without someone, then the moment they step into your life, you forget how it was before and cannot even fathom going back; yet when they do, it's as if they took something with them, something you can't live without.

I guess was I getting used to having someone that really understands how I'm feeling or at least truthfully tries to. Not that Jeremy isn't understanding, or even Valerie, not to mention Joe and Michelle, even Faith and Hope. But Ben is just ... on a different level, if it makes any sense.

Four months ago, I was mostly on my own. The friendship with the twins has always been pretty easy, we just talk about trivial stuff, and they come see me or try to convince me to go to a party. It was apathic for the most part, with the twins just loosely orbiting around me, and Joe coming over almost every Monday for a pizza night.

Then Ben happened. And it's as if his appearance unlocked a new chapter, adding new characters into the mix; from Michelle, the friendly yet a bit intimidating NYPD officer, to Valerie, the curvy goddess that other than make me feel even worse about myself, actually inspires me to be a better version of who I am. And Jeremy ... oh, Jeremy. The sole thought of him brought a silly smile to my face.

"Oh, Romeo, Romeo ..." Valerie chanted, laughing as she pinched my cheeks.

I blushed, pulling away. "I was just ..."

"Thinking about Ben?" She winked.

I gulped. "No!" I cleared my throat, lowly correcting her: "Jeremy ..."

"Jeremy, Benjamin ..." she weighed the two names with her hands, "not that far."

"Why would I think about Ben?" Considering he doesn't even care enough to let me know when is he coming back, or if he is coming back at all.

Valerie shrugged, pulling back on her chair and rubbing her belly, satisfied of her ice cream. "I don't know, maybe you miss him." Tsk. Why would I? "He's been gone quite a bit."

"Maybe he decided to stay." I thought out loud.

"At home in Nebraska?" Valerie laughed, skeptical. "Not a chance. The Ben I know hates monotony, and believe me, our hometown is everything but surprising. Every single day is the exact same as the one before. Ben would go nuts if he had to live there for life. It'd be like a prison sentence."

"Well, he has family there." I pointed out, shrugging. "Maybe he decided he wants to stay with them."

"Nah." She shook her head. "The Harris are lovely, but Ben has always been a dreamer, and dreamers don't thrive in such a small town."

"You know his family?" I wondered, mildly envious. Valerie did know Ben long before me, why am I even surprised she knows his folks.

"Back in high school Benny and I were tight." She grinned, pegging down the clerk to get another whipped coffee ice cream sundae, which arrived pretty swiftly, even though the girl at the counter seemed busy arguing with a cute nerdy guy.

"What happened after?" I couldn't help myself asking.

Valerie shrugged. "Life, I guess. You know that saying? The friends you make until the age of 23 are usually temporary."

I guess that's true. I had a close friend in high school, too, but then I moved out because of college, while she stayed at first, then left, too. We kept in touch for a bit, but I've never been too good at that, so we soon lost each other. I kind of regretted it, but I guess it was just meant to happen.

"It's pure luck that we met again here." Valerie went on. "I truly believed he would be off to who knows what grand city or travelling around to make the covers of National Geographic. It's always been his dream."

"What happened?" I inquired. Maybe it wasn't right of me to quiz her like that, it was Ben's life, not hers. With Ben it was always all about me. Sure, at first he would do monologues, telling me about his family and everything, but then he would ask me all sorts of questions just to get me to talk.

"Again, life." Valerie went serious. "I don't really know the details, like I said, we lost contact." She sent me a knowing look, though. "You could always ask him."

"Between one how are you and the other, you mean?" I blurted out sarcastically.

Valerie arched one of her perfectly cured eyebrows. "I take it as there's troubles in Paradise?"

I gulped, shocked at her words. What Paradise? "Jeremy and I are hardly friends, it's not ..."

"I meant Ben."

"Oh. He's ... uh ..." if they were so close, how come she doesn't know? "Ben is ... gay." I would have sworn she did her best not to laugh, but maybe I imagined it.

"Yeah, I know." She stretched a bit. "What I meant is, you two seemed so close, is there a problem now?" She didn't sound too sure of her words, but I shrugged it off.

"Well, we haven't been talking much." I confessed. "Just a random good morning or how are you every few days."

Valerie smiled reassuringly as she stood, ready to restart our girl day. "Don't think too much of it, Jo, he's probably busy. As I remember them, the Harris are quite a handful, and Ben was always the one taking care of everything, especially for his brothers."

Suddenly I recalled what Ben told me about this family. That he never knew his dad, and that his mother married his stepfather when Ben was 9; his brothers came a bit later. I guess that makes family life a bit awkward, at least in the beginning, although Ben always talked dearly about his stepdad. As if she'd read my mind, Valerie went on:"Mr. Harris dotes on Ben, believe me, Jo. Ben's mom told me it was like love at first sight."

"What do you mean?" I stood up as well, and we headed over to the counter to pay our bill. Well, Valerie insisted on paying for me, despite my protests.

"Ben was 9 when they got married." She said as we headed out.

"Yeah, he told me." I followed her, coyly mirroring the polite smile that some guy that entered the shop while we exited it sent me. I facepalmed myself when I remembered Valerie had just passed by, he was probably smiling at her, not me. Duh.

She froze in her steps when we were a few steps away from the ice cream parlor, and I nearly crashed into her. "I left my sunglasses in there, could you ..."

Without arguing, I went back into the parlor. The clerk was busy with another customer, while the nerdy guy was still standing there – either waiting for his order or to restart the argument with the girl. I checked the booth we'd been sitting in, but there was no sign of Valerie's sunglasses. Think of it, she wasn't wearing any when she picked me up earlier.

"Hey."

I nearly jumped when I heard a male voice behind me. "Hi." I greeted awkwardly when I found myself face to face with that same guy that I thought had smiled at me.

"Did you forget something?"

How about minding your business? Would have been my first response, but I just nodded. "My friend says she left her glasses here," you know, that beautiful girl you were staring at and whose number you probably wanna ask me – because why else would a random ice cream parlor customer just come up to me like that –, "but I can't find them."

The guy – a bit taller than me, but shorter than Ben, black hair, cute smile – nodded, then started looking for the sunglasses as well. "I don't see anything here," he said as he checked the booth, then looked at me, a cheeky smirk covering his thick lips, "other than a beautiful lady." Say what now?

I gulped, pretty audibly too, "I-I'm sorry, what?"

"Do you think your friend would mind if you ditched her to ... let's say get coffee with me?"

Uh ... did I step through the looking glass? Inevitably, I blushed, albeit unsure whether that truly happened or I just dreamed of it. "I ... I gotta go." I scuttled out of the parlor without answering him, and reached Valerie at the speed of light. Valerie who was waiting for me just outside, a Cheshire cat grin on her face. Did she set me up?

"So?" She asked, excited. "Did he ask you?"

"What ..."

She hooked her arm to mine, and dragged me away from the parlor – thank God! –, "that cute guy! Did he ask you out?"

"How do you ..."

"Oh, silly girl!!" She playfully slapped my shoulder. "You think I didn't notice the onceover he gave you when we passed by him?"

"No, he ..."

"Baby girl, I know that technically you're seeing that cop, but you gotta live a little!"

"What ... do you mean?" I let her drag me along the street, probably to yet another boutique where she'd spend an hour wandering around to check out the competition. I didn't know how to tell her that I don't exactly enjoy physical contact and her squeezing me into her like that was making me feel awkward. It's not like she's Ben and everything comes naturally. I mean ... no, I just hate being touched.

"Okay," she feigned an exhausted sigh as we turned a corner, "Womanhood 101, part two: learn to notice when a guy checks you out."

What the hell was she talking about? Nobody checked me out. "He was smiling at you." I pointed out.

"Uh ... no, he wasn't!" Valerie exclaimed, excited, as we came to a stop – case in point, in front of yet another boutique, cue the eye roll. "He gave you a onceover and smiled at you!"

"What?" I finally managed to slide out of her grip. "No, that's not possible ..."

"Joanna ..." Valerie grabbed my shoulders from behind, and made me stand in front of the boutique's window. "Look at yourself, baby girl. You're a knockout."

"Valerie ..." I sighed. Not this again.

"I mean, ok, he wasn't that cute ... but not bad either." She winked, but I just ignored her. "I know you're used to other types, but he really wasn't so bad."

I glanced at her, mildly confused, but also embarrassed because we were in the middle of the street, let me remind you. "I don't understand ..."

"Tell me, what are you wearing?"

"Uh ... just jeans and a shirt."

"Exactly!" Valerie exclaimed, as excited as if she'd just received the best news ever.

"Exactly what?"

She chuckled, finally letting me go. "Easy outfit, knockout result! Do you understand what I'm saying?"

"Not really ..."

"It just took some care, Jo!" Some care is a little reductive, considering she sat me by the mirror for half an hour to do my makeup and hair. Fortunately, she let me wear my own clothes: jeans, shirt, white t-shirt under it. Couldn't have been any easier than that. I mean, ok, maybe it was a little bit less shabby than my usual, but nothing to fuss about like Valerie was doing now. Sometimes I wonder whether I'm really female, because I don't understand women at all.

But wait ... "did you send me back in on purpose?" I inquired, mildly annoyed.

"Of course!" Valerie, I like you, but let's take the enthusiasm down a notch. Sometimes she's too happy and energetic for me to handle.

"Why?"

"I told you! Experiment!"

"What?" I frowned.

"The guy gave you a onceover."

"He didn't ..." I rolled my eyes.

"He did, you stubborn girl." She flicked my forehead. "Onceover plus smile equals flirting."

"Oh, come on ..."

"Yes! He did ask you out, didn't he? And I'm sure he would have asked for your number, hadn't you run away like that!"

"He was just being polite because he wanted your number." I blurted out in a sigh.

"Oh, please. What did he tell you?"

I rolled my eyes once again. "Some lame line about a beautiful lady."

"So ..."

"Nothing."

"Ugh, you're so stubborn!" Valerie rolled her eyes, albeit smiling. "But we're on the right path. I know it."

I wanted to ask what path, exactly, but she dragged me into that boutique before I could say anything else. Is there something I'm missing here? Ben disappearing for two weeks, Valerie calling me to hang out, being all up in my business, being ... well, pretty much a Ben. And this experiment she said today. Is Ben really not coming back and she's just trying to sugar the pill before telling me?

22. Would I ever lie to you?

"So ..." Jeremy cleared his throat when we got to my door. Well, my building's door. Close enough, I guess.

"Thanks." I smiled bravely. "I had fun." Feels like I say that at every date, and every date ends the same way. I don't know whether to be glad we're still doing this or confused as to whether we're stuck in a loop or not.

"Me too." He grinned, hands stuffed in his pockets. This time, however, he did something that took me off guard. Jeremy, who had always kept a somewhat safe distance between us at every date – other than hands casually brushing here and there –, this time almost closed the gap between us.

It was enough for me to have to look up, him being slightly taller than me, and enough for him to probably spot the imperfections behind Valerie's perfect makeup art. I may be a complete ignorant when it comes to people, but even I knew what was about to happen. It was about time, may I add. After 4 weeks, at least a dozen dates, it was time, it had to be time.

Jeremy looked evidently nervous, though. During the time spent together I discovered that he's just as socially awkward as I am, which is a blessing and a surprise, but also makes things a bit more difficult between us. Introvert

+ Introvert equals Super Introvert and barely any steps taken while dating, you know. That's why after so many dates, so much time spent on super nerdy dates and equally nerdy texting, we still haven't kissed.

It'd be funny if it wasn't so frustrating: number of times I kissed my allegedly gay neighbor that apparently dropped off the face of the earth? two; number of times I've kissed the guy I've been dating? Zero. Even I know there's something off with that count, at the very least it should be the opposite.

"Would it be too ... cheeky of me if I asked to come up?" Jeremy wondered, his voice lowering a bit. Before I could answer, however, he pulled slightly back, justifying: "I just don't want this perfect night to end." He blushed the slightest. "I'm not ... uh ..." ah, there it is, the Jeremy I know, awkward and shy. He scratched the back of his head, clearing his throat nervously. "I'm sorry, I realize it sounded like I want ... you know ..." Yeah, yeah, I know. "But ... I just thought we could, I don't know, have a drink, talk some more?"

I mean, why not? "Okay."

"Really?"

I chuckled. I think I may have found the one guy that's even more shy than I am. Or rather, he's not truly that shy, just he's nervous, as if terrified he'll say the wrong thing and ruin everything between us. I can't deny I understand that fear all too well. However, I promised to Valerie that I would do everything in my power not to retreat into my safe cocoon. I need to live a little, as she says.

And maybe Ben has been gone for weeks now, but doesn't mean I can't go on and get out of my shell like he so wanted me to. I shook my head slightly in order to chase away the thought of Ben. We text, sure, but he always ignores me when I ask if/when he's coming back and what is he up to.

"Let's go." I told Jeremy, smiling boldly, and unlocked the door. This has to work. 20-year-old me would scream in delight, our crush finally coming over, finally talking to us, paying attention to us, which, now I know, he already did back in the day. He just was too shy to really act on it.

Jeremy and I walked to the elevator in silence. I don't know whether he was trying to think of the next steps or he just likes silence as much as I do. Maybe the latter. These four weeks I found out we have a lot in common, from the love for books and overall learning new things, to all that nerdy stuff that most of the people around us don't understand. I can't help but regret my actions even more now, we could have connected really well back in the day, if only I'd been braver. But I guess it's better late than never, right?

"Did I tell you? I have this weekend off." Jeremy mentioned when we got to the elevator.

"Really? What are you going to do?"

He pursed his lips, as if not sure whether he should ask or not. "That's the thing ... I was thinking-uh ... we could, get away?" I gulped, probably not very quietly, as his nervous laugh told me. "Yeah, I mean ... I don't know if you've noticed, but-uh ... it's been a month."

A month that we're dating, sort of. Oh, yeah, I definitely noticed. I got used to his good morning and good night texts, to him dropping by before and after work, to our afternoon dates because he's still on night shift. I'm getting used to his presence in my life, and I don't know whether that's a good thing or not, but I definitely love it.

There are only 2 stains in this unlikely period of my life: one is, obviously, Ben's absence; two is the fact that, much to my dismay, I had to go back to

Scott and beg him to hire me back. I know, I know, I was finally rid of him. But, well, after a week spent nursing that scalding wound to my hand, I did some Math, and I was nowhere near finding a new job, so I had to swallow my pride and go back, tail between my legs.

However, Michelle and Jeremy drop by the diner pretty often, and I don't need to tell you what seeing police uniforms does to Scott. He's been nicer, if by nice you mean he ended the verbal and somewhat physical abuse. Of course, he left me on the night shift indefinitely, thinking I'd hate it, and doubled my tasks for the night, making sure I go home absolutely worn out. What he doesn't know is that I like the night shift, and I probably will until Jeremy has the same shift.

"So, what do you think?" Jeremy asked again, which meant I was spacing out.

"About?" I asked, smiling kindly as I turned to him after having pressed the button to go up to my floor.

"The Berkshires?" He proposed.

"The Berkshires?" I repeated, confused.

"Yeah, I thought it'd be nice to spend a weekend there ... there's this nice antiques fair and I know you love antiques, so ..." Jeremy explained.

Sounds very romantic, which I don't know how appropriate it is after only 1 month, but it also sounded interesting. However ... "Scott would never give me the time off." I sighed.

"I can ask him nicely," he chuckled, exposing his badge, to which I laughed, "or I could send Michelle after him ... no one can dare say no to that woman."

"I thought you said police was only a temporary choice but you seem to enjoy it." I commented as we got off the elevator once on my floor.

Jeremy shrugged. "Well, yeah, but it's probably just that Michelle makes it interesting. I can't really see myself doing this permanently." I nodded in agreement. I don't see him as a cop for life either, to be honest. Jeremy is more like the scholar type.

"What would you prefer?" I asked as we headed to my apartment.

Jeremy cleared his throat, a bit embarrassed. "It'll sound super-nerdy, but ... I was thinking paleontology."

"Paleontology?"

"Yeah, I mean, I always loved dinosaurs ... I did major in Archaeology after all, I just didn't find anything to back it up so I had to adjust."

I understand that feeling all too well. "I think you should pursue your dreams." I stated as we stopped at my door.

"I could say the same to you." Jeremy smiled. "You did say your dream was to write."

"Yeah, but it's ... complicated."

"It always is, but you never know if you never try." Somehow that sounded like it held deeper meanings that had more to do with us than with our career problems and dreams.

In fact, Jeremy brushed my arm, tilting his head to the side. "I like being with you, Joanna." He admitted, to which I obviously blushed, lowering my glance. "I'm often nervous because I don't wanna lose this second chance we got, but ..." he cleared his throat as he neared me, and I held my breaths, "I really like you, and ..." closer, always closer, he caressed my cheek, "maybe I should have done this weeks ago," Jeremy mentioned as he leaned in, and pecked my lips at first, as if testing the waters.

Seeing I responded positively, he went in, more decisive but always gentle. A month ago, I would have been scared and anxious, now ... well, I was. But just a little braver. Enough to wrap my arms around his neck, deepening the kiss. Oddly enough, that one practice kiss with Ben served to its purpose – or at any rate the purpose I convinced myself it had, in lack of an answer from him. I learned, more or less.

Normally, this would be happening after a long date night, but with our schedules it's a bit difficult. I'll admit I've never been more interested in breakfast than when I started having it with Jeremy, and now this ... I don't know whose life I'm living right now, because it definitely doesn't look like mine.

--

Tell me, how do you sleep after something like that? After a long night shift, I should have crawled to my bed the moment Jeremy left, but ... how? He didn't even come in. After the kiss, we both got super-awkward, so he decided to go home to get some sleep.

When you put together 2 awkward nerds it's only normal that this kind of stuff happens, to be honest. And I don't mind. But, try sleeping after that. Hence, I decided to do laundry. It does take me more ever since Valerie decided I'm a charity where she leaves clothes she, allegedly, doesn't sell. Pretty sure it's a lie, but there's no way of convincing her otherwise.

After having changed into a more comfortable pair of sweatpants and oversized t-shirt and having removed my makeup – believe it or not, now I wear makeup every day –, I grabbed the hamper with my dirty clothes, and stepped outside my apartment.

Hadn't I ever. The moment I opened the door, I found the oddest sight. "Ben?"

"Yeah, who else?" He laughed sarcastically, lowering his arm which had been about to knock on my door.

I let my hamper fall as I dropped back against the wall, overwhelmed. I felt like I was seeing a ghost. "Where ... what ... when ..."

"You ok?" Ben looked at me, worried.

"Of course not!" I slapped his hand away when he tried to place it on my shoulder. My breaths were hitched so much that I felt like I was gonna pass out. "Where the hell have you been?!" I blurted out, unable to retain myself.

He chuckled – the bastard had the nerve to chuckle! –, "away."

"You don't say?" I scoffed.

"Oh, look who found her claws."

I sent him a dirty look, almost ready to tell him all the things I thought to myself throughout these weeks. Like, why did you leave out of the blue? Do you normally drop off the face of the earth for days? Is disappearing from someone's life what you call being there for them? But I kept it all. Both because in the end it wasn't worth it, and because maybe I had no right to get mad. It's not like he really owes me an explanation, does he? Besides, with all those calls at whichever hour of the day, why didn't I think of it sooner? He was with his boyfriend.

So, I just retrieved the hamper from the floor, and bypassed him to go do what I was supposed to. There wasn't really anything I could say, other than a chilly: "Welcome back."

"JoJo ..." Ben called as I walked away, but I didn't even turn around.

He disappears for a month, barely texting, dodges every single question about what he's up to, and then suddenly comes back, acting like nothing happened. Seriously? I have no right to be mad, but I inevitably am. These four weeks would have been wrapped in my paranoia, hadn't it been for Jeremy. I spent most of my free time with him, and the rest with Valerie, so it was somewhat easier to force out any Ben-related thought. At some point I just decided ok, he's not coming back, I can delete his number.

"Joanna ..." he called again, this time taking swift steps to the elevator, where he stopped me before I could step on.

"I've got stuff to do." I replied, always chilly.

"Can't it wait? It's been a long time."

"Oh, really? I hadn't noticed." I scoffed.

"Come on ..." the fact that my arm burned when he touched it didn't convince me, neither did the faster beats of my heart. Maybe I missed him, but so what?

Ben sighed and, after having snatched the hamper away from my hands, he gripped my arm, and pulled me into his, hugging me tight. "I missed you."

No, no, no. You don't get to say that. You don't get to just appear out of the blue and hug me like nothing. You don't get to make me feel glad I'm even only setting my eyes on you again. No. It's not fair. "I didn't." I blurted out, cold and stiff in his arms.

"I don't believe that for one moment." Ben claimed, not letting me go. "You called me."

"Yeah, so?"

He chuckled, his hot breath against my left ear making me feel chills for some reason. "You hate phone calls, JoJo. Yet you called me."

"Well ... Valerie was worried." I lied.

He shook his head. "Valerie called too, so you didn't have to."

"Well, I ..." I cleared my throat, embarrassed to have been caught in a lie, "I ... I didn't know she did."

Ben insolently placed a kiss on my cheek, then spoke softly in my ear: "I'm sorry I've been gone so long, I didn't mean to."

"You don't need to justify." I didn't move, even though he was squeezing me hard into him, as if to physically tell me he missed me. I resisted the temptation of wrapping my own arms around him, I just stood there, awkward. I'm not a hug person.

"You're mad at me." He stated matter-of-factly.

"No."

"Yes."

"No." I rolled my eyes, trying to find the strength to pull back.

"Yes."

"Stop it."

He laughed. "Only if you admit you missed me."

"And what good will that do?"

He hugged me tighter. "I get to hear it."

"So?"

"It means you care."

"Ugh."

Ben impertinently kissed my cheek again as he sought my hands, entwining them in his. "I would have never stayed away this long, hadn't I been forced to." He claimed. "Can you forgive me?"

Ugh, why did he have to use that nice voice of his, that tone where he can ask me to do just about anything. And when did I become so weak and so incline to people invading my personal space? "Fine." I squirmed a bit, trying to pull back, but he didn't let me. "But let me go."

"Do I have to?"

"Ben ..."

"No touching, yes, I know." He laughed. "But that rule doesn't apply to me, does it?"

"Yes, it does." I sent him a dirty look. "Especially when you go missing like you did."

"I had to."

"Yeah, yeah ..." I finally wiggled out of his grip, and could breathe properly. "When did you arrive?"

"Just a few minutes ago." He pointed at his suitcase still in front of his door. "I came to you first of all."

I rolled my eyes, to which he grabbed my left hand again, once more entwining it in his. "JoJo, come on ... I'm sorry."

"Sorry doesn't cut it. I was worried." I freed my hand from his grip, finally regaining my senses. How could I let his stupid hug intoxicate me like that? So what, he hugged me. Big deal. Hugs mean nothing but an awkward pair of seconds to me.

"Ok, how can I make it up to you?" He tilted his head to the side, giving me a pleading look.

I sighed, raking a hand over my face. "Next time you go missing, at least call me."

He grinned cheekily. "I will." Somehow, I doubt that. "I got busy with some clients."

"Clients?"

Ben hooked his arm to mine and, after having grabbed the hamper for me, he made me turn back towards my door. "I'm hungry, should we get breakfast?"

"I just had breakfast." With Jeremy.

"Second breakfast then?"

"Ben ..."

"Fine, fine ..." he let me go, "but will I see you later today?"

"I've got a night shift." He arched an eyebrow, not understanding, so I explained: "I went back to the diner ..."

"Oh, come on ..."

"I had no choice! I needed a job."

Ben sighed, disappointed. "There are so many hiring."

"I needed something fast." I shrugged, walking back to my apartment. "Not all of us can afford to drop off the face of the earth every now and then."

"Come on, I thought we were past that ..."

I shrugged. "Just saying."

"Alright." Ben sighed. "Well, so can we have lunch together maybe?"

I pursed my lips. How do I tell him I'm getting lunch with Jeremy? It shouldn't be a problem, right? You don't need to lie to your gay friend about the guy you're seeing, do you? Especially when it's not even a secret relationship. It's not like Jeremy is married and I'm the other woman. Yet I didn't know whether I should tell Ben I'm still seeing him. "I can't."

"Why not?"

"I'm ... I'm seeing Valerie for lunch." Goddamnit, Joanna. Why lie? Why?

"Good, two birds, one stone. I was supposed to meet Valerie too one of these days." Ben shrugged.

Ugh. "Well, it's ... it's a girls day."

"A what?"

"Valerie and I, we have these ... girls days once a week. We have lunch together and we go ... well, shopping." At least that was true.

"Since when you like shopping?" Ben chuckled.

"I don't." I rolled my eyes. "But ... I like hanging out with Valerie." I really do. Outside the times she unnerves me with her "Womanhood 101" lessons and the fact that she always insists on doing my makeup and hair and checking my outfit every single time, she's a great friend. And, she has been great help with this whole new game called Dating The Guy I Had A Crush On. It's really a bit Valerie's merit if I'm not as much of a frozen burrito as I usually would be around Jeremy. Well, most of the job was done by the right now annoying light-brown-haired photographer called Benjamin I Come In And Out Of Your Life Whenever I Please And You Let Me Harris.

"And ..." Mr. Annoying came closer, and mildly worried he might hug me again, I backed up against the wall, which gave me a mind's eye of that freaking kiss he gave me that one time. That was enough to make my knees feel like jelly. "You can't make an exception just this once? For me?" He pleaded, giving me a puppy look that was worth melting for.

"Ben ..." I sighed for the umpteenth time in a short interval.

"Come on ..."

No, no, no, no, Joanna, no. You can't bail on your date just to meet up with a friend that clearly doesn't deem you important enough to share his whereabout throughout these four weeks. Besides, Jeremy and I just kissed, if I bail now, he'll think it's exactly because of that kiss.

"Would it help your decision if I said I have to leave again tomorrow?" Ben interjected into my thoughts while I was trying to convince myself not to give in to his pouty look.

"What?" My eyes snapped to him.

"I'm a freelance, I gotta go wherever my clients want me to."

"Are you sure you're not lying just to convince me to say yes?" I inquired out loud, skeptical.

Ben chuckled. "Not this time. I've got a double wedding in Connecticut this weekend, and they want me to capture the preparations the days before. It's actually a pretty big gig, you know. They pay well." There was an underling of, I really need the money that I understood all too well. "Actually ..." he added, a bit mischievous, "because it's such an important client, I kinda need an assistant ..."

My eyes widened. "No." I blurted out immediately.

"You'd only have to help me carry and set up the equipment, and with the lighting and other stuff to make sure the photoshoot goes well."

"I know nothing about photography." I argued.

"You don't need to know stuff about photography. It's really easy and you get paid."

There it is, the magic word. I pursed my lips. I could really use the extra money; it would mean an extra step towards being able to finally leave the diner for good. Scott even cut my salary for the first month, as a welcome back fee, he said. "Well ..."

"Yes?"

"Ben, you know Scott will never give me the time off." I argued. I couldn't dare ask for a weekend to go with Jeremy, imagine a week.

"JoJo, let me make this clear for you ..." he said, hands now on my shoulders, staring straight into my eyes, which didn't help the whole jelly knees situation, of course. "These people are crazy rich." Ben explained. "They want a photoshoot for the whole week, arrival of the families, rehearsal and all included. The only things they don't want photographed are the bachelor and bachelorette parties, really. That means we get 1 day off for which we will still get paid. And they pay a lot."

"Define a lot." I squinted my eyes, thinking of the money I could get.

"It's 2 grand."

"For the whole photoshoot?" That doesn't seem like much.

"A day." Ben grinned, finally removing his hands from my shoulders.

"Are you serious?" I quickly did the Math in my head. "That's ..."

"12 thousand dollars." He finished for me.

"To split?"

"Nope, 12 grand each."

"What!"

Ben laughed. "I know right? Told you, they're crazy rich and don't care how much they spend. This whole double wedding thing is so big, it'll make William and Kate blush."

"But it wouldn't be fair of me to take as much as you, you're the one that will actually do the job ..."

"So you're agreeing?" He grinned, absurdly happy.

"Well, I can't exactly say a straight no to 12 thousand dollars, can I?" I chuckled. It's what I make in 6 months at the diner. "But why can't you just hire some student like you?"

"Why would I want a student when I've got my JoJo?" He winked charmingly, the bastard. For being gay, he sure knows how to make a woman weak to her core, I'll admit. "I know you need the money, too." Ben said. "This gig allows you to quit that stupid diner once and for all." It would indeed give me some breathing space. "And consider there's other rich people invited at this wedding, so that means ... potential new clients."

"Where did you even find them?"

"Oh, those Italians I did a wedding photoshoot for some time ago, they spread the word. That's why I got so much work this month, JoJo."

I frowned. "Are you gonna give me the I was busy excuse now?"

"Hey, I did answer your calls, didn't I?"

"Only because I forced you to."

He grinned cheekily. "JoJo, come on, you're never a duty, I told you. I missed your voice." Why does he have to be so charming? It should be illegal for a gay man to be charming with a woman, it wakes up thoughts he can't translate into actions. Then again, in my case it wouldn't happen regardless, but ... damn!

But this job he was offering, though. Six days in Connecticut alone with Ben yet surrounded by posh and shallow rich people. I don't know how to feel about that. Not to mention what would I tell Jeremy? No to the Berkshires with him but yes to Connecticut with my gay neighbor? That doesn't send the right message, does it?

"So, what do you say?" Ben insisted.

"There must be a catch." I mentioned, doubtful.

He gave me a puppy look. "Would I ever lie to you?"

Ugh, he and his guilt tripping tricks. "No ..."

"So ..."

"Okay, fine. But I hope I will really get paid, because I'll have to quit at the diner. Again."

23. From Cinderella to Jay Z

"**D**id you take everything?"

I rolled my eyes. "Yes, for the hundredth time, yes, I did ..." I sighed, to which he chuckled.

"Hey, I'm just trying to be careful."

"Why do we need to use the car?" I asked, still confused as to why couldn't we just fly to Connecticut but had to wake up super early to load the car, and then drive all the way to Woodbury.

"Because it takes longer." Ben chuckled. "We'd have to fly to Boston then from Boston go to Connecticut, how is that worth it?"

"Fine, fine." I raised my hands in mock surrender. "You don't need to lecture me."

He laughed as he finally closed the trunk after having placed in there his equipment as well as our suitcases. "You need to travel more, JoJo."

"I wish." I sighed, getting into the car. I don't know much about cars, but Ben's seemed pretty cozy, and I liked that it was navy blue, my favorite color. He joined me in the car a moment later, and we both fastened our seatbelts in silence for a moment.

"Have faith in your dreams," he claimed as he started the car, "and one day your rainbow will come smiling thru; no matter how hard your heart is grieving, if you keep on believing, the dream that you wish will come true."

I furrowed my eyebrows, staring at him. "Cinderella, really?"

He laughed, shrugging. "It does the trick."

"I didn't know you were into old fairy tales."

"I'm not," he started driving, "but it's one of Elle's favorites."

"Elle?" Who's Elle now? I don't think he's ever mentioned a girl with that name. He did say he has brothers, but he never mentioned a sister.

Ben glanced at me, a bit flushed. "Oh, uh ... my friend. We casually saw each other again when I went back home for my mom's birthday."

I nodded in understanding. Seems he has a lot of female friends. Valerie, Elle ... I've never really heard him talk about male friends. Then again, he doesn't talk much about his life in Nebraska, just about the stuff in New York. It's as if he were deliberately keeping that side of him hidden. Is he ashamed of it? Maybe there's something in his past that he's not particularly proud of?

I took the chance to stare at Ben for a long minute while he focused on the road. Does he look like someone that's hiding a secret? He's pretty open about everything, the only dodging is related to his life in Nebraska, like I said. But I can't see what could he be hiding. I mean, after all this time and seeing how we opened up, I'm mostly surprised he still hasn't told me a word about the person he's always on the phone with when he's at home, but I can't really demand he tells me, can I? Especially not when I didn't tell him about Jeremy either.

Speaking of Jeremy, he was bummed when I told him I couldn't go to the Berkshires with him, but he was happy I found an opportunity that would allow me to leave the diner. He said, and I quote: "that place doesn't deserve you, the sooner you run away, the quicker you can start cleansing your soul from the stench of that hellhole". He's pretty poetic at times, I like it.

So, yeah, he was disappointed that we wouldn't get away for the weekend and that I even had to leave for about a week, but he was happy for me. In the end, it's 12 thousand dollars. I don't think I've ever seen all that money all together.

"I ... didn't thank you for this opportunity." I murmured, biting on my lip.

"Huh?" Ben answered distractedly, focused fully on the road. He didn't even have time to shave, the stubble was becoming a beard, and his glasses seemed thick as ever. Did he ever look so, I don't know, normal? I mean your regular cute nerd that doesn't care about how he looks. I can't tell whether he was always like that or it's just that it's been so long and I almost forgot the odd mix of handsome and sweet that Ben is. "You're staring at me." He chuckled.

Blushing, I looked away. "Sorry."

"You don't need to thank me, JoJo. In the end you're doing me a favor. It's a big gig, I couldn't do it on my own."

"Yeah, but ..." how to tell him that 12 thousand dollars aren't exactly small change for me?

"I'm lucky, you know." He mentioned, catching my attention. "I never told you, but ... things weren't going so well."

"What do you mean?"

"Well, I came to New York for the same reason everybody does ... you know, it's the concrete jungle where dreams are made of there's nothing you can do ..."

I couldn't help but let out a short laugh. He's so cute sometimes. "From Cinderella to Jay Z. Wow, that's quite the leap."

Ben mirrored my laugh. "Technically I was quoting Alicia Keys, but yeah. I'm not a snobby nerd like someone ..." he winked at me, "I take my inspiration from anywhere."

"Hey, I'm not a snob!" I protested. "I can go from Mozart to Taylor Swift."

"Ok, name one trivial song that talks literally about nothing but has a good beat."

I blinked my eyes, confused but also annoyed, because I couldn't think of anything, no matter how I racked my mind for it. "Uh ... well ..."

"See, you only look for things that have a deeper meaning. You look for the lyrics, not the music."

"But I knew the song you quoted."

"Oh, come on!" He laughed loudly, "this is New York, JoJo! They probably play this song at every other corner."

"How would I know if I don't go out other than when I go grocery shopping or to and from work?"

"You live in Brooklyn."

"Yeah, and?"

"He literally starts with I'm out that Brooklyn ..." of course he kept laughing, "you wanna tell me you've heard it nowhere in the neighborhood? Not once?"

I rolled my eyes, mildly annoyed that he was right but also amused. "Fine ... maybe I've heard it blasting from a shop or something like that. Doesn't mean I'm a snob." I pouted a little, crossing my arms.

Ben took the chance to glance at me for a long moment when we stopped at a red light, and he pursed his lips, his eyes raking over my frame. I would have sworn his gaze lingered a bit more than due, but I was probably imagining it. "It's not a bad thing, you know." Ben said, looking back at the road when the light went green.

"Being a snob?"

He smiled. "Maybe snob isn't the right word. Let's say ... you don't stop at the shallow. I mean ..." he pursed his lips, "in a chaotic, loud, noisy world that only looks for the superficial meaning of everything, you dig deeper. It's not a bad thing."

"Why are you always analyzing me?" I asked, blushing a bit. He always sees through me like an open book, I don't get how's that possible. It's not like I've ever given him much to go by.

Ben grinned. "I don't analyze you. I just ... pay attention. Is that a bad thing?"

"Well, no, but ... I mean ..." no one's ever paid this close attention to me, seeing my moods, reading between the lines, looking for a deeper truer meaning ... most people only stop at the shell, the introverted, mostly shy, quiet shell of a fat girl that doesn't know how to behave among people. "I mean ... we'd barely met and you were already all up in my business, trying to talk to me despite my silences, trying to get me out of my shell ..."

"Do you realize how far you've come?"

"Only because I'm having a whole conversation with you? We're friends, I-"

"You made new friends, without my help. And you look just ... freer, you know."

"What do you mean?"

"I mean how you carry yourself around, there's an added self-confidence that wasn't there when we met." Ben pointed out. "And it's not me, or Valerie. It's just you. It's as if you're blossoming, finally. And it's a nice sight, I gotta say," he glanced over at me, his smile unfaltering, "it's a gorgeous sight."

My cheeks went full red this time, because I did catch what he meant. Maybe some time ago I wouldn't have understood, or pretended not to, but, be it Valerie with her 'Womanhood 101' lessons, or the time spent with Jeremy, or obviously Ben himself and his efforts at making me see what I had remained so stubbornly blind to ... I became a bit more, I don't know, self-observant. I'm more aware of myself and who I am. And of course, I'm a long way from finding my true self, but I gotta say, this is a great start.

And it's not about the clothes, or the makeup, or having a boyfriend, or new friends. It's just about the fact that I feel finally ready to give myself a chance. I'm ready to lift the iron curtain and finally explore the world outside my inner self. Slowly, but steadily, cautious and maybe anxious but not afraid. Hell, maybe I'm even ready to dust off the cobwebs from my dreams, and restart pursuing my ambitions.

When I was a kid, I was somehow sure that my future would hold something grand. Why did I stop believing I could make it? Was it the environment? 12 hours a day in a place where you're hated and belittled aren't ideal to thrive, right? But it wasn't just that. It can't have been just Scott and his abuse. Whatever it was, however, I feel ready to move past it, and finally do something with my life. I don't know what yet, but it's going to be 100% me. No more compromising, no more hiding behind the odds.

"You're right." I said, finally, after a long silence. "I think I finally feel myself again."

Ben nodded. "And where's this old-new Joanna headed?"

"Forward. I don't know where I'm gonna go, but it's time to be on my way."

24. It's just Ben

"Woah." I gasped the moment we stepped out of the car. "You weren't kidding, this place is huge. How are we going to manage?"

Ben shrugged as he walked to the trunk. "Realistically, only a small portion of this kind of venues is ever used. What's important is that we're wherever bride and groom are." He grabbed a small paper from his back pocket, and handed it to me. "Complete schedule for every photoshoot, with times and dates, locations and how to get there."

I gulped, suddenly realizing what I got myself into. "Uh ... I don't know if I can do this."

Ben smiled and walked over to me. He placed his hands over my shoulders, which made me back up against the car, against which he kind of caged me – he definitely has a thing for invading my personal space, but I guess I don't mind all that much, since it's him. "All you need to do, is stick to me, and everything's going to be okay. Alright?"

I chuckled a bit. "If you thought I was gonna ever leave you out of my sight this week, you're nuts."

"You sure about that? I'm gonna have to shower at some point ..."

I blushed, looking away. "I didn't mean ..."

"Relax, JoJo," he pulled me into a hug – yeah, he's decided that hugs are also a thing between us, which I don't mind either; it's one way to get used to it –, placing a small kiss on my cheek, "I'm just messing with you. It's gonna be a long week, but it'll be worth it."

12 thousand dollars kept ringing my ears. 12 thousand dollars. That's enough to give me some breathing space while I work on a plan to move forward in my life. Of course, after settling some things, not much will be left, but it'll still be enough for a couple of months at least.

"Awwww! Look at those two! So cute!" A shrill female voice screamed, followed by a clap of hands.

Instinctively, I pulled away from Ben, mildly blushing. She probably wasn't talking about us and our hug, but you never know. When I looked to my right, I found a skinny girl in a pretty colorful dress grinning from ear to ear as she stared precisely at us. Case in point.

"Good morning, Ms. Wharton." Ben greeted, going to shake her hand, which she didn't accept, presenting that same hand for him to kiss its back. Rich people ... "I'm Benjamin Harris, the photographer your fiancé hired. And this," he pointed to me, "is Joanna Brooks, my assistant."

She nodded in my direction, still grinning like a Cheshire cat – or like a psychopath, which is all in all the same, if you ask me. "You make a lovely couple." She exclaimed, to which my cheeks reddened only more.

Ben cleared his throat, a bit uncomfortable – and with reason! –, but he didn't correct the girl. "Yeah, so ... we'll just settle in our rooms, and then we can start."

"Do you have everything you need?" The stern woman beside Ms. Wharton asked, her expression and pose so tense that I almost thought she would break at the tiniest sneeze. Then again, a woman like that probably doesn't even sneeze.

"Yes, ma'am." Notice how Ben's tone went from friendly polite to Downton Abbey servant kind of well-mannered.

"The schedule?"

"Yes, ma'am."

"Good. Now get a move, you're already late."

We arrived in advance, actually, but try telling her that. This week is going to be intense, but again, the thought of all that money gave me a pretty solid motivation.

✧✧ ✧ ✧✧

"She sounds like a real peach." Jeremy laughed when I finished telling him about Mrs. Wharton, the bride's mother and our major pain so far. One day and I already hate her. It's like, every minute we breathe, she's annoyed. She sees Ben not taking pictures for a moment? Oh, stop slacking! With how much I pay you! Blah, blah, blah. Ugh. Again, rich people ...

"I know, right? Maybe she doesn't agree with the marriage."

"Wasn't it supposed to be a double wedding?" Jeremy asked.

I lay in bed a bit more comfortably, fluffing my pillow a bit. "Yeah, it's both Wharton sisters, but different mothers, so Mrs. Wharton – namely the current wife – really only pays attention to the younger bride." I laughed to myself. "I'm sure the other one could get married in a shed, for all she cares."

"Upper class drama, huh?"

"Yeah ..." I sighed, leaving my arm over my eyes, to protect them from the light, and because I felt sleepy. There's different kinds of tired, you know. There's diner tired, where you're worn out and fed up with life, but still have to keep going; and there's this kind of tired, where you're exhausted and can barely move a muscle because you've spent the day running up and down a gigantic venue, but ... you feel at peace. It's not that the job is easier – in the end all I have to do is carry the equipment and set it for Ben while he takes care of the lighting and of the clients –, it's just the idea that this job will actually give me something other than self-doubt and self-loathing.

"You ok?" Jeremy interrupted my line of thought.

"Yeah, just a bit tired." Ben and I had to scuttle from one place to the other, because Mrs. Wharton wants to be sure every single moment of every single event is captured. This family is so large, even only the arrival of the relatives on all sides took up half a day, and the dinner at night passed midnight. Of course, the brides went to sleep early to make sure they don't ruin their beauty sleep, but the rest of the families stayed, and we couldn't get away.

"Think of the ultimate goal." Jeremy suggested. "It should make everything easier to endure."

"You're right." I smiled, feeling sleepy.

"I'm glad you called back." He mentioned. "Surprised, but glad."

"Why surprised?"

"Well, I know you don't really care for these things."

"Why does everyone say that?" I chuckled. "I mean, I don't like phone calls, that's true, but when it's worth it, it's different."

"So ... I'm worth it?" Jeremy implied cheekily but clearly hopeful.

I blushed, even though he couldn't see me. "Well ..." yes, yes, you're worth it and I even miss you.

"I know I shouldn't say this, we're still on uncertain territory here, but ... I miss you." Jeremy admitted.

A long silence followed, because I didn't know how to reply to that. Or rather, maybe I knew, I knew I could have and should have told him I missed him too, but I just couldn't make myself. I'm still navigating this ... new-ish self that's more open to the world, you know. It's still difficult to express myself.

Jeremy cleared his throat. "Well, maybe you want to sleep, you're tired ..." he didn't give me time to reply, just hung up. I can't blame him, he was disappointed. I sat up, and opened the messaging app, thinking maybe I can't voice it, but via text it should be easier. In the end, it's just 3 words, right? Not that bad. And it's not like it would be a lie. On the contrary, it's a real truth, maybe a bit scary, because I remember that my crush on Jeremy back in the day cost me a lot of pain, but it would be the truth nevertheless.

I typed 4 words – I miss you, too –, but before I could hit send, there was a knock on my door. Leaving the phone on my bed, I went to open, well aware that it could only be one person. Our rooms are next to each other and far from those of every other guest, after all. "You should be sleeping." I chuckled when I opened to Ben. Normally I wouldn't let a guy in my bedroom, but I mean, it's Ben. If there's one thing I know by now, is that that kiss was just a way for him to push me out of my comfort zone.

He shrugged, coming in with 2 bottles of beer in his hands. "I know," he said, "I just wanted to celebrate your first day on the job."

"I don't drink." I reminded him when he offered me a beer.

"Come on, you did great, you deserve it."

"Yeah, but ..."

"One single beer won't get you drunk, JoJo," he chuckled, "pizza should arrive soon anyway."

I rolled my eyes, sitting on one side of the bed so that Ben could take the other. You'd think that, for being so rich and staying in such a grand venue, they'd at least pay meals for the people they hire. But I should have gotten the hint when we were told we'd sleep in the staff wing. In rich people terms – aka Mrs. Wharton – we're "in the same quarters as the help". I didn't know the term "help" was still used after the '60s.

"We shouldn't be eating at this hour, though." I pointed out as Ben uncapped a beer for me.

He shrugged, laying back against the headboard. "I'm starving."

"Yeah, but we have to get up early, and-"

"You can take the good girl out of her shell, but deep down she'll still be a dutiful good girl, huh?" He laughed, taking a sip of his beer. "You need to relax, JoJo. Rich people don't get up before 10 am."

"But ..."

"Anything that needs to be done for the wedding, it's up to-"

"The help. Right." I scowled. A moment later, someone knocked on the door, and I when I went to open I found one of the bellboys holding our pizza. He smiled politely when I tipped him, then left. I put the pizza carton on the bed, and Ben sat up straight.

"It's not Joe's, but we'll have to make do." He grinned, digging in quick.

"I'm not much hungry," I admitted, going to sit on my side of the bed.

Ben rolled his eyes. "Don't tell me you're on a diet now."

"Well, it wouldn't hurt." I raised my hands in mock surrender, half grinning, when he shot me a deadly glare. "I'm kidding, chill."

"Well, you'd never refuse pizza. So there is something." He eyed me quizzically.

"Not really," I shrugged, eyeing the beer in my hands, unsure whether to drink it or not. I've never had much of a social life, so I've never really drunk alcohol. Even my 18th birthday and my graduation ceremonies were spent with family only, so no chance for alcohol.

"Then eat," Ben inched a slice of pizza pretty much in my face.

"Hey, sometimes even I don't feel hungry."

"Pizza is not hungry food, pizza is pizza."

I rolled my eyes, chuckling, and took the slice from his hands. "Fine ... but just so you know, if I really wanted to go on a diet, you're the worst friend ever to have near."

He laughed. "Good."

"Don't you think maybe I just want to be healthy?"

"Can you run?"

"Yes.""Do you breathe heavily when you climb stairs?"

"No ..."

"Then you're healthy. So, shut up and eat your pizza." He scoffed, making me laugh.

"Is this Grumpy Ben?"

"This is Diets Are Nonsense Ben." He stuck his tongue out, then dug into another slice of pizza. "I don't know what you're complaining about, Valerie tells me you're having quite the success with the opposite sex ..."

I blushed, feeling suddenly embarrassed. "I'm not ... I mean ..."

"She says when you girls have your ... day out, you get some pretty significant looks."

This time I scoffed, then took a sip of the beer. It felt strong, but nice. "Sometimes I think our girl days are just all an experiment for her. For her Womanhood lessons."

He laughed, finally done with the pizza, and sat back against the headboard, which I mimicked, both of us with the beers in our hands. "Val says you're a knockout, you just need to acknowledge it."

I rolled my eyes, then took another sip of my beer. "I don't need the attention."

"Then what do you need?"

"Well, a job, for starters. Or rather, a career." I left my head against the headboard, to stare at the ceiling. "I need to seriously start thinking about what do I want, where do I want to end up. I mean ... ten years from now, where do I see myself?"

"That's a question people our age struggle with constantly."

I nodded. "I turn 29 next week. So I have exactly 1 year to make something of my life."

"Why 1 year?"

"Well, I was sure that by 25 I would have had everything figured out, you know. But it didn't happen. So I guess 30 it is. Besides we are pressured into having some sort of stability by that age."

"Stability is overrated." Ben scoffed. "Who says everyone wants the same thing? Some people want to travel the world until their bones let them."

"Is that what you wanna do?" I inquired, tilting my head to better look at him.

He smiled. "Well, I did. And I guess these new clients do allow me to travel more. But ... I'll have to set my roots somewhere, too."

"You just said stability is overrated."

"It is. But you still need a place where you can rest, you know. I mean ... a home to rest in between."

"Is that why you came to New York?"

Ben nodded. He placed his half empty beer bottle on the nightstand, and lay down, arms behind his head, eyes on the ceiling. "I needed somewhere to use to lay the foundations for my future."

"What future?" I couldn't help asking. I put down my beer, too, at this point I was only interested in finally knowing more about him, and it felt like Ben was finally ready to open up a little more.

He rolled onto this side, to face me, and, smiling faintly, he patted on the side of bed I was supposed to lie on. I'd been sitting in a corner, pretty much. Instinctively, I did as asked, so that we lay real close, our faces just a few inches away. He was clearly sleepy, and that's probably why he felt free to open up. I wasn't sure whether I should take advantage of it, but I've always died to know more about Ben. I mean the Ben before New York.

"I wanted a better future," Ben said, smiling at me, "life was never much kind to me, so I thought it was time I took something back."

"What do you mean?" I whispered, unconsciously moving a tad bit closer to him. When he grabbed my hand, I flinched a bit, and my heart did somersaults, but I didn't pull back. I was getting sleepy, too, but I was craving to know everything I could about him.

"I had dreams, but you know how it is, one thing or the other gets in the way, and life takes a turn you'd never expected." His smile was unfaltering as he entangled our hands. "Not that I regret it ... despite everything, I wouldn't go back. But ... I needed more, so New York was the answer."

"In the car ..." I mentioned, "you said things weren't going well ..."

He nodded. "Yeah, I was only getting some small jobs at weddings and other ceremonies, nothing big. Things that kept me above water, so to speak."

"But you want more."

"And who doesn't?" He grinned as his thumb traced the back of my hand. "Society as it is trains us to always want more. Nothing is ever enough." How true. "I could just keep on freelancing like that, it pays my bills and leaves me enough not to be anxious every month. But it's just not enough."

"What about National Geographic?"

"Oh," he laughed, "that's a dream long gone. Never gonna happen."

"Why not?"

"Because it brings you all over the world, and I can't do that." He stared at me, now serious, his hand squeezing mine. "I've got reasons to stay."

He didn't mean ... well. No. How could he mean ... "Is ... is he going to uh ... join you in New York?" Why did I ask, why did I ask! I shouldn't have.

Ben frowned. "Who?"

"The ... the person you're always on the phone with." I felt like color drained out of his face, and I'm pretty sure I heard him gulp.

"That's the idea, yeah." He admitted. I don't know why, but I felt something odd in my chest. I wanted to let go of his hand, tell him to get up and go to sleep, we have work tomorrow, but I didn't. Ben didn't move either. "You're special, Joanna. Did you ever realize that?" He smiled as he pulled me closer. I didn't protest, I just let him engulf me in a hug.

Day 1 of a week all alone with him, and I'm already here sharing a bed as we stare at each other without speaking. In any other circumstances, I would have felt dirty, it would have meant half-cheating on Jeremy just when he pretty much decided we are indeed a couple. But ... it's just Ben, right?

25. What could he be possibly hiding from me?

"Joanna?"

I heard my name coming from a familiar female voice. I swiftly turned around, so quick that I almost felt my head spin. "Hope?"

The tall blonde girl I hadn't seen in a while grinned, coming my way. "What are you doing here?" She wondered as she enveloped me in a tight hug. I had some photography equipment in my hands, so I tried to do my best to hug her back without breaking anything. She wore a green silk dress that made her absolutely stunning, I gotta say.

"I'm ... working." I mentioned as I pulled back.

"Working?"

I pointed at Ben, who was busy talking with brides and grooms. "Ben was hired for the photoshoots, I'm here as his assistant."

"That's wonderful!" Hope grinned, truthfully happy. "I'm here because Mr. Wharton is daddy's CFO," she rolled her eyes, "his wife is insufferable, and Libby Wharton is a nightmare, but ..." she shrugged, we had to." Rich people problems.

"Is Faith here, too?"

"I wish!" Hope scoffed. "That bitch made up some silly excuse not to come." She rolled her eyes. "It's probably for the best anyway, Libby and Faith ... well, better not have them in the same room."

I couldn't help but chuckle, nodding. I don't know what happened between the two, but 10 to 1, Libby Wharton wouldn't get out of a match with Faith alive. "Well, I gotta say it's nice to see a friendly face." I admitted.

"I know right!" Hope grabbed my hand, squeezing it. "You've been quite busy lately." She eyed Ben. "I guess love triangles tend to do that to a girl."

My eyes widened in shock. "What? No!" I unconsciously glanced at Ben, who was actually heading our way. "No, no ... we're ... I mean, he's gay!" Joanna, seriously. Your first answer should have been, I'm with Jeremy. Jesus, what is wrong with me?

Then again, am I with Jeremy? It's only been a month and we only kissed once. I mean, sure, he's called me every night this week, and we spent at least an hour talking, but ... in the end, did we define our relationship?

Hope took a long look at Ben, as if she was seeing him for the very first time. He was wearing black jeans, with a grey pullover over a white shirt – same as I was: on day 2, Mrs. Wharton presented us with a "uniform". I would wonder how did she find out my size, but I'm not sure I even want to know.

"Hey, Hope." Ben greeted with a tired smile. Only a few hours into the wedding day and we were both already exhausted, yeah. It was the last day, thankfully. We didn't even get out day off, because Mrs. Wharton decided we ought to make her money – or rather, her husband's money – worth, so while brides and grooms were having their bachelor and bachelorette parties, we had to all the way to the Wharton mansion in Hartford and take all the pictures we possibly could. It was totally unrelated to the weddings, actually. But, according to Mrs. Wharton, she was allowed to ask because her husband had been way too generous with our pay.

"Hey, Ben." Hope smiled politely, yet staring at him as if expecting something. A hug? They don't know each other well enough for that. Or maybe she was expecting him to gulp and faint at the sight of her heart-stopping beauty. She's still not convinced he's gay, it seems.

Ben took off his glasses for a moment, and raked a hand over his face. "Well, JoJo, it turns out we wasted the last 3 hours of the day." He sighed.

"What?" I turned to him, on the verge of a heart attack, because I don't think I can redo everything – again!

"Yeah, one of the brides doesn't like the photos we took by the fountain. She wants to redo them all."

"You gotta be kidding me ..."

Hope chuckled. "Yeah, that sounds like Libby. I'm betting Caroline isn't giving you the slightest headache."

I nodded. "Caroline Wharton is the ideal client. She just leaves everything up to Ben."

"Come on, let's go." He said dryly. "They're waiting."

"Ok, boss." I tried to cheer him up, but he was so worn out he didn't even smile, just walked away. "Sorry, I have to go, Hope, before he hangs himself with the camera strap."

"The Whartons are making every single penny count, huh?" She laughed.

"Yeah." I stretched a bit. "I'm gonna sleep for a week, after this."

"As you should." Hope laughed. "Well, I'll let you go. But ... I'm glad to see you like this, you know."

"What do you mean?"

She shrugged. "I mean happy and open, talkative ... you look different, a great kind of different."

I half smiled. "Thanks." I didn't really know what else to say, so I started following Ben. "I'll see you at the reception."

She nodded. "Yeah, Nate is here, too. I'm sure he'll be glad to see you." He doesn't even know me, but okay. Thank God, Jeremy arrived at the perfect time, so Faith stopped trying to set me up with her impossibly out of my league brother. Nothing against Nate, but I don't think we really have anything in common. We can't be friends, imagine being what her sister wanted us to be ...

✧✧ ✧✧ ✧

"Do you think ... if the weddings are cancelled, we get paid anyway?" I wondered, eyes on the scene in front of us. Ben had stopped photographing. And for a good reason. It turns out that, during her bachelorette party, Libby slept with some guy, and one of the bridesmaids had the brilliant idea to tell her groom. Needless to say he flew into a rage, storming out of the church right before the weddings started.

Right now there was a whole commotion about it, with Libby running after her groom, Mrs. Wharton whisper-yelling – because a lady never raises her voice even while being as sharp as a knife with her tongue – orders here and there, and the guests overall gasping and murmuring that it was typical of Libby, and that Chuck – the groom – maybe dodged a bullet.

For the thousandth time this week, I gotta repeat myself by sighing and saying: rich people.

Ben sighed as well, but not very amused. "Maybe we should talk to Mr. Wharton before his wife starts focusing her rage on 'the help'."

"You think she'd deny us what's owed?"

He shrugged. "I don't know. Maybe?"

Great. A week of nonstop work, and now it's possible we don't even get paid. "I need a beer." I grunted.

Ben chuckled, eyeing me while he cleaned his lens. "I thought you didn't drink."

"Well, it's your fault, you started this ... beer tradition."

"One beer and you're already an alcoholic, JoJo?"

"Who wouldn't be, after a week spent around Dolores Umbridge there." I hinted at Mrs. Wharton.

Finally, for the first time in a couple of days, Ben really laughed. He's been so tense and drained of every energy, we've pretty much swapped roles for the past couple of days, with me being the talkative one between us, in an attempt at cheering him up.

"I don't know what's Chuck complaining about." A voice murmured from behind me. When I turned around, I noticed a frowny Hope staring at the scene, arms crossed over her chest. "We all know this marriage is just a business deal."

"What do you mean?" I turned to her.

She shrugged. "Their mothers have competing companies, in a very old-style move, Mrs. Wharton decided that a marriage would sanction the merge that's been in the works for a few months now."

Repeat with me: exasperated sigh ... rich people. "What about Caroline?"

"Oh, that one's true, I'm sure. I introduced them. Caroline, Faith and I grew up together. I introduced her to Anthony last year, during the Fashion Week. Of course, her stepmother was against it." Of course, she would be. She's against anything that brings people joy, like a proper Umbridge.

"You." Mrs. Wharton spat, appearing in front of Ben. "Keep doing your job."

"But, ma'am ..."

She hinted behind us, where her daughter was standing, sporting a bright fake smile. "Delete anything you had on the scandal or I will sue the hell out of you. Now get on with your job, or do I have to do it for you?" Then she stormed away.

"Yes, ma'am ..." Ben grumbled, turning towards the entrance, hinting for me to do the same, since I was holding the equipment for the lighting. At least we're almost done.

✧✧ ✧ ✧ ✧

I recoiled when Ben screamed at the top of his lungs. "Are you ok?"

He nodded, plopping down onto the sand – because of course, such a grand venue is right be the ocean. "I'm just letting out some steam. You should try it."

"Scream at the top of my lungs in the middle of the night? No, thanks." I sat beside him. "But I'm glad it's finally over. I don't know how you manage."

He chuckled, taking a handful of sand to play with it. "Well, most of my clients are regular people. Nothing like this."

The wedding was over pretty soon, believe it or not. And because they had to deal with the whole ... scandal, Mrs. Wharton decided to be kind for once in her life and, after having paid us, she let us go. Since technically we can sleep here, because the wedding was supposed to go on until late night, Ben and I decided to relax a bit, so we came to the beach nearby.

"Don't you ever get tired of weddings?" I asked.

"Oh, I hate weddings. That's why I'm so good at photographing them."

I frowned, confused. "How does that make sense?"

"Maybe it doesn't. Not everything has to make sense, you know."

"You're a weird one." I chuckled, staring at the ocean.

"Says the queen of weirdos."

I laughed. "Touchée." He mimicked my laugh. "But seriously, thank you for this."

"I told you ..."

"Yeah, I know, but ... it's important to me." I eyed him carefully. "I was in neck-deep. Without this, I would have stayed in that stupid diner forever."

"And now ...?"

"Now I can breathe a little easier. Take some time to clear my head, ponder over my next moves."

"Make a plan."

"Yeah. Do you have a plan?" We never really finished that talk we started having the first night here. We both fell asleep, then we got to busy with work, Ben didn't come knocking on my door anymore.

He nodded, leaving his hands back to lean on the sand as he stared at the horizon while the sun was getting ready to set. "I could open my own photography agency, but I won't."

"Why not?"

"Agencies do mainstream stuff, and a lot of it has to do with posh people like Wharton or simple models. I didn't get into photography just so I could capture a living mannequin wearing some overpriced dress they wanna convince young girls is necessary to get into with that exact mannequin size."

I blinked my eyes, surprised. "That's quite the statement."

He sighed, his gaze now fully lost on the horizon. "I knew someone that was ruined by society's obsession with skinny."

Oh, shoot. Opening up, Ben before New York was about to make an appearance again. It's always a one in a million moments, I never feel ready for it, no matter how often they've start to come. So, I didn't know what to say, and remained silent, hoping he would continue.

"Pretty hurts. Isn't that what they say?"

"Perfection is a disease of a nation." I mumbled, unable to retain myself, which gained me Ben's quizzical look, despite the amused smile that was to erupt on his lips. "What? I like Beyoncé ..."

"Of course you do. You can go from Mozart to Taylor Swift, after all, right?" He mocked.

I slapped his arm, half laughing. "Don't make fun of me."

"You know the odd part, JoJo?" Ben claimed, sitting up as he stared at me. "We're here witnessing one of the most beautiful sunsets, yet all I can focus on, is you."

I gulped, totally caught off guard. My heart started beating fast, both because of his words and because I was frantically trying to think of something to say. I didn't know what. His words had no meaning either, because why would he focus on me, why would he forget a whole sunset, one he should have been photographing, as beautiful as it was, to look at me instead. "Who was she?" I asked, in a foolish attempt at relenting the tension that seemed to be building up between us, not to mention trying to calm down my heart.

Ben sighed, dropping onto the sand. He lay there for a long moment, eyes closed, then, finally, spoke: "Someone very important to me." A sister?

"What ... happened to her?" I wasn't sure I wanted to know, but anything that served to distract me from his words a minute ago was welcome.

"She had a dream."

"To be a model?"

He shook his head. "Actress." He corrected. "She gave up on ..." he hesitated for a moment, "something that meant the world to her. But it wasn't enough. These days, skinny isn't enough."

"Is she ..."

"She overdosed."

"I'm sorry ..."

He shook his head. "Diets are nonsense, JoJo. It's just society's way of reminding you you're not good enough. It doesn't matter what size you are, you'll never be good enough, yet they keep on telling you to get better, to want more, be more." He spoke softly, his voice lowering, as if he were falling asleep. "My friend, she, someone pointed her to some pills that would help her become what they wanted her to be. It would open up the doors of Hollywood for her, they said." His jaw clenched. "It killed her."

I remained silent. When it comes to these things, there are no words that can relieve grief. What could I possibly do or say that would help him? Nothing. So I just listened.

"I don't want to be a wheel of that same system that killed her." He said. "You think that, once in New York, I couldn't have made easy money just going after celebrities? Selling photos to gossip magazines?" He scoffed, as if the words were poison in his mouth. "I'd rather starve than feed the monster."

"Ben ..."

"It's very idealistic, I know. And maybe foolish. Hadn't I gotten lucky with those Italians, by now I would be back in Nebraska for good. But better that than losing myself and ... soiling her memory."

I don't think I've ever heard him speak so ... heartfeltly, fervently; enraged yet grieving, weary yet fully earnest. It's as he'd just bared his soul to me, and I had no idea what to do with it. Speaking would have ruined the moment, but remaining silent might have told him I didn't care. Hence, I did the only thing I thought was possible, the only one that really only he is getting me used to. I lay down beside him, and hugged him.

Ben circled my frame, pulling me into him, and I left my head on his chest. His heart beat erratically, same as mine, especially when placed a small kiss on the top of my head.

Months ago, I would have never thought something like this would happen to me. I would have never been so spontaneous. But now ... it might have been the whole setting – sunset, ocean, weariness from an entire week of work –, or just the fact that Ben has become the one person I trust and rely on the most, but it all felt ... natural. And it was a pure kind of natural.

It was easier, because I didn't even need to worry about any possible repercussions on our friendship. It felt liberating, in a way, to be able to just do anything, say anything, knowing it won't come back to bite me, that I won't be judged for it.

I closed my eyes, thinking I'd rest for a minute, instead my eyelids drooped, and I fell asleep. I barely heard Ben murmur something about "the truth" and "being honest". I probably heard wrong. What could he be possibly hiding from me? He's the most sincere person I've ever known.

26. Old dreams and uncertain futures

"**A**re you sure you don't want any help?" I wondered, yet without getting up. I was pretty comfortable, lying on the couch, watching him cook. I wouldn't get up for anything in the world. One week working for Mrs. Wharton killed me almost as much as working at the diner did, my bones have been achy all day.

Jeremy shook his head, his back turned to me, so I had no idea what was he making. All I know is that he came over early this afternoon, and started cooking. I had time to take a shower, feed the cats, lock them in my room so they don't try to murder him, and rest comfortably on the couch. And still, he wasn't done. "That would defeat the purpose, wouldn't it?"

I chuckled. "I know, but I feel bad ... you're doing all the work."

He turned to me, only to send me a sweet smile of his. "That's the whole point, Jo. Besides, you said you can't cook."

"Well, I can ... just ... basic things."

He laughed. "No basic tonight. You deserve something special."

"What are we celebrating?"

He shrugged, turning back to the kitchen counter, I bet not to let me see he was kind of blushing the same as I would. "Your newfound determination to pursue your dreams?" Jeremy asked rhetorically. "Or your new job? Or maybe ... the fact that after a month we're still here. Your pick."

My stomach flipped at the mention of us. It's already been an entire month. And I guess now with this ... romantic dinner he decided to ambush me with, there's no doubt: we are indeed a couple.

I'm not sure how to feel about it. It's something that 20-year-old me day-dreamed about every single day, it almost distracted me from my studies, so much that I forced myself to avert my attention from it, in fear that it would ruin my plans, my ambitions. If I think back, I don't know whether to laugh or what. It wasn't just deep shyness and crippling self-doubt, it was also the absolute certainty that I needed to keep my eyes on the prize, otherwise I wouldn't have made it. Well, guess what, I did keep my eyes on the prize, but I still didn't make it.

"Where are Reese and Shaw?" Jeremy asked, chopping something on the counter.

"Sleeping in the bedroom."

"No dinner?"

I smiled lazily. "You can try to feed them, but they don't really like people." Except Ben and Hope. For some reason my cats only like those two.

"Last time I went near Reese, he decided we're enemies for life." Jeremy chuckled, showing his left hand, which that little rascal had scratched the moment he'd tried to pet him.

"Sorry about that."

Jeremy shrugged. "He'll get used to me. They both will." Did he just imply what I think he did?

"Where did you learn to cook?" I couldn't help asking after one of the most delicious dinners of my entire life. I've never had much of a refined palate, I'm a pretty easy type when it comes to cooking, and I'll admit my mom was never great at it either, so this dinner ... my God! From croque monsieur to pasta with vodka sauce, then chicken piccata with lemon sauce, and now ... French madeleines.

"It's always been a hobby." Jeremy said. "But I don't really know how to bake."

I grabbed a madeleine. "Is that why you planned a cooking class if we went to the Berkshires?"

He chuckled, nodding, guilty. "Yep ... you caught me. How did you know?"

"I saw the flyer in your car."

"How come, I'm the cop, yet you're the one doing the detective work." He joked, and we laughed together.

You'd think that, me being so helplessly awkward would have ruined everything between us, and at first it almost did, the same as when we were 20. But ... between Ben and his pushing me to get out of my comfort zone, and Valerie with her 'womanhood' lessons, but more importantly the fact that Jeremy is just as awkward as I am, if not worse, I guess we ... work.

There's really not much to say about it. We have a lot in common, and we have fun when we're together, easy fun, without pressure. Actually, the moment we realized we didn't need to put too much pressure on things to go somewhere specific, we started really enjoying our time together. Sometimes things are just as simple as they seem.

"Have you thought about your next move?" Jeremy wondered as he took a madeleine for himself. I already had a couple too many, they were just too good.

I shrugged, leaning back. "With the money from the Wharton gig, I settled some things, and then set aside some for expenses. Ben says he might have something else this weekend. It won't pay as much as the Wharton, but still good enough."

"Weekend, huh." Jeremy grimaced. "I thought I'd have you to myself this time ..."

Cue the reddening of my cheeks. The more confidence he gains, the more he drops these smooth lines I never know how to respond to. "Well, most weddings are on the weekend." I said, trying to sound nonchalant. To cover my anxiety, I drank some water.

"So, you only join him for the weddings?"

"Yeah, only those gigs where he needs help with equipment and stuff."

"Every weekend?" Jeremy inquired, seemingly disappointed.

"I don't know, it really depends on him, you know."

He smiled faintly. "So your neighbor is pretty much your employer now."

I chuckled. "In a way, yeah, maybe. I don't mind, Ben isn't really demanding, although he's fully focused when he works. This week he was so stressed out, I didn't know how to cheer him up. When he screamed like that, at the beach, I really worried for a moment."

"You went to the beach with Ben?"

"Yeah, there was a whole scandal at the ceremony, you know," I munched on a madeleine, "the reception was cut short, we got half of yesterday off, so we went to the beach, to see the sunset."

Jeremy nodded without a word, but all of a sudden, he seemed preoccupied, doubtful. I'm not sure why. He likes Ben, they've talked a couple of times, but at the sole mention of the beach, he kind of clouded over. It's not like he has anything to worry about, I mean ... it's Ben.

"So you have every Sunday off?" I asked, to restart the conversation. Jeremy remained silent for a couple of minutes, which might not be odd for two like us, but it's odd when you're having a date, isn't it? "Jeremy?" I called when he didn't answer. "You ok?" I touched his arm lightly.

He almost jolted awake. "Huh?" He looked at me. "Oh, yeah, I was just ... thinking."

"Thinking?"

"Does Ben have anyone?" He asked abruptly.

I frowned. "You mean family? Yeah, in Nebraska."

Jeremy shook his head. "No, I mean, is he seeing anyone?" He arched an eyebrow quizzically. "Does he have a girlfriend?"

I almost laughed, I swear. So this is why he remained quiet for a few minutes? Me and Ben at the beach together made him think weird things? Come on. Actually, I did laugh, which had Jeremy stare at me confused, so I explained: "Ben has a boyfriend." I pointed out.

"What?"

"He's gay." Jeremy didn't seem convinced, so I explained further: "His boyfriend should join him in New York soon, or at least that's the plan. I'm not sure about the details, Ben didn't say." Personally, I would have told the guy to just come over and try to get a job in New York, live with Ben in the meantime, but maybe they're not at that stage of the relationship yet. Ben doesn't even talk about him, I only know they have these phone calls every night, sometimes it's animated phone calls, as if they're arguing.

"Oh." Jeremy let out a shaky breath after a long minute. "I ... didn't know."

"Well, despite what it may seem, he's a pretty private guy, doesn't talk much about himself."

"I see." Jeremy smiled slowly, finally back to himself. "Well, maybe we can have a double date sometime soon."

I grimaced. "That would be a terrible idea."

He laughed. "Why?"

"Because I prefer to be alone with you." Oh. Did I really say that? Out loud even? Was it the wine? "By the way, I ... I never told you, but ... you know, I missed you this week." Yep, I must be drunk.

Jeremy's countenance seemed to brighten both in surprise and in joy. "Really?"

"Yeah, I ... I didn't know how to tell you, but ... yeah." I chuckled nervously, then stood up to change the subject; in fact I cleared my throat: "I should wash these dishes ..."

"Jo ..."

"You did the cooking, I'll do the washing, it's only fair." I said nervously before he could speak. I grabbed the plates on the table, and brought them to the sink. I felt my heart beating fast in my chest, my cheeks reddening by the minute. I don't know why I said what I said, it was just sitting there idle in my mind, and suddenly it came out. He probably thought I was desperate.

I nearly screeched when I felt Jeremy grab my hand, and turn me around to face him. He smiled gently and, without a word, he kissed me. It felt more intense than last week, more passionate, as if this time he was sure it was the right move. And it was. I relaxed in his arms, and responded to the kiss, slowly and gently. I don't know how to describe this, I don't have much experience with these things, if any at all. All I know, is that it felt like Jeremy had been holding on for ages and was pouring his all into that kiss, and it only felt right for me to do the same.

✧✧ ✧ ✧ ✧

BEN

"Yeah, no, I get it, it's just ..." I sighed, rubbing the bridge of my nose, "it's too early."

"It's been 5 months, almost 6 now."

"I know, dad, but ..."

"You have to understand, your mother and I already have our handfuls with your brothers. It's not that we don't want to, it's just that we're running out of excuses."

"I know, I know, and I'm sorry to have left it all on you, but ... I'm just trying to make sure it's all as it should be, you know."

"Maybe you should just stay here." And there he goes again. "You don't even come on weekends anymore, you need to understand how hard this is ..."

"I do, dad, I do ... but you also need to understand the difficulties I'm facing here. I'm still building up my business. How am I supposed to work around the clock to build us a future, and at the same time stay at home with her?"

"That's why I'm telling you to come back here."

"Dad, come on ..."

"I know you always had big dreams, son, but it comes a time when a man needs to put his family first."

As if I've never done that. It's exactly because I've always put my family first that I had to give up on my dreams and ambitions. And I don't even mind, in the end I wouldn't go back, but at some point I'd like a break from family, too. I don't mind supporting my family, being the main breadwinner, I've done that for over 10 years now, since my dad got sick and my mother couldn't make it on her waitress salary. It's how it is, your family is there for you, you're there for your family. It's natural. But I'm not even 30 yet, I'd like to grab the little chances I still have.

Ugh, who am I kidding. That train is long gone. It would be selfish of me to think of myself when there's Elle. Hence, I sighed. "I'll come pick her up on Monday."

"You don't need to drive all the way here; your brother can take her to New York."

I nodded. It's probably better, I need to sort out everything before she arrives anyway. "Okay, I'll book the flight for both. Now give the phone to Elle." I didn't mean to sound harsh, but I'm exhausted. I've been working long hours to make sure I actually build up something, and I thought my family could hold on at least a while longer, but between my stepdad's sickness, and my brothers, my mom can't really handle it anymore.

"Daddy?"

I grinned at her sweet voice. "Hey, honey. Did grandpa tell you?"

"Yes! So, it's true?" Of course, Elle was excited. She's been dying to come to New York since forever, I just kept on delaying because I wanted to be sure.

"Yes, it's true. You happy?"

"YES!!!"

I laughed with her, but I spaced out a little when she started talking about all the things she should take with her, and the stuff she'd do once in New York. I could hear Joanna sing in her apartment. She's been happier lately, I don't know whether it has to do with this newfound faith her in future, or with Jeremy. Maybe both. I'm afraid that finding out I lied, is gonna ruin all the progress she's made. How am I supposed to tell her that not only I lied about being gay, but that I've got a whole 9-year-old daughter to prove the exact opposite?

27. Liar, liar pants on fire

JOANNA

Tic. Tac. Tic. Tac. Tic. Tac.

Even the clock doing its job unnerved me. I was sitting in my living room/kitchen/the only other room of the apartment besides bedroom and bathroom, staring at my laptop screen, a Word page open. A blank Word page, more specifically.

You see, I decided that, in order to go forward, I need to have a plan, and to have a plan, you need to make one. But to make a plan, you need to know what do you want, where do you want to end up. And here comes the big question: do I know what I want?

I mean, years ago, when I was a naïve schoolgirl, I thought the path was clear:

1.Get into a good college.

2.Get Bachelor's and Master's fast.

3.Apply for a PhD.

4.Start working.

Pretty straightforward, huh? If only it'd been so easy. Oddly enough, getting into a good college was the easy part. The problem was affording one. I got a scholarship only for one, so it was kind of a forced choice, but a good one. Especially if you consider I met Jeremy there, not to mention two of my best friends. The Master's was harder, because no scholarship ... my parents did somersaults at first, but then I just went for the most obvious choice: student loan, which I'm still repaying and it's where most of the money gained from the gig with Ben went.

I did graduate somewhat fast, that is true, but because I was in neck deep with student loans and everything, I never applied for a PhD. That's where my nightmare at the diner started. Working 12 hours a day in a hellhole isn't exactly a great source of inspiration and hopes for a better future. I guess I let myself go, and in the end forgot what was my goal when I started.

I wanted to be a journalist, back then. But if I look at myself now, there's no way I can be a journalist. I don't think I even want to be a journalist anymore. I do still like writing, but how doable it would be to get a job a publishing house, I don't know. I've been rejected quite a few times already in the past.

Not to mention that I kind of lost touch with that Joanna, the Joanna that was always writing, that edited typos in any written thing she read, that catalogued her home library in different ways, the Joanna whose favorite place in school was always the library.

But even reading became difficult, mostly because on a minimum waitress salary and different expenses to face, books are indeed a luxury. A luxury I tried to carve out a budget for regardless, sure, but when I got Reese and Shaw I had to stop: between vet bills and their food, it was take care of my cats or buy books. I did still have quite the list of unread books in my library anyway.

Now, as I was saying, trying to come up with a plan for the future was proving more difficult than I thought. I mean, how do you answer such a question? What do you want in life? It's not like choosing your flavor of ice cream. It comes with other different questions, like, can you make it? Are you actually able to do that job? How many are the chances you'll be hired?

Okay, maybe I didn't try that hard, back in the day, but it's also true that it's a difficult world. Publishing isn't much open when it comes to hiring, you know. I remember the last one I applied for. They were looking for an editor for fantasy novels, but I was rejected so quick, I barely had time to figure out what happened. Funny enough, I saw that same publishing house looking for the exact same figure a few months ago. I almost applied, there's a different chief now, but at the time I was way too lost in my hopeless pity party. Talk about missed opportunities, I guess.

Sighing, I stood up to go refill my cup of tea. Reese and Shaw were cozily sleeping on the couch beside me, hugged to each other. Jeremy was finally able to switch to day shift, so he'll come over after for dinner, which I guess means I should maybe, possibly, start thinking about cooking for him. But you know, I don't think he should find out my worst flaws just yet, he can discover them gradually.

I haven't seen Ben in a couple of days, he's been busy with work, but this morning he sent me an odd text.

There's something I need to tell you before someone else does

I racked my brain over and over, trying to understand what that could possibly mean, but I couldn't find an answer. Old-ish me would have obsessed over it, thinking the worst, like, is he sick? Is he getting married? Did he break up with his boyfriend? Or, worse of all, he's he leaving for good? I even asked Valerie if she knew whether something was up with Ben, but she said he seems his usual self.

I have to disagree there. I don't know how can someone like Valerie, who's known him so long, not see that Ben has been acting weird. He seems antsy, worried, anxious, as if there's something that's eating out at him and he doesn't know how to come to the bottom of it. I did ask him if everything was ok, if maybe he got bad news from his family – with his stepdad being ill, you never know. But he said everything's fine, he just needs to talk to me, four eyes, just the two of us.

He made it sound like impending doom. Like it's something that may pull us apart forever, which really worried me, but then Jeremy made me notice that it was probably way less than what it felt like, and that it's just that "we need to talk" in whichever version tends to alarm us way more than it should.

I guess he's right, but it still remains that whatever Ben needs to tell me, it's nothing good. Otherwise why would he say he needs to tell me before someone else does? It must be something I need to know directly from him, and that can only be one of the things I thought. Maybe he's really leaving.

As selfish as it may sound, I really hope it's not true. I'm only now starting to piece my life together, and I don't think I could do it without Ben. I mean, sure, Valerie is huge help, and Jeremy is so supportive it's really amazing, but ... Ben is the one that started it all, so to speak. Not to mention that there is this odd bond between us, something that's more than friendship yet it's not, you know, sentimental.

I laughed to myself, thinking about it as I walked back to the couch. More than friends, less than lovers. That's Reese and Carter. Are we Mr. Reese and Detective Carter? Ben doesn't look like the dark and stormy type that keeps dangerous secrets and hides a deeply troubled past. And I'm not a tough and determined single mother with a moral compass that never strays from the right direction, am I? But it's true that we're more than friends. And I like it.

I've spent most of my life alone, partly my choice, partly my shyness' choice, so having people around me now, and I mean people that really care, is both odd and reassuring. It makes me think my life really can take a detour for the right direction.

If 9 years ago, someone had told me that Jeremy Fahey and I would be a stable couple, I'd have laughed hysterically in their face. Hell, if someone had even only told me that Jeremy had a crush on me and he wasn't acting on it simply because he was just as shy, I would have never believed it.

Nine years ago I was an ambitious nerd that knew what she wanted and was sure she'd get it. Today I'm a confused 29-year-old that's only starting to come out of the mist.

Oh, right. Happy birthday to me. 29 years. I have exactly 365 days to make something of my life, to lay down the first bricks of my new path. That's why I decided that today would be the right time to make a plan ... it turned out to be way harder than I thought it would be. I sat back on the couch, and restarted staring at the same blank Word page. What do I want in life? Where do I see myself, 5 or 10 years from now?

✧✧ ✧ ✧ ✧

"Are you sure you don't wanna celebrate?" Jeremy pouted a little. The fact that he was sprawled on my couch, still wearing his police uniform made my heart smile. For a simple reason: it means he's getting used to me, us, my home, being in my life. And I love that.

"You need to wake up early." I reminded him, eyes on the gift he got me: a beautiful print with a simple quote "inhale the future, exhale the past".

"Yeah, but I can still take my girlfriend out for dinner on her birthday."

My heart skipped a few beats at his words. That's the first time he ever called me his girlfriend. I guess that's one way to make it official between us.

Because I didn't answer, Jeremy winced a bit: "Too soon?" Of course, he read between my silences, like I would have.

I bit on my lips, eyes still on the print. "I'm just ... not used to that word."

He looked for my hand, and took it in his. "We're here, though, finally. I don't care about labels, I just care that we're finally here."

I turned to him, mildly blushing. "So you don't mind um ... well ..." how do I say it, "I mean, you don't mind ..."

"Waiting?" Jeremy smiled faintly. "No, I don't."

"But ..."

"There's more to relationships than sex, Jo. And that's what we have."

I nodded in agreement. It's true, we started really slow, but we're progressing. I have no idea how to be in a relationship, to be honest, but Jeremy makes it easy. We just spend time together, we kiss, sometimes we cuddle, we text a lot, we even have calls, it's just ... natural.

But I was beginning to be worried he might soon get tired of all this, without the other side of things. I'm not saying I'm not ready for it, I mean, I'm 29, it's about time, I've been ready for ages. But I don't wanna rush it either. What we have, it's too precious to spoil it by rushing things.

"Are you gonna say the same thing in a year or two?" I joked awkwardly, trying to relieve the tension.

Jeremy laughed. "Well, I was hoping it'd be less than that, but it'll be what it'll be."

I turned to him, tilting my head to the side, slightly frowning. "You think I'm that bad?"

He slid closer, so that he could hug me and kiss my temple. "I think I'm lucky to be here, as corny as it may sound. Besides, it's not like I've had this incredible sex life so far." He laughed. "You overestimate my charms, baby." Seeing me grimace, Jeremy chuckled, nuzzling my neck. "Right, no nicknames."

"No, it's fine" I lied, half giggling because his nose was tickling me.

"Liar, liar, pants on fire." He recited, pulling me closer into him. We laughed together, like silly kids, until I turned to him, and we kissed. Yeah, we kissed, like, you know, one of those corny cliché movies where the underdog protagonist finds the love of her life randomly and casually, as casually, as easily as I lose hairbands. We kissed like a real couple, like people that actually do enjoy being together, not because forced by politeness, but because they truly choose each other.

I don't know how did this happen. How did I go from a lonely sad New Year's Eve with my cats, to spending my 29th birthday with the one guy my 20-year-old self dreamed about day and night. How did I go from having absolutely no prospect, slaving away in a filthy diner under the thumb of an abusive employer, to finding the courage to start over and pursue my dreams.

When we both found ourselves short of breath, we pulled slightly apart, grinning like idiots. Jeremy did that thing he usually does when he's nervous – he traced the small of my back with his fingers –, and I didn't understand why was he at first, but then he cleared his throat. "Jo … I … will you think me insane if I tell you something?"

Did I jinx it? I just finished saying how my life turned upside down and it was partly because of Jeremy, too, and now he seemed downcast and worried. Why did all the men in my life decide that my birthday is the perfect time to give me bad news? Should I expect a call from my dad telling me he and mom are getting divorced? Or that he's got a second family we didn't know about? Or that he's sick?

"Jo?"

Damn spacing out. "Go on ..." I whispered, half hoping I could close my ears same as I did with my eyes when I lowered my head.

"It's nothing bad ... I think." Jeremy said, unsure, lifting my chin with one of his hands, which forced me to reopen my eyes and look at him. He attempted a smile. "I ... just promise me you won't run for the hills?"

I furrowed my brows, baffled. What could possibly make me run away? Unless ... "You have a wife, and kids, and I'm the one you cheated with?" I blurted out, realizing I had only when I saw Jeremy's bewildered expression.

"No." He chuckled, pulling me into him when he encircled my hips. "No, of course not." He placed a soft kiss on my cheek, which was just an excuse to be able to whisper in my ear: "But this, your ... creative mind, the way you look at things from an unusual perspective, this ... this is why I love you, baby."

28. The first one hits you differently

JOANNA

Laugh. Come on, laugh, I know you want to. It must be so challenging to keep all those face muscles restrained from laughing, I won't be mad if you just give up. Laugh. It's easy. Or smirk, I don't know. Just ... don't look at me like that.

Jeremy stared at me, somewhat hurt. Because he had just told me he loved me and I had just frozen like a corpse in his arms, consequently causing him to pull back. I did spend the last 5 minutes in utter silence. If what he said was true, if that I love you wasn't a joke, then of course he's hurt.

But how can it not be a joke? How can someone as sweet and kind as Jeremy actually fall in love with someone like me? If he were to start laughing, I wouldn't even blame him.

"I know it's way too soon," Jeremy finally spoke, but in a sigh, "I just ... well," he pulled back entirely, scratching the back of his head as usual, "I mean, it's been years, you know, and ..." another sigh. He stood up, and started pacing.

"Jeremy ..."

"No, ok, I mean, I get it, you're freaked out, hell, I am freaked out myself," he said, then raked a hand over his face, sighing once more. "I thought if I said it smoothly, it'll sound less ... well, I mean ... you know, pathetic. But ...." He groaned lowly.

"You ... you mean it?" I heard myself whisper.

"Of course, I mean it." I guess I spoke loud enough for him to hear me. Jeremy turned to me, tilting his head to the side. "Why wouldn't I mean it?"

Well, do you want me to list the reasons alphabetically or just by category? Because there's a whole archive ready for me to open.

He plopped back on the couch beside me, albeit frantic. "How can I not mean it?" Jeremy went on. I kind of flinched when he grabbed my hand and entangled it in his. He bit on his bottom lip, sucking on it, which is another one of his nervous tics. "I may have ... downplayed my crush back in the day a little."

"What ... what do you mean?"

Jeremy squeezed my hand. "I may have been further down the road to bigger ... feelings than I let on."

"But ..."

"Yeah, we never spoke much, I know, but ... well, I actually don't know, but ... yeah, I mean, from that almost nothing to this, I ..." He left my hand abruptly, jumping up again, and started frantically pacing back and forth. He kept muttering to himself, I wasn't even able to catch what he said, something along the lines of, 'crazy' and 'what was I thinking'. Of course, he would have such a reaction. I shouldn't even be surprised. I did say he's just as awkward as I am, if not even more, didn't I?

"Jeremy ..." I tried to call, but he kept shaking his head. Obviously, he was blaming himself for his own feelings, telling himself how stupid it was to confess what he felt. I didn't hear him, I just know because that's exactly what I would have done. "Why?" I finally asked, loud enough to reach his hysterical self.

"Why what?"

"Why ... why do you ... feel what you feel?"

Jeremy stopped his pacing, and faced me. He looked at me as if I was insane. "Because you're you." He finally said, which took me off guard. "I mean, you're awkward and you have a really weird obsession for serial killers, your cats hate me and after a whole month we've only kissed, but ... how can I not love you?" He grabbed my hands, so that I stood up to face him directly.

The fact that his eyes were fixated on me made me slightly uncomfortable, but I wasn't sure how to get out of it. "It's easy with you, Jo." Jeremy said, squeezing my hands. "I haven't often felt comfortable in my own skin, but with you, it's just ... different. I feel like I can be myself without fear."

Now, what do you answer to that? How do you properly react to such a heartfelt confession? I've never been in this situation, with someone bearing their heart to me, I ... I don't know how to deal with it.

✧✧ ✧ ✧ ✧

BEN

I kept tapping my foot on the floor, trying to gather the courage to finally knock. But how am I supposed to break out the news to her? Oh, hey, sorry

I've been gone for a few days, I just had to deal with some stuff and by the way, I have a 9-year-old daughter I never told you about. If she was violent, Joanna would just punch me, which is the least I deserve.

Sighing, I raked a hand over my face. I can't avoid this any longer, Elle is coming to New York tomorrow. I spent almost a week making sure everything is ready for her, I signed her up for school and found a babysitter. Obviously, I avoided Joanna. I don't even know how to look at her. Selfishly, I'd have hoped to have more time to finally find the guts to tell her, but as always in my life, nothing goes my way.

Taking a deep breath, I finally knocked. I wait a few seconds, but no one came to open. I checked the time: almost 10 pm. Maybe she's out with Jeremy? I knocked again, nothing. I called her phone, but it went straight to voicemail, clear sign it was turned off.

"This doesn't sound right ..." I muttered to myself, furrowing my brows. Her phone is never off, she needs it because her grandmother used to call her at weird hours, she remained used to being always available. Unless she doesn't want to be available, that is.

I knocked a fourth time, then left my ear against the door, trying to detect any sounds. I could hear Reese and Shaw scratching the door. I'd made up my mind to just open the door by force, when finally I heard it being unlocked.

"Yes?" Joanna murmured, leaving the door ajar. I could only see the top of her head, bangs and glasses hid her eyes, a sign that she was staring at the floor, not looking at me.

"JoJo?"

"Ben ..." I would have sworn her sigh hid some signs of tears.

"Are you okay?" I pushed the door a little, to open it, but she resisted.

"Yeah, I ... I was sleeping." Now, I could clearly hear traces of tears in her voice.

"It's early."

"I was tired. I ... can we talk tomorrow?"

"No." I pushed the door open, unsure of what I would find or what hoped to find. I don't think I'd have ever been ready for the sight before my eyes. Joanna was wearing old pajamas, her hair was ruffled, her face puffy, her eyes red – the glasses just couldn't hide it.

"This is really not the time, Ben." She whined, barely able to hide the distraught tone.

Without a word, I just grabbed her hand, and pulled her into my arms, hugging her tightly. "I'm here now, you'll be ok."

She fought it a bit, claiming she was fine, but I didn't budge, and in the end, she relaxed, or rather, gave up. When she returned my hug, pretty much clinging onto me, I knew she was really hurt.

The first breakup hits your differently, that's just how it is. It's not a matter of whether you loved them or not and how much, it's just that the first one hits you like a full iceberg colliding with your ship. I didn't even need to know what happened, I was 100% sure the tears that started wetting my shirt were for Jeremy and the relationship that died way sooner than it should have.

I guess now it's not a good time to add more grief to her plate, is it?

29. Because it's you

B^{EN}

"But what happened?"

I rolled my eyes for the third time, but I couldn't raise my voice, because Joanna was sleeping peacefully on the couch. Peacefully after having cried her heart out. "I'm asking you, Valerie."

She scoffed, loud and clear through the phone. "Well, you would know if you paid more attention."

"It's not my fault if I was busy."

"Busy doing what?" That accusatory tone, sharp yet with not loud – typical Valerie.

"Work, Val, what else?"

"What about your boyfriend?"

"My what?"

"Your boyfriend, the mystery guy you're always on the phone with, the one that's coming to New York soon ... the love of your life despite it being a complicated relationship, according to what Jo says."

What the hell. "What are you talking about? I don't have a ... I'm not dating anyone."

"Well, that's not what you told Jo."

"I didn't ..." I sighed, rubbing the bridge of my nose, "it doesn't matter, I'm asking you, what happened? Why is she like this?"

"I have no idea, she was fine last time I saw her."

"Which was?"

"I think ... on Friday? Maybe Thursday ... yeah, Thursday."

"No texting? Nothing?"

"Hey, don't come at me, Harris. Let me remind you you're the one that has a habit of disappearing out of thin air." She got on the defensive, as usual.

"I'm not accusing you, Val, I'm just trying to understand what happened." I sighed for the billionth time.

Valerie remained silent for a few moments, almost half a minute, then, she inhaled deeply. "Is it that bad? Last I talked to her, she was okay."

"Define okay." I demanded, knowing full well that Joanna is all too well used to hiding what she really feels.

"She seemed happy, you know, new hopes in a new life, a boyfriend, new friends and all." Valerie clicked her tongue. "The only cloud was you."

"Me?"

"Yeah, she was worried about you, you know. Like, he works too hard, he's been distant, is he okay ... that kind of thing."

"Oh." I had no idea she'd picked up on so much. I always focus on her, what she needs, how to help her, I've never really opened up about myself, except that day at the beach.

"She really cares, you know." Valerie said, and I could hear that accusatory tone in her voice again. "She cares a lot about you, Ben."

"I know."

"No, you don't."

"What's that supposed to mean?"

Valerie sighed. "I don't think you fully grasp the depths of it."

"If you're thinking she ..."

"No, not that." Valerie cut me off bluntly. "I'm just saying, you have a habit of cutting ties abruptly, and I don't think Joanna can handle that." She inhaled deeply.

I remained quiet, knowing that it wasn't just about our mutual friend. Glancing at Joanna, I made sure she was still sleeping, then I spoke: "I'm sorry, Val. I never said it, but I am."

"Yeah, yeah, I know ..." she faked a laugh, "but it wasn't easy to get over it, you know."

"Val ..."

"No, no, I get it ... people take their separate routes after high school, I get it. But that's the thing, you know, I thought we were inseparable."

We both did. "You know it was ... Val, you know us, our ..."

"Oh, that was a mistake." She laughed but I could hear a bit of pain in her voice. "We were never meant to be a couple, Benny, we both know that. I'm not mourning what never was. But I would have preferred we didn't lose each other like that. You were my best friend, as corny as that sounds."

Sighing, I dropped back against the wall, sliding until I sat on the floor. Reese and Shaw were balled up at Joanna's sides, as if in protection. I should have probably left the room to have this conversation with Valerie, but I didn't want to take my eyes off of Joanna, in case she woke up and needed me. "A lot of things happened." I mentioned, which wasn't an excuse, of course not, but I just wanted Valerie to be sure I didn't mean to just cut ties with her out of the blue.

"You've always had a lot on your plate, Ben, I know that."

With my family, she meant. First it was just me and my mom. She worked triple shift to make ends meet when I was a kid, so she was pretty much never home, I learned to take care of myself pretty soon. Then she remarried and it was a little bit easier, but my brothers arrived, and because both my mom and my stepdad worked hard, I often took care of the boys.

I don't regret it at all, I love my brothers, but of course, doing that didn't give me as much time to focus on myself, especially when my stepdad got sick. He's been battling with it since I was in high school, and he's better now, but the first years were difficult for the whole family, so I did what I could to help, both financially and with housework, everything. "Yeah, but I shouldn't have let you down like that." I admitted.

"Ben ... that's not what I'm saying nor why did I bring it up." Valerie said sternly.

"I know, I'm just trying to explain."

"Oh, Honeybooboo, you forget where we grew up." She laughed, this time truthfully amused. "You think I didn't hear about her? My mom told me."

For a moment I felt like the ground under my feet was shaking, as if the biggest secret of my life had just been revealed. It wasn't a secret at all, but the fact that Valerie knew about it, I'd never imagined. "She told you everything?"

"She just told me you had a new girlfriend and things were pretty serious between the two of you." Valerie explained. "But when I told her I didn't want to hear about you, she had mercy of my poor wounded heart, and stopped mentioning you entirely."

"Val ..."

"Yes, yes, you're sorry, I know. But that's exactly my point, Benny. It hurt me, remember me? The tough kid that learned how to face her bullies? It hurt me ... imagine just how bad would sweet, naïve Joanna feel in my shoes."

That hit me deep. I finally realized what she was saying. This wasn't about what happened, but about what she thought was going to happen. "I'm not leaving Joanna." I said firmly.

"Can you say you're 100% sure about that?"

Well, not 100%. Both because my life is all but predictable, and because once I tell her the truth, the chances that she'll see me again are pretty much zero. "I ... I can promise I'll do my best."

"That's not enough, Ben, not for her."

"Are you saying she spent the past 10 minutes crying because of me?"

"I'm saying you took a girl with no strings attached, and entangled her life with yours. That leaves a mark, Ben, a heavy mark. So be careful how you disentangle that web."

JOANNA

Slowly, I opened my eyes, still groggy. When, upon trying to move, I heard some meowing, I realized my kittens were curled up on my stomach. I smiled at them. Whoever said cats don't love you clearly never had one. They get attached, they love you, just ... in their own, somewhat distant, maybe a little cold way. Kind of like me, I guess. Maybe I was a cat in a past life.

I tried to sit up as slowly as possible, not to wake them up, but my feet seemed trapped. When Reese rolled over, ending up on my side, I was able to see what was keeping me prisoner. Or rather, who. Much to my surprise, Ben was asleep, had shot back against the couch, his hands firmly holding my feet on his lap. And here I was hoping I had dreamed of that outburst.

I literally cried my heart out on his shoulder, of course the dummy would stay here to take care of me. It's possible he even cancelled on some plans just to stay with me. I will never, for the life of me, understand why does he care so much, why is he so affectionate, so protective, so thoughtful.

I don't know, maybe it's that I'm used to being on my own for the most part, having few friends that don't really get all up in my business, that don't dig deep, but I just ... don't get it. I mean, what it's to him if I'm okay or not? Does it really matter if I'm balled up in my room, crying? Sure, friends care about these little things, but ... he takes it one step further, and I just don't understand why. We're as close as if we'd known each other since childhood, and at the same there's a lot I don't know about him, or rather, his past. I guess we really are like Reese and Carter.

I tried to move my feet, but Ben stirred a bit, so I remained still, just staring at him. I shouldn't have let myself go like that, I shouldn't have just wept like a little kid, in the end it was nothing incredibly big. I was nervous and tired, working out a plan for my future is proving to be way more difficult than I thought.

And there's Jeremy. How do I factor Jeremy in all this? Should I? I mean, yes, he said he loves me, but still, it's one month. I'm the type that agreed with Rory when she rejected Logan's proposal, you know. I thought it was smart of her to choose not to settle and aim for her biggest dreams. Well, okay, the revival ruined it, but still.

It was an emotional day, I guess. Between the bad news I received from home, and the anxiety about my future, I guess I got overwhelmed, so I wound up crying. It happens, you know. But somehow Ben is always there whenever I'm down. It's like he has a sixth sense for my negative moments, so that he always shows up to make it better.

I really don't know what is it with him, what binds us so closely, but I know that I can't see my life without him anymore. It's Reese and Carter again, after all. Outside the banter and after the initial 'do I arrest him or not?', they grew incredibly close. More than friends, less than lovers. That simple phrase keeps ringing in my head every time I think about Ben.

I've learnt not to rely on people, they leave, every time, but Ben ... I don't know, I guess he convinced me he's here to stay. On one side, it feels nice to finally ease up, rely on someone, lean on them without fear they won't be there to catch up. On the other side ... like I said, people leave. One day, he's gonna forget me the same as every other "friend" I used to have.

Ben stirred some more, finally starting to open his eyes. I wanted to take my feet off his lap, but he was still holding them. "You're awake." He said with a groggy smile.

"I've been busy looking for freedom." I joked, hinting at the feet.

He chuckled. "Well, I guess now you're in my power." He claimed, feigning an evil smirk.

I half laughed, but then he started tickling me, so I had to force myself to remain calm not to risk kicking him. "No, no, no ... Ben, no ... you have no idea the danger you're in!"

Because he stopped to have a good laugh, I was able to finally free my feet. The dirty look I sent him served to nothing, he just stuck his tongue out, like the silly boy he is.

"I hate you when you do that." I rolled my eyes, standing up. I hate being tickled, ugh.

"So ..."

"What?"

He followed me along the extremely short path from the couch to the kitchen, where I went to make some tea. "How are you?"

I half smiled. "I'm okay, I was just being overdramatic."

"Heartbreak is never overdramatic, it's just normal."

I frowned. "Heartbreak?"

"It was a short relationship, but ..."

"Is that what you thought? That Jeremy and I broke up?" When he nodded, I almost laughed, to be honest. "No ... I just had a bad day, that's all."

"Oh." There was a hint of disappointment on his face and his tone, but maybe I was dreaming it. Ben likes Jeremy. I mean, they don't talk much, but only because Ben just doesn't talk all that much in general. That's one thing I never understood, how he's so open with me but isn't much sociable otherwise. "Then what was it?" Ben inquired.

I could feel him following me with his gaze as I moved around the kitchen, trying to find something to cook dinner with. I've never been much of a cook, but watching Jeremy, I kind of started getting interested in it. Well, maybe only because he wants to teach me, but still. "I told you, just a bad day." I debased it.

"A bad day doesn't make you depressed like that." He pointed out.

"I wasn't depressed, just ... worn out." I corrected as I stared into the fridge. The thing about having a boyfriend that cooks, your fridge is always full of leftovers. Maybe too many.

"Worn out." Ben repeated, skeptical.

I turned to him. "Why did you assume it was about Jeremy?"

"Well, what else could it be?"

"Anything." I shrugged. Having decided to just make a sandwich – I haven't had my first cooking lesson yet –, I went to the cupboard to grab bread and peanut butter. "Or do you think that, just because I'm a girl, the only thing that can make me sad is a boy?" I teased.

"First of all," Ben claimed, coming to stand beside me, "you're not a girl, you're a woman." He said, leaning against the counter to face me. "Secondly ..." he bit on his lips, "well, never mind."

I frowned. "What?"

"Nothing, nothing."

I rolled my eyes. "Come on, say it."

"Well," Ben shrugged, stuffing his hands in his pockets, "if you want my honest opinion, I don't think you and Jeremy will last much long."

That's one rude awakening. "What? Why not?" Also why did you push me into him if you thought it wouldn't work out.

"Call it sixth sense."

I rolled my eyes, focusing back on my peanut butter sandwich. "Well, he told me he loves me." I didn't intend to spit out the words aggressively, but they came out like that regardless.

"Oh."

"Yeah, shocking, isn't it?" I pretty much attacked the sandwich when I cut it in half. "That someone would actually fall in love with me. How truly scandalous."

"Not really." Ben stopped my hand, so that I was forced to look at him – mostly because he didn't let go as he spoke: "Loving you is easy, JoJo, tearing down your walls, that's a whole different beast."

"I guess you would know," I muttered, lowering my gaze.

Ben let go of my arm, sighing, "more than you'd be ready to accept," he claimed, stealing my sandwich.

"Hey!" I complained.

"You shouldn't be eating carbs."

"I thought you said I don't need a diet."

He grinned cheekily, stretching his arm towards me, half eaten sandwich in his hand. "Come take it back, then."

I scoffed, crossing my arms over my chest as I leaned back against the counter. "As if."

Ben came closer, and left the sandwich on the counter, so that he could – surprise, surprise – cage me against it by placing his hands at my sides. "You need to loosen up." He chuckled.

"And you need to stop caging me against things," I rolled my eyes, half amused.

"I can't, it's the only way."

"To do what?"

"To be close without you wiggling away."

What does that even mean? I furrowed my brows. "Why do you always talk in riddles?"

Ben laughed. "I don't, you're just too blind to see what's right in front of you." He reached behind me, I thought to take the sandwich back, so I moved slightly to the side, but that way Ben took the chance to pull me into his arms. The amount of time he spends breaking my boundaries and invading my personal space, anyone would have already been pushed away – literally and figuratively. But ... it's Ben.

"Am I making you uncomfortable?" He wondered.

"You're all up in my comfort zone, how can I not be uncomfortable?" I scoffed, yet unmoving.

"So why aren't you wriggling away?"

"Because it's you." Even I was shocked at the words that came out.

Ben looked amazed. "Have I finally made it? I'm inside your bubble?"

I rolled my eyes, half smiling. "You can be so corny sometimes."

He laughed, pulling slightly back. "Corny is fun sometimes." He flicked my head, "especially when I get to tease you." I stuck out my tongue to him, and we laughed. When it died down, Ben went serious. "So, what really happened?"

"I told you-"

"Ah!" He held up a finger. "Only the truth."

"Fine." I sighed. "Well, you know my family ... I mean, we're not exactly rich." A bit of an understatement. "And this month, my parents had more expenses than expected, so I helped." I shrugged. "Long story short, I'm broke."

"And that caused you to cry ... why?" Ben wondered.

"Well, you know, things start getting better for me, and then immediately stuff happens ... it's just how it always is with my life. I guess I kinda had a bit of a breakdown."

He smiled faintly. "I understand that feeling all too well." He caressed my cheek. "But, as I love being so corny, you said," he winked, "I need to remind you, you'll be okay."

I looked up at him. "Because you're here?"

"As long as you'll allow me to be."

That's a funny statement. "Why wouldn't I want you to stay?"

Ben shrugged, looking disillusioned. "Maybe you'll find out things that'll make you hate me."

"That's something I would say." I chuckled. "Don't be silly, Ben, I would never hate you."

He sighed, pulling back abruptly. "JoJo ... there's something I need to tell you."

30. Do it like the French

"What is it then?" I asked, more and more confused. Ben spent the past 10 minutes pacing the living room, sighing and cursing under his breath. I was getting worried because I've never seen him so antsy. "Ben, come on, it can't be so bad." I tried to pacify, but nothing, he went on sighing and pacing and muttering curses. "Ben ..."

"I don't know how to say it!" He blurted out in a short breath, finally stopping and turning to me. "Hell, Joanna, I don't even know how to look at you."

I gulped. "What ... what do you mean?"

Ben growled, covering his face with his hands. "I lied! Okay? I lied." He yelled in his hands, his voice therefore muffled.

I blinked my eyes, marveled. "Lied about what?" I almost chuckled, because, come on, what could Ben possibly lie about? His eating preferences? Or maybe he's not really a Slytherin, just a closet Gryffindor? But hey, maybe I was right and he's really a secret agent. I could barely hide the laugh as the last thought crossed my mind. Ben a secret agent. How crazy I was to think that. And how much I've changed since we met, even though it was only a few months ago.

"It wasn't meant maliciously, okay?" Ben went on, now looking at me, which made me a bit anxious, causing me to lose my good humor.

"What wasn't?"

"I ..." and there he goes again, sighing.

"Ben, at some point you'll have to spill the beans, come one. It can't really be as bad as you think." I kind of spat, frustrated. It started off as somewhat funny, but the confusion was making me anxious.

"But it is." He corrected, head hanging low, shoulders deflated, as if he'd given up on finding the right words to say. "It's as bad as you could possibly imagine."

"What, you're secretly a murderer? Or a stalker?" I try to light up the mood, but Ben's lips barely twitched in what was the vague resemblance of a smile.

"You remember what I told you when we met?"

I rolled my eyes. "Ben, you told me so many things altogether the first days, you need to be more specific."

"About ..." he swallowed, "who am I ..."

I frowned, but didn't say anything, hoping he would go on without as much of a fuss. However, I was starting to feel this talk was going to go in the wrong direction. I guess it figures. Like I said, when things starting going well in my life, something bad hides in a corner to ambush me.

"I am ... Joanna, I am not-"

"SURPRISE!!!"

Oh, come on, not now. I sighed at the two blonde hurricanes that just irrupted in my living room, obviously half drunk. I should have expected it, it's Sunday.

But I wasn't gonna let Ben off the hook. "Hey, girls." I smiled, standing up. "You know where's everything," I told them, well aware that they – especially Faith – were after more alcohol. "We'll be back shortly," I said, grabbing Ben's arm. I ignored their puzzled looks, and dragged Ben outside the apartment, determined to get this appalling truth out of him, one way or the other.

Once we were out, I carefully closed the door, and dragged Ben a bit closer to his apartment, because I know Faith loves eavesdropping. I didn't really have much time, Jeremy said he'd come over after the dinner with his parents – a tradition for them on Sundays, but he skipped the past few because we were together. It's like Ben picked the worst time possible to confess his unspeakable truth, with the whole world against him. If I was a superstitious type, I'd have thought the universe was sending us signals, telling us not mess with fate by unraveling truths that are supposed to remain hidden.

"So?" I asked, crossing my arms over my chest. "You were saying ...?"

Ben sighed, dropping against the wall opposite from me. "There's a lot I haven't told you about myself."

"Oh, I know. You never open up." I scoffed. "You let me do all the work." Nope, he didn't smile this time either. Damn, this secret must be really awful.

"Joanna, I ... I'm sorry."

"Ok, but what for?"

I expected him to still deflect, maybe go around, apologizing again, instead, he grabbed my hand, and crashed me into him. I barely had time to catch my breath that he crashed his lips on mine, effectively cutting my breaths short.

Taken back, I kind of wiggled a little bit, trying to pull back, but Ben cupped my cheeks, deepening the kiss. And when I say deep, I mean really deep. Do it like the French, my only friend in school used to say: the right one will take you off guard, he will crash into you or you into him, cage you in his arms, and do it like the French.

I was tense, though. As much as that kiss was stirring every single fiber of me, compelling me to melt in his arms and just bask into the passion that was ready to devour me, I didn't respond. My back may have arched against him, my heart may have been crazier than cat high on catnip, but I didn't respond. Or not as much as everything inside me wanted to force me to.

Okay, maybe I did use a bit of tongue. Maybe I did close my eyes, letting my other senses guide me. Like the smell of Ben's perfume mixed with natural scent, which I could have spotted anywhere. Not because I understand anything of fragrances, but because I was used to it, it was halfway between the scent of new books and citrusy smells.

My fingertips tingled in an attempt at forcing me to grip his t-shirt, but I resisted. I was, however, beginning to feel lightheaded, be it due to the lack of air or to the whole situation. I didn't have the courage to pull back, though, I'm not sure why. Countless questions were spinning in my head, yet the only one I could find an answer to was the same one I'd been asking Ben for the past half hour: what did you lie about?

As if hearing my inner talk, Ben murmured against my lips: "I love you, JoJo."

No. No, Ben, that wasn't the answer, no. The correct answer was literally any other, but not this. Breathing heavily, I leaned against him, not because I wanted to hug him, but because the dizziness I'd been feeling was causing me to almost faint.

Ben took it as an encouragement, though. In fact, he encircled my hips, pulling me into him. "I shouldn't have lied, but I was afraid you'd run away."

And making me think you're gay was supposed to make me less wary of you. I'm not that stupid, Ben. I'm not. I may have been refusing to see it, lying to myself, but I'm not that stupid. A gay friend doesn't kiss you like you kissed me the very first time. I've always been in deep denial, but 90% of the time, I know what happens around me, Ben. I know. Same as I know what's coming next. "But you're married." I muttered, my face half hidden in his neck.

Ben stiffened, his grip on me tightening. "What?" He asked, uncertain, his voice shaky.

"The phone calls, the secret, the whole lie about being gay ... you're married." I pulled back, eyes still closed. I didn't have the courage to look at him. "I kept telling myself it was a boyfriend, because I really wanted to believe you. I thought, why would he lie to me? What could he be possibly want from me that would make him lie like that?"

"Joanna ..."

I took a step back, feeling tears well up in my eyes. "Did you think a kiss would solve everything, Ben?" I wondered out loud, my voice breaking. "Did you honestly think that I'm so easy to manipulate?"

"No, of course not, I just ..."

"Didn't resist?"

"I didn't know how to say it." He murmured. "Joanna, look at me." Ben demanded, but I kept my eyes closed, and when he tried to reach for my hand, I retrieved it. "I'm still me."

I scoffed sarcastically. "And who is you? Who are you, Ben?"

"I'm still the same guy you opened up to, JoJo. I'm still the guy that listened to your rants every time."

"For all I know, you could have a whole family back in Nebraska. If you're even from Nebraska."

"I am. I didn't lie all the way through."

"Oh, so you just picked the things you could say, like a game. True, false, true, false ... is that how you decided what to tell me?" I spat, feeling anger rise up. I clenched my fists at my sides, trying to force myself not to cry. "I believed in you, Ben. And you didn't even have the decency to say with your own words."

"Joanna ..."

"Save it." I shook my head. "I don't even want to know what's true and what's false anymore. It doesn't matter."

"But it does ..." I flinched when he grabbed my hand, but once again, I forced my eyes to remain close. "You always say it doesn't matter, but we both know that's when you're the most upset."

The nerve. I took a step back, gritting my teeth. "Don't. Don't you dare pretend you know me."

"You know I do. I know you better than you know yourself." Ben claimed unabashedly. "That's why I know you feel the same as I do."

"Delusional more than just a liar, I see." I scoffed.

"JoJo ..."

Finally, I opened my eyes – literally and figuratively –, and walked back to my apartment. Once at the door, I stopped before opening it. "Is Valerie in on it, too?" I couldn't help ask. "Does she know?" It would be so fitting, wouldn't it?

"No ... no, she doesn't."

I nodded. At least there's a silver lining in all this. I should have known, though. I should have known nothing was ever true. I should have known he wasn't who he said he was.

After all, how realistic could it be? That your new neighbor turns out to be the one person that changes your life for the best? That that same neighbor would come to mean so much to you, that it's as if a hole were carved in your heart the moment you part from him. What are the chances that in my meaningless life I would find someone that really cares?

31. Now they know you're alive

Are you ok?

Please answer me

I knocked and knocked but nobody answered

Baby please call me, I'm getting worried

Four of the twelve messages Jeremy sent me after I cancelled our plans for the night. On one side it's cute, on the other ... a bit asphyxiating. But I understand it, I just bailed on him out of the blue last night, and refused to take his calls or answer his texts. Because he is like me, I am sure Jeremy is afraid I reconsidered our whole um situation, that his love declaration freaked me out so I'm ghosting him until he finally realizes we broke up. That's what I would think.

I'll deal with him sooner or later, too, same as I'll answer Faith, Hope, Valerie, even Michelle, who keep sending me messages. It's a bit exaggerated, if you ask me. It's not like I dropped off the face of the Earth for 6 months, it's just been 1 day.

Then again, Faith probably already told everyone except Jeremy. Not that I gave her and Hope any account of what happened, I just told them I wanted to sleep, but Faith carved out of me a simple sentence: Ben is a liar. That was enough to unleash them. Faith started ranting and cursing loudly, claiming she knew, there was something odd about him, there had to be something, while Hope tried to come comfort me.

All I did was crawl on my bed, and curl up in a safe cocoon. It's where I've been since last night. Even Joe texted me, saying Valerie asked if he'd heard from me. For being friends with such an introvert as I am, these people sure have a knack for drama. When you know someone like me, you should expect a couple of days of silence every now and then, but I guess I got them too used to a different me.

The fun fact is that I thought this was really a new-old me, but the truth is, it was just a silly, naïve girl that Ben manipulated. I spent night and day thinking about everything he ever told me and, surprise, surprise, I found quite a few inconsistencies. Stuff that anyone would have picked up, had they been not as stupid as Joanna Brooks.

Why did he always take his phone calls alone? Why was I never allowed to even catch one single word of it? Joanna The Dumb One thought sense of privacy; anyone else would have said he's hiding something.

Why did he never tell me about his past? Why was it always bits and pieces? Like random childhood stories, but never anything past high school? Why, to this day, even Valerie doesn't know why did they pull apart?

All this, I thought he was just a private person, that he didn't feel comfortable talking about himself and his past. How wrong I was. He didn't talk about it simply because it was a whole parallel life he was trying to hide.

This isn't just any lie, you know. It's not like he said he hates pineapple pizza, instead he loves it and eats it secret when I'm not around. This is a whole different Ben.

I don't get it, I honestly don't. What was the purpose of this lie? He said it was just so I wouldn't run away, but run away from what? I'm not an abused woman that is wary of straight men, therefore could only trust a gay one.

Social awkwardness is about people in general. Sure, at first I felt a little bit freer knowing he was gay, and it was probably a bit silly of me, but soon enough it became simply about how comfortable I felt around him because it was him.

I thought I knew him. I've never cared about people's past. Sure, I was curious and confused as to why he didn't say anything, but in the end I didn't care. It was my friend, my best friend – if such a definition doesn't sound corny coming from a 29-year-old.

I had a friend in high school, my one and only friend. Yet we weren't as close as I am with Ben. Well, as close as I thought I was, because you can't really say you are really friends when the other lies to you all the time, can you?

☆ ☆ ☆ ☆ ☆

I woke up abruptly, having heard a sudden noise. Normally, I'd have thought it was Reese and Shaw causing a ruckus until I wake up to give them breakfast, but my kitten were right there beside me, half asleep, as startled as I was.

Frowning, I blindly reached for my phone to unlock it and see what time it was. Ah. I thought it would be the middle of the night, but no, it was 4 pm. Obviously, there were a lot of messages and missed calls, some even from my parents. My conscience told me to at least put a status where I tell everyone I'm fine, I'm just hibernating from the world for a bit, but I didn't feel like it.

I dragged myself out of bed, deciding that maybe I should eat, or at any rate the cats should eat. When I went into the kitchen, the noise I heard before was repeated, but this time it was accompanied by some chatter. I felt a sharp pang to my heart when realization hit me: Ben.

He wasn't alone, though. Maybe that's why he wanted to have that talk exactly yesterday, not a day later. He did say that whoever he was always on the phone with would come to New York at some point. I guess it's time for Mr. and Mrs. Harris to begin their new life in the big city. Well, pardon me if I feel like puking.

I gave Reese and Shaw their lunch/dinner, which, needless to say, they pounced on. Poor babies, I've been so lost in my depressed bubble that I didn't even feed them as much as I normally do. Not that they starved, I left them enough food for a day, at least.

While I was rummaging my mostly empty fridge to find some food, I hear another noise – this time one I recognized easily: the door. Someone was knocking insistently on my door. In fear it would be Ben – as unlikely as that would be, since now he's busy with his better half –, I ignored it. The person on the other side kept knocking, but I wasn't gonna budge.

I dug deep into the peanut butter jar to make one last sandwich before having to mandatorily go buy groceries, and headed back to my room – the only safe haven in this turmoil of betrayal and deceit. However, before I could enter, I heard the front door opening, or rather, being forced open. Somebody pretty much broke it down.

Rolling my eyes, I went ahead and entered my bedroom. Let burglars steal what they want, it's not like there's anything valuable in here. But I was sure it wasn't robbers.

"Joanna!" A shrill voice called louder than dogs could bear.

I winced, recognizing it instantly. "Paris ..." Like the city? Like Gilmore Girls iconic character? Nope. Like Paris Hilton. I sighed. My youngest cousin. "What are you doing here?" I turned around, rolling my eyes. Even more when I noticed the tall jock she was accompanied by.

"You ask???" She yelled – because Paris Hilton Williams – yes, her middle name is the celebrity's last name – doesn't know the meaning of calm and posed. It's either overdramatically over the top, or nothing. The Sir Lancelot beside her was too busy playing with his phone to even try to fix the door he'd just broken down with his brute force.

"Yes, I'm asking." I replied in a monotonous voice, not at all incline to extend this obnoxious visit any longer than it needs to be. Paris moved to New York last month with her boyfriend, which was the compromise my aunt had come to after her daughter had giddily announced she'd get married after high school.

It wasn't much of a bargain, if you ask me: Paris still gets to sleep with her boyfriend, despite her conservative mother's protests, and she doesn't even need to sneak around like she used to. But for my aunt it's better. She says it's because she hopes Paris will see what a deadbeat her boyfriend is when he can't help her pay rent, but I think it's because if shame has to be, then let it be far from everyone.

Paris rolled her eyes theatrically, admiring her nails. "You went missing."

"Uh ... no, I didn't? I'm right here."

"Well, you didn't answer your phone, your mother told my mother, my mother bugged me." She scoffed, then took a pic of me – in all my absolutely indecent splendor. "There." She claimed, after having presumably hit send. "Now they know you're alive." She sent me a disgusted look. "I'd rather be dead than wear that," – she pointed at my attire, made of a grey extra-large t-shirt with more stains than I could count, and extra-large tracksuit pants, which were paired with messy hair and puffy cheeks. Have I been crying? Oh, why would I? Only because of Ben – assuming his name really is Ben?

Paris didn't linger in small talk – thank God –, once she'd replied to her mom – or mine? –, she snapped, her fingers, and her Sir Lancelot came back to real life, swiftly leaving the apartment. "I'm not dragging my ass to this dumpster again." My cousin scoffed. "You better start talking to your mother." And just like that, she left.

Once I was sure they were really gone, I sighed, and went over to the door. It wasn't severely damaged, but it still needed some fixing. Normally, I'd need a locksmith, but growing up in an overdramatic family teaches you to do housework, even the "manly" ones.

A bit of manual work later – luckily, I didn't need to change the look –, the door was the same old one as it used to be. I stood there, staring blankly at it for a moment. I've lived here for over 2 years now, and nothing has ever changed.

Ben pushed me to believe I could actually make something of my life, and even though something would compel me to say that part of me never really existed, since the Ben I thought I knew never did either, I don't think that's true.

That Joanna isn't simply Ben's JoJo. It's Jeremy's Jo, it's Joanna Brooks, the ambitious freshman that took the world on, aiming for the moon, not wanting to make do with the stars. That Joanna isn't a dream, she did exist, and she was coming back. Why should she give up?

So what if Ben lied? So what if nothing of what we had was ever true? Does that mean that I should go back to quiet Joanna that accept abuse from

Scott and had forgotten all her dreams in favor of a lifelong agony slaving away in a diner?

32. Your regular career woman

NOTE: I started this book before my break from writing, so it's set in 2018

NOTE 2: In this chapter there is a crossover that may spoil one of my stories for you, if you wish to avoid that, on my wall you find a reading order

✧✧ ✧✧ ✧

32. Your regular career woman

"Hello, may I help you?"

I swallowed. I couldn't have her repeat the question a third time, she'd call security thinking I'm just another nut job come to spy on her employer. "H-Hi ..." You can do this, you can, Joanna, you can.

The woman at the reception nodded, albeit annoyed. "Are you here for a reason?"

"Yes, I ..." Come on. I swallowed my anxiety, and spoke clearly: "I'm here for the interview."

The receptionist sent me an exhausted look, clearly thinking my IQ was way less than what she's used to in this marvelous building. My cheeks did redden, but I had a small needle hidden in my pocket, meant to stab me every time I thought I should give up. "What interview?" The woman asked in a sigh.

"Uh ..."

"This building hosts the offices of one of the biggest companies in the country, Ms. Brooks, there are job interviews every day for different positions. You need to be more specific." The receptionist spat, clearly sick of me.

Gulping down my fears again, after having stabbed my thigh with the needle for the 12th time in 5 minutes, I nodded. "The publishing house. I ... I am here for the interview as ... editor." I don't know whether she looked at me with bewilderment mixed with mockery, as I thought she did, but I'd have probably deserved it. However, all she did was press a button on her phone, and start talking to someone about interviews, giving my name.

Being dressed decently – black pants, white shirt, black jacket, very business-like, even perfect makeup thanks to Valerie as usual – didn't take away the feeling of being in the wrong place.

What was someone like me doing all the way to Manhattan, seeking an interview in one of the most exclusive buildings? I said I would still try to get my things moving for my future, but I should have started way smaller than this.

"You can go up." The receptionist said in a flat tone. "27th floor, you'll find someone greeting you to escort you to her office."

Swallowing my saliva for the umpteenth time, I nodded. She pointed me to an elevator, and I headed there. All the way up, I kept thinking I should just run away.

Stabbing myself over and over again with the needle served to nothing: the closer I got to my floor, the more I felt like a fraud and a fool. I have little to no experience as editor. It's true that this is a fairly new publishing house, but the name of the company it belongs to ...

"Good morning." A guy in his early twenties greeted. He was dressed somewhat informal – jeans and shirt – but still looked highly professional.

"Hi."

"Are you're here to see Ms. Benedetti?"

I nodded without a word, and he gestured for me to follow him, which I did quietly. It was a pretty large place, but not many people around. The job offer did say it was a freshly founded publishing house: they literally started a couple of months ago.

That's why I went for it, thinking maybe they wouldn't be as picky as others would, but then I googled the address ... I don't read magazines and I don't watch TV other than movies and shows, so it took me a bit of research to understand who would I be dealing with.

The well dressed 20-year-old guided me along a somewhat long corridor, until we reached the last door in the corner, pretty much the last office on the floor. He knocked lightly, and a soft female voice said to come in, which he did, with me on tow. "Joanna Brooks, she's here for the editor position."

The woman sitting at the desk nodded, so the guy gestured for me to go sit across from her. Hesitantly, I did, and he left us alone. I didn't dare speak for a few moments, because she seemed busy with some papers – she hadn't even looked up from them yet. All I could see was a messy braid, a pencil lost in it as if to keep it from falling apart, while a pen was in her hands, and thick rimmed glasses on her nose.

I don't know what was I expecting, but certainly not this. I mean, I don't know anything about rich people and their world, but you'd assume that the guy they call the "Golden Bachelor" would be marrying someone uh less normal?

You'd think his future wife would be a Blake Lively that's perfect in every instant of her life, not a regular woman with her tics – like biting on her nails as she reads, which she was doing now – and disheveled moments. I read about his ex – because obviously magazines interviewed her when word about the marriage got out –, and ... she's completely different.

It made me catch a breath, though. I was expecting some soul-sucking, man-eating vampire, instead I found the most regular career woman you could ever expect.

"I'm sorry, just a sec ..." Ms. Benedetti said, holding up a finger while still intent on reading and editing not sure what on those papers before her.

Her one second lasted another minute, and I had time to take a look at the office, which was in fact what you'd expect from Manhattan: windows covering the whole wall behind her back – with a breathtaking view on New York's best skyline, may I add –, huge desk made of who knows what expensive wood and that yet still wasn't enough to contain all the paperwork, laptop, tablet and everything else she kept on it; on the side walls, huge shelves still half empty – in fact there were boxes scattered around, most of which were labeled books.

The only thing that really stood out in perfect order were the photos in a corner of her desk: despite the mayhem, that only corner was immaculate. No wonder, those photos displayed the happy family that the Grants are forming, as pretty much every single magazine I found mentioned.

"Okay." Ms. Benedetti finally said in a sigh, slamming the pen down on a paper to finally look at me. She gave me a polite smile, and fixed the glasses on her nose. "I'm sorry about the mess, we're still uh ... working things out around here."

"It's ok," I murmured, because what else could I say?

"Ok, so, I'm Samantha," she introduced for some reason, "yes it's Benedetti not Grant, and it will remain Benedetti after the wedding; yes, he works in this same building but no, he has nothing to do with the publishing house; yes, you may see him every once in a while because we do have lunch together like a normal couple, but no, he doesn't like signing autographs, so don't ask or I'll have to listen to him complain about how people don't understand he's not a rock star, he's just a regular guy that's worked hard for what he achieved." She blurted out all at once, in a tone that gave away just how many times she had to repeat the same things. Ms. Benedetti sighed heavily, rubbing the bridge of her nose. "Any questions?" She sent me a side look. "About the job you are interviewing for, not about my fiancé, please."

How do I tell her I don't really care about who her fiancé is? "I-uh ... the ad said you need an editor?" Oh, really smart question, Joanna, congrats.

Ms. Benedetti nodded, squinting her eyes – clearly all that reading hurt them –, "we are just starting," she said as she reached for something in the mess that was her desk, "the people you saw outside work in different departments, but what I need is an editor that will literally edit manuscripts as they come. That means correcting grammar, punctuation, run-on sentences, yes, but also fixing the content if needed. We are a small publisher, and as such we wouldn't expect famous authors, but ... well," she pointed at the ceiling, "big name on the building door, so we've gotten a lot of inquiries and manuscripts."

She uncapped the eye drops bottle, then took off her glasses. I didn't need an explanation, but she said it anyway: "I had some problems with my eyes a few years ago, so now when I tire them too much, I need this," she pointed at the bottle, then she applied a couple of eye drops. Ms. Benedetti blinked slowly, then put the bottle down, and wore the glasses again. "Do you have experience with editing? Writing? I didn't see much on your resumé."

Ah. The question I was dreading. I could lie and say I've done this and that, but how fast do you think it would take her to find out? "Not ... really ..." I cleared my throat nervously, "I-uh ... did some editing for our newspaper back in high school, and I wrote articles for the one in college."

"But you wouldn't really know where to start if I gave you a book to edit?" Her voice didn't sound judgmental, just surprised – surprised I would even apply for the job if I didn't know how to do it.

"I followed a course on content editing in college," I mentioned, trying to save whatever I could, even though it was futile.

"What have you been up to since you graduated?"

"I worked at a diner," I mentioned, a bit ashamed, lowering my glance.

"So nothing related to your studies?"

"No ..."

"Is it because you couldn't find anything or you didn't like what you found?"

How about, it's because I got tired of rejection letters, and decided I could just rot in that hellhole called a diner? "It's ..." I sighed, wondering whether I should just leave now before making a fool of myself.

But then I thought of the odds: I don't have a job, I counted on those gigs with Ben to keep the money flowing while I worked on my plan for the future, but ... that's gone now. That means I don't have a choice: it's either I find a good job now, or I move back home, as my mother repeated over and over when I called her after Paris' visit.

"Miss Brooks ... Joanna, if I may," Ms. Benedetti started, "there's nothing shameful about accepting whatever job out of necessity." Said by the future wife of a billionaire, it does sound funny. The woman took a deep breath, pondering, then, finally, she said: "Would you consider an internship, instead of the job you applied for?"

I blinked my eyes, marveled. "What ... do you mean?"

"Well," she bit on her lips, "unfortunately, because the work load may be heavier than you might be able to bear, this being your first experience, I cannot hire you as editor," I knew it, "however ..." what? "I do believe you have potential," she eyed a paper beside her – my curriculum, I realized –, "and given the opportunity, you could become way more than even you think you're capable of." How did she ... "If there's one thing I've learnt from my fiancé, Joanna, is to believe in your abilities. Confidence is key."

I'd love an internship, especially here, but ... "will I-uh ... is it paid?"

Ms. Benedetti offered me an understanding smile, so that I didn't need to explain anything. "Yes, of course." She roamed her desk with her eyes, then grabbed a folder with written 'expenses'. "Let's see ..." she curled her lips as she read, "between me and you, Joanna, I'm trying to make this work without my fiancé's help, so money's a bit ... tight," she looked up at me, "he provides the name that granted me the bank's loan – pun unintended –," she chuckled to herself, "and the offices, but everything else is on me."

"I understand."

"Of course, if we were to fall, Grant Enterprises would soften our landing," she laughed, "but I'd hate to be his damsel in distress once again." Again?

"I appreciate your help." I mentioned, because she was literally giving me an offer I couldn't refuse: a chance to have a job that reflects my studies, one that at the same time would give me experience I could use in the future, and even get paid for it, which is something internships don't always give.

Ms. Benedetti smiled candidly, "don't thank me yet, Joanna ... even as intern, your workload will be rough."

"It can't be worse than slaving away in a diner 12 hours a day." I blurted out without thinking, which caused her to laugh.

"Well, it's only 8 hours here. I won't ask you to bring your work home, unless we really are on tight deadlines and I need everyone to pull their weight." Something tells me she almost never leaves this office, working way more than everyone else. Ms. Benedetti scanned a paper that looked to be some financial statement, then exclaimed: "Ah-ha! I knew I could squeeze it in." For some reason that made her happy. "

Ok, so, I need to draft a quick contract, and ..." she glanced around, "ugh, where did I put it ..." Maybe she needs an assistant, more than an editor. "This was for an editor, but I guess I can tweak it a bit ..." she bit on her lips, "but I'll need Lucas' lawyers to take a look at it ..." she sighed. "Okay, uh ..." she looked up at me, "can you start ... tomorrow? You'll find the contract to sign first thing in the morning, I promise." Ms. Benedetti offered me a gentle smile I couldn't help but mimic.

Feeling a huge load off my chest, yet at the same time another one adding onto my shoulders when I realized just what was I getting into, I nodded. Fingers crossed, things will go well for once in my life.

33. Cop instincts, huh

We need to celebrate!!!

Uh, no, we don't. I rolled my eyes – Valerie and her over-enthusiastic self, as usual.

I'll bake something! Ben can go grab drinks, maybe Joe can provide the pizza?

Ugh. How do I tell her that Ben and I aren't friends anymore? If I even try to mention the issue, Valerie's going to start pouting and going on and on about how we should fix it, and friendship lasts forever, and she got over the fact that Ben pretty much ghosted her after high school but they met again because fate, and blah, blah, blah.

It's just not the same situation. Pulling apart after high school is mostly normal, but faking an entire friendship, that's a whole different animal. Okay, maybe he didn't totally fake it, but it still remains that he lied about the most basic things and a lot of others.

So tonight at 9?

I sighed, dropping the phone onto the table. When I left the Grant building, I wasn't sure where to go or what to do. I mean, what to you do when you get great news? You tell your loved ones – normal people would say. Well, I've never done that. I mean, when I got good grades, when I won awards or got accepted into colleges, I never told anyone.

Okay, mostly it's because I didn't exactly have anyone to tell other than my parents. I've never been much close to my cousins, except when we were very little, and I don't have siblings, plus I've never really had close friends, other than that girl I mentioned. So, I never felt the need to tell anything to anyone. Hell, nobody even knows about my plans about the future.

Well, no one except ... well, Ben. Yes, I did mention something to Jeremy, but in the end, it was Ben that helped me with the planning, Ben pushed me, challenged me. I mean, this whole ...sort of transformation really started with him. So, I guess it's mostly been something between the two of us. That's why, regrettably, the first person I wanted to tell when I got the job, was Ben. And I couldn't.

It's only been what, a couple of weeks? Only now I'm starting to feel it – feel his absence. Sure, everything's happened fast: decide to actually do something to start off my plans, apply for a job, prepare for the interview ... it was all so hectic that it was even easy to leave out every other thought and to mostly avoid talking to people.

Obviously, I did answer my mother's calls – I didn't want Paris' australopithecine boyfriend to knock off my door again –, and my boyfriend's ones just so he wouldn't think I decided to break up without telling him, but in the end, I kept to myself. It was also the only way to cope. Because people would ask questions: where is Ben? How come he's not around anymore?

Anyway, the point was, after the interview I didn't know where to go and I didn't feel like going back home, so I did the weirdest thing for someone like me: I walked into a coffee shop, which is ironic considering I don't even drink coffee. It was vintage enough to attract my attention, not to mention the wall-large bookshelf full of books. I just like hang-out places with bookshelves, they give me the sensation that it's not for everyone's taste, which means it'll be cozy and tranquil. And this place was exactly like that that.

I was lucky enough to find a spot in the corner, right by the bookshelf, so that's where I went to sit, back to the window. I ordered a tea and a pastry just so they wouldn't complain, but I wasn't really hungry – I know, I know, how is it possible! One like me that isn't hungry! –, but I spent the past 10 minutes half replying to Valerie's texts, half deep in thought.

Am I happy I got a job even though it's just a paid internship? Yes. Am I happy that I'll finally do something related to my studies? Damn, yes. But at the same time, I don't know, I felt odd. I should be, if not happy, at least content. I have a boyfriend that loves me – a guy that, with all his quirks and awkwardness, is smart, kind, even cute and, amazingly (or appallingly, depending on the perspective) loves me. Of all women possible, Jeremy loves me.

And then there's Valerie. We haven't known each other long, but she's an awesome friend more than just an inspiration for me as a woman. Joe is like the brother I never had. Faith has been a little aloof since she got engaged, but she's still a good friend, even though we're so different – same as her sister. And I guess I can even say I have a family that cares. My parents maybe haven't been the greatest as I grew up, but they still care.

And now this new opportunity to actually make something of my life. I made a 5-year plan that sees me starting as the smallest wheel, and ending up a successful writer, and the internship at Dante's Friends – Ms. Benedetti's publishing house – is the greatest beginning I could have asked for. Well, okay, maybe it would have been more instructive if I started in a bigger place, more famous and with a way longer history, like that Lion's

Publications in Boston – which I also applied for, by the way, but didn't get an answer yet. But it's probably easier to start really from scratch.

So, I have a family – not perfect, but still, they're there for me –, I have good friends, a great boyfriend, and now the start of career I had been longing without hopes for years now. I should be happy. Or at least I shouldn't feel so empty.

Yes, yes, I know, the reason for this feeling is what happened with Ben. But there's nothing I can do about it, is there? Part of me wants to give him a second chance, but how can I trust him?

If I think about the fact that he said he loves me, I almost want to laugh. Love. I don't know much about love, but even I can tell it doesn't involve deceit and lies. It's not love when they blatantly and unabashedly lie to you for months, without ever taking up one single chance – despite having had many, since we did spend a lot of time alone – to come clear.

All the time we spent alone, all the nights spent on my couch watching movies and eating pizza, laughing and chatting together. All the times I showed my weaknesses, opened up, he had the chance to say his truth, and he didn't. Jesus, he even kissed me!

How am I supposed to feel about that? How am I supposed to feel about a married guy kissing me and, actually, subsequently making of me a cheater? I should probably tell Jeremy, but I don't know how. The time he seemed jealous of Ben, I assured him my neighbor was gay, how am I supposed to come up to him and say hey, he's not actually gay and we kissed, is that a big deal for you? Come on.

I have zero experience in relationships, but I'm pretty sure that somebody kisses you and you sort of, kind of, not quite but still respond to it, it does count as cheating. Could be vaguely related to cheating, but a vague relation is still a relation. Heavily treated and mostly chemical food is still called food, isn't it?

Maybe Bridget Jones was right when she said: it is a truth, universally acknowledged, that when one part of your life starts going okay, another falls spectacularly to pieces. I take the first step for my career? My love life seems okay? My family isn't a complete nightmare? It seems only fair that the friendship department falls apart.

Think about it, it's all entangled. Ben and I are no longer friends. That means Valerie and I might fall out, since she's primarily his friend. And due to the kiss scandal, Jeremy and I might fall out. So, a few minutes are able to make me lose 3 of the people I'd come to count as irreplaceable pieces of my life. Just like an unstoppable domino.

My phone kept buzzing with messages from Valerie about a party tonight, but I didn't even want to answer anymore. I don't know what to do, or if I have to do anything at all. Should I tell Jeremy about the kiss? Probably. Should I give Ben a second chance? It's not like he's even tried to talk again.

I don't even hear him much anymore, probably because his sweet other half is here now, no need to be so much on the phone, right? But you know, as much as I appreciate being left alone in peace, I would have expected him to insist a bit more.

"Can I get you anything else?"

A soft female voice broke into my trail of thoughts. When I looked up, I saw the waitress staring at me expectantly, which made me blush a bit. I must have been here for hours. "Oh, uh ..." I quickly did some mental Math to be sure I could spend more, "another tea, please."

She nodded, grabbing my empty cup. "I'll be back in a jiffy." She claimed, for some reason smiling. Waitresses actually smile? I know I never did.

Then again, there's a difference between working in a hellhole and working in a cute coffee shops for nerds.

I grabbed my phone, and unlocked it, only to find all the messages Valerie sent me:

So tonight at 9!

I'm baking!

Can you ask Ben? I tried to call but he didn't answer

As if. I don't know why I haven't deleted his number yet, but maybe I should. Sighing, I scrolled through my chats. When suddenly "is writing" appeared under Jeremy's name, I instinctively closed the app, feeling nervous. It's not that I don't want to talk to my boyfriend, it's that right now I really don't want to talk to anyone. I shouldn't have even told Valerie about the job.

My phone buzzed again – Jeremy, of course.

How did it go?

Right. I told him about the interview beforehand, Valerie only got to know after the result.

I got the job

I replied quickly.

Awesome! We should celebrate!

Ugh, what is it with people and their obsession for celebrating? I didn't even celebrate my graduation. In other circumstances I'd be okay just spending the night with Jeremy, that would be enough of a party, but ... I really don't feel like seeing anyone today.

BEN

"Can we get Pop Tarts?" Elle asked, hopeful.

I sighing, pushing the cart past the snacks aisle. "You already got Oreo."

"Can I change?" And there goes the pouting. She definitely learned these tricks from my brothers.

"Elle ..."

"Pretty please, daddy?"

I sighed once more. "Fine." I stopped the cart, and reached inside to grab the Oreo she'd already begged me to buy. "Go swap them. But this is the last time. You know you only get 1 of these snacks."

She grinned cheerfully, and walked back to the shelves she needed. I took the chance to check my phone, and noticed I had a couple of missed calls from Valerie and other messages, but nothing from Joanna. It's been 2 weeks, but she still doesn't even want to see me, and how can I blame her.

"What if I get Doritos?" Elle yelled from the other side of the aisle.

There goes my umpteenth sigh since we entered the store. "Only 1 snack, Elle. Just one. Choose wisely." Cue their excited shriek that made some other clients chuckle. I bet they assumed I'm her brother. People never think she's my daughter, both because I'm not even 30 yet, and because, truth be told, she doesn't look all that much like me. She's her mother's copy. It's a pity she doesn't remember much of her.

My phone rang – Valerie again. I picked up only because I know if I missed it again she'd call the police. Problem is, I haven't told her about Elle either.

"Val?" I answered when I took the call, eyes on Elle and her careful selection of snacks.

"Where have you been?"

I half smiled. "Been busy."

"You always say that." Valerie snorted. "Are you coming tonight?"

"Where?"

"To Joanna's!"

My eyes widened a bit as my heartrate increased. Did I miss a message from her? Did she ask to see me? Ignoring Valerie and her rants, I rechecked my messages and missed calls one by one, I even checked emails and – long shot – social media, hoping I would find a single sign that Joanna finally is ready to talk to me again. But nothing. Predictably, my heart dropped just as fast the same pace it'd picked up.

"Yes or no?" Valerie yelled enough for me to hear even though the phone wasn't against my ear. Meanwhile Elle was walking back to me with her final choice in her hands – Cheetos. She grabbed my free hand, and together we walked back to the cart, while Valerie was calling me through the phone.

"Yes, I'm still here." I said, placing the device between my shoulder and my ear, so that I could still grab the rest of the groceries and pay attention to Elle – luckily, she's a tranquil kid, doesn't go running around giving me a heart attack. That's something she took from me, actually, her mother was a force to reckon with, never staying put for one second.

"Are you coming or not??" Valerie groaned. "You have to! It's a big thing, we need to all be there for her!"

"What?" I wish I could say I had even an inkling of what she was talking about, but even stalking Joanna on social media didn't give me any hints about what she's up to – she barely uses them and her posts are never personal.

"Joanna!" Valerie repeated, clearly exasperated. "She got the job! Didn't she tell you?? I told her to call you for the party!"

"Uh ..." How do I tell her? Luckily Elle was too busy awing at everything she saw – coming from a small town in Nebraska, a simple New York store is enough to make her gasp – to pay attention to my phone call with a woman she's never even met. As long as my daughter is concerned, really, I've never been and never will be with a woman that isn't her mother.

"What's going on?" Valerie inquired. "Joanna has been avoiding me, you've been avoiding me ... what's going on?"

"I've just been busy." That's not even a full lie. Between work, classes, and Elle, I've barely had time to breathe. Yet somehow my treacherous mind was able to torment me with thoughts of my JoJo.

"Yeah, yeah, that's always your excuse for everything." Valerie groaned. "What really happened?"

"Nothing ..."

"Benjamin. Don't make me spank you."

I half smiled. "Listen, I gotta go now. We'll talk another time." I hung up before she could protest.

Elle was already looking at me quizzically. "Who was it?"

"Just a friend."

My daughter tilted her head, doubtful. For being only 9 years old, she sure is perceptive. "Is it the lady that called the other day?"

I gulped. "What?"

Elle shrugged, walking to the shelf where juices were kept – we need to buy her favorite one in packs, since she brings it to school and drinks it in the afternoon with her snack. "A lady called when you were cooking and I was playing Angry Birds on your phone."

Valerie didn't say anything about it. Could it be ... "What did she say?"

"Nothing." Elle replied distractedly, roaming the shelf in search of apricot juice boxes.

"Nothing?"

My daughter shrugged. "I answered how grandpa taught me." I couldn't help smiling. "This is the Harris house, who am I speaking to? She hung up."

Valerie wouldn't just hang up. She'd inquire about who was on the phone. I bit on my lips, daring to hope. "Did you say who you were?"

"No."

Ugh. If really it was Joanna calling, that answer must have just confirmed her I'm married. Great, I'm a deeper hole than I was to begin with.

"Was it wrong?" Elle asked, perplexed and apologetic.

I shook my head. "No, honey, it's okay. Now, what do you want to eat tonight?" The fact that Joanna tried to call me means she was almost ready to open the talks, but if now she fully believes I'm married, I've got no chances that she'll ever even look at me again. Glancing at my phone, I wondered whether I shouldn't dare. Granted she won't answer, but an attempt wouldn't hurt, would it?

I thought giving her some time would be a good idea, because I know her, and pushing too hard with her gets you nowhere. But at the same time, not trying at all probably told her I'd given up.

"Daddy?"

I jolted awake when Elle called me. "Yes, honey?"

"Why is that man staring at us?"

"What?"

She pointed at a guy waiting in line at one of the cash registers, his cart half full. I've only seen him a few times, so without the uniform it was a bit of a struggle to recognize him, but not impossible. "Hey, Jeremy." I greeted, faking nonchalance, as we walked up to him.

"Hi." Tight smile. His gaze darted from me to Elle, back and forth, as if trying to understand what was going on. What would be more plausible? "I didn't know you had a sister." Case in point. Like I said, people never guess I'm actually her dad.

I thought about lying, but Elle prevented me: "This is my daddy." She claimed, clinging to my leg, as if offended that anyone would think otherwise.

Jeremy's eyes widened in surprise. "You have a daughter?"

I sighed, nodding. "Elle, this is Jeremy, a friend. Jeremy, meet Elle."

My daughter eyed him carefully before nodding, while he smiled at her sweetly. "Nice to meet you, young lady." He tipped off his imaginary hat. Then turned back to me. "Does Joanna ..."

"No."

"I see." He pondered for a moment. "That explains a lot of things."

"What do you mean?"

"Well, you have been around these past weeks, she hasn't mentioned you, no weddings ... you two don't talk anymore, do you?" I was a bit surprised, I'll admit. Maybe I underestimated him. As if reading my mind, Jeremy chuckled, shrugging. "I may not enjoy it much, but being on the force does teach you some things. Like learning how to read between the lines."

"Are you going to tell her?" I couldn't help but ask.

"Of course, not." Jeremy seemed offended by my statement. "I'm not a snitch. She needs to know, and you two need to work things out, but it's not my secret to tell." He furrowed his brows, this time looking at me accusingly. "Especially since she believes you, well, gay."

"I know, but ..." Instinctively, I glanced at my daughter, who was looking in between us, puzzled. "I don't know how."

Jeremy shrugged again. "Words will come out." He glanced at his watch, then at Elle, and kneeled before her. "A friend gave me tickets to the zoo," he squinted his eyes, I bet eying the plush toy my daughter always brings with her – cop instincts, huh –, "but I don't know much about penguins, I bet you could help me." He smiled kindly.

Elle grinned – she's always excited when she gets to talk about her favorite animals, penguins –, then looked at me. "Can I go, daddy?"

I should be worried that my daughter trusts the first stranger she thinks to be her dad's friend, but I guess this is a good chance as any. It's not like I really have anyone to leave Elle to, since none of my friends here know about her. "Yeah, sure." I wonder, if Jeremy knew I told his girlfriend I'm in love with her, would he be so willing to help us patch things up?

JOANNA

"I know you like tea, but ... 4 cups in a row is a lot even for you."

When I heard his voice, my heart seemed to stop. I don't know whether it was because of the shock or because I had too much theine in one afternoon. "How ... how ..."

Ben smiled. "Find my phone, silly. How else?"

"Oh, so you're a stalker, too, more than just a liar." I scoffed, turning my head towards the bookshelf just not to look at him.

He sat in front of me, instead. "You gave me the password when you lost your phone at the theatre and it was on silent." He reminded me. Ugh.

"What do you want?"

"To talk."

"We already talked enough."

"No." When Ben grabbed my hand, I felt my heart once again seemingly stop. "It's time for you to start listening, JoJo."

"I-"

"I have a daughter."

34. Ellie and Elle

"You have ... what??" I whisper-yelled – because we were still in a public space –, eyes as wide as my cats' when they're in a mischievous mood.

Ben pursed his lips, yet without leaving my hand. I should have probably snatched it away, but part of me, as astounded by the depth of his lies and appalled by the enormity of his revelation as I was, I still was dying to know every single detail of the story.

And Ben seemed to perceived that – or probably read it all over my face, since I can never hide him anything, unlike him –, because he took a deep breath and, squeezing my hand, he started talking.

"As you know, Valerie and I kind of ... lost contact after high school."

I nodded, even though I wanted to remind him her version of the story: he ghosted her, plain and simple. Whichever the reason, whatever the bigger, greater distraction he found, he pretty much dropped his best friend right after they graduated from high school.

Obviously, she is a little dramatic, but in the end it is true. And these past weeks I thought I wasn't even surprised. Someone that is able to lie so blatantly to your face every single day for months obviously has no qualm in dropping you like a hot potato whenever it suits him. Cue my attempt at freeing my hand, given the line of thought my mind had taken.

However, Ben once more read me like an open book, and, squeezing my hand more – enough for it to become a tad bit red –, he scoffed: "Just listen, okay? No prejudices, no back-thinking, no jumping to conclusions, no deeming me an unredeemable bad guy just because of what happened between us." His tone was stern – the nerve!

"You can't come demanding after-"

"JoJo, please." Ben squeezed my hand and because I moved it a bit, hurt – in more ways than one –, he took the chance to entangle our fingers. His blue eyes were pleading with me, and as much cold as I always considered myself to be, I still had a hard time not melting. "I don't have a right to demand anything after what I did, I know, but … can you please just listen? Once I've told you everything, you can decide whether you still want me in your life or not, but for now, just … listen, okay?"

There wasn't much I could reply to that. I could have slid my hand out of his, without a word, which would have been the same as saying no, I do not want to listen, there's nothing you can say that may actually work. But maybe there is, that's the problem.

I thought and thought and thought, what could possibly drive someone to make up an entire life or at any rate hide key points of it? The only reason I could come up with – based on the evidence I had, namely the phone calls and his secrecy –, was that he was married. Because if someone claims to be gay, when it's not true, then having a whole family at home is the only possible explanation, no? "You have a daughter and a wife?"

"Joanna …" Ben sighed, shaking his head. "Just halt that derailing train of thought of yours, for once, okay?"

"I thought you liked it, the fact that I am so ... creative."

"Of course, I do. But not right now. Right now, that overly creative mind of yours is what stands between us."

That's not the only thing, Ben, come on. "That's not true." I finally pulled back my hand. "What separated us are your own lies."

"That's what I'm trying to-"

"But what really stands between us, Ben, in your way, it's the fact that I do have a boyfriend." I stood. "Someone that loves me for who I am, not for the me he built."

"You're jumping to conclusions again." Ben scoffed, standing up as well.

I shook my head, rummaging through my wallet to get the money to pay for all my teas. "You have a daughter and a wife, what's there to add? There's not much room for assumptions when you present me with such a fact." I threw some money onto the table, hoping it would cover my bill, and stormed out.

"You're running away again." Ben froze me – literally, because I was just about to step foot out the door. "Like always. Every single time you get any close to really feeling something, you run away." His voice was too loud for my tastes, because I could already feel the glances of the other customers and some staff on me.

I wasn't gonna wait for him to humiliate me in front of everyone, though, no. I just walked out, ignoring my red cheeks as much as I could, and hating Ben even more for submitting me to such a mortification. It's clear he doesn't know me, if he thinks the theatrics work with me. They have the exact opposite effect, actually.

Being the center of attention is the one thing I loathe the most, and he should know. He should know how I am, and he should know that the worst possible thing you can do to a shy/introvert person is to put them on the spot like he just did.

Sighing, I grabbed the earphones in my back pocket, hoping music would absorb my feelings and thoughts. I guess maybe it's indeed time to delete his number.

"Joanna." This time it was whisper-yelled at the same time as something gripped my arm.

I closed my eyes, forcing my heart to stop its silly somersaulting. "Don't." I merely murmured. Don't embarrass me, don't make me the center of attention, don't prove me one more time that I was right and you never cared, you've never really known me, you just guessed based on your typical, generic shy fat girl.

"I'm sorry, ok? I didn't mean to embarrass you earlier." Ben admitted. If only he knew how little his apologies matter at this point, and how hard it is to believe a single word that comes out of his mouth. "Can we go somewhere private?"

"Why?" I tried to free my arm, but his response was pulling me back towards him. "Just let me go."

"You'll run if I do."

"I wouldn't run in the middle of a busy street."

"You know what I mean."

"Do I?" I scoffed, turning to him only because talking while he stared at my back was awkward. "I don't know anything anymore."

"Just listen to me, please ..."

"I did."

"No. You ran away. As you always do." Ben claimed, and without giving me time to argue, he went on: "Did you ever even stop to think about what I said last time?"

"I have thought about your lies even for too long." I rolled my eyes, hating myself not only for still listening to him, but for having wasted so much time on him and his deceitful self.

Ben sighed. "Not that." He glanced around for a few seconds, which I almost considered using to walk away. The road was as trafficked as you can imagine – it's New York, after all –, and the noise would be deafening to anyone that isn't used to this city. "Let's go."

Before I could ask where, Ben dragged me towards an alley behind me. I would have thought it dangerous – a New York alley is where Batman's parents were murdered after all –, but the fairy lights above our heads and on the door we reached told me this was actually a kind of fancy place. It was a restaurant, in fact, as the sign above the glass door read. Luckily, it was closed.

"Why are we here?"

"Far from the madding crowd." Ben quoted jokingly, but I wasn't in the mood to laugh. Nor was I feeling, well, whatever those fairy lights and the whole ambiance were supposed to make me feel. Hence, he turned serious. He finally let go of my arm, but remained standing in the middle of the alley, blocking my only way out. "Here we can talk." He said. "A friend works here," he hinted at the restaurant behind me, "we could even have dinner when they open."

"Dinner?" I scoffed. "You plan on keeping me prisoner all day?"

"If that's what it takes to finally make you listen, sure." He shrugged –
again, the nerve!

"Don't treat me like a child." I rolled my eyes, crossing my arms over my
chest. Then I quickly undid that when I noticed Ben's line of sight. Did
he ever look at me like that? Did his eyes ever go any more south than my
collarbones?

"Can we just talk? Instead of running around the city, or rather, me having
to run after you? Do I need to handcuff you to my wrist to actually force
you to listen?" Ben groaned, rolling his eyes.

"What do I need to listen to? More lies? You already said your truth, what
else?" I scoffed, going to lean against the wall on the left.

"I haven't even started."

"You said you have a daughter. That usually implies the presence of a
wife or girlfriend – you know, the person that actually gave birth to said
daughter."

"She's dead!" Ben shouted at the top of his lungs, so much that some
pigeons nearby flew away.

I don't know whether it was the shock of the revelation or the fact that
he never really lost his patience with me, but my back pressed against the
wall so hard it actually hurt. "She ... she what?" I asked in a murmur – an
ashamed murmur, to be exact.

Ben took a deep breath, and walked up to me, mirroring my position
against the wall. His gaze on the sky we could hardly see, as high as the
buildings around us where – but still, the small stripe of blue sky that
emerged brought some feeble sun rays.

"Eleanor, her name was Eleanor." He started, and I felt my knees already quiver. The pain latched in his voice felt ancient yet ever so fresh, as if it renewed itself every single day. "Ellie, for everyone," he cracked a small smile, "which is why she wanted to name our daughter Elle. She thought it would be cute – Elle and Ellie, Ellie and Elle."

"How ... how old is she?"

"Elle is 9." He turned to me for a second. "I didn't mean to keep her a secret, I just wasn't sure how to tell you about her."

Telling me you're gay isn't a great idea to make up for that, I wanted to say, but I kept it. Instead I just nodded. Feeling like my knees wouldn't be able to sustain the weight of his story, I slid along the wall, and sat down. I didn't care if it was lurid, after this I'm going to need a long, long shower anyway. "I'm ready." I murmured after a few seconds.

Ben sat beside me. When he grabbed my hand, entangling our fingers once more, I thought about pulling back, but it wasn't the right time. "Like I said, Valerie and I pulled apart after high school. Partly because I stayed at home, she went to college, so it was easy to lose contact, partly because ... well, that summer, the summer after graduation, I met Ellie."

Love at first sight, I bet. "It wasn't instant." He contradicted my thoughts. "Like ..." Ben turned to me, pressing his lips as if he wanted to say something but wasn't sure whether he should or not. He opted for no. "She moved with her family from Omaha. A downsizing plan her dad was adamant on – something Ellie hated."

"She wanted to be an actress." I murmured without thinking, connecting the dots, for once.

Ben's gaze shot to me, but he wasn't surprised. He nodded. "Leaving the city to go to a small town is the exact opposite of what you need to get to Hollywood." I can imagine. "We butted heads for a while. The first time we met, all I saw was an insufferable client that fussed about her salad – I worked as waiter back then, photography didn't give me enough to provide for my family." He paused. "I don't deny I got caught up. I don't know what it was about Ellie. Maybe we just found each other at the right time – two lost souls that needed a direction."

I don't know why but those words made me feel some sort of pang to my heart – but not at the tragedy of his story as much as at the emotion still latched in his voice as he talked about her. To have loved like that, I wonder if I know what it means and if I ever will.

"We weren't careful," Ben went on, shrugging, "nine months later, Elle arrived." He pursed his lips. "Eleanor, she ... well, none of us was ready, but she, I told you, she had dreams. I won't pretend, having a child so young, it has a tendency of cutting off your wings pretty ruthlessly. Especially when your ambitions revolve around such a plastic world as the star system, where everything and everyone is fake and obsessed with appearance." It was impossible not to spot the hatred in his tone.

"We had long discussions about it. Many people over the years blamed Ellie for choosing her career over her own daughter – but they didn't know." Ben sighed. "They didn't know the weight of that choice, how it nearly crushed Eleanor, keeping her chained. They didn't – they don't – know that she made a brave choice. It's easy to give up on your dreams, you know, follow the concrete road ahead of you.

It's the reason why people end up bargaining, making do, stopping halfway or worse, when they've almost reached their destination. It takes more than courage to follow your dreams," he glanced at me, "it's not just about your own fears, it's about everyone in your life, society, everything.

It's like climbing Mount Everest, really." He chuckled for a moment. "You're not sure you'll make it to the top, but you can't go back and you can't stop. If you stop, you die. If you go back, either you die or you live with regrets."

Somehow, I felt like he was referring to me as well. The way I just stopped pursuing my dreams, crushed by the weight of the "real" world, the expectations, the responsibilities. It's not easy to think ahead, build imaginary castles in the air, when you're busy worrying about concrete things like food, bills, and rent.

"Everyone always blamed Ellie, claiming she was a degenerate mother for leaving her daughter – 3 years old at the time – to go chasing a dream that would never come true." Ben sighed noisily. "You understand just how deeply sexist our society is when you think about how many times I heard people tell me: children need a mother; single mom is natural, but single dad ... cue the disgusted or worried face; or, why did Eleanor leave? Didn't you provide for her and Ellie? Like a real man?"

Ugh. I felt like puking. A real man. What does that even mean anymore? "Idiots."

Ben smiled slightly, his thumb starting to trace the back of my hand, which, now I realized, he was staring at, closer and closer to leaving his head on my shoulder. "If I had left them, people wouldn't have been so judgmental, you know."

"Because boys will be boys." I recited, scoffing, rolling my eyes.

"The thing is, nobody ever understood that Ellie, she ..." There you go, he did lean his head on my shoulder as his voice broke a little. "She didn't want to leave. I know it's easy to judge, like, oh she leaves her daughter to go be an actress, such a terrible mother. But it wasn't like that. The plan was the very same as I had when I came to New York, you know?" Ben explained. "Ellie was unhappy, post-partum depression hit her hard, but she was only 20 ... you cannot ask a 20-year-old – a free spirit, a dreamer like her even

– to give up on everything and just keep paddling through. Yes, she loved our daughter, of course, she did, but ... for some people children aren't everything."

That's understandable. Not everyone is made to have a family, and not everyone can handle witnessing their dreams – especially if they were close – fall through. We're not all made of steel, you know. Actually, no one is, we just have different levels of endurance.

"We agreed that she would pursue her dreams, and when it was time, Elle and I would have reached her." Ben sighed heavily once more. "I didn't think that world would swallow her whole. I didn't think she would get in so deep that she couldn't reemerge anymore. She was asked for more, always more. Lose more weight, smile more, train more, be more. And she couldn't handle it."

"Hence the pills."

Ben nodded against my shoulders. "Hence the pills."

"I'm sorry." I squeezed his hand, not knowing what else to say. What do you say in such situations?

"My family helped me with Elle." He went on. "I worked long hours – I had 2 jobs, one as a waiter, one as bartender, and photographer on the weekends. Luckily, I could bring Elle with me on the photography gigs, so we could make up for the lost time. My mom took care of her after school, sometimes my brothers babysat."

"That's nice."

"But you know, one thing Eleanor and I had in common, is that we both had big dreams."

I nodded, remembering what Valerie told me about Ben feeling like a lion in a cage in their hometown. He always wanted to travel. "Hence New York."

He shrugged. "It's not the best place to raise a kid, to be honest. But ... you know, the city of possibilities."

"If you can make it here, you can make it anywhere." We quoted in unison, only to then smile.

Ben raised his head, to look straight into my eyes. "I didn't mean to lie. But ... you were so shy and scared, I thought maybe, if you believed I wasn't uh ... if you believed I wouldn't ... that I couldn't be interested in you in that sense, maybe you'd relax."

I let out a small snort-laugh, only to then cover my mouth. Ben rolled his eyes, I bet knowing where my line of thought was going. "I would have never, not even in a billion years, thought you were trying to get with me. Even if you downright told me, have sex with me, I would have never even considered you actually meant it."

"Yeah, I know that now ..." he sighed, "and you know how wrong you were ..."

I frowned, tilting my head to the side. "I wasn't-"

"I kissed you, JoJo." He chuckled, cheering up a bit.

"Yes, but that was just uh ... I don't know, the heat of the moment?"

He rolled his eyes once more, but this time half smiling. "You're on a level of denial humanity hasn't discovered yet, I swear."

"It's not denial, I just don't think you know what-"

"For God's sakes, did you even hear me when I said I love you?"

Oh. Oh! I ... no. I totally uh, removed that part. Um. I mean, I did hear it, yes. But ... he didn't mean ... uh ... "But that was ..." my cheeks reddened, so I had to lower my glance. "Like ... you meant ..."

"If you tell me you thought I meant it platonically, I'm gonna start tickling you."

I sent him a dirty look. "You wouldn't."

"Try me." He laughed. Well, at least he cheered up.

I tried to free my hand from his, but obviously in vain. Of all the things I heard two weeks ago, I didn't exactly focus on his uh confession. I mean, yes, I did hear it, but I dismissed it as nothing, like, I mean, it's something you tell your friends anyway – the English language doesn't really give you many choices in that sense, does it? "Ben, you can't ..." I murmured, voicing my thoughts. "I mean ... you," shouldn't you be still loving your long-lost Eleanor? Isn't that how romance works? When you lose your sweet other half, you find yourself unable to move on and love somebody else, no?

Ben's laugh died down slowly as he stared at me intently. "If your objection to us," he pointed at me and him, just to be clear, "is that I couldn't possibly fall for you, then," he flicked my forehead, "you're crazier than I thought when we first met."

"Oh, so you did think me crazy."

He rolled his eyes, albeit smiling a bit. "Once again, Miss Joanna Brooks, I literally declare to you, and you don't see it!"

I opened my mouth to say something, to argue that he wasn't declaring anything, that he's out his mind if he thinks he loves-LOVES me. But I didn't. I closed my mouth, and took a deep breath, leaving my head against the wall. I closed my eyes, trying to make sense of all this. How many are the chances that after a life spent mostly alone and invisible, feeling inadequate and worthless, in a matter of months, I would have not one, but two guys declare they love me?

That's fiction material, not real life. The girl that never believed in herself, finally starts doing so, and attracts attention. She gets friends, a new job, a boyfriend and her new best friend confesses to be in love with her. I'm pretty sure I've seen something like this in those crappy soap operas nobody watches.

So many things have happened altogether, I can't believe it's real. Any of it.

"You don't believe me, do you?" Ben murmured. "I guess I deserve it after all the lies."

"It's not that." Well, not just that.

"Then what?"

"I ..." I sighed, and shook my head. "This isn't real." I stood up, dusted off my pants.

"What do you mean it's not real?" Ben questioned, standing up as well. "How can it not be?"

I kept shaking my head. "No, this isn't ... no."

"JoJo ..."

"I ..." my breaths hitched, I was finding troubles even only thinking straight, imagine actually speaking and explaining the turmoil that was my head.

Ben took my hand in his once again, and brought it to his lips. "This is as real as ever."

"Ben ..."

"No, you have Jeremy, I get it. That is a good enough reason." He said. "But don't tell me it's not real, because it is, always has been."

Again I went with the shaking of my head. "What do you mean always ... you're not making any sense!"

"Why not? Why does it make sense for Jeremy but not for me?"

"It doesn't for him either!" I nearly yelled, pulling back from him. I felt tears welling up in my eyes, and I hated it. "Don't you see? This cannot be real! This is probably just me writing yet another stupid love story." I said, while he looked at me bewildered. "I can already see the blurb:

Joanna Brooks had her life all planned. She'd have graduated in time, got a great job, had a successful career. In the middle there would have been a relationship or two maybe, but by the age of 25, she'd have been happily in a stable relationship, working for a well-known newspaper as journalist.

She'd have never guessed, when she was 12, that none of these plans would work out.

28 years old, stuck with a crappy job and no love life whatsoever. Future seemed as bleak as ever. With two new kittens, Joanna was readying herself to start her life as crazy cat lady...but her new neighbor, handsome and lovely photographer Ben Harris, doesn't seem to think it that way, as he gets ready to revolutionize her whole existence.

Trouble is, his own life is not as crystal clear as he pretends it is.

Don't you see, Ben?" I gave in to a few tears. "All of this, it sounds exactly like a fictional book. Even where we are right now!" I gestured for him to pay attention to our surroundings: the fairy lights, the cute and romantic restaurant somewhat hidden away at the end of a Brooklyn alley. The only thing missing is the right music. This is exactly how I would end one of the sappy romances I wrote in secret, without ever telling anyone.

35. We're friends

B^{EN}

I remained there staring at her for the longest time after her outburst. A book. This feels like a book. Why am I not surprised? That she would start convincing herself none of this is real? Any girl would maybe think I'm lying – would be understandable after all that happened –, but not Joanna, no. Joanna believes it's not real. I don't know whether to laugh or worry. I heaved a deep sigh, trying to gather as much calmness as I could. Then, I pinched her arm.

"Ow!"

"There, did you feel that?" I asked.

"Of course, I did!" Joanna protested, rubbing her arm while sending me a dirty look.

I chuckled. "Then it's real, you crazy girl! Or should I believe you have hallucinations?"

"Ben, that's not what I was saying ..."

"What is it with you? Why does everything need to have a reason? Some things just don't have an explanation! There's no why to everything!"

"But why-" she stopped herself mid-sentence, well aware that she was proving my point, and I couldn't help but laugh, gaining yet another dirty look from her.

"Ok, let's see," I pursed my lips for a moment, then pushed her against the wall – gently, of course, I'm not a savage, come on –, caging her. "You wanna know why I love you." I said out loud, just so she would finally register those 3 words she keeps on rejecting.

"You don't-"

"I do." I smiled faintly.

"Ben ..."

"No, listen to me." I cupped her cheeks, invading her personal space by closing the gap between us – not because I intended to do who knows what, but because I know that when I do this type of thing she gets flustered and loses control over herself. That's when she's the most truthful, namely when her repressed mind doesn't have time to tell her what to think or say. "You are amazing just the way you are."

"If you're gonna start quoting Bruno Mars, I'm out." She scoffed, causing me to chuckle.

"You know what I mean."

She rolled her eyes. "I've done nothing to ... deserve it."

"Who says love is deserved?"

"Well ..."

"It's not meritocratic, JoJo. Love is just ... love."

She grimaced. "Can you stop saying that word ..."

"Why? Is it making you uncomfortable?" I pushed against her. "Am I making you uncomfortable?"

"Yeah, is he?" A third voice interjected. When we both turned to the left, we saw a tall beefy man in his late 30s staring at us – or rather me – sternly and suspiciously. The owner of the restaurant, I'm guessing. "Did anyone ever teach you that no means no?" He spat.

"It's not what you think ..." I tried to mend, well aware that he was getting the absolutely wrong idea.

"Yeah, yeah, never is ..." he scoffed, taking a few steps closer to us – or rather, again, to me who was still invading Joanna's personal space.

"It's really not what you think." She murmured, but taking the chance to slip out of my grip. "We're friends." Somehow that sounded more intended for my ears than for his.

✧✧ ✧ ✧ ✧

JOANNA

The walk back home was more awkward. I tried to focus on literally anything else just to avoid talking to Ben, but it was all in vain. His words kept racing in my mind, over and over again. I'm kinda glad that man from the restaurant interrupted us – very chivalrous of him, by the way, to come in my aid thinking I was being harassed –, and after that, Ben got a call and he needed to come home, so our talk was cut off; but because we live near, we walked. A taxi would have taken us home in a couple of minutes, sparing us both the awkwardness, but no ... we walked. Ugh.

When we got to our building, Ben stopped at the door, almost causing me to crash into him. "Do you ... think you're ready?" He asked in a sigh.

I frowned. "Ready for what?"

Ben rolled his eyes. "JoJo, who do you think called me earlier?"

"You didn't say-oh! Right." Damn, am I dumb. Who could possibly have him rush home so quick? Jeez, Joanna, sometimes you're dumber than the fly that keeps smashing against the closed window when the other is open. Ugh.

"Yes." He turned to me. "So, I'm asking you, do you think you're ready?"

To meet her. Meet Elle. I pursed my lips for a moment. "I ... don't know." How horrible can it be to meet a 9-year-old? I mean, I hate meeting people and I'm not exactly great with children, but I'll have to meet her at some point ... I guess. That's if Ben and I will still ... ugh, I don't know anything anymore.

"That's alright." Ben spoke softly, nodding. "I don't wanna force you." He cracked a small smile.

"No, I ... I should."

"You sure?"

Not at all. But I need to push myself, don't I? I mean, if we're to be uh ... if Ben and I will still ... see each other, then I should meet his daughter, shouldn't I? But the thing is, I am not that certain I forgive him yet.

The story about Eleanor was sad and heartbreaking, but it doesn't change the fact that he deliberately lied to me for so long. For months. I may sound heartless, but a sob story as explanation (which it isn't quite) and an I love you aren't enough to restore the trust and faith that were broken. Not for me.

"JoJo?"

"I ..." I took a step back. "I need some time."

"Oh."

"I'm sorry, but ... this ... everything is ... it's a lot to digest. I ... need a break."

"That's alright, you can meet her another day."

"No."

Ben's face morphed into such a pained, hurt, disappointed look that I really felt my heart burn. "What ..."

I raised my hands, shaking my head. "I think we should ... I think it's better if we stay away from each other for a while."

36. Now I can pass out for real

"**A**re you okay?"

I flinched when I saw a hand being waved before my face. I blinked my eyes, realizing where I was. "Sorry." I murmured, lowering my glance.

"What's going on?" Ms. Benedetti asked, tilting her head to the side. "You've been distracted all week."

Where do I begin? My neighbor and best friend, who I thought was gay, is not only as straight as a damn arrow, but also has a 9-year-old daughter and he – incidentally, unbelievably, absurdly – confessed he's in love with me. Me, me!

On top of that, I have a boyfriend that also said he loves me, and he hasn't received an answer in weeks. He pretends he's cool with it but I can see the hurt look on his face every time we kiss or part – he hasn't repeated those words, but it is evident that he is waiting for me to say them back.

And how about the fact that my boyfriend not only still talks to my neighbor, but he's become friends with the daughter! Apparently, Jeremy and Elle spent some time at the zoo while her dad came to talk to me – the irony of this! My boyfriend literally playing wingman for his rival!

"Joanna?"

"Yes!" I blurted out without thinking, only to blush when I noticed my boss' weird look. "Sorry." I murmured again. "Uh, is there ... anything else?"

Ms. Benedetti eyed me for a long, long moment. "Am I overworking you?" She asked, seemingly concerned. She fixed her glasses on her nose, then added: "I know we're doing crazy hours, but unfortunately it's required for now, until we really take off. But if you think it's too much for you ..."

"No!" I exclaimed, afraid she was about to fire me. I straightened up, shaking my head. "No, it's fine."

"You've been doing a lot here, Joanna, more than what is, technically, required of you."

"That's ok. I enjoy working here."

"You sure?"

"Yes."

Again, my boss studied me carefully for a few moments. It's true that, being technically an intern, I do more than edit texts; actually, editing texts is one of the last things I do, more as a way to teach me than really as part of my job. Mostly I do grammar editing, but the actual editor checks again every time. Mainly, I do pretty much everything is needed, including taking coffee orders for everyone, yeah.

"Do you feel valued here?" Ms. Benedetti asked me, which took me off guard.

Do I feel valued? Has anyone ever asked me that? Scott would never even dream of it. "Yes ..."

She pursed her lips. "Because I've been thinking about it, and ... maybe you need something different."

Please, don't sack me, please, don't sack me, please don't sack me. I badly need this job. I unconsciously pressed my eyelids, wanting to make myself as little as possible. Was my work so bad that I get fired after barely a month? Maybe it's a sign I need to downsize my expectations and dreams.

"Oscar!" She called, well, yelled, for her assistant, namely the guy that took me to her when I came for the interview. I don't know him much, same as I don't know much any of my co-workers, me being the usual asocial I am, but he seems nice. I'll think the same even if he brings my resignation papers.

"You called?" The tall, slim guy in a suit appeared like a genie at the door. He's incredibly efficient.

"Yes." Ms. Benedetti grinned, gesturing for him to come in. "I have thought about your question," she said, directed at him, "and I think you're right, you should be able to do more." Wait, is she firing both of us now?

"Really?" Oscar grinned like a Cheshire cat, his eyes brightening.

Our boss nodded, crossing her arms over her chest. "It was part of our deal, after all, wasn't it?" She said to him, then turned to me. "Oscar was um ... kind of stolen," – cue his chuckle –, "he had originally applied to work with ..." she raised her index finger to point up, namely the last floor of the building, namely the place where her soon-to-be-husband's main offices are, "but there was no uh vacancy at the time. I happened to be there and ..."

"She took pity on me." Oscar laughed. "Offered me a job as her assistant until I either found something else or ... well, a spot freed ..." he hinted upstairs as well.

I nodded, still unsure what was going on. "So, you're leaving?" I asked him. I didn't intend to say it coldly, but it probably came out that way, because we really don't know each other enough for me to care if Oscar goes to work elsewhere or not.

"That's the thing!" Ms. Benedetti said, excited, grinning. "With Oscar going to work for Lucas, I ... am going to need a new assistant ..." she beamed, this time directed at me.

I blinked my eyes, still a bit perplexed, but now kind of putting two and two together. "So, you want me to ... replace him?" That came out wrong. But they both smiled, nodding, meaning I did get it right, for once.

Ms. Benedetti went on explaining that as her assistant I would more clearly see how all of this – publishing – works, because I would be in contact with pretty much department. It's as if she were outlining my plans before my eyes without me even knowing I had them.

Not that I ever really thought that far. My 5-year-plan wasn't that detailed, it was more along the lines of: be self-sufficient, have a more stable life, do at least a few of the things I've always dreamed about.

Like traveling, seeing more of the world – or rather, seeing the world per se, since I've only really seen New York so far. Ben and I even talked about this – about traveling together, going places, like Europe or ... ugh. No. No, no, no. No thinking about him.

"You okay, Joanna?" I realized I was shaking my head repeatedly when my boss placed her silky hands over my shoulders, staring at me worriedly.

"Sorry, I ..." I cleared my throat, taking a step back because I'm not very comfortable with people invading my personal space. "I was uh ... thinking."

"You don't like the idea?"

"No, I ... it's a great plan." It really is. "But ..." how do I ask her about money without sounding demanding or just ... plebeian? Before being the fiancé of the Golden Bachelor, based on what I read, Ms. Benedetti was wealthy nevertheless – her mom is a lawyer, her dad is a cop, they have this ... mansion in Italy, where they spend every summer.

It's also true that you can't really believe gossip, but the point is, to her ears I may sound like ... I don't know, Jane Eyre with Blanche Ingram. Well, maybe that's not a fair comparison, Ms. Benedetti is the exact opposite of that little conceited harpy that Blanche was.

"But ...?" My boss repeated, expecting a full answer. Meanwhile Oscar had disappeared out of thin air.

"But uh ... how does that change my position?" Oh, very diplomatic, good idea.

She smiled. "We can review an example of the contract signed by Oscar, and start from there. And yes, my personal assistant gets paid more than an intern." She rolled her eyes playfully, kind of causing me to chuckle – I restrained myself in time, it's still my employer, after all. But I felt relieved. I guess at least one side of my life might actually go well. If only the rest didn't follow Bridget Jones' theory.

✧✧ ✧ ✧ ✧

"You should meet her." Jeremy said out of the blue.

"Huh?" My glasses were fogged because I was draining the pasta, since my crazy boyfriend had 2 insane ideas at the same time. One: invite my employer over for dinner to celebrate my "new" job. Two: cook Italian.

Now, it's already insane to invite over your boss who also happens to be one of the most known women in the city due to not only her rising company but also to whom she is marrying.

But to cook Italian for an Italian woman ... that passes every level of crazy known to humanity. Cherry on top of the most insane cake ever, Ms. Benedetti actually accepted! She actually accepted to spend a Friday night having dinner in the shoe box I call apartment, just me, her, and my boyfriend. I don't know who is in more dire need of psychiatric help, really, her or Jeremy.

"You know who." My boyfriend answered enigmatically while I was busy trying not to scald my hand – again.

"Jay, you either have me help you cook this irresponsible dinner, or you test my brain with your riddles. Pick one." I grumbled, finally draining the pasta the way he said – because like Hell I would know how to do it. I've never once cooked any kind of pasta if warming up noodles doesn't count.

He laughed of my pain, obviously, then made me jump by coming over – well, pretty much appearing behind me, placing a soft kiss on the back of my neck once he'd circled my hips. You know, the boyfriend stuff you see in movies.

Turns out Jeremy has a thing for the romantics once he's at ease. Not that I mind, it's actually really nice, but ... not quite appropriate when I'm in the verge of a panic attack because my employer will be here soon. "Do you trust my cooking abilities?" My boyfriend asked, kind of cockily, because I guess he didn't quite grasp the full depths of what he'd done by inviting Ms. Benedetti here.

I turned my head to him, who was still grinning. "You're an incredible chef, Jay, but that's my employer!" I whined for umpteenth time since this afternoon.

"Yes, and?"

"She's Italian!"

"And ...?"

I pointed at the whole mess that was my small kitchen, with ingredients on one side – stuff he was working on –, and tools on the counter where I was. "You're making Italian dinner for the Italian woman that can be my fortune and my undoing!" I whisper-yelled dramatically. "Not to mention that she's probably used to who knows what haute cuisine!"

"And?"

"Uh ... do you know who is she marrying?"

"Yeah, and?"

I rolled my eyes. "Will you stop with and ..."

Again with the laughing. Then he kissed my cheek. "Baby, they might be ultra-rich, but they're human, too, you know. Actually, what I heard is that they're pretty down-to-earth."

I sighed, half relaxing in his arms – not because I was actually relaxed, but because it felt nice to be lulled for a moment, before I gave in to my anxiety. "Well, at least it's just her ... I don't think I could handle her fiancé." I'd probably pass out right here before his eyes if I were to meet Lucas Grant in flesh and bones.

Not that I'm a fan of his, I understand nothing of computers and the only famous people I could possibly be interested in are writers – and

Chris Hemsworth, because, well, Thor! But ... I saw the pictures on my employer's desk more than just on the magazines and everything else, and I understood quickly why everyone is so awestruck by him. Luckily, I've never once crossed his path even while working just one floor beneath him.

"Well, about that ..." Jeremy pursed his lips.

"What?" Before he could answer, I heard a knock on my door. "Oh. My. God! I thought Italians were always late!"

Jeremy laughed, finally letting me go – but not before having kissed my cheek one more time, of course. "Baby, maybe ... easy with the stereotypes in front of your employer?"

I brought a hand to my mouth, covering it, when I realized what stupid thing I said and how loud! Ms. Benedetti hates stereotypes. Dear God, tell me she didn't hear anything. "I will hate you forever if this goes wrong." I blurted out, shooting daggers at Jeremy.

He bit on his lips. "Well, hate usually implies love ... I guess I can work with that." He winked.

And there goes my heart skipping beats again while at the same time the angel on my shoulder started singing no, no, no, don't phunk with my heart ... yeah, apparently, I have a pop culture loving conscience.

Luckily, he went back to cooking without adding anything, and because the knock on the door was repeated, I shook my head to wake up. I didn't even change yet. Hell, she's not just punctual, she's even early! Who does that!

Taking a deep breath, I walked over to the door, and opened it right when the third knock ended. "I'm sorry, Ms. Benedetti, I-" Wait, where is she?

"Can you give this to Shawy, please?" A young voice asked gently.

My eyes opened wide when I looked down. There she was standing, head tilted to the side, a pack of treats for cats in her hands. I don't know much about kids, but she definitely looked about 9-10. Oh, no.

"Elle!" What was unmistakably Ben's voice called from next door. Ah. There you go. In case I had any doubts on who this blonde little girl that brought treats for my cat could possibly be. Now I can pass out for real.

37. When did my life become a soap opera?

"**I**'m here." The little girl answered when her dad called a second time.

All the while, I remained there staring, unable to think or speak. I did hear Ben gulp from his door when he saw where his daughter was. "Elle ..." he sighed.

"I just wanted to give this to Shawy before we go." The kid explained, showing him the treats she had in her hands.

I should have probably thanked her, or even only question how did she know my cat, but all I could do was stare at her. Long honey blonde hair, light brown eyes, she wore a cute white skirt and a white t-shirt that had a cute stamp on.

She looked adorable, no question. I tried to see resemblances between her and her dad, especially when he walked over to us, but all she had of him were the eyes. You really wouldn't say they're father and daughter. At the most, you'd think he's her brother, and it's not just about the age, it's simply that she doesn't look much like him. Other than the eyes, like I said.

If you merely focused on those light brown eyes, then definitely, you would have no doubt who she is for him.

"I'm sorry ..." Ben murmured, flustered, hand on his daughter's shoulder. She seemed confused at his apology. I wonder if he's ever talked to her about me.

However, what caused me to jolt awake, was Jeremy poking my hips from behind. Before I could complain, he appeared next to me, smiling, Shaw clinging onto his shoulders – Reese is still on the fence about my boyfriend, but his sister likes him. "Hey, Ellie Jelly." Jeremy greeted grinning. "Ms. Shaw was wondering when you'd come back."

The child beamed at my kitten, and gladly took her in her arms. Amazingly, Shaw didn't argue, she actually welcomed the embrace, even happier when Elle opened the bag of treats for her.

Ben and I looked at the scene, baffled. We were the only two unaware of what was going on, it seemed. Jeremy winked at me, even when I sent him a dirty look, and especially when he invited Elle inside my apartment with the excuse of needing help with dinner.

"I didn't know ..." Ben cleared his throat. "She just ran off, I didn't know she would ... sorry."

Oh, Ben. I sighed, shaking my head. "It's ok."

"How uh ... how are you?"

I shrugged. "I'm okay. You?"

He shrugged as well. Then there was silence, awkward silence. Well, not total silence, because in the kitchen, Jeremy and Elle were busy half preparing dinner, half playing with Shaw. Reese just stared at the scene, unbothered at first, but when Elle went to him as well, he was happy. Cats do love kids, after all.

"They get along well." Ben mentioned, hinting at Jeremy and Elle. "I hope you don't mind."

"Why would I?"

He shrugged. "I don't know, maybe you don't like seeing my daughter with your boyfriend."

"Why wouldn't I?"

Ben sighed, raking a hand over his face. "Let's not play this game, JoJo. We both know you're way more perceptive than you let on."

Am I, though? If I'm so perceptive, why didn't I see the lies behind his cheery façade? If I'm so perceptive, why did I never even see that he felt something for me? Is he that good of an actor or am I that dumb?

"Elle! We need to go." Ben called.

"Just a minute!" She replied, still playing with my kittens.

"Not a minute, now. We need to go now." He sounded stern – fatherly stern – but also pretty frustrated.

"She can ... stay." I murmured. "My boss is coming over in about an hour, but meanwhile she can ... play with the cats."

"No."

"Ben ..."

"I have a gig, I need to go."

For a moment, I thought I'd tell him to leave her here, but more than just the awkwardness of it, the trouble would be the dinner with Ms. Benedetti. "She's cute." I blurted out instead. "She has your eyes."

Ben seemed taken aback by my statement, as if he hadn't expected me to notice the similarity or, Hell, to even remember the color of his eyes. It's been a while, after all. "Thanks." He said lowly.

"Ben, I uh ..." I cleared my throat. I'm sorry for being such a horrible friend? I'm sorry for rejecting you? I'm sorry for putting us both in such a situation?

"Joanna?" A female voice called from the elevator.

My eyes widened because I recognized it instantly. "Ms. Benedetti." I greeted, trying not to start hyperventilating for at least 2 reasons: a) I wasn't dressed appropriately for the dinner yet; b) she wasn't alone. As they walked over to my door, I felt like making myself as tiny as possible. Is that how everyone feels in front of this mesmerizing couple?

"Hi." My boss smiled. "We're a bit early, it's just that we went out sooner to be sure to be punctual ..." she eyed the man she was clinging onto – tall, dark-blonde hair, drop dead gorgeous –, who smiled, "this one attracts a lot of attention ..." they both laughed. I would have wanted to laugh, but I was trying not to feel like any man in front of Medusa. "So, Joanna, this is my fiancé, Lucas. Lucas, this is Joanna."

"Nice to meet you." He smiled politely – a pearly white smile that was blinding – stretching his hand to shake mine. Did I say drop dead gorgeous? Man, the pictures online don't make him justice.

He's like, a mix between Chris Hemsworth and Chris Evans. It's like God took all the beauty in the world and used it to make this particular specimen. Jeez. No wonder they call him the Golden Bachelor. He's super rich, super smart, super-duper hot and even a nice guy, based on his charity work.

"Uh ... hi ..." I only said when Ben – having providently slid beside me, elbowed my side lightly, to remind me not to look like a dead fish in front of my boss and her soon to be husband. "Oh, uh ... this is Benjamin Harris, my neighbor." I introduced him, much to his dismay. Ha. You suffer with me, Harris.

Ben nodded politely, not much fazed by the posh sight in front of us. "Nice to meet you." He shook Mr. Grant's hand, then Ms. Benedetti's. I guess that, with his job, he's kind of used to super rich people, not even the so-called Golden Bachelor can stun him.

"Uh ... come in ..." I murmured, stepping aside to let them pass, albeit awfully ashamed. They're probably used to who knows what mega-mansion, the shoe box I live in is probably as big as one of their bathrooms.

Much to my surprise, Mr. Grant smiled when they entered my apartment. "Does this remind you of anything?" He told his fiancée.

She giggled, bringing a hand to her mouth. "You're right." Then she turned to me. "This place looks so much like the apartment I lived in when I first came to New York, Joanna! If I wasn't sure I actually bought it, I would think this is it!"

"Well, the street is the same." Mr. Grant said.

"You lived in Brooklyn?" I asked, a bit confused. The Grant building is in the heart of Manhattan.

"Oh, yeah, I couldn't afford Manhattan." Ms. Benedetti and her fiancé laughed together, as if reminiscing stuff only they were privy to.

"Hi." Jeremy came to greet, wiping his hand on a cloth before shaking their hands. "Thanks for coming."

"Thanks for inviting me." Mr. Grant said with a polite smile. "I don't ... often get invited to uh friendly dinners." What does that mean?

Ms. Benedetti laughed, nudging him. "It's difficult to manage normal parties with friends when your face is all over the city." Cue everyone's laugh. I merely smiled. I felt back to awkward and shy me that couldn't utter a single word.

"And who's the little one?" Mr. Grant wondered, eyes on Elle who was still playing with my cats, as if totally unaware of the celebrities that just entered the apartment. Then again, why would she care.

"That's Elle." Ben replied firmly, yet sending me a side glance.

Ms. Benedetti seemed to catch that, because she looked in between us, then smiled. "I didn't know you had a daughter, Joanna."

Ah. Oh, no. No, no, no. Wrong thing to say, wrong, super wrong thing to say. "I ... don't."

"Elle, let's go." Ben called gruffly. She huffed a bit, but then joined her dad. "Sorry, I have a gig and we're getting late." He grabbed the kid's hand, so that they could walk swiftly to the door. "Have a nice dinner." He didn't slam the door, but he might have as well, given his rough tone and hasty departure.

"I said something wrong, didn't I?" Ms. Benedetti bit on her lip, apologetic.

"No, it's ... fine." I smiled a bit, albeit embarrassed. "Ben is my neighbor, like I said, and ... Elle is his daughter, not ... mine."

"Oh!" My boss half gasped, bringing a hand to her mouth. "I'm so sorry!"

I didn't know what to say, so I remained quiet. In the end, there's no way to explain it, especially not without causing troubles in my relationship as well. Thinking back, maybe I should have told Jeremy about the kiss with Ben and what he confessed. My boyfriend is the one that offered to babysit Elle so that her dad and I could talk ... if he knew what happened and what Ben told me, I doubt he'd be too happy about it.

Ugh, when did my life become a soap opera?

38. Are you ready to become a stepmom, Joanna?

"So, Joanna ..." Ms. Benedetti-well, Samantha, since that's what she insisted on being called, sneaked up on me while I was washing the dishes. Somehow, I convinced Jeremy to let me do it on my own, just to take a break from this whole ... happening.

Did I say I'm an introvert? Well, I am, and as such, I need my batteries recharged now and then. The evening went great, even I conversed somewhat fluidly, but at some point, I just needed a moment to myself. Not to mention that detail about meeting Ben's daughter ... I'm still shocked.

"Thanks for coming." I said politely while soaping some plates.

My employer smiled, then grabbed the dishes I'd already soaped, and washed them under the faucet. "Thanks for inviting us."

"You don't have to ..."

"I want to." We both were talking about helping me with the dishes, of course. "They're having fun on their own anyway," she hinted behind us, where Jeremy and Mr. Grant – I will never, for the life of me, manage to actually call him Lucas, even though he insisted as well – were conversing amiably about history. Yeah, history. Not football, or baseball or whatever, but ... history. Jeremy majored in that, after all, and Mr. Grant said he's always been interested in ancient civilizations.

"Thanks." I said.

Samantha just nodded, and we both went on washing and soaping the dishes in silence for a few seconds – relative silence, since our respective partners weren't much quiet. "I wanted to say ... sorry again about earlier." Samantha mentioned. "I put you on the spot, I didn't mean to."

"Earlier?"

"Yeah, with ..." she hinted behind her.

"Jeremy?" I had no idea what was she talking about, the dinner actually went well.

"He doesn't know, does he?"

"What ..."

My boss neared me a little bit, pretending to grab a soaped plate to wash it, which gave her a chance to whisper in my ear: "About you and your neighbor."

When I say I gasped out loud and broke a plate, I'm not joking. I literally did. Luckily, Samantha had the calmness to tell our respective partners everything was okay, we'd just been clumsy, so they went on with their discussions. "You ok?"

"Yeah, I ..." I cleared my throat, staring at my hand, "just clumsy ..." that's one word for it. I picked up the pieces of the broken plate – luckily all in the sink – in silence, hoping that she would not ask questions or worse, make assumptions. But when do I ever get what I want?

"I don't judge, Joanna. You're young and ... they're both fairly handsome, it's understandable that you're torn between them." Samantha said. "But ... Jeremy seems like a nice guy, he doesn't deserve it."

"I ... I'm not ..." my voice broke a little, and when I spotted Jeremy's concerned gaze, I covered it up with a small cough. "We're not ... Ben and I, it's ..." complicated? It never even started because he never even tried?

All he did was come out saying he's gay, lying about everything, and then randomly kiss me and come up claiming he loves me. That's not exactly the recipe for a mature relationship, is it? Hell, it's not even the recipe for a friendship, but I'm trying hard to forget about the lies and really forgive him.

"I had a neighbor." Samantha said, half smiling. "He was the first friend I made in New York, he was genuinely nice with me, something that back then, for me, was hard to grasp."

What does that mean? She clouded over for a moment, but then, as if it were the source of her strength, she turned to gaze at her fiancé – who was laughing and chatting with my boyfriend on the couch, not looking like one of the most powerful men in the city at all. "I thought Sean felt the same as I did." My employer went on, turning to me. "I thought he considered me a friend. But ... he didn't."

Now that sounds familiar. But what was she getting at? "Ben is a friend." I guess that is the absolute truth, more or less. I am still trying to decide whether or not I can keep being around him. The surprise meeting tonight with his daughter only made things more real.

As long as I didn't actually see Elle, I could pretend this was just a mistake, Ben and I were still the same close friends/confidantes that told each other everything. But she is proof that not only he had a life before New York, but that he also completely lied to me about it. It'll sound dramatic, but I do not take very well being lied to.

"Sean was a friend." Samantha countered, always with that small smile of hers. "But ... he wanted to be more."

"And he was?"

She chuckled. "Of course, not." Duh. Who could ever even only hope to win against the Golden Bachelor, right? "I had never even realized he wanted more, only when he told me, I actually acknowledged it. But ... it was too late." Cue the gazing at her fiancé again. It's been like that all night, really. It's like they can't take their eyes off each other for more than 5 minutes or they'll fear the other fades away.

I won't deny I envy the kind of complicity and boundless love that oozes off them. It's like they were made for each other. When I did my research on Ms. Benedetti, before my interview with her, I read different things, some even implied she had pretty much brainwashed him.

And I don't know anything about celebrities nor about relationships, but I don't think I've ever been around a couple that's more perfect. Then again, I don't know many couples, most are family and they're not a great example.

When Mr. Grant caught his fiancée's gaze, they smiled at each other, and he winked, making her blush lightly. To think they've been together for years and they even have children.

Samantha cleared her throat, turning once again to me. "I was saying ... when my neighbor confessed his interest, it was too late."

"You were with Mr. Grant already." I finished for her, mostly because I don't think I can handle more of their mushiness. It's cute and all, but at some point it just rubs salt in the wound. It's like hanging a juicy steak in front of someone that's been fasting for a month.

"It's a bit more complicated than that, but yeah." Samantha confirmed, nodding. "My point was, I can see why you'd be torn between two handsome guys that both adore you." Say what, now? As if she'd read my thoughts, she laughed lowly. "Come on, you wanna deny Ben is mad about you?"

"I ..." Yes? No? Maybe? I have no clue?

"I can't really say I've been there, to be honest. The moment I stopped denying it, I didn't have eyes for anyone else other than Lucas." Cue the lovesick sigh. "But in a relationship, moments of uncertainty are normal, you know, you shouldn't be ashamed." She lowered her voice. "And like I said I don't judge, but Jeremy is a nice guy and he clearly loves you, you should make up your mind without ... well, you know."

"I know ... what?"

Samantha pursed her lips. "Look, I don't have a right to say anything, I just think Jeremy is a great boyfriend, you shouldn't cheat on him."

If only a sound had come out of my mouth. Oh, I did open it, and inside my head I did scream, but no sound came out. My eyes were wide as saucers, my mouth was agape, and I would have broken another plate, hadn't Samantha swiftly taken it off my hands.

"You ok, baby?" I hear Jeremy call from the couch, but I didn't know how to answer.

"Yes." Samantha replied for me. "She just uh ... cut her finger with a glass shard. You have some disinfectant and band-aids in the bathroom, you said, right?" I didn't even have time to nod, she just grabbed my hand, and dragged me to the small corridor towards my mini bathroom. Once there, she sat me on the toilet seat. "Phew, that was a close call."

"I ... Samantha, what ..."

"No, no, Jeremy should never find out, it would break his heart."

Is she high or something? "I ... what are you talking about?" I finally gasped out, blinking again.

She furrowed her brows. "I'm talking about you and Ben, that tension between you two earlier. The fact that you're going behind Jeremy's back ..."

"Why would you assume such a thing!" I whisper-yelled, leaping to my feet. "I would never do that to Jeremy! Or to anyone! Who do you think I am?!" I was offended and insulted.

"You're telling me there has been nothing between you and Ben? Absolutely nothing?"

I gulped, kind of loudly even. "How ... what ..."

"Like I said, tension."

"But ... it was ... just a kiss." Or maybe two or three. Ugh, here I was playing innocent, taking it all out against Ben for lying to me, and I totally bypassed the fact that, basically, I cheated on my boyfriend.

Not that I didn't know, I just didn't even have time to think about it, and I guess that hearing it said out loud was different. It made it actually real. A fact, not just a random rambling of my messed-up mind.

"Just a kiss?" Samantha tilted her head to the side.

I took a deep breath, not wanting to make a fool of myself in front of my employer. "Yes." I murmured, nodding slowly. "Just a kiss."

"Oh."

Oh? That's all? Oh? After she almost gave me a heart attack and I pictured myself enveloped in the flames of Hell in the circle of the lustful?

Samantha sat on the toilet seat, pondering for a long moment. "Tell me everything from the start."

"I don't think it's appropriate ..."

"Have you talked about this drama with anyone, Joanna?"

"The only person I'd talk about this stuff with is ... well, the only one I can't say it to." I confessed.

"Ben?"

"Yeah."

"I see. Well," Samantha stood up, "we can't stay in here all night, they'll get suspicious, but ..." she glanced at her watch, "we can take a walk, say we need fresh air."

"They won't buy it." Mostly because Jeremy knows I barely go out.

She chuckled. "You're right, Lucas would worry."

It's true that Brooklyn isn't the most peaceful area of New York, but this neighborhood is pretty tranquil and it's barely 10 pm, he wouldn't have much to worry about, most shops are still open. But I didn't say anything, I preferred to keep my story to myself.

"Well, tomorrow at work?"

"Samantha, I ..."

"Joanna, one of the things I neglected in my life is the dire need of having someone you can talk to. Especially woman to woman."

Well, I'd have Valerie for that. But she's still kind of pissed that Ben didn't tell her anything about Elle either. Plus, I wouldn't even know where to begin. Joe is too young. Faith and Hope ... we don't really have that kind of friendship. As for Michelle, she's friends with Jeremy. Taking a deep breath, I nodded. "Okay. Let's talk about this."

Samantha had a great idea. She said I was out of band aids and there was a bodega nearby, we could just walk over there quick. Of course, her fiancé protested – she isn't as famous as him, but her face still is on some magazines, people could recognize her, he said, making it sound like he was terrified they'd abduct her or something –, but she persuaded him somehow. Considering she whispered something in his ear and right after he looked at me, I suspect she explained the situation to him.

It took less than I thought, really. Just 10 minutes: home to bodega, bodega to my apartment was enough to give a full recount of everything that happened.

From when Ben and I met, seeing Jeremy again after years, the crush I had on him back in the day, our dates, how he told me he loved me. And then Ben and his being gay yet not exactly, and his lies, and the revelation about Elle and Eleanor, and his feelings for me. All of that only took 10 minutes. Incredible, right? The biggest drama in my life could be summed up in a 10 minutes talk.

"Well, Joanna, it's quite the dilemma." Samantha said, arms crossed over her chest, as we walked to my apartment. "But I think choosing to stay away from Ben for a while was a good choice."

"Really?"

"Yeah, you need to clear your head. Actually, I think that, ideally, you should take a break from Jeremy as well."

My eyes widened and I halted my steps. "I don't want to break up with him."

"You don't have to. Just ... take a few days off, maybe a week."

That's easier said than done. Jeremy is a sweet and caring guy, he doesn't suffocate me with messages – he learned soon that I need my space, which sometimes he needs as well, being an introvert, too –, but he does care about hearing from me every day at least once. I can't just disappear out of thin air and expect him not to worry.

"I may have what you need." Samantha said. "Lucas forced me to accept a vacation. He says that, between work and the kids, plus his needy self – his words, not mine –," cue her smitten laugh, "I may be soon burning out, so when his sister offered a girls only trip, he said yes on my behalf."

"Nice." But what does that have to do with me?

"You come with us."

"What?" How do I tell her I cannot afford whatever fancy place she and her sister-in-law plan on going to?

"Why not?" Samantha shrugged. "It'll be fun. And you get to relax a bit."

"Uh ... I can't."

"Don't worry, I'll pay."

"I cannot accept that."

She smiled. "Ok, take it this way ... you come as my assistant, it'll be overtime ... better?"

"Still, it's ... I can't ..."

"You're finally back." Mr. Grant interrupted us when we were at my door. "Were you trying to run off?" He engulfed his fiancée in a tight hug, gently kissing her cheek, which made her giggle.

"Not tonight, but this weekend." Samantha said, which confused both Mr. Grant and Jeremy. "Joanna and I are going to take a few days off, recharge batteries. Work has been super-hectic, we deserve it." She grinned sheepishly at me. I guess this is happening.

Jeremy. Ben. Jeremy. Ben. Jeremy. Ben. Nope, peeling the petals off a daisy didn't work. The whole weekend with Samantha and her sister-in-law didn't work. Nothing served to clear my head. If anything, I got even more confused, because Samantha and Rachel only enhanced my doubts.

a)If you loved Jeremy, you wouldn't have so many troubles telling him already. He confessed weeks ago.

b)If you were indifferent to Ben, you wouldn't have kissed him, abandoning yourself to him.

c)Jeremy feels like safe cocoon, Ben triggers the passionate Joanna you've been repressing.

d)Are you sure Jeremy isn't your what-if? The relationship you wanted years ago and now you can't give up because you feel you owe it to your past self?

e)Is Ben really available? He has a daughter, children swallow every second of their parents' life, and he's even a single dad!

All weekend my head has been a continuous ping pong between Jeremy and Ben. It's as if my life depended on this choice I didn't even know I had to make.

I hadn't even considered breaking up with Jeremy until Samantha mentioned this "tension" she said she noticed between me and Ben. I hadn't even considered IF I have feelings for Ben.

Do I? Or not? And how do I feel about Jeremy? Is he just a safe choice because he makes me feel good whereas Ben challenges me, he "awakens my wild side", as Rachel put it. Whatever that means.

It's unfair towards Jeremy to say he's a safe choice. It's not like he's this closed off guy that wants me chained to him. He's always supported me with everything: the interview with Samantha, my idea of restarting to write, and when I said I wanted to travel, he didn't laugh, he said "sure, where do you want to go first?"

Jeremy supports me. He is there for me every single time. He hasn't pushed me into anything, even though it's been almost 2 months and we still haven't, well, consumed – if you know what I mean. He respects my boundaries and is willing to wait, he believes in me.

And it's not true that we live a boring life. We do what we both like most: watching movies, reading, going to museums. It's stuff we both love. Just because we love nerdy things, doesn't mean we're boring. Maybe to everyone else we're a passionless couple, but as far as I'm concerned, this is the kind of stable relationship I've always wanted.

What could Ben offer me? I don't even know IF I want anything from him. His life is already as complicated as it gets, I don't think he has room for me.

I'm sure Elle already takes up enough of his time, not to mention his family. Set aside whether I have feelings for him or not – which I still don't know –, a relationship would be way more complicated than I could handle. Because f) Are you ready to become a stepmom, Joanna?

39. Valerie The Evil One

"This is incredible." I awed, grinning from ear to ear. "How did you manage?"

"A friend of a friend." Jeremy replied enigmatically.

I frowned, tilting my head to the side. "This friend of a friend doesn't happen to be marrying my employer, does he?"

My boyfriend laughed, pecking my lips. "Maybe." He hinted behind me. "Don't think about it, focus on that."

And how could I ignore it? Before our eyes, there was the most beautiful sunset I've ever witnessed. Back home I was always getting lost in it, I purposely went outside for it, it was one of the very few things that brought me joy back there. And to find something just as incredible here now ...

When Jeremy convinced me to get away for a weekend, I had no idea what was he planning, and given my recent dilemmas, I was reluctant. But when we reached the lake house, I forgot about everything else. I guess Elizabeth Bennet was right when she said, what are men to rocks and mountains? We hassle and fret, still thinking we're the center of the universe, but in the end, we're nothing compared to Mother Nature. Nothing. It's not that we lose meaning, though. If anything, we gain more.

"Thank you." I murmured, unable to take my eyes off of the last traces of sun, which was going to sleep.

"Anything for you." Jeremy said, embracing me from behind, to place a small kiss on my left cheek.

Anything, he said. In other circumstances that promise would have been void of any meaning, but when faced with the grandiosity of our world, it's difficult not to read into three simple words more than I would normally allow myself to. If I ever had any desire for romance, any dreams at the very back of my skull, Jeremy nailed it 100%.

I guess that's why I turned around in his arms and, having placed my hands on his shoulders, I nodded against his forehead. "Okay."

He was puzzled. "Ok, what?"

I chuckled a bit, feeling lightheaded yet ever so sure of my choices. "Jay, we're all alone in a lake house in Canada, and that was the most beautiful, most romantic sunset ever seen ..."

"I'm glad you enjoyed it, I ..."

"Jay ..." I pecked his lips, grinning. "Read between the lines, silly."

"That's never been my strong suit."

I chuckled. "Okay," I lightly raised on my tiptoes because he's taller than me, and I whispered in his ear: "I'm ready."

"You ..."

"Yes."

"No." A different voice interjected. Behind Jeremy, I could see him, looking at me expectantly, as if waiting for me to make up my mind. "We both know that's not it."

Time seemed to freeze, because Jeremy wasn't moving, he didn't move an inch even when I let go of him. "This isn't fair." I sighed.

"And choosing comfort over love is?"

"I'm not ..."

"Now who's the liar ..."

"I am ... I am ... I am ... I am ..."

"You're what?"

I screeched when, upon opening my eyes, I found someone in my line of sight, staring at me so close that I almost felt violated. "Valerie!" I screamed, sitting up and covering myself with the sheets, even though I was fully clothed. Stupid dreams.

"Surprise ..." she feigned enthusiasm. She was clearly mad at me.

"What are you doing here? How did you get in?"

She shrugged, standing up properly. "Ben gave me your key."

"What ..."

"You'd given him a backup key, he gave it to me ... why didn't he return it to you?" Valerie inquired.

"Well, I-uh ..."

"Cut the crap." She crossed her arms over her busty chest, looking at me sideways. "What's going on between you two? He comes telling me he has a daughter that's living with him now, and you two broke off, you don't want to see him ... what the hell is happening here?"

I wish I knew, Val, I really wish I knew. Sighing, I raked a hand over my face. "Ben, he ... aside from all the lies about being gay and hiding Elle from me, he ... well, he ..." I couldn't even bring myself to say it out loud.

"He what?"

I sighed once more, lowering my glance. For some reason I felt ashamed. "Ben told me he loves me."

"And?" Valerie scoffed, impatient.

"What do you mean, and? What's there to add?"

"Well, when a guy claims to love you, usually there's either a messy heart-wrenching breakup or a super mushy recount of how you two declared undying love to each other."

I frowned. She wasn't surprised, at all. "You knew?" I looked up at her.

Valerie chuckled for the first time today, sitting on the side of my bed. "Oh, honey, everybody knows."

"Everybody?"

"Well, everybody except Jeremy, I assume, otherwise he wouldn't be so chummy with his rival's daughter." Valerie claimed, then laughed to herself. "Then again, your boyfriend's such a nice guy that he probably would be regardless."

"There's nothing wrong about being a nice guy." I defended.

"A little bit boring, if you ask me, but sure, nothing wrong at all."

"Val ..."

"Get up. You slept for a whole weekend, the first thing you need is a shower."

"How ..."

"Jeremy." She shrugged. "God, he's such a goody-two-shoes. Don't you get sick of it?"

I rolled my eyes. She prefers the bad boy type. "Not at all."

Valerie sent me a side glance that I would have sworn was hiding a half impish smirk. "Does that mean you wouldn't mind enduring it for the rest of your life?"

When I say I gasped, I probably don't fully convey just how loud. Valerie laughed when I covered my mouth with my hand, in shock. "Are you crazy??!"

"What? At this point, you should know."

"You're being unnecessarily mean, Val." I shot her a glare. "You know how ... well, it's ..."

"That's the point. I don't know." She scoffed, rolling her eyes. "You and Ben have locked yourself within your own selves, so I don't know."

"I just told you ..."

"Everything?"

"Well, yes, I mean ... the general lines."

"Case in point."

"Val ..." I sighed, raking a hand over my face. "I'm sorry."

"Yeah, yeah ..."

"No, I really am sorry. I guess that ... between Jeremy, and the drama with Ben, not to mention the new job, I kind of fell behind in other things. I'm sorry."

Valerie stared at me for the longest time, trying to force herself not to budge, but in the end she did, smiling. "Ugh, when you pout like that, it's impossible to stay mad." I protested a bit when she ruffled my hair the way you do to a puppy, but she ignored it.

It's true that I haven't been a great friend. Most of my time was spent either working or with Jeremy, or trying not to go insane thinking about the disaster with Ben. Faith and Hope are used to us not hearing from each other frequently, but with Valerie we started off already being always together, having our girls only days. I actually miss those.

As if on cue, Valerie said: "Come on, get ready. It's Pink Ladies time!"

I hate that name. Don't get me wrong, I like Grease, but I absolutely loathe the color pink. However, Valerie was all too happy about it, so I just let it be. I guess some time alone with her might do me good.

"I hate you so much." I groaned, directed at Valerie. As a response, she grinned. When she said our day out would be in Coney Island, I was a bit confused, because normally it's all about shopping and pampering ourselves: a theme park sounded unusual. And there was a reason for it. The reason was walking up to us right now, hand in hand with his 9-year-old daughter.

"Hi." Ben greeted, clearly feeling awkward.

"Hi!" Elle greeted mostly Valerie, hugging her tight. It's kind of ironic that pretty much anyone else is bonding with this little girl, yet the one person that should, namely me, is avoiding her at all costs.

Then again, her dad keeps out of my sight as much as it's humanly possible, the only reason we see each other sometimes is because Jeremy and Elle have become friends and do spend time together.

Again, the irony: my boyfriend becoming best friends with his rival's daughter. I wonder if Valerie is right, if Jeremy really has no clue about the situation between me and Ben, or he's just pretending.

While Valerie and Elle hugged, Ben sent me an apologetic look. Clearly, he didn't know about this meet up either. Our mutual friend probably guilt tripped him into spending a day in Coney Island to bond with his daughter.

"Joanna, you remember Elle, right?" Valerie The Evil One said, so that all eyes fixated on me, including the little girl's ones.

"Of course." I nodded, embarrassed, attempting a smile. "How are you?" I asked the kid.

She shrugged. "How is Shawy?"

Apparently, she spends a lot of time with my cats. "She's at home with her brother, they were sleeping when I got out."

"Can I come see her later?"

Uh oh. "Of course." How can you say no to such a cute and polite 9-year-old? Needless to say, Elle grinned, beaming with happiness, and turned to her dad, confirming her glee with him. I released a breath I didn't know I had been holding back, which Ben noticed. I tried to remain calm, but this day would be long and exhausting.

✧✧✧✧✧

I was right. A day spent in Coney Island is exhausting on its own, when you add that it's spent with who you thought was your best friend yet turned out to be a) a liar; b) a potential love interest, given the feelings he confessed; and with his daughter, you understand that I couldn't wait to crawl on bed and wake up next week.

I'll admit that it wasn't as terrible as I thought it would be, that is true. Valerie tried to sneak away, to make sure just the three of us would spend the whole day together, but I managed to avoid that. However, I did spend some time alone with Elle. She's a nice kid.

I'm not great with adults, imagine with children, but Elle is smart and cute, not to mention open and kind. You can see a lot of her dad in her character. She may be physically all her mother, but everything else is Ben to a tee.

"She's incredible." I murmured to him while we watched Valerie and Elle on the carousel.

"Thanks." Ben replied dryly.

When I turned to him, I noticed he wasn't even looking at me. He's been mostly quiet for the whole day, actually. I would have wanted to do something about it, talk things out, but I didn't know where to start, and even if I did, his daughter was always nearby. "Ben ..." I started, biting on my bottom lip.

"Please, don't." He shook his head. "I'm glad you and Elle get along, but you and I, it's fine. Leave it be."

"But ..." Did that mean what I think it meant?

"Look, Joanna, I'm sorry I lied. I faced things in the worst possible way, and I apologize for that. I should have been upfront."

"I know, and I understand, but ..."

"We're moving to Boston."

"WHAT??" Oh, I definitely screamed, so loud that people nearby heard me even over the noise of the amusement park.

Ben shrugged. "Elle doesn't like New York."

"That's not true, and you know it." I blurted out. She told me she loves New York. Yes, it's different, she can't really go wherever she wants because you know, it's a dangerous city and her dad never leaves her unsupervised, but she loves it here. She's made friends in school, she and Jeremy have fun together, more than she does with her babysitter, and she loves spending time with my cats.

Ben turned his back to the carousel, sighing as he leaned against the balustrade behind us. "It's better this way."

"So you're gonna deprive your daughter of her friends, you're gonna take her away from something she loves, just on a whim?" I couldn't help myself. It's not fair. First, he says he'll wait, then he just goes and decides to leave. Yes, I can be a pain, yes, I am difficult, and these weeks have been absurd.

I know I didn't go easy on him. But did he expect me to take everything in a stroll? Be happy he lied, or content he apologized? Did he expect me to just drop Jeremy in the blink of an eye the moment he snapped his fingers? He was the one that pushed me into Jeremy in the first place! It's better this way, he said, after that kiss. Now I know what he meant.

"A whim?" Ben spat, angry. "A whim? You think this," he pointed at me and him, "is a whim?!"

Us? Me? I'm the reason for him to want to leave New York? "I ..."

"What happened to you, Joanna? Why is it so difficult for you to understand? What makes you so damn obstinate and blind?"

"Hey, I ..."

"Your boyfriend tells you he loves you, and what's your answer? Nothing. Your best friend has feelings for you, and you say it's not real. What could possibly have made you so blind to everyone else's feelings, including yours??"

Where do I begin? "You wouldn't understand." I murmured. He didn't quite yell, but there were a lot of people around us, and for the second time, he made me feel like hiding in a corner or turning invisible.

"Try me." Ben scoffed, turning to me, now slightly calmer, albeit still ticked off.

"Ben ..."

"I'm serious." He said. "I'm the person that knows you the most, compared to everyone else, your parents included," that is true, "yet I still have no clue as to why are you so closed off? Why is there such a barrier between you and whoever tries to love you? Why is it so hard for you to actually believe that someone freely and unconditionally wants to be in your life?"

I felt the tears prickle behind my eyes, but I didn't want to cry, nor did I want to admit it out loud. It wasn't the right place nor the right moment. If there would ever be one. "You claim to know me," I murmured, voice somewhat broken, "yet you keep on doing this, you keep on putting me on the spot."

"I didn't mean to raise my voice." Ben sighed, raking a hand over his hair. "But you need to understand how frustrating this whole situation is."

"I do. But do you see my side of things?" I forced my self to swallow the tears that so badly wanted to fall, and I looked up at him. Suddenly, it felt as if we were alone, no one else around. "Do you understand how complicated it is for me?"

"No." Ben dug his hands in his pockets, his penetrating gaze was scorching. "No, I don't. Because again, I am not privy to that insane world that hides behind your shy girl façade."

That's bullshit, and he knows it. "You are." I bit my lips to stop those stupid tears. "You always have been."

"As much as I tried, I still failed." He shrugged. "And it's probably my fault. I went at it wrong."

"No ..." Ugh, stupid tears were starting to fall. "I ..." I looked around, feeling my cheeks enflame because people were staring at me, or at least I felt they were. I felt as if the whole world was staring at me, making fun of me, and in my ears I kept hearing my mom scoff "what are you crying for? Are you a child? Only children cry". God knows I love my parents, but they've never understood me.

"Staying will just be worse for the both of us, Joanna, you know that." Ben went on.

I shook my head forcefully. "No ..." I had so many things to say, yet I didn't know how to, or where to start. When tears began falling ineluctably, being visible, I covered my face with my hands, feeling overwhelmed, close to hyperventilating.

I could feel it coming, but I wasn't gonna put on a show for all the tourists around me, no. However, I couldn't leave either. Not until I fixed things with Ben. I couldn't let him leave without making amends. Actually, I couldn't let him leave at all.

40. Took you long enough

Blindly, because tears were fogging my sight, I grabbed his hand, and started running. I wasn't sure where to go, I just ran, Ben on tow, until I found a secluded enough place for us to speak privately. Unfortunately, that place turned out to be a not particularly pleasant bathroom, but oh well.

Sighing, I fell against the wall of a stall where I'd dragged Ben. It was way smaller than I thought at first. It was hard not to brush against each other, but luckily the bad smell averted my attention from that. I placed my hand over my heart, trying to catch my breaths. Ben was busy being a dad – calling Valerie to let her know the aliens hadn't abducted us, his daughter wasn't orphan.

I didn't think things through, though. When Ben looked at me expectantly, wanting to know why did I drag him into a smelly bathroom stall, why were my cheeks tear-stained, I felt cornered.

He knew it was an anxiety attack, and he knew there wasn't much to do other than the one thing he always did – hug me. This time, however, he didn't try to. However, before I could think the worst, he read my mind: "If I touch you now, I'm not gonna be held responsible for what follows."

I frowned, baffled. "What ..."

He leaned against the wall opposite to me. "We're in a small bathroom stall, barely inches away from each other."

"It was the first place I found, it's smelly, but ..."

"JoJo." He stopped me. "If there's one thing you've never even noticed, is just how difficult it was not to kiss you every time you were in my arms. You think the smell of a dirty bathroom would be a deterrent? Not even your vomit that time you almost threw up on me was enough."

"Gross."

He chuckled for the first time today, and my heart slowed down a bit after the frenzy of the race and the quasi-anxiety attack. "It's called love." Ben claimed cheekily, his light brown eyes fixated on me. "For the billionth time, silly woman, I love you." Contradicting his own words, he grabbed my hand, and pulled me into him. "And you love me back."

And there goes the heart restarting its race. "I ..."

"Tell me you don't." Ben demanded defiantly, cupping my cheeks, eyes always fixated on mine. "I dare you."

"That's ..." I sighed, trying to lower my glance, but he didn't let me. So, I just closed my eyes. "You're leaving."

"Only if you let me."

I reopened my eyes, this time looking straight into his light browns. "You mean it?"

"On one condition."

Somehow, I knew what he wanted. "I ... Jeremy, he ..."

Ben fainted a smile, caressing my cheek. "No offense, JoJo, but we both know Jeremy is just a parenthesis."

"That's unfair ..."

"Maybe, but true."

"You pushed me into him."

"Because my life is a mess." He cupped my cheek, our lips nearing. "I have a daughter and a family that demands a lot of me."

"And?" I scoffed.

"And ... you're a crazy cupcake that needs to let out some of her craziness. I can't cage you within family life when you haven't even had a chance to live."

"Seems to me, you don't have your ideas much clear either."

He laughed, pecking my lips. "I know I love you." He claimed. "And I understand now your main concern is that I might abandon you."

"You did."

"I gave you space."

"You messed up."

Again, Ben laughed. "Indeed I did. But ..." He paused for a few seconds.

"What?"

"I was trying to give you a choice."

I furrowed my brows, confused. Maybe he needs a recap of all that's happened in these crazy months. "First you make a point of being everywhere I turn, basically deciding on your own that you have a place in my life,"

I reminded him, thinking of the first weeks, when I was too shy to speak yet he still hung around, doing everything and beyond to carve a spot for himself in my small circle.

Ben chuckled, his thumbs stroking my cheeks. "Believe it or not, in the very beginning, it was indeed about helping my shy neighbor let out her true colors."

"Like you did with Valerie."

"She told you?" He was taken off guard, maybe even a bit worried. Probably because he was wondering whether she'd told me everything.

"Most of it." Ben gulped when I said that, which made me half chuckle, for a moment forgetting our predicament. Valerie told me how she was like me in high school: shy, overweight, awkward; and how meeting Ben was providential because he helped her find her true self. It was an inspiring story, I'll admit.

"Oh, uh ... well, it was nothing, you know, just teen stuff." He justified, seemingly embarrassed.

I frowned, not sure what he meant. "She said you helped her find herself."

"Oh ... that ..."

"What did you think I meant?"

"Well ... it's not really the right moment for this, we were in the midst of something ..." Ben pulled a hair lock behind my ear, caressing my cheek. "Like me reminding you, for the umpteenth time, that I love you."

"Are you saying that just to distract me or because you think if you repeat it a thousand times more, you'll finally convince me?" I wondered out loud.

He laughed. "Maybe both."

"Cheeky."

"Says the girl that dragged me into a tiny bathroom stall to be alone."

I blushed. "Well, I ..." I cleared my throat, lowering my glance. "I didn't think things through ..."

"Clearly not."

I took a deep breath. We have the attention span of a worm. "The point is ... you can't just leave."

"Well, why not? You have Jeremy." Even with those words, Ben didn't pull back.

"Elle likes it here." I completely ignored him mentioning my boyfriend. Because had I acknowledged it, I'd have had to face the fact that I was basically cheating on him.

"She's 9 and this is the first city she sees, she'll like Boston, too."

"What's in Boston for you?"

Ben shrugged. "I have a cousin there. He sells cars."

I scoffed, rolling my eyes. "Cars? You don't even understand cars!"

The jerk laughed, obviously, still stroking my cheeks. "It's a job as good as any."

"What?"

"Well ..." that's where he pulled back slightly, "having a daughter is expensive, you know? Not to mention she requires attentions, and ... I mean, it was nice while it lasted, but ... I can't keep doing this." He sighed. "It's a dream long gone, how could I think it would work?"

"It has so far."

"With many struggles." He eyed me attentively. "Thanks to your boyfriend as well."

"Jeremy? Why?"

Ben shrugged. "He stays with Elle while I'm at work if the babysitter can't make it. It's a huge help."

"Oh."

"But, like I said, children require presence. I'm all she has here, I can't spend most of the time traveling, don't you think?"

"And Boston is the solution?"

"It's something. Having a stable job will allow me to be more with Elle."

"What does she say?"

Ben frowned. "She's 9, she has no saying in this."

"She does." I rolled my eyes. Is he serious? He's the dad here, yet I'm the one that needs to give him advice? I crossed my arms over my chest, leaning against the wall – basically taking the chance to once and for all defuse the highly dangerous moment we'd been having. "Elle is a smart kid, she will understand."

"Maybe, but ..."

"You are unbelievable, you know."

Ben arched an eyebrow at me, seemingly shocked. "What?"

"First, you say you leave because of us. Then it's about Elle. Maybe you're the one running away."

"That's not true ..."

"Given the records, you do have a tendency to disappear now and then."

"You're being unfair here ..."

"Am I?" I don't know where I was getting the courage, but I was sick of the drama. "First you were all up in my business, then we kissed, you basically threw me into another man's arms, claiming it was better that way. Every time we shared moments, you pulled back right after. From the very first moment, you didn't even give a chance to make up my own mind, you lied right away, thinking I would oh so desperately fall for you and it would ruin me because you're a single dad and all that."

"JoJo ..."

Nope, not this time, Ben. You gotta hear it. You gotta hear everything my mind's been tormenting me with. "You ask me how can I not believe what you feel is true. Well, how can I? How can I believe you love me when one day you're here, and the next you're gone?"

Ugh, stupid tears prickling behind my eyes again. But this time no, I wouldn't let them stop me. It was just me and Ben in a secluded place, to hell with precautions, let tears fall, let him understand how much his behavior messes with my head and heart.

"That's not true, I've always been there for you." He defended, albeit weakly.

"You've been there as long as there was no one else. Then when Jeremy came, you took a step back."

"For obvious reasons!" Ben protested.

"It wasn't obvious to me!"

"Because you're so blind you can't even read your own heart!" He hinted at the bathroom stall we were in. "Why did you drag me in here? Did you even ask yourself that? What does it mean? Why do you not want me to leave?"

"I ..."

"We both know the reason, but you're the only one unable to admit it, even to yourself!"

"How can I??" For one of the very few times in my life, I actually screamed, loud enough for people even outside the bathroom to hear, but I didn't care. "How can I admit it when you're so unpredictable!"

"What? I have been here all the time, you-"

"Given how many times you pushed and pulled this cord between us, given how many times you said one thing then took a step back, how can I admit to loving you when I'm not even sure you'll be there to catch me?!"

"How can you not? I assured you in every way I could!"

"And then you backed off!"

"I had to!"

"Bullshit!" I groaned. The stall was becoming increasingly too claustro-phobic for us and for the weight of the words we – especially I – were throwing around. I don't think he even quite realized what I just said. I barely could. "First you claim to be gay, then when you kiss me, you throw me into someone else's arms. Then you disappear, and when you come back you drop such a bomb as the whole having a daughter. You expect me to be ready whenever you want me to be, yet you're not!"

"I'm the one that's always been open about how much I care."

"Care being the key word!" I groaned. "Put yourself in my shoes, Ben, were you ever clear?"

He didn't answer. Instead, Ben stared at me for a few long seconds, as if finally seeing me for the first time in – well, I don't know how much time had passed since we'd entered the bathroom stall.

I was expecting him to try to justify himself, or even leave. Instead, a small smile started forming on his lips. "Wait a minute ... did you just say what I think you just said?"

Ugh. I rolled my eyes. "Took you long enough." I grumbled, turning to the side because his stupid smile was unnerving.

Ben pulled me into his arms – something he seems to really enjoy, apparently –, and cupped my cheeks. When he spoke, his voice was low yet needy, demanding yet hopeful. "Say it ... this time clearly."

"That's not the point, I ..."

"That's exactly the point, silly girl." He chuckled, stroking my cheeks. "I love you, JoJo. How many times do I have to say it?"

"As many as it takes."

"For what?"

I bit my lip, trying to be lucid enough to really see what was ahead. But you know, I could only see one thing, or rather, one person. The moment he said he would leave for Boston is the moment the fog in my head cleared and I could hear my heart loud and clear for once. Sighing, I hid my face against his chest, and murmured something, barely audible.

"Louder." He demanded, clearly amused.

As a response, I pinched his sides, causing him to laugh, but I also took the chance to do something I never really have. Hug him. Weird, I know, but I never really let myself go when he embraced me.

This time, I circled his hips, leaving my head on his shoulder. And I spoke clearly, not stuttering, no hesitating, not rambling, no spacing out. I said it: "You can't leave me."

"Why not?"

"Because I love you, Ben. And I want to be with you."

Epilogue

"You okay?" Ben asked for the billionth time.

I rolled my eyes, albeit smiling. "Yeah, yeah, I'm fine. It's just ..." I glanced at the building one more time. "It feels weird, that's all."

"It's normal, you've lived here a long time." He said, loading the last piece of luggage.

"Yeah." Four years of my life. Of course, the last ones were odd, but the first two ... it was a shoe box, sometimes stuff didn't work and the landlord didn't want to pay for it, but in the end it's been my home. The one place I called home because I was all by myself and free.

Living alone is not the same as living with family, you know. Family has a tendency to invade your personal space, in one way or another. I may be an only child, but between relatives and neighbors, not to mention family friends, I never really had privacy. So, this place was my true home. And to leave it now, after everything that's happened even, it feels odd.

Ben put his arm around my waist, and kissed my cheek. "We're still in time to change our minds." He said comfortingly.

I looked at him smiling, knowing full well he was just trying to make me feel better. "You know we can't." I reminded him. "I have a new job, you have new clients, Elle has been enrolled in a new school. Hell, even my cats have said goodbye to their old home!" I chuckled. "It's done."

"No second thoughts?"

I shook my head. Ben nodded, and placed a soft kiss on my forehead. We'd have lingered more in that mushy moment, but Elle knocked against the window from the back seat, anxious to arrive. I smiled when I looked at her.

I'm not sure if I'll ever be able to wrap my head around it, but I'm lucky. Not only my stepdaughter – as weird as that word sounds to my ears – has accepted me without problems, but she's a sweet, smart kid. Of course, she's a bit of a hurricane, hyperactive, as most kids are, but it's not that difficult to handle. If anything, it makes me feel ... more alive, if that makes sense.

I pulled away from Ben, reminding him: "We better get moving, there's a lot to be done." He agreed, so we parted, but he still managed to steal a kiss before getting into the car.

These have been some crazy months. It's been a full year since Ben and I confessed what we felt for each other. What followed, differently from fiction, wasn't pretty.

✧✧ ✧ ✧ ✧

A YEAR AGO

"Well, I can't say I was expecting it." Jeremy said flatly, shaking his head. "I thought we had something."

"We did!" I protested. "But ..."

"But Ben is Ben?" He scoffed.

I sighed. There was no way this could go well. After I told Ben what I felt, I made clear that before everything else, I would need some time to talk to Jeremy.

Deep down, I hoped the breakup would be civil, which it was, but I could have never been prepared to the heartbreak brimming in Jeremy's eyes. "I'm sorry ... I really am," I said for the billionth time. "I wasn't ... I didn't expect it either. I ... what you and I had, it was real and I enjoyed it. But ... in the end, I ... well ..."

"Please, spare me the excuses, Joanna." Jeremy stood up, then dusted off his jeans, as if he'd been sitting somewhere impure and ghastly. I couldn't blame him, I felt disgusting.

"Jay ..."

"I want to be happy for you, Jo, I really do." Jeremy said, tears choking up his voice. "But ... I don't deny this is a lot to take."

"I know." I agreed meekly. "I wasn't hoping for anything, but I wanted to be clear with you. First and foremost."

"Have you?" He sent me a side glance while trying not to cry.

My heart trembled at the thought of him crying for me. "Yes."

"You said there was only a kiss." Oh, no. "Is that true?" Technically, yes. But it wasn't just one kiss. If we sum everything up, it's at least 3 kisses. "Joanna?"

"I ..."

"I deserve the truth, at the very least."

I nodded, agreeing. "There were kisses here and there."

"When?"

"What difference does it make? It was-"

"It makes a big difference to me. So, when did it happen?"

Sighing, I tried to recall those moments. "The first kiss was before you and I met." It came out as an attempt at justifying, and I felt even more disgusted with myself. It's as if the worst side of me wanted to tell Jeremy that no, I didn't cheat because in the end, Ben came before him, so if anything he was in the wrong. Just how messed up is that?

"Does that mean it started even before me?"

"No!" Oh, God, no. I sighed, running a hand through my hair. This has to be one of the most difficult talks I've ever had. If not the most difficult. "It's ... complicated."

"Just tell me, Joanna." Jeremy spat, clearly angry – and with reason –, "I deserve the truth."

He's right. Of course he's right. "We kissed the day after our first date." Cue the low gasp that escaped his lips. "It was ... I don't know, I was high on painkillers because of the scalded hand, and Ben helped me with everything, and ... I just ... kissed him."

"You kissed him?"

"Yes."

Jeremy let out a wry laugh, starting to pace the room. "Well, this is brilliant. We've gone painfully slow for months, even a kiss was difficult, yet you go and kiss your neighbor. Fantastic."

"Jay ..."

"He's always been there." My ex pointed out. "Ben was always there, even if you didn't know or realize. He's always been a constant presence."

I frowned. "He was my friend."

"Your gay friend. Right?" Jeremy spat, becoming somewhat aggressive. "Isn't that what you told me? Oh, don't you worry about Ben, he's gay."

"He told me he was!" There I went again with justifying my heinous crimes.

"So, you're picking a liar over me. Well, that makes me feel even better." Jeremy scoffed, shaking his head. "Unbelievable. This is unbelievable." He muttered to himself. "The guys at the precinct couldn't understand why was I so stubborn about you," wait what? "I said, she's worth it, believe me, she is. They couldn't understand why would I want to wait so much ... I guess they were right."

"You told your friends about ... our intimacy?"

"You told Ben, after all. And Valerie. And everyone else."

"I didn't tell anyone anything." I corrected him, now offended. "It's called intimacy for a reason." When you enter a relationship, you assume that what happens between you and him, will be private, no? You expect him to keep a secret, maintain the privacy of your moments, not share them with his friends. I didn't share anything with my friends, even though they insisted.

"Relax," Jeremy said, "they kept asking how was it, so I gave in to peer pressure and told them no, we hadn't had sex yet."

"Why would they need to know?" I rolled my eyes.

"That's not the point, is it?"

"Yes, it is." I stood up. "It's a breach of privacy, my privacy."

"Are you seriously trying to lecture me on relationships after you cheated on me?"

"I'm not." I responded without missing a beat. "I'm not justifying myself, nor will I try to. What I did was awful. Even a kiss is cheating, and I thought about telling you after the first time, but then things happened, and I didn't have the courage-"

"That sounds a lot like an attempt at justifying yourself, Joanna." Jeremy spat venomously.

"It is not." I said clearly. "I am sorry for what I did. You have been amazing."

"Oh, come on ..."

"I mean it. First relationships aren't normally as ... perfect as ours was."

"Our relationship wasn't perfect at all, considering you had a side piece before we even started, don't you think?"

I sighed, closing my eyes for a moment. He was dead set on believing that Ben was always there, that I was with both of them all this time. But it's not true. It's not true at all. "Like I said, we kissed a couple of times." I restated, as calmly as possible. "Three in total. The first time was after our first date, I was high on meds. The second time ... it's when he told me he loved me. He took me by surprise, I barely had time to realize what was happening. And the third one was, well, yesterday, with the whole ... everything."

"Is that supposed to make me feel better?"

"You asked ..."

Jeremy shook his head. "I don't get it, Joanna. I don't. We were fine!" He threw his hands in the air. "What happened?! You said Ben was a friend, and yet his presence was always lingering between us. Even when he wasn't there."

"Jay ... I was with you because I wanted to be with you."

"But now you want to be with Ben. How does that make sense?"

"It doesn't! It's just the way it is! And I don't know how to make you feel better, I just want you to know that you did nothing wrong. You've been the most perfect boyfriend, and you're a great guy ..."

"Oh, come on!"

"It's true," I said calmly. "I'm sorry things went how they went. I wish I could change it, I wish I could go back in time and do things differently, but I can't. All I can do is apologize and wish you the best."

Jeremy didn't speak for the longest time. All he did was stare at me, dead in the eye. I would have normally averted my gaze, but I owed him anything he would find comfort in, so, I forced myself to remain there quiet, despite my heart beating rapidly.

I don't know what I was waiting for, or if I should speak at some point, but Jeremy didn't give me time to. Shaking his head, he quietly made his way to the door, and left, slamming the door for good measure, of course. That signed the end of my very first relationship.

Releasing a breath I didn't know I had been holding, I collapsed onto the couch.

"Done?" Ben asked, appearing at the doorframe. As much as he tried to stay serious, the silly grin on his face was impossible to contain.

I nodded, laying on the couch. "It was exhausting."

"I heard the shouts." He said, entering my apartment.

"Yeah," I sighed, covering my eyes with my arm, "he didn't take it very well."

"And who would?" Ben chuckled.

"Don't laugh." I reprimanded. "It was sad and I feel terrible."

He came to sit at my side. "Because you're a good person." He said, rubbing my belly, which made me half smile. "You did something bad, you apologized for it, and you took the shit he threw at you."

"It was the very least I could do." Then I frowned, removing my arms from my eyes to look at him. "Did you eavesdrop the whole time?"

Ben laughed, leaning over me. "Of course," he pecked my lips, "I was dying in anticipation."

"Anticipation?"

He kissed me deeper. "You're finally mine."

"Didn't anyone ever tell you that people don't belong? What am I, a bag?" I protested teasingly, albeit cupping his cheeks.

"Yeah, yeah ... you're mine, I'm yours. As it should be."

PRESENT

Despite the stain on the first pages of our book, everything ran smoothly. For the most part. Turns out that pretty much everyone was sure Ben and I would end up together. Valerie, of course. Joe was certain from the get go that Ben felt something for me. Faith and Hope said the same. Michelle was disappointed, for obvious reasons, since she's Jeremy's partner and friend. However, much to my relief, she didn't stay mad at me for long.

Jeremy dropped out of the NYPD, in the end. Based on what Faith told me, he restarted college. I don't know anything else because I don't want to know. I thought it would be counterproductive for me to still keep tabs on my ex. Both because I would think about him, and because it wouldn't be fair to Ben. I'll never forget Jeremy – after all, it's true that you never forget the first one.

I turned to check the backseat. Elle was asleep, Reese and Shaw around her as in in protection. I basically have a daughter. How crazy is that? Glancing at Ben who was driving, I adjusted myself on the seat, wanting to nap or just be more comfortable. We still have a few hours on the road.

"What?" He smiled, taking a glimpse.

"Nothing ... just taking you in."

He pursed his lips, half smirking maliciously. "Oh, I think you did that already."

Blushing, I kicked his ankle. "Watch it ..." I hinted behind us, in the back-seat."

"She's sleeping."

"You never know."

I rolled my eyes, albeit smiling. The thing is, our beginnings were messed up, but ... we're here, and I am, truly, happy. I can't think of one single time before Ben that I said I was happy. If anything, I was always quoting Jane Eyre: I'm not unhappy. But this ... what we have, our small crazy family, it's more than my heart could have ever hoped for.

We would have stayed in New York, but we decided to move in together, and either apartment, mine or his, weren't big enough for all of us.

We tried to find another place, Samantha even helped me, but ... abruptly, I got news from that Lions Publications in Boston, for which I had applied at the same time as I did for Sam's company. A position as editor had become available, and they wanted to interview me.

It was stressful, I had to prepare in depth on subjects I had almost forgotten since college, but in the end, well, I made it. I got the job.

Leaving Sam was sad, I'll admit, but we promised to keep in touch, which apparently won't be that difficult, because the chief editor at Lions Publications is one of her close friends. Or he's friends with Lucas, I wasn't really listening, too lost in my thoughts.

I guess this is what happens when you give yourself a chance. There's no doubt I was lucky, finding amazing people that decided to stay in my life for good, but I would lie, if I said my efforts had nothing to do with where I am now.

I got the job of my dreams because I am good at what I do. The relationship with the man I love has its ups and down, like every other, but in the end we're more than happy – we're a family.

Me, Ben, Elle, even my fur babies, Reese and Shaw. This all started with them as kittens, being my sole comfort in my worst days, and it continues with them being my stepdaughter's best friends.

In the end, the point is, I believed in myself. I furthered a process Ben had sent in motion. Simply, I became the maker of my own fortune, and I will be reaping the fruits of what I sowed for a long time to come. So, the moral of the story is, it's never too late if you decide to believe in yourself.

THE END